PENGUIN BOOKS

If It Makes You Happy

Julie Olivia writes cozy love stories filled with humor, spice, and friendships that feel like a warm hug. She is a roller-coaster fan, avid romance reader, and rainy-day enthusiast. Julie lives in Atlanta, Georgia, with her husband and their very opinionated pets.

Praise for *If It Makes You Happy*

"Pure rom-com magic. For the nostalgic girlies who want a hit of nineties romance comfort, you'll be kicking your feet and giggling. Get ready for Julie Olivia to be your new favorite."

—B.K. Borison, *New York Times* bestselling author of *First-Time Caller*

"Every page of this brilliant book is filled with tenderness, warmth, and nostalgia that will wrap readers up in a giant, cozy hug. Highly recommend for fans of gentle love stories with heart, wit, and spice in equal measure."

—Hannah Bonam-Young, *USA Today* bestselling author of *Out of the Woods*

"Julie Olivia has written the perfect cozy romance. In *If It Makes You Happy*, [Olivia] has distilled the best parts of the autumn season and paired this with the ultimate small-town setting that will have every reader wanting to pack a bag and travel to Copper Run."

—Lauren Connolly, author of *PS: I Hate You*

"*If It Makes You Happy* is a delicious romance full of yearning, hope, and second chances." —Thien-Kim Lam, author of *Something Cheeky*

"*If It Makes You Happy* is a nostalgic tale of love, friendship, and finding happiness. A sweet, slow burn that's worth every aching moment. Cliff and Michelle are absolute perfection."

—Teagan Hunter, author of *Best Friends for Never*

"Julie Olivia has created a charming small-town romance with perfectly imperfect characters you can't help but root for. *If It Makes You Happy* has just the right amount of tension and banter between single dad Cliff and newcomer Michelle, and the delicious slow burn of their growing affection had me turning the pages late into the night." —Jillian Liota, author of *Sweet Escape*

TITLES BY JULIE OLIVIA

STAND-ALONES
The Fake Santa Apology Tour
If It Makes You Happy

NEVER HARBOR SERIES
Off the Hook
Out with the Tide
On Midnight Shores

HONEYWOOD FUN PARK SERIES
All Downhill with You
The Fiction Between Us
Our Ride to Forever
Their Freefall at Last

INTO YOU SERIES
In Too Deep
In His Eyes
In the Wild

If It Makes You Happy

JULIE OLIVIA

PENGUIN BOOKS

PENGUIN BOOKS

UK | USA | Canada | Ireland | Australia
India | New Zealand | South Africa

Penguin Books is part of the Penguin Random House group of companies whose addresses can be found at global.penguinrandomhouse.com

Penguin Random House UK,
One Embassy Gardens, 8 Viaduct Gardens, London SW11 7BW

penguin.co.uk

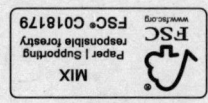
Penguin
Random House
UK

Originally self-published by Julie Olivia 2024
First published in the United States of America by Berkley,
an imprint of Penguin Random House LLC 2025
First published in Great Britain by Penguin Books 2025
006

Copyright © Julie Olivia, 2024

The moral right of the author has been asserted

Penguin Random House values and supports copyright.
Copyright fuels creativity, encourages diverse voices, promotes freedom
of expression and supports a vibrant culture. Thank you for purchasing
an authorized edition of this book and for respecting intellectual property
laws by not reproducing, scanning or distributing any part of it by
any means without permission. You are supporting authors and enabling
Penguin Random House to continue to publish books for everyone.
No part of this book may be used or reproduced in any manner for the
purpose of training artificial intelligence technologies or systems. In accordance
with Article 4(3) of the DSM Directive 2019/790, Penguin Random House
expressly reserves this work from the text and data mining exception

Book design by Devan Norman
Interior art: Autumn illustrations © DiVIArt / Shutterstock
Printed and bound in Great Britain by Clays Ltd, Elcograf S.p.A.

The authorized representative in the EEA is Penguin Random House Ireland,
Morrison Chambers, 32 Nassau Street, Dublin D02 YH68

A CIP catalogue record for this book is available from the British Library

ISBN: 978-1-405-98394-5

Penguin Random House is committed to a sustainable future
for our business, our readers and our planet. This book is made from
Forest Stewardship Council® certified paper.

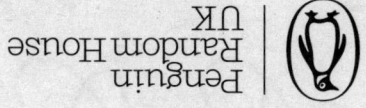

This one is for me.

To six-year-old Julie, who bumbled her way through a talent show performance of "Spice Up Your Life." Nobody remembers. Hopefully.

Author's Note

This book is my love letter to both the autumn months and the late nineties. There are cozy harvest festivals, crunchy leaves, Halloween celebrations, and Thanksgiving pies! Be prepared for a couple of nineties rom-com clichés as well. I couldn't help myself.

While this book is full of fun nostalgia and autumn spirit, I would also like to note the following content warnings:

- Descriptive sex scenes
- Explicit language
- Death of a parent from heart attack (off-page)
- Grieving of a loved one
- Parental abandonment and estrangement
- Divorce
- Cheating (off-page; not main characters)

Be kind to your heart as you read, friends.

Now grab a blanket, light up a cozy candle, and revisit the autumn of 1997!

xo Julie O.

Playlist

1. "One Headlight"—The Wallflowers
2. "There She Goes"—Sixpence None the Richer
3. "No Rain"—Blind Melon
4. "Dreams"—The Cranberries
5. "Real World"—Matchbox Twenty
6. "Say You'll Be There"—Spice Girls
7. "Black"—Pearl Jam
8. "I Want You"—Savage Garden
9. "I Put a Spell on You"—Nina Simone
10. "Sex & Candy"—Marcy Playground
11. "Lovefool"—The Cardigans
12. "Linger"—The Cranberries
13. "You Gotta Be"—Des'ree
14. "Come as You Are"—Nirvana
15. "You Were Meant for Me"—Jewel
16. "Save Tonight"—Eagle-Eye Cherry
17. "Head Over Feet"—Alanis Morissette
18. "Uptown Girl"—Billy Joel
19. "If It Makes You Happy"—Sheryl Crow

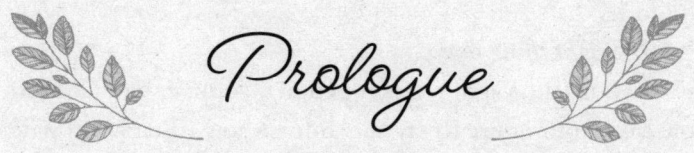

Prologue

MICHELLE

JULY 1997

I prepared for today the best I could—set out my simple black dress, picked up flowers, met with the priest—but telling my family I'm divorced at my mother's wake wasn't on my list.

"I'm leaving in five minutes," Allen whispers sharply in my ear.

"I know."

"I will tell them if you don't."

I grit my teeth. "I know."

Allen can't miss his flight. Sure, my ex-husband *could* have booked it for tomorrow after the vigil, but if you're no longer legally tied to a family, I guess it's irrelevant whether you pay respects to your ex-mother-in-law.

I run my pendant along the thin necklace chain, watching the long line of visitors snake through the chapel. I force a smile at someone I don't recognize.

I inhale sharply and evenly let it out. "We shouldn't do this today."

Allen looks away. His lip curls. "Yes, but we *should* tell

them together. Today is our only option. It's the right thing to do."

The right thing to do.

Two months ago, a much peppier, younger woman than me called our house to say she didn't know Allen had a wife. Like him, she also said telling the truth felt like "the right thing to do."

I don't point out his moral inconsistencies. There's no point in arguing if I can't win.

We should have told my family about our decision to get divorced. His family knew weeks ago. But when my mom's health suddenly declined, it never felt like the right time. I was dotting the last *i* in the paperwork when Dad called, telling me she'd passed.

Allen clears his throat, running his palms over his beautifully tailored suit jacket. Most men might nervously fiddle with the buttons of their suit, but Allen isn't the kind of man to show weakness in public. Not in his white coat at the hospital. Definitely not at a wake.

A lot of those in attendance are from Mom's former nursing days, and some are even my employees at work, but there are many more I don't recognize. These strangers mourn in loose suits and abandoned fashions, like they scrambled to find appropriate garb. An older woman beside the last pew is wearing plum stockings. The man beside her is in glasses from the seventies that swallow his cheeks.

"Who are these people?" I murmur.

Allen shrugs in response.

A family approaches the coffin—a man, a woman, and two daughters. They're some of the new faces. The man wraps a large arm around a skinny teenage girl with stringy blond hair curtaining her blotchy, tear-soaked face. A much younger girl is hiked on his hip, gripping his tie. The woman—I assume his wife—stands behind them with crossed arms and a bouquet of flowers.

I wonder if they're happy. Allen and I decided—as a *unit*, like we always did—to not have children. We protected our careers and the nice townhome that couldn't withstand crayons on the walls. Our rugs were too expensive for spilled milk. Children were too wild, and we were too . . . *not*.

I watch the dad set down his reaching little girl. He takes the bouquet from his wife, peering over the bobbing heads traversing their way through the small chapel. I wonder who he's looking for. He swivels his eyes toward us, and his gaze lands on mine.

It *snags*, like a stuck zipper in fabric, jerking against my stomach and taking threads with it. My gaze can't budge. His doesn't either.

In some ways, he's traditionally handsome—very much like Allen. His defined jaw is freshly shaved. The high cheekbones cut creases into his cheeks. His Adam's apple sticks out from a thicker neck, dipping into a protruding collarbone, exposed through his unbuttoned white shirt and the loose tie his daughter tugged earlier. He's taller than the other men in line. His broad shoulders fill out his suit. Yes, very traditionally good-looking.

But then there are other ways he's attractive—the non-Allen features. His dark brown hair isn't trimmed close—*loose* is the best way to put it, like maybe he tried pomade but ran a stressed hand through the strands too many times. His nose is slightly crooked at the bridge. And even though his lips are pulled in a taut line, there's a small crease along one side of his mouth. It's a laugh line that doesn't know how to disappear, even at a wake.

His eyes relax, like he's mentally extending a chair for me to join him in our silent, all-seeing space. He's kicking his feet back. He's not going anywhere.

I inhale a shaky breath. How can he seem so at ease, staring at a stranger? He lazily flicks his eyes to Allen, then back. I can feel his stare in the pit of my stomach, like maybe he can see what I'm hiding—like *he* knows about the divorce.

"Psst."

My heart jumps into my throat at my sister's voice. Sara's head pokes out from the side door in the vestibule behind us.

"Shelly, come here."

Allen rolls his eyes as Sara tugs me backward into the room. I attempt to steal one final look at the other man, but the door shuts in my face before I can.

In better circumstances, this room serves as a bridal suite. An oval cheval mirror is propped in the corner. Padded mahogany chairs circle a small table. I can still picture my three bridesmaids sitting in the corner five years ago—Sara, Allen's sister, and my old college roommate. I don't know the last time we spoke.

"You've got to talk to Dad," Sara rushes out.

I blink and nod. "Okay."

"I've tried, but—"

"It's fine," I interject. "Don't worry."

The corner of her glossy pink lips tilts up, but the smile doesn't reach her eyes. "Thank you. I don't know how you stay so"—she waves her palm at my tall posture—"composed. You always seem like you have it together."

My little sister is the softer one between us. She's petite with the type of platinum-blond hair women pay big bucks to re-create—the opposite of my and Dad's brown hair. But while I got a double dose of brown eyes, Mom's woodsy eyes, she inherited Dad's beautiful blues, and now they shimmer with tears hanging on by a thread. She has enough emotions for the both of us. I love that about her.

"How are you?" I ask.

"I'm good." Sara aimlessly reaches out and fluffs my hair. "Stuck in gross black. How are *you*? Allen is acting totally weird. But I guess he always does."

I hum noncommittally in response as my stomach smarts.

She sighs. "A lot of people out there, huh?"

Sara's rambling, so I try to soothe it with a casual "Did you invite some of your art school friends?"

She huffs out a laugh. "As if. They'd give you a heart attack." Both of us freeze. Her eyes instantly widen as my lips purse together. "That was . . ."

"Unintentional," I finish for her. "I know." I attempt a smile. "It's fine, Sara."

She quickly nods to herself, eyebrows tilting in. "Um, anyway . . . I think those are people from Copper Run. You know Mom was really involved in the town."

"I know."

One year ago, our parents retired to a small town in Vermont to open a kitschy bed-and-breakfast. It was technically both of theirs, but it was Mom's heart and soul. It makes sense that Copper Run residents are here. Mom was the kind of person who could be revered and loved in only a year. Give me two years in a single room with one person, and we'd still be strangers. Maybe that's where I went wrong in my marriage.

"They drove all the way to Seattle?" I ask. "Across the country? Did the town shut down?"

"Don't be mean," Sara says, smiling. "They're good people."

"Irresponsible people," I tease with a small smile. It fades as quickly as it arrived.

I tug at my earlobe, twirling the small pearl earring.

"Where's Dad?" I ask.

Sara pulls her thumb up to bite on the nail. "In the corner."

"Hey," I say, quickly tugging her hand down. "It's fine. I'm fine. *You* will be fine."

Sara nods slowly, then quickly before jerking me into a tight hug. I hold her as long as she needs until she finally pulls away. I pat her shoulder. "I'll be back."

Across the bridal suite, Dad sits in the far corner, looking out the tall window to the city outside. This cathedral is on a corner block, right at an intersection where honking is at its peak and a green light means you should have accelerated five seconds ago.

Dad rests his hand on Rocket's back, absentmindedly stroking down the dog's feathery black-and-white fur. After a couple of pats, the border collie ducks his head out of reach. He traipses to the opposite wall, shooting a look at me, as if to say, *There. I comforted him. Happy?* before dropping to a sit with more force than necessary.

It was Allen's job to find a pet sitter for Rocket today. Of course, he couldn't be bothered, just like he couldn't be bothered to tell me until yesterday that I'd inherited *his* dog in the divorce because he couldn't take Rocket out of the country. Rocket doesn't listen to me. He barely lets me pet him. But what was I supposed to do? Rocket's fate came down to either staying with me or following Allen into the Humane Society. Rocket's prima donna disposition would have been appalled, and I'm not even remotely that heartless. Realistically, Rocket shouldn't be in the chapel, but he won't bother anyone—even if he does give me the cold shoulder.

Dad's hand hangs limply at his side where Rocket once was. I reach out and take his palm into my own.

"Hey, Shellfish," he murmurs under a frail smile.

"How're you holding up?"

"Good." The bags under his eyes say otherwise. "You?"

"Fine," I answer.

He drops my hand, reaching up to trace the pendant on my chest. "Is this your mother's?" He follows the thin chain as it snakes down the divot in my collarbone. "You're getting too skinny."

"I'm fine," I repeat.

"She was really good at picking out pretty things," Dad muses more to himself than me. "The necklace. The sheets at the inn. Y'know, there are these doilies she loves. The little linen ones with the—" His voice cracks.

"Dad . . ."

He winds his hands together and glances at the closed door that leads to the quickly filling chapel. "Who all is out there?"

"Apparently the entire town of Copper Run."

"Oh," he says, a hint of a smile at the edge of his lips. "Good people, that bunch."

"So I hear."

"How's Allen taking this?" he asks.

I involuntarily clench my jaw. "He's fine."

"Is *fine* your answer for everything today?"

A huffing laugh reluctantly backfires out of me. "Yes."

From the corner of my eye, I can see Rocket staring at me through slitted dog eyes. I curl my fists. The dog knows I need to bring up the divorce, just like the strange man outside does.

How do I tell Dad and Sara though? *Hello, I'm your almost-thirty-year-old workaholic daughter/sister who can't hold up a marriage.*

Allen is forty-two, moving overseas for medical work, and thriving with a woman the same age I was when we met.

Sara will be distraught, but I don't want someone to feel sorry for me. Allen doesn't want me anymore, and I won't make him stay. It was a reasonable decision. A good one. But I don't want balloons and confetti either.

"How am I supposed to go back?" Dad whispers on a breath.

"Out there?" I ask.

"To the inn," he clarifies through shaking lips. "I have no idea where she put everything. She was in charge of the bills, the calendar—oh God, I can't call the guests. It's the busiest season. We're almost fully booked. I can't . . . I can't . . ."

I inhale. "Hey. We'll figure it out. We always do."

"*You* always do," he says. "You got all your mother's strength."

"No, Sara has it too. She has that, plus her energy. She'll do great with the inn."

He nods over and over, rubbing his temples. "You're right; you're right. She'll be a natural. You're right."

We both know Sara possesses Mom's good traits. Her gentleness. Her positivity. Her excitable, creative side. Those are the traits of someone who inherits a beloved bed-and-breakfast—not the frigid eldest daughter. Not like I wanted it anyway.

Sara will finally graduate from school in December. She'll seamlessly step into the role afterward—as long as Dad can handle it until then. He doesn't look as if he's in control of anything right now though.

The chapel door creaks open, and the low hum of conversation flows in. My body tenses as Allen smoothly strides into the room, each step of his Valentino oxfords snapping on the linoleum. Rocket runs over, tail beating up a storm. Allen placates him with a pat, then nudges him away.

"Are you ready, Shelly?"

Maybe it's the lack of sleep, but my mind is foggy at the request.

My dad starts to rise. "Do we need to go—"

"No," I interrupt, placing a hand on his shoulder.

Allen and I are practical people. His rational mind is one of his most attractive features. Yes, he's a little cold, but so am I. We understood each other once—respected each other. At least until today. His misplaced need to keep up appearances matters more than my family's mourning.

Sara walks over with her eyebrows tilted in. She carries a bouquet of flowers. "This is from some man outside."

She holds them out to Dad. I intercept them so it's one less thing for him to handle.

Sara's eyes dart between Allen and me. "Everything okay?"

Allen exhales impatiently.

Please, not today, I mouth to him.

He shakes his head. "Shell—"

I pinch my eyes closed. "Give me one second."

"Let's not make this difficult," Allen drawls.

"What's going on?" Dad asks.

"Dad, it's nothing. We just—"

And that's when Allen announces, "We got a divorce." The words bounce off the walls and low ceiling.

His eyes widen, and so do mine. I don't think he expected it to be so loud, and I didn't expect it would sound so unceremonious.

"I won't be here tomorrow," he continues, adjusting his lapels. "I'm leaving for the airport."

I can feel my pulse in my neck, my hands, and my legs. There's a cut in my palm from one of the flower's thorns.

"I'm sorry you had to find out this way," Allen says in our

extended silence, checking his watch. "I need to go. I am very sorry for your loss." Allen says it like he wasn't part of our family for five years.

He starts to casually walk away in the same manner. Rocket attempts to follow, but Allen shakes his head.

My blood feels like lava, bubbling up to my throat and cheeks. My chest hurts from the heat. I can't tell if I'm sad, scared, or angry. Unfortunately, in fight or flight, I'm not proud to say that fight is the default.

I stride after him, emerging from the side room into the main chapel again. The hum of low conversations surrounds me. The cool air from the open chapel door whips through my hair, crinkling the bouquet's paper.

"We should have waited," I snap.

Allen turns on his heel, looking side to side as he stalks closer.

"No, we should have told them earlier," he murmurs under his breath.

"When exactly?" I grit out, my body tense with anger. I'm getting louder, making him fidget more. *Good. Be uncomfortable.* "At the hospital, after her heart attack? Before the bypass? Or in the waiting room, when your colleague told us it failed?" Allen's blond hair, once gelled back, is now fraying. I can see the white streaks coming in along his temples. He attempts to swipe a strand back on a sucked-in breath.

"We should have told them the day we decided," he says.

"You see, this is your problem, Shelly—"

"I don't have a problem."

"I should have known you'd keep this from them for as long as possible. You don't tell anybody anything. Not me. Not your family. You keep all your emotions bottled up until they explode. Well, congratulations. Here's your explosion."

I blink quickly, standing taller, clenching my fists. "I do not—"

He leans in and hisses, "Why do you think I had to find *someone* who made me feel like a partner?"

My head jerks back so fast that it feels like someone fisted my hair and yanked.

I can barely whisper out, "What did you just say?"

"You're so uptight. You're not fun anymore." He's counting my flaws on his fingers now. "You have to take charge of everything. Ever think I didn't want that? Ever think *nobody* wants that? And you hold everyone to such impossible standards. God, you couldn't even forgive your mom for—"

Crack!

At first I think that's the sound of my heart breaking. Then I realize my palm pitched back and collided with Allen's cheek.

I gasp. I can't breathe.

Allen blinks at me as my pink handprint slowly takes shape on his face.

Still as stone, he breathes, "You deserve to be alone."

The words—definitive and concise—ring in my ears.

I rush past him and out the chapel's double doors. The wind whistles through my hair. A bead of sweat dribbles down my lower back. The thorns from the bouquet gnaw into my skin. The first fall leaves flit down from the trees.

Honking cars. Loud music down the sidewalk.

He's right.

I'm bubbling with anger, and here's my explosion.

My world is out of control.

Everything is out of my control.

September 1997

Chapter 1

CLIFF

I have a bad habit of staring at the phone. Arms crossed. Tongue in cheek. Foot tapping. Maybe it's unfair, but the thing doesn't ring when I need it to, so who's really the victim here?

"You sure there were no messages for me this morning?" I ask, leaning over the bakery counter, where my sister is staring as intently as I am at a framed cupcake painting. "Carol?"

"It doesn't look good," she announces.

"The painting?"

"It doesn't look good," she repeats.

"Sure it does," I answer. I swing open the half door to the linoleum-tiled lobby and wipe my hands on my apron. "It's great."

I honestly can't tell the difference between this and the last painting she picked, but with Carol, there can't be hesitation.

Carol's been redecorating the bakery's interior for weeks now. Green walls became pink, then yellow. Iron chairs were traded for dark wood, then light. The display cases have somehow remained untouched, but I give her another week until those are gone too. This place could have neon beer signs for all I care, but that's why she's in charge of presentation and I'm not. My job is to bake.

She's Burke's Bakery's brains; I'm the hands.

Carol swivels her eyes toward the bakery's floor-to-ceiling windows. Winston, our resident painter, is perched on a small stool on the sidewalk, creating the final strokes on our seasonal window art. It's a mural of autumn leaves, scarecrows, pumpkins, and apples. I told him to add a pie, but he said he couldn't draw pies, so plain apples it is.

Carol lets out a wistful sigh. "I couldn't do that."

"Of course you couldn't. That's why we hire Winston. The art looks *fine*," I reassure her again.

I look at the counter phone. I thought I'd heard a ring. Maybe I didn't.

"It's not working." Carol snatches the cupcake painting off the wall, places it on the floor, and power walks outside. I follow her out, leaving the door cracked open so I can hear if the phone rings.

A breeze picks up. I tuck my hands into my denim pockets. Copper Run isn't even remotely as cold as it will be in future months. It's the beginning of September, and the leaves have begun shifting from summer greens to deep auburn and burnished golds. It's the first real blustery day, wind knocking leaves down around my feet.

"What do you think?" Winston asks from the sidewalk, gesturing to the glass mural, paintbrush poised in the air.

"Stunning," I say. "Your best work yet."

"Carol looks stressed."

"She's upset she's not as talented as you."

Winston chortles. "Everyone wishes they were as talented as me."

I clap his back in passing. "Good job on not getting a big head, buddy."

He salutes me in response.

I follow Carol across the street to the town square. She reaches into her back pocket and pulls out a pack of cigarettes. I raise my eyebrows.

"Shut up, Clifford. I'll quit tomorrow."

I hold up my hands. "I didn't say anything."

Carol flicks her lighter, takes in a breath, then blows the smoke through the corner of her mouth in the opposite direction.

"I'm a basket case," Carol moans.

If people were pastries, Carol would be a cannoli. When you take a bite of a perfect cannoli—even though it's perfect—it cracks apart, and all that's left is a gooey center. Carol is always on the verge of showing her soft side.

I sigh, dropping my arm over her shoulders. "You're not a basket case."

"I never get anything right."

Carol's always critical of herself, but she's been *too* critical lately. We've all been on edge since Birdie Cadell passed this summer, and we all cope in different ways. I overbake. Carol smokes. At least she does it far enough from the bakery that the smell of her smoke won't permeate the store.

She flicks her hand around, smoke trailing with it. "Do you ever feel like that? Like a loser?"

"No."

She shoots me a look, and I grin.

"Listen, we make sure the croissants are fluffy and that the door opens at six." I grip her shoulder with my palm and shake. "If we get that right, there are no problems. It's *just* a bakery, Carol."

She tilts her head to the side. "*Just* a bakery," she mocks. "You're such a liar."

She's right. Of course it's not any old bakery; it's *our*

bakery—a bakery I dived into headfirst two years ago and one that thrives more than it has any right to. Burke's Bakery is both my biggest accomplishment and one of my biggest problems. I love it.

"The cupcake painting doesn't matter, all right? You're doing great. Promise."

Carol gives a weak smile. I pull her in for a side hug.

"Thanks," she mumbles.

"Now, let's get going."

Carol scrunches her nose. "You're not the boss of me."

I bark out a laugh. "Technically, I am."

"I hate you sometimes."

"Not as much as Emily does."

She snorts. "Are you kidding? Emily *idolizes you*."

"Oh, right." I snap my fingers. "Forgot it was the *opposite*. My daughter loves me."

"You ass," Carol hisses through a reluctant smirk, pushing my shoulder. "One day, she'll be a normal teenager and see the light."

"Don't jinx me."

"Maybe she'll turn out to be a mess, like her dear ol' aunt," she muses, taking another inhale of her cigarette. "Oh God, I'm a mess."

I take the butt from her fingers and press it into the ashtray on the park's trash can.

"I do hate you," she says through narrowed eyes. "I mean it this time."

"I'm sure you do."

I lean against the lamppost but startle as orange lights wound around the pole stab into my back. Copper Run's square is decorated for the Harvest Festival. Haystacks line the walkways, scarecrows stand erect beside the white gazebo, and crowds of pumpkins form a small patch in the corner of the park. I need to decide what I'll bring to my booth this year. Last year, Burke's Bakery sold out of our apple crumb cakes.

Carol kicks out a foot, scratching fallen leaves on the sidewalk. "So . . . has the evil queen called?"

I rap a fist against the lamppost and tongue my cheek. "That's not nice."

"Has she?"

"No," I answer. "And there were no messages for me, right?"

"Nope."

I nod to myself. "Then no. Nothing."

"That's normal though."

"Unfortunately."

My ex-wife makes weekly calls from New York to our daughters, but it's not uncommon if she misses one. I've called her twice since Sunday, but I reached her answering machine both times. It's been two years since Tracy left Copper Run, and I worry about her, but I worry about her relationship with our daughters more.

If Carol is a cannoli, Tracy is a yule log—more difficult to bake than it needs to be and only seen by me at Christmas.

Carol places a gentle hand on my shoulder. I give a half-hearted smile.

"Let's go," I say. "Smoke break is over."

"You got it, *boss*."

"I knew you'd come around."

We move to cross the street, but down the sidewalk, striding toward the bakery, are my two daughters. I consider that maybe my watch is slow, but when I look—*no*. School is not out yet.

"What the—" I stride across the pavement, holding out a palm to stop our florist, Sandra, from hitting me with her van. She playfully honks, but her smile drops when she spots my worried expression.

"Sorry, Cliff!" she calls out the window.

I give a passive thumbs-up.

I catch up to my sixteen-year-old daughter, already sliding her backpack down one arm, key chains rattling on the concrete.

"Emily, what happened?" I ask, darting my eyes between them.

Emily shrugs. "I saw Brittany outside the video store."

"And you didn't think to send your sister *back* to school?" I ask, rushing toward my six-year-old. I squat down to her level.

"She was crying," Emily explains.

"How'd she even leave without someone seeing?"

She shrugs. "Recess? I don't know."

Although both girls have their mother's honey-blond hair, they couldn't be more different. Emily inherited my pin-straight locks, and it's longer than it's ever been, cascading over thin headphones hanging around her neck and hitting halfway down her jean jacket. She's wearing a striped, cropped T-shirt, a sliver of exposed skin above her denim pants. I definitely told her not to wear that, but she's always been a little defiant, and I love that about her.

On the opposite end of the spectrum, there's my six-year-old, Brittany, wearing white overalls and sparkly sneakers. Her curly ponytail is pulled back with a neon-pink scrunchie. She's not nearly as rebellious as Emily, but she mimics her sister enough that confidence isn't a problem.

I cup Brittany's cheek, thumbing over the streak of tears. "Britt, what happened?"

"Luke said . . ." She rubs her sniffling nose with the back of her hand. "He said that Steve was going to lose his match."

I squint. "Steve? Who's Steve?"

"Steve, Daddy." She pokes at her T-shirt. Peeking above the top flap of her overalls is a bald man in a leather vest.

"Oh." I playfully knock my palm against my forehead. "D'oh. *Steve*."

Brittany giggles through a sniffle.

I forget we're on a first-name basis with the wrestler of the year. Carol got her hooked on Steve Austin—*of all people, Christ*—and he's edging higher on my six-year-old's list of admirable men, right over those Backstreet Boys. Either way, her mother would kill me if she knew. If she ever called on time.

I squeeze Brittany's shoulders. "Now, come on. You *know* he's not going to lose."

"But Luke says he will."

"Okay, well, you can tell that little punk Luke that he's wrong, and he'll always be wrong, and he should just get used to it now, okay?"

My daughter starts mouthing my words back to herself, as if reciting lines for a play.

"Don't actually tell him that," I rush in. "What's said in or near the bakery is kept in the bakery, all right?"

"But we told Birdie everything."

Emily and I exchange a look.

"Right," I say slowly, swiveling back to Brittany. "But remember that Birdie was an exception. What's said in Bird & Breakfast also stays in Bird & Breakfast."

Birdie Cadell and her endearingly quiet husband, Paul, ran Bird & Breakfast for the past year. Since we live next to the inn and because Brittany's never seen a yard she didn't like to run through, we grew close to the Cadells quickly. Birdie would watch Brittany after school, and Emily would take advantage of their biscuit surplus. It's been a weird adjustment for my girls since she passed.

"I miss Birdie," Brittany murmurs.

Emily cringes.

"Hey, she's in a better place now, remember?" I tell her, though I hope my words carry to Emily too.

Brittany nods slowly, and I wonder if she's reliving our conversation about death outside the chapel at Birdie's wake. We took a big summer road trip out to Seattle to pay our respects, but I have no clue how much Britt remembers about death. All I know is, she loves bringing it up.

"Do you think Sara will be fun?" Brittany asks.

I shrug. "I don't know. Hopefully."

When we called Birdie in the hospital before her bypass surgery, she mentioned that her daughter Sara would take over the inn. I jokingly told her it was too early to make contingency plans, but she must have known something I didn't. I can only assume Sara will show up eventually, but with no calls or letters from Paul yet, we're in the dark.

"Cliff!" I look up to find Betty peering out her sandwich shop door. "You need help?"

I wave with a grimace. "We're all right, Bets."

She glances down at Brittany, then back up. "Are you sure?"

I shake my hand harder. "I'm good, Bets!"

"Well, let me know—"

"Sure will!"

My face heats. Betty is only the start; more heads will poke out from their stores soon. Copper Run residents insist on helping like that. Hell, *I* insist like that. But the last thing I want is to burden my kind neighbors with our silly issues.

"Do I have to go back?" Brittany asks.

"What, to school?"

She nods. I sigh. God, my kid looks pitiful with her puffy eyes and out-of-breath chest rising and falling like she ran a marathon.

"No," I say on an exhale. "You don't have to go back to school. Head inside. I baked cookies." I playfully tug on her ponytail. "I'll call the school so they don't think you're dead."

Her eyes light up. "Really?"

"Really."

I pat her on the back, and like I've flipped a light switch, she's laughing with her arms straight out by her sides, making airplane noises as she zooms into the bakery.

"Only one cookie, okay?" I call out, but she doesn't hear me—or doesn't want to.

I click my tongue and peer at Emily. "I just got played, didn't I?"

She smiles. "Duh."

I groan as she slides her headphones back over her ears. I hook a finger in the side to tug them back down.

"Aren't you supposed to be at work?" I ask. "Lisa is gonna kill you."

"I finished up everything," she responds with a shrug.

Emily's afternoon work-study is at the post office across the square, and it's the only reason she should be out of school. But Lisa, the elderly postmistress living on a breath and a prayer, is of the mindset that you can leave when your work is done. Normally, I'd agree, but I know my daughter. Hell, I know about being a *teenager* in Copper Run all too well.

"You said you saw Brittany outside the video store." I narrow my eyes. "Why were you at the video store?"

She stiffens and shrugs. I know that gesture.

"I went to see what came out this week," she says.

She's a terrible liar.

"You were seeing that kid again."

Emily's eyes widen. "No!"

My eyebrows fall into a single line. "Really?"

She tilts her chin up. "Really."

"So, you weren't visiting James—"

"Josh."

"Right. That's what I said."

She narrows her eyes to match my own. But I know what she's thinking, and she knows I know.

"Fine," she concedes. "I was hanging out with Josh."

"Uh-huh—"

"But I was thinking . . . since my grades are good . . . I was wondering if—"

"No," I groan, placing my thumb and forefinger over the bridge of my nose.

Emily slaps her thighs. "Oh, come on! We've been dating for two weeks now!"

"And that's not enough time for him to grace my doorstep."

"Like you're some king—"

"You said it."

"Dad—"

"I'll send you to your room, Em."

"We're not even at home!" she says, gesturing to the sidewalk.

"I'll launch you there."

That makes her pause.

She bites her bottom lip to hold in a laugh. "In a cannon?"

"In a cannon," I confirm with a grin.

She folds her arms over her chest. "You're not the boss of me."

Carol snorts. "That makes one of us."

"What*ever*, Carol," Emily shoots to her.

Carol holds both hands up in surrender.

When Tracy left, Carol tried to be the supportive aunt, but at the time, she was just another female authority figure Emily didn't want. At this point, it's a joke Emily won't drop.

I turn back to Emily. "I definitely *am* the boss of you until you're eighteen. And last time you blew out candles, I recall you turning sixteen. And James—"

"Josh."

"Isn't even in school anymore. What is he, thirty?"

"He graduated in May!" Emily groans. "He's only seventeen! If you let him come over—"

"To do what? Play Monopoly?"

"He's probably great with money."

"Because he's saving for retirement, right?"

Emily's head falls back as she lets out an over-the-top groan. "He's not *that* old!"

"I'm going on another break," Carol says, digging into her front pocket for her pack.

"Can I bum one?" Emily calls to her.

I tip my head to the side. "Did D.A.R.E. teach you nothing?"

Emily shrugs. "It made smoking sound cool actually."

I can't hold back my grin as I shake my head. "You're such a little snot. And it's *not* cool. How cool can it be if Carol does it?"

"I'm standing right here," Carol says.

"Your aunt is an adult," I continue. "She's allowed to make terrible, life-ruining decisions."

"When can I make terrible decisions?" Emily asks.

"When you're fifty."

"Oh, wow, maybe by then I'll be old enough to date Josh too," Emily says sarcastically.

I smirk. "He'll be dead by then, the old geezer."

Emily reluctantly smiles as she pulls her headphones back over her ears.

"I'm making your least favorite meal tonight," she says.

"The absolute worst one."

"Can't wait, kiddo."

I hold up my hand for a high five. Emily can't resist slapping it before pulling out her Discman from her jean jacket pocket, pressing play, and trudging down the sidewalk, away from the square and to our street.

I look at Carol as a hiss of smoke rises between her fingers.

"Her lipstick was smeared," she says.

"It was," Betty chimes in with a solemn nod. She's outside her sandwich shop, pushing a dustless broom.

Nosy.

"I saw it too," Dolly, three more doors down at the bookstore, tips her empty watering can over dry flowers.

Winston chuckles from his stool. "You're in trouble."

It's impossible to have a one-on-one conversation in this town.

"Yeah, I know it was smeared," I mutter to all of them.

It hasn't been easy, raising a teenage girl. It's not like there's a class on which tampons to buy or how to say, *No, you can't sneak out of school to see your boyfriend. Please stop asking.* Emily claims her mom gave her *the birds and the bees* talk. I'm not sure if I believe it because Tracy likes difficult conversations even less than I do, which means I should probably talk to her soon. Add it to the list, along with reminding Brittany not to fight over a grown man's fake winning streak.

I raise my girls day by day, week by week. It's always something new, and I always hope the problems get spread out over the course of weeks or years. But sometimes they happen all at once on the same day.

Carol crosses the street again, and I follow. I steal the cigarette from her hand and put it out on the ashtray on top of the town trash can.

She eyes the sizzling butt before murmuring, "Thanks."

"You're welcome."

Inside, the phone rings.

I thread my fingers behind my head and stroll back to the bakery. "That'd better be Trace," I mutter.

"You're not that lucky," Carol says.

"Tell her I said hi!" Betty calls.

I throw a lazy thumbs-up back.

Crossing behind the counter, I take a deep breath and pick up the receiver. "This is Burke's Bakery."

I wait for my ex-wife's apologetic voice.

Instead, I'm greeted with a gruff, "Hey, Cliff. How're you today?"

I let out my held breath. "Oh, hey, George. What've you got today?"

I take the pen tucked beside the phone's cord and scribble George's usual catering order on the notepad. But the more he talks, the more it dawns on me that Tracy still hasn't called.

Again.

The Burke family is held together by duct tape, glue, and the old wood of this bakery. But we are held together, and I suppose that's all we can ask for. It'll be my ex-wife who sends me into a stress-induced early grave. Maybe I can hang out with Birdie in heaven.

A flash of yellow glimmers through the bakery's floor-to-ceiling glass windows. I look up and watch a taxi pass by. I don't know the last time I saw a *taxi* rumbling through Copper Run.

I lean over the counter with George continuing to murmur in my ear, peering through the car's back window. Inside, a stiff border collie watches the town square buildings pass. And beside the dog, a beautiful, familiar woman flips over a map.

MICHELLE

When I left Seattle, I intended to disappear completely. Thankfully, Copper Run is in the middle of nowhere, Vermont.

It's been two hours since I rumbled away from the airport in a musty taxi. The chain-smoking driver peers through the rearview mirror, as he has been doing every five minutes since picking us up. His eyes won't leave Rocket. The taxi's floorboard is littered with fast-food wrappers and sticky CDs, yet he's concerned about the well-trained dog sitting sentinel in his back seat.

"You're paying extra for the mutt," he told me amid throwing my suitcases in the trunk.

I swear Rocket grumbled under his breath at the borderline slur, assuming dogs could have such emotions.

"I know," I said, side-eyeing the driver's peeling name tag behind his headrest, reading LOUIS.

I shoved a folded clip of cash at him that would overshoot the meter's cost by a hundred bucks at least, including his trip back to the airport. He rubbed a thumb over the layers, then pocketed the stack without another word.

Two hours later, trees accented in burnt orange and maroon zip past the taxi window. In Seattle, buildings overshadow the already scarce trees. But out here, it's all foliage and fences. Not a skyscraper in sight.

Rocket stares out the cracked window, a light breeze rustling his fur. He doesn't stick his head out. That would be too undignified. Instead, he observes.

When our driver rumbles roughly over old train tracks, Rocket swivels his eyes to me, as if to say, *You can't be serious, Shelly.*

He readjusts in his seat with a huff of breath. I don't bother to pet him. He wouldn't like it anyway. Hating touch is the one thing we have in common.

"This it?" Louis growls from the front seat.

I lean over the center console, watching the hills of autumn gold and red slowly part to reveal a white lattice sign.

WELCOME TO COPPER RUN!

"Yes."

Past the sign is a covered red bridge—short and one-way—emptying into a town square.

"Jeez-us. It's practically *Happy Days* out here," Louis says, peering over the wheel through the windshield.

A quaint park, lined with shops, is covered in hay bales and pumpkins. Orange-and-white bunting hangs between lampposts. A white gazebo, smack-dab in the center of the park, is wrapped in orange string lights and a garland of autumn leaves. Two propped scarecrows sit on the bench inside.

Along the sidewalks are A-frame chalkboards listing daily specials. Hanging wooden signs from awnings point out shops, like a pharmacy, a video store, and a bakery. Most floor-to-ceiling glass storefronts are decorated with window murals of more scarecrows and pumpkins. Another lattice sign beside the park reads COPPER RUN, as if we might have forgotten already.

"What're you gonna do all the way out here?" Louis asks.

"I'm running a bed-and-breakfast." A sentence I would have never uttered thirty days ago.

He chortles out a "No kidding?"

"No kidding," I echo.

I unfold my map, tracing my finger along the roads highlighted in yellow and blue. This place is minuscule on a map. I bet there are only two stoplights, and we've probably passed both of them.

"Left up here," I say.

The square transitions into long sidewalks lining two-story houses with turrets and wraparound porches. Leaves collect on the ground, some yards raked and some not. A group of kids fly past on their bicycles, sitting high on the pedals. A toddler waddles past a tree swing. A woman aims a camcorder behind him. On the opposite side of the street, an older couple walks hand in hand.

"Cute little place, eh?" Louis muses.

I glance down at the map again. "Turn right up ahead."

I fold up the map, but when the creases don't line up perfectly, I shove it haphazardly into my bag. My hands are shaking, and I know exactly why.

My uneasiness reaches a pinnacle in my throat when I recognize the large white house at the end of the street. Swinging on two chains from a white post is a wooden sign painted with the cursive words *Bird & Breakfast*.

The two-level colonial house is immaculate. A white picket

fence closes off the cobblestone walkway, leading toward the wraparound porch, where two chairs and a swinging bench rock in the breeze. A bay window protrudes on one side, and through the glass, I spot a bench seat and lace curtains. Perfect rosebushes line the driveways between the inn and the house next door.

I'm so distracted that I almost forget to say, "This is it."

Louis slams on the brakes, and I fling my arm out to block Rocket from barreling onto the floorboard.

I swear his brown eyes narrow with an expression of *I hate all of this.*

"Yeah, yeah," I mutter.

When we're fully stopped, I grab Rocket's leash from my purse and hook it onto his collar. We both slide from the car.

The crisp air is a reprieve from the smoky taxi. Copper Run smells like crunching leaves and breezes that bite. There's a hint of something warm in the air too—baked bread of some kind. Maybe a pie or biscuits in the oven. Mazzy Star hums from my neighbor's open window.

Louis opens the trunk, unceremoniously dropping two suitcases onto the sidewalk. Not a single goodbye is exchanged. It isn't until he pulls away that the weight of my decision finally hits me.

Shit.

Rocket glances up at me.

I raise my eyebrows. "I'm fine."

Stepping forward, I swing open the gate in the white picket fence. Rocket reluctantly trots through before me. We crunch across the newly fallen leaves on the rocky path as I roll my patter-pattering suitcases behind me, stopping only to lug them up the creaking front steps with a bag slung over my shoulder.

I dig in my pocket to pull out the key ring my dad gave me before I left.

He'd thumbed through them with a stressed "This one opens the front door. This one opens the back, but you have to give it an extra jiggle. This one is the cellar, but don't mix it up with the attic—they look the same . . ."

I told him I'd figure it out and not to worry.

I eventually locate the front-door key, turn the lock, and push the stained-glass door inward.

A rush of stale air hits us. I wonder when the last time was that someone walked in, if it was my dad locking up after my mom's hospital visit two months ago.

Rocket gingerly steps inside, sniffing the air.

"See anything?" I whisper.

His ears twitch backward, as if to say, *Don't rush me.*

I hold up my palms. "All right, all right."

I walk inside and flick on the lights. The foyer is illuminated by a chandelier above. To the left is a front desk with wooden cubbies. A stairwell ascends to a bare landing, then rotates up to a second floor. A carpeted runner paves a path to the parlor past the front desk, where sunlight filters in through the pulled-back sheer curtains over the bay window. Decorative china plates and teacups are locked inside glass cabinets in a large hutch. In the center, a floral rug is tucked underneath beige furniture with low skirts and padded arms.

I can work with this. I've advertised much less appealing things.

I trail down a small hall to the right, pushing inward a door that reads STAFF ONLY. Past it is a decent-size kitchen. Tan hand towels adorned with grapes and vines are folded on the counter. Dark purple half curtains hang across the window to the backyard. An empty coffeepot is plugged in.

I walk to the back door and open it. Another stone footpath trails through a small garden, ending at an enclosing white fence that separates the grass from the gravel parking lot. The lot fits maybe four cars. A single car—my mom's silver Honda—takes up the space farthest from the house. The hood is coated in a thin layer of curled brown leaves.

Rocket tugs against his leash. I unclip it and let him run in the fenced area.

Before stepping out myself, I walk down a narrow hallway to the right. At the end is a closed door with a framed cross-stitch sign reading Home Sweet Home. I gently twist the handle, and the door whines open. A quilt-covered queen bed sits against the wall. A small TV with a built-in VHS player is on the dresser in the corner. On a side table is a cordless phone and a small stack of Chicken Soup for the Soul books, topped with a tiny Precious Moments porcelain figurine—one of many Mom collected.

I breathe in. I breathe out. But no amount of air will dissipate the tightening in my chest.

I want to be here, I have to remind myself.

I take a seat on the edge of the bed and wind my palms together.

I chose this.

"You really don't have to do this," Sara told me before I left, holding my bag close to her chest like a bargaining chip. "I can put off graduation."

I gently took the bag from her. "Sara, if you argue with me one more time, I'm gonna burn the inn down instead."

"I promise I'll move there when I'm done," she quickly interjected.

"I know you will. But until then, I've got it covered."

I didn't tell Sara about the extended leave I was taking from work. She didn't need to know.

Sara grinned. "I've got a whole speech prepared. Don't underestimate me." She went quiet for a moment before adding, "Really though, you have a super-adult advertising job. And a super-adult life."

"And I've got it figured out."

I glanced into my living room. Dad sat in the recliner, his sock-covered feet on the extended footrest.

"Take care of him, all right?"

Sara grinned, joking, "He'll be partying with the college kids in no time."

I gave a weak smile.

Sara jerked me into a hug, whispering, "Call me once a week. At a minimum."

Mom gave the inn to Sara, but my little sister has one semester left in art school, and she's already taken a couple of gap years. Dad can barely get out of bed, let alone run the love of his life's dream business. So, I'm doing what I always do—whatever needs to be done. Which means running this place until Sara graduates in December.

My company gave me a small leave of absence—probably because they felt bad about both my mom and my untimely divorce, but mostly, they let me leave because they had to. Nobody else knows how to do my job the way I do.

I knew what havoc would ensue if I came here, and I've

already gotten three pages on my beeper because of it. My company put Mark in charge of my main account. It's a terrible decision because Mark is about as competent as a wet paper bag, but his golf handicap is thirteen, so that's all that matters.

I peer out the lace-curtained window to my left.

Great.

My room directly faces my next-door neighbor's kitchen, where a teenage girl with stringy blond hair bops in front of the sink to the loud music I heard earlier.

I close the curtains and unpack my suitcase, tucking clothes neatly into drawers and hanging my nicer shirts in the closet—stopping short when I see that a lone wooden rod is the only space I have. Slung over a hanger on the end is a plum leather clasp purse. I run my fingers over the long crossbody strap. Mom's artsy dresses matched Sara's style, but sometimes Mom's tastes overlapped with mine. Only sometimes.

I lay the purse on the bed and transfer my makeup and wallet from my large bag to this one. Not like I'll need the big one anymore anyway.

I go back to the kitchen and brew evening coffee. As the coffee maker gurgles, I peer into the cabinets, spotting chipped mugs and crinkled bags of flour. I'll have to go shopping.

Once the coffee's done, I take it upstairs and sort through the guest rooms and the hall closets, then head back down to the parlor and front desk, trying to get the lay of the land. I find a black three-ring binder on the front desk. In the clear front slip is a tan paper with my mom's loopy cursive.

Bed & Breakfast Information

I carry it into the kitchen with my coffee, looking out the back door, expecting to see Rocket's bored face, but—

At the edge of the yard, a little girl's arms poke through the picket fence, wrapping around Rocket's black-and-white fur. His snout is buried in her neck. And she's squealing.

Oh God.

I drop the binder and my coffee, barreling through the back door.

"Rocket!" I scream.

My heart races. My nerves kick into my throat. I know he wouldn't hurt her. He's stubborn, and he doesn't listen, but he's not violent.

He's not violent.

My chunky loafers kick up crunched leaves and dead grass. I grip his collar and pull him back.

Once they're separated, I realize the girl isn't screaming. She's giggling. Her cute button nose scrunches up in overwhelming laughter. Her curly blond hair, held up high with a scrunchie and little sparkling butterfly clips, bounces with every breath.

"He likes me!" she exclaims.

A car door slams shut, pulling my attention to the red truck idling in my neighbor's driveway. Heavy boots fall against the pavement, and then someone breaks between the rosebushes separating the inn's small lot from my neighbor's house.

"Brittany?!"

Emerging from the other side is the most concerned-looking man I've ever seen. Dark, furrowed eyebrows pinch in. The edges of his mouth tug down into a twitchy, exaggerated frown.

I feel like I've been caught, but I'm not sure why.

"What's going on here?" he asks, and his formerly shaking voice is now flustered. His brown hair sticks out where the tree limbs dragged strands back, and even his orange flannel, rolled up at the sleeves, is loose around his veined forearms, like they were pushed up in a rush.

The man's gaze finally meets mine, and suddenly, my shoes feel rooted to the ground. My stomach barrels down to the dirt.

This is the man from Mom's wake.

That same sensation—the feeling of being *seen*, our eyes *snagging*—overtakes me once more. His eyes scan my own before tracing over me—from my cheeks to my lips and farther, to my fist clutching Rocket's collar.

Closer now, I can see his eyes are a light blue, reminiscent of a summer day devoid of clouds. Bright. Happy. Nothing like today's overcast sky, a day almost filtered in sepia from all the falling leaves. Faint freckles dot the bridge of his nose while the nose itself sits slightly crooked, like maybe he's been punched once or twice in his life. A small, faded scar adorns his upper lip, probably confirming my theory. But aside from that, his cheeks are smooth-shaven, and that little crease beside his mouth is just how I remember it. Handsome. Like he's on the edge of a laugh.

"He's so soft!"

We both dart our eyes back to the little girl. She pushes her arms through the gate toward Rocket. I pull his collar back right as he jerks forward. The man grips a fistful of the girl's overalls, pulling her up in the air. She giggles uncontrollably.

He spins her to face him. "What did I say about petting dogs you don't know?"

"Don't do it," she answers through laughter.

His mouth tips into a lazy smile. His full bottom lip crooks up on one side more than the other, exposing a sliver of straight white teeth. That little crease deepens as he chuckles with her.

"Exactly." Gently, he places her back down and jokingly says, "Stay."

The man's eyes find me again, sticking me in place once more.

"You know," he says, running a free palm through his hair, "I'm not exactly familiar with how to handle someone kidnapping my child."

"What?" The word comes out sharper than I intended it to.

"Should I call to report you and your"—his eyes trail down to Rocket—"attack dog?"

He smirks.

It's a joke.

He's joking.

Dumbfounded by the whole *suddenly talking with a neighbor* scenario—which was not on my to-do list today—I respond with, "He doesn't normally like people."

The man clicks his tongue and squints playfully. "Somehow, that doesn't make me feel any better."

I close my eyes, cringing at myself with a nod. "Yep, I just registered that."

He chuckles as the girl reaches out again.

"Can I pet him?"

Rocket sniffs closer. *Can I sniff her?*

I finally notice crumbs littering the girl's overalls pocket. I sigh. "She must have food. That's why he's sniffing her."

"Ah." The man takes a step closer and closer, one after

another, until I mirror his steps backward. Once he's close enough to touch, I bumble out, "Wait, what are you—"

Then he reaches *past* me. He bends at the knees and picks up a bright pink plastic lunch box from the ground, which I completely missed in my fumbling to get out here. Smacked on the front is an amalgamation of sparkling colors, bright stars, and a unicorn with a rainbow mane.

He pats the lunch box. "Well, it's either bread or drugs in here. Which do you reckon?"

My head jerks back. "Why would *drugs* be in there?"

He shrugs. "Maybe he's a drug dog."

"Rocket's not a drug dog."

"Hey, you can tell me if he has a drug problem."

The girl giggles. Maybe she's used to this weird man's charades, but I'm far from laughing.

"That's not—" I clamp my mouth shut in quiet frustration.

"You're telling me drug dogs don't have a drug problem?"

He pops open the lunch box. Leftover bread crust topples out. Rocket promptly gobbles it off the grass, sending the girl into another laughing fit.

The man cocks his head to the side, strands of hair falling with the motion.

"I've been planning to meet you," he says. "You're Sara, right?"

For some reason, that jump-starts my nerves once more.

"No," I say. "And how do you know—"

"I was told Birdie's daughter would be here to—"

"I am her other—"

"She was going to take over—"

"I'm here to run the—"

There's a beat of silence where, finally, neither of us talks over the other.

I exhale. "I'm running the inn now."

He squints. "But your name isn't Sara?"

"No, I'm the other daughter."

He lifts his eyebrows as his lips kick up into a smile. "Right."

Our staring contest is broken by a loud gasp on his side of the bushes.

"Shut. Up. Are you *near a dog*?" The teen I saw in the kitchen window crosses the property line, the untied shoelaces on her Converses snapping on the walkway.

"I'm *allowed* to be near dogs," the man counters with a laugh. It's the type of laugh that seems like it's been on the edge of his teasing lips this whole time. Like it belongs in that little crease beside his mouth.

"You hate dogs," the teenager says.

He scoffs. "I don't *hate* dogs."

She stares at me. "Who's this?"

"Figuring that out. Will you take Britt inside?"

"Is everything okay?" she asks.

He smiles. His expressions are so gentle toward these girls. "Yes. Go back inside for a second."

"But I just got out here."

"And you'll have just as much fun taking the walk back inside," he says, shaking the lunch box by its handle. "Enjoy the crunching leaves. The breath of fresh air."

The teenager rolls her eyes so far back that I can see the whites of them, but it's accompanied by a smile.

She holds out her palm. "C'mon, Britt Britt."

The little girl scrambles to her feet, giving a wave to Rocket. "Bye, doggy!"

Rocket resists me, as if to follow them, but I continue gripping his collar.

Linking hands, the girl and the teenager walk to their back door, but not without a few extra glances back at us before disappearing through the snapping screen door.

"Teens," the man mutters with that crooked smile.

He stares back at me. I didn't realize he'd stepped closer. He leans forward to rest his forearm on the fence. It's so close to my shoulder that I can feel the warmth of his palm. This man has zero concept of personal space, but I'll be damned if I move away first.

"I didn't get your name," he observes.

"Michelle," I answer.

"Cliff," he responds, extending his hand. "Cliff Burke."

I take it. His hand is bigger than mine. A faded pink burn embellishes the back. His shake is firm but somehow gentle, yet not soft enough to be insulting. He doesn't shake my hand with half his palm like I'm frail, but instead like I'm an equal—something most men at my company struggle to balance.

"So, why isn't Sara here?" he asks, continuing to shake my hand.

"What?"

"You're right. Too personal a question."

Shake.

"Why isn't my sister taking over, you mean?" I ask.

"Yes."

Shake.

"She's busy," I answer.

"And you aren't?"

"Not now."

Cliff's teasing smile rises once more. "What does that mean?"

"I wanted the job," I lie.

He snorts. "No, you didn't. So why take it?"

He's too perceptive, which has my nerves spitting fire as I blurt out, "Because my mom clearly can't do it anymore."

It isn't until he stops moving that I realize we were still shaking hands. His eyebrows tilt in, and embarrassment sluices down my spine.

"I'm sorry," he murmurs.

I pinch my eyes closed and sigh. "No, I'm sorry," I echo. "It's been a long day."

I open my eyes again to peer at him and find his boyish, lopsided smile grinning back. My chest tightens.

"I can only imagine." He glances down at our hands linked together. "So, are you going to let go first or me?"

I quickly slip my hand from his. He watches the motion, that nettlesome grin plastered on his face.

"It was very nice to meet you, Cliff."

I walk backward. Rocket is on my left, and I swear he's giving Cliff the side-eye. I feel myself doing the same.

"You too, Michelle." But when I turn to leave, he calls, "How about you come over for dinner?"

I halt in place, whirling back around. "What?"

"Yeah," he says. "A big neighborly welcome. We tend to do that here."

"That's—"

"Trust me, it'll be fun. And"—he blows out a breath with a smile—"I'm sure you'll get to know us eventually if Britt has anything to say about it. She makes friends quick." Before I can refuse the offer, he twists at the waist and yells toward their screened back door, "Emily! Set the table for one more!"

"You don't have to—"

"It's no trouble. You don't have groceries yet anyway. Right?"

I look down at Rocket at the same time he peers up at me. *Shelly, what the hell?*

As if on cue, my stomach growls. Cliff flicks his eyes down, then back up. A cocky smile is paired with raised eyebrows.

I don't see any other option, so I say, "Sure."

CLIFF

Michelle enters my kitchen cautiously, like she's been invited to dinner with Satan in Hell. And I swear that border collie following her is ready to steal my pitchfork.

"The dog!" Brittany runs past me.

I whip my hand out, but she slides slightly out of range, so I can't grab the straps of her overalls in time. When my daughter skids to a halt in front of that border collie, he lowers onto his haunches on the tiled floor.

"Rocket, be nice," Michelle commands.

The dog's ear twitches, but he doesn't deign to turn his head.

Michelle remains stationed by the door, back straight, arms crossed. Crimson lipstick matches her equally crimson nails, anxiously tapping the crook of her arm.

I remember her from Birdie's wake. She looks the same. Confident. Stunning. Tense. But also alone. I check for a ring on her fourth finger. There isn't one.

Huh.

I assumed she was married to the equally stiff man standing beside her at the wake. Then again, she slapped him, and the impact echoed through the whole chapel. No love there.

"She's so cool," Emily breathed afterward.

The drama distracted Emily from tears for just a moment, so I'll need to thank Michelle for that at some point.

Michelle's lips part as she looks around our kitchen. I follow her line of sight. Our house is nothing fancy. There are probably too many magnets on the fridge, holding up graded homework, finger paintings, and glossy photos smeared with fingerprints. Our kitchen nook is piled high with books and mail, and our hutch is stacked with Emily's CD collection. But Michelle looks at all of it with some type of awe.

I'm in some type of awe too.

There are lots of beautiful women in Copper Run, but I can't remember the last time I saw someone as breathtaking as her. Even now, out of her black funeral dress and in a more casual—notably, black—outfit, Michelle commands the space. Her brown hair, blown out below her shoulders, looks straight out of a catalog. A lighter brown colors her eyes, but they're shadowed by long, dark lashes. Sure, she has soft features—a curved jaw, delicate cheekbones, and smooth pink cheeks—but this gentleness is contrasted by the intensity of her arched eyebrows and full lips, straightened into a single line.

"Can I guess?"

Michelle blinks at me. "Can you guess what?"

"The city," I continue. "I'm assuming Baltimore."

"What?"

"Where you're from. Boston, then?" I squint. "No . . . Seattle. You work in Washington, where your mom is from."

She's quiet for a moment before confirming, "Yes. Seattle."

She seems like a city girl.

I bite back my grin in satisfaction and call out, "Emily, how's that soup lookin'?"

"I threw in some extra squash for you."

A shiver rolls over my spine, and I exaggerate it to get the point across. Brittany beams from the floor, hands now coursing through the dog's black-and-white fur.

Michelle walks toward the window over the sink, parting our frilly curtains between two fingers.

"You guys can see into my bedroom," she observes.

"Birdie liked to put on a show for us."

Her eyes snap to mine. I laugh.

"Kidding."

Then I realize maybe that was insensitive. I know Birdie would have laughed though. Her daughter? Clearly a more serious sense of humor. Her deadpan attitude and dark polish are so different from Birdie Cadell's laugh lines and pastel floral dresses.

I cross the kitchen to the cabinets. "So, you're taking over your parents' bed-and-breakfast?"

She opens her mouth to answer, but Emily interrupts, "Wait, are you Birdie's daughter?"

"Yes," Michelle answers.

Emily instantly frowns. "I'm really sorry about . . . y'know."

I think I see Michelle swallow. "It's all right."

"What about Mr. Cadell?" Emily continues.

"My dad's living with my sister at college for now."

"Oh . . ." Emily's words fade away.

I'd be lying if I said I didn't deflate as well. Birdie's husband was a common presence as much as she was. Sure, he didn't talk much, but he made up for words with actions. Waiting at the bus stop for Brittany when I was running behind at the bakery, grilling out in the summer, sitting on the porch with us in the evenings . . .

One look at Michelle reminds me that, while we lost our neighbors, she lost her mom. It's not even remotely the same.

When Michelle's attention is turned away, I mosey to the stove and lean toward Emily.

"Hey, maybe let's not interrogate her," I whisper.

"But you *just* did."

"Yeah, but I'm a dick, and you're not, kiddo."

I creak open the cabinet above and pull down a stack of plates. Michelle suddenly crosses the kitchen tiles with little *claps* of her black shoes. She extends a hand.

"So, you're going into the busiest season alone, huh?" I continue as if our conversation didn't have an awkward pause.

"I'll manage," she answers, flicking her fingers toward herself.

I grin, looking at her hand and back up. "You're our guest. You're not gonna set the table."

She moves her fingers again, silently arguing my point.

I slowly smile wider, finally placing the plates in her hands. "All right, then. Thank you."

"Where do they go?" she asks.

I nod toward the dining room through the closed doorway. "We'll set up in there."

But I can't stop staring at her and grinning from ear to ear. She's so bold and unapologetic.

Emily snickers. "We never sit in the dining room."

"Well, we have a guest now, don't we?" I say.

"So, the dining room?" Michelle clarifies.

"Yeah, through there."

But before she can push the door, it swings in toward us. The door narrowly misses Michelle. She stumbles back, and I place a hand on her lower back, along with another under her palm to help balance the wobbling plates. Not that they're particularly special china, but they're the only plates we have.

Carol emerges, unloading her purse onto the breakfast

nook. "If your pal Lars stops by one more time, asking for you when he *knows* you're not there, so help me—oh. Hi."

My sister freezes, finally spotting the stranger in my home. It's about the same time I realize I'm holding said stranger. Being this close, I catch a hint of amber and cloves in her hair. No, burnt sugar. Over time, as a baker, a lot of smells grow sickly sweet, but burnt sugar never gets old.

I step back and wave my palm toward my sister.

"Carol, this is Michelle. She's Birdie's daughter. She'll be running the inn. Michelle, this is my sister. She lives in a constant state of distress."

Carol extends a hand to Michelle. "That's my brother. He's a dick. But it's nice to meet you."

"Likewise," Michelle says, reaching her free hand out to shake.

The corner of her lips kicks up. I think that might be the first smile I've seen from her. I return the gesture even though her smile isn't aimed at me.

"I forgot to introduce you to everyone," I realize, threading my palm through my hair. "Right here is Emily." I drop my arm around her shoulders. "She's studying for home ec, so we keep her by the stove."

Emily pokes her wooden spoon at my chest. "He's a misogynist actually. Big one."

"Huge," I sarcastically agree. "She's gotta learn her place now while she's young."

Emily barks out a laugh, but Carol admonishes me with a "Jeez, Clifford."

"And that's Brittany over there."

My daughter is splayed on the floor next to the dog now, way too close to his mouth. *God.* I swear my heart rate triples.

"Hey, Britt Britt, back up a bit, will you?"

Without breaking her giddy eye contact, Brittany scoots away a millimeter.

"How many sisters do you have?" Michelle asks.

"Why? Do you wanna take one?" I joke. "Actually, these two are my daughters."

It's a blink-and-you-miss-it moment, but I swear Michelle's eyes snap to my fourth finger. I'm the one huffing out a laugh this time.

No ring here. Not even a summer tan line of one.

Emily claps the pot again with the wooden spoon. "All right, it's ready! Extra squash chunks. Just for you, big dog."

I whip open the fridge. "I'm not ready. How'd you get ahead of me?"

"You got distracted," she accuses.

I flash my hand, palm up, toward Michelle. "By being a polite neighbor."

Michelle arches a single eyebrow at me again—an *I'm not your excuse* eyebrow. I chuckle at the small hint of playfulness.

"I'll get the toast started," Carol says, shucking off her jacket, hanging it on the door hook next to Britt's pint-size one.

My family and I bustle around the kitchen, getting the last of the meal prepared. Michelle disappears through the swinging door with the plates. When she comes back, she pulls open a random drawer until she finds utensils. She gathers those up as well without a word. I smile. She doesn't like to stay idle. I can respect that.

Before long, we're in the dining room with soups and sandwiches, side by side, atop frilly place mats. Spoons clink into bowls. Brittany's soup slurps echo. Emily was right. We never eat in here—and for good reason. The mahogany table, the uniform chairs with stiff, padded seats, and the bronze-framed photos of beaches are relics of my ex-wife's decorating. We much prefer the kitchen nook, marinating in the oven's lingering warmth, with Emily as our DJ, playing music on the boom box.

"So," Carol says, "Michelle, how do you like it in Copper Run so far?"

"I've only been here an hour."

"An hour?" Carol gawks.

"I stole her," I say nonchalantly.

"I did too!" Brittany adds.

"Is the inn yours now?" Emily interjects, crisscrossing her legs in the chair.

"No," Michelle answers, dipping her spoon in the ginger soup. "I'm only staying until after Christmas."

"When are your first guests?" Emily asks.

I click my tongue and say out of the corner of my mouth, "What did I say about interrogating?"

"Tomorrow," Michelle answers.

I freeze. "Wait, you only have one day to learn the ins and outs of running that place?"

"Thought we weren't interrogating," Emily mumbles.

"I'm a fast learner," Michelle responds with raised eyebrows once more. I like the way they touch the wisps of her brown hair. It's almost delicate. "I didn't want to cancel on guests at the last minute."

"Daddy can help," Brittany chimes in, slurping the soup from her spoon. "He promised."

"Sure did," I agree. "We were pretty close to your mother," I explain. "There weren't enough bushes to keep out this kid." I shuffle my hand through Brittany's hair, sending her ponytail lopsided. "So she and your dad were forced to put up with us."

"My mother was a very giving person," Michelle says. It

might be a sentence that's usually paired with a wistful smile, an echo of a delightful memory from childhood. But she only gives the slightest twitch in the corner of her mouth. Not terrible, but tainted by something.

"I believe that," I agree skeptically.

Carol sighs. "She loved this town."

"Birdie won the costume contest last year," Brittany blurts out.

"Oh yeah!" Emily says. "She dressed as Freddy Krueger. It was so rad."

"Have you met Lisa and George yet?" I interject.

Michelle shakes her head. "Who are Lisa and George?"

"Good friends of your parents," I say. "And nuisances."

"George and Cliff fight like cats and dogs," Carol pseudo-whispers to Michelle with a grin.

"Maybe if he didn't demand *fresh*-baked goods in the afternoon, I wouldn't have to," I announce—not as much of a whisper.

From below, I hear a dog's inhale, followed by slobbery teeth gnashing. I pull up the floral tablecloth and balk at my daughter feeding the border collie pieces of her sandwich. He licks the remainder from her fingertips.

"Britt, don't feed the dog."

Michelle's cheeks flush a deep red as she shifts her head under the table too.

"Rocket!" she hisses. "Be polite."

The dog, once again, does not pay his owner any mind. Michelle tongues her cheek. Our eyes snap together underneath the table.

"He likes to ignore me," she says.

Carol sputters out a laugh.

"Sorry," Carol says. "The dog having a personality—that was a little funny."

Suddenly, the phone rings from the kitchen. Every person stiffens, including me. Michelle's eyes swivel over all of us.

"We don't answer the phone during dinner," I explain.

"But it might be Josh," Emily pleads.

It might be Tracy, finally calling for her weekly check-in with her daughters.

I force a smile. "Can't wait to hear what he has to say, then. Think it's about savings?"

"You're so mean."

"And you're *so* laughing."

Emily harrumphs, but my ears catch each subsequent ring.

I want to answer the phone, but I'd be a hypocrite if I stood up now. She could leave a message, but would she pick up if I called back?

Another ring.

And finally a click, followed by my own muffled voice.

"You've reached Cliff, Emily, and Brittany," Answering Machine Me says. "Leave your name and number after the beep, and we'll call you back." Then a three-person chorus of me, Emily, and Brittany yells, "Bye-ee!"

There's a beep. An inhale of breath from all of us.

"Uh, hey. This is Josh."

Exhales around the table.

"Calling for Emily. Um . . ." Emily shifts in her chair eagerly as Josh slowly continues, "Yeah. I'll call back later, I guess."

I decided weeks ago that Josh was undeniably a fig roll. Dry and boring.

He hangs up on his end, and I give her a side-eye.

"He seems nice," Carol says.

Emily bites her bottom lip. "Can I be excused? Please?"

I'm not in the mood to argue, so I nod.

"But, hey, no more than one hour on the phone. And if you hear call-waiting, switch over!"

Emily is already out of her chair, swinging through the kitchen door with her dishes before I can finish.

I grimace at Michelle. "Anyway—"

"I should get going too," she says. "Thank you for dinner. It was great."

It wasn't. Emily's soup was atrocious, but Carol and I smile at her politeness anyway.

I scoot my chair out from the table. "I'll walk you out."

We walk through the kitchen, passing Emily with the kitchen phone pressed to her ear. I squeak open the screen door, allowing Michelle and her dog to pass in front of me. The amber scent of her hair catches me once more.

I lean against the doorway. "Thanks for putting up with us. And I'm sorry. We really loved your mother."

"I appreciate that," she says, and I believe her.

"Y'know, I promised Birdie I'd help you. Well, Sara, but also you."

She raises an eyebrow.

I can't help but chuckle. "What?"

"I should be fine," she says, looking away. "But thank you. I just need to get by until December."

Interesting.

Her aversion to this town reminds me of my ex. The people, the trees, even the leaves—she assumed the whole town, including nature, was conspiring against her.

"Copper Run isn't so bad," I say, tilting my head to the side. "Did Birdie leave you any instructions?"

"I found a binder, but I haven't read it yet. I was hoping to review it tonight, but—"

I lean back, clicking my tongue. "Ah. My fault again."

"It's fine."

She continues to not make eye contact, and my eyes rove over her of their own accord. Somehow, her being annoyed with me only makes her prettier. Flushed cheeks serve her well.

I nod slowly. "Well, this was fun."

Her eyes swivel to me, and I think I see a bit of humor there. "Absolutely."

"I'll see you tomorrow, I guess."

"Wait, why?"

Then it's my time to pause. "For . . . breakfast? At the inn?"

"Why?" she repeats, more direct this time.

I laugh. "Well, normally, I drop off pastries each morning."

I wonder what pastry she likes. I wonder if it smells like the burnt sugar on her neck. Maybe her favorite is obvious, like crème brûlée—on the fancier side with literal burnt sugar—but something tells me it's not that simple.

"There are pastries every morning?" she asks.

"For breakfast, yeah. I'm the baker *around these small-town parts*," I joke with a faux accent. "Birdie was never too great at baking herself, so . . ." My words fade off at her confusion.

Michelle stares at the empty inn through the crowd of bushes. I've never seen a person think so loud.

"You all right?"

"Yeah," she says, blinking back. "I have a lot to learn."

"I was serious before. I made a promise to Birdie that I'd help," I say.

She shakes her head. "I don't need it."

"It's not an offer. I'm fulfilling a promise. At least let me help during your first couple of weeks."

"Really, I don't—"

"Then at least let me drop off recipes."

She nods. "All right."

"All right, then."

"Thanks again for dinner."

"Anytime."

As she walks away, patting her hip for her dog to follow, my eyes dart to her ringless finger once more.

Chapter 4

MICHELLE

I miss the honking cars and bright city lights beaming through my townhome window at night. It took four hours of not sleeping among wind and silence—deafening silence—for me to turn on the TV in my suite. I woke up three hours later to an infomercial selling ladders.

One groggy shower later, I start coffee and crack open Mom's thick instructional binder, which I tucked beside the well-loved cookbooks and chopping block.

My chest pulls into a knot. Everything is so . . . *her*. The floral scrapbook paper. The thin cursive. The Sharpie ink hasn't blurred along the edges yet, like she could have written this yesterday.

I flip the crinkling page protectors and find phone numbers, a daily task checklist, cleaning supply restocks, and then a letter.

Dear Sara . . .

My breath catches in my throat as I slam the binder closed.

Sara.

I understand why my sister inherited Mom's pride and joy. Her bubbly personality is perfect for hospitality.

I'm the woman who gets things done—not the fun daughter.

I know who I am. I'm *proud* of who I am. I built my advertising career from nothing. I was the first female manager in our office and the first advertising manager in our company overall. I've worked very hard to be in a position where people do what I tell them.

Sara got Mom's carefree, optimistic gene. She even helped pick out this property. When Mom bought it, I didn't find out until after the signature had long dried.

I close my eyes. *I just have to be here until Sara graduates. That's it.*

I slip a finger back in the binder and open it, bypassing the page with the letter. There's a slip with numbers to different newspapers' advertising offices. I exhale with a smile. Good. That's my forte. I can tackle that this afternoon. I turn another page, spotting the daily to-do list.

"We'll start there," I announce to nobody but myself and Rocket.

He stretches out on the back door's welcome mat, peering up at me as if to lazily say, You *will start there. I'm napping.*

I snap yellow rubber gloves halfway up my forearms and scrub every surface. I toss bedsheets and pillowcases through the upstairs laundry chute. I vacuum, dust, and cough.

Three months ago, I was in my large corner office. I never would have guessed I'd be elbow-deep in a toilet with my ex's dog blinking at me from the bathroom's threshold. Rocket's laughing internally—I can feel it.

By lunchtime, I whip open my bedroom window, letting the outside autumn air filter in. I fall onto the bed. Its squeaking mattress springs feel like a whine of misery. Or maybe those are my own noises.

Dear.

Sara.

I roll my head to lay one cheek on the quilt and check my watch. It's three hours until the first guest checks in, and I've barely looked at the reservation or even the instructions on how to log his visit. I need to call the office back in Seattle once they're awake too. There's no time to rest.

Sitting up, I glance out the window and notice the Burkes' window propped open. Cliff paces through the kitchen, and my body freezes. Quickly, I stand and shut the window.

It's not that I dislike my new neighbors. The little girl, Brittany, already has Rocket wrapped around her finger. The teenager, Emily, was funny and sarcastic. And Carol, the sister . . . well, she's a mess, but she reminds me of my own sister on a bad day.

The women aren't the problem though.

It's the brother—Cliff Burke—who keeps drifting through my mind.

Cliff Burke, with his veined hands raking through loose brown hair. Cliff Burke, with his crooked smile and deep laugh. Cliff Burke, who doesn't understand personal space.

I shake out the irritated feeling in my hands, the remnants of warm sparks that skittered over my skin when he touched me once, twice, who knows how many times yesterday. The palm curled around my waist. The breath in my ear when he steadied the uneasy plates in my hand. The solid body behind me when I fell into him.

The bedside phone rings, and I jump before grabbing it off the base.

"Bird & Breakfast. This is—"

"Shellfish!" my sister's voice squeals through the phone. "You're actually there!"

I laugh. "Hi, Sara."

"Ugh, it's so weird, not hearing your voice every day."

"I've only been here a day."

"That's twenty-four hours too long."

It's been a bit longer, but I don't correct her. Between my drive and her commute back to college in California, it's been closer to two days.

"Wait, what are you doing up so early?" I ask. "It must be . . ." I check my watch again. "Nine in the morning."

"Don't go all big sister on me. I'm fine. I've been painting all night. God, I don't want to graduate," she says on a laughing whine.

"Haven't you put off graduating enough already?"

"Yeah, but I could *live* in school forever."

I grin to myself. I adore my sister's love for the arts. It's so different from how I think, and I wish I could bottle that fascination for myself.

"Get your degree already," I tease.

"I should have called earlier."

"This was perfect timing."

"Yeah, but another day, and you'd have totally forgotten about your little sister, and that's not acceptable."

I huff out a laugh. "I'm always thinking of you. How's Dad?"

"He's . . . fine." Sara's voice lowers to a murmur. "Still watching a lot of *M*A*S*H*."

"Yeah?"

"Yeah." There's a moment of silence before she asks, "How are *you*, Shelly?"

"Good. Yeah, it's fine over here."

"Wow. Convincing," Sara says with a laugh. "Met anyone?"

I swallow. "Mm-hmm." Sara will only ask more questions, so I add, "My neighbor invited me to dinner last night."

She gasps. "You went to dinner? With the hot neighbor?"

My face heats. "I didn't say he was hot."

"Yeah, but Mom always said he was. The guy with daughters, right?"

I look over at the open kitchen window. I almost choke on air as Cliff passes by again.

He looks so . . . *casual*. He's not like the men I'm accustomed to, with blazers and snug ties. Cliff's wearing a white tee layered under an unbuttoned long-sleeved corduroy shirt. The sleeves are rolled up his forearms. The little line beside his mouth is creased.

I feel ridiculous, holding my breath as I watch him, phone pressed to his ear like mine is, flipping a pen through his long fingers. After a moment, he tucks the pen behind his ear and pushes the free hand through his hair. He mouths words I can't hear, then walks out of view.

"Shells?"

"Yeah, sorry. It's . . . a little weird, being here."

"Oh . . ."

That sticks in my chest more than it should.

Dear Sara.

"I should go," I say. "I've got a lot of work to do."

"Hey," Sara says, suddenly quiet. "Do you wanna talk about it or something? The inn? Mom? . . . Or Allen?"

I shake my head, then realize she can't see me. "I really should go, Sara."

"Mm-kay," she says, then softly adds, "Love you."

"Love you too."

I place the phone back on its base, reaching up to trace Mom's pendant over the thin chain. Rocket stands in the doorway again, staring at me.

"I don't need your judgment right now," I murmur.

Rocket huffs and walks down the hall.

Across the yard, Cliff paces in front of the window again. I pull the lace curtains closed.

"Drive safe," I say.

I receive a mumbled "Thanks" in response.

This is only my second set of guests, but they left the same way the first group had—with a cold shoulder and grumbling under their breath. To add insult to injury, the guest book is, once again, unsigned.

My parents never told me their guests were rude, but after four days of hosting two reservations under my roof, I'm convinced the busy season brings the worst kind of tourists.

The week started out fine. The first man arrived with a suitcase in tow and a beaming smile. He said he traveled here often, which was obvious by how casually he leaned on the desk with his elbow, almost nudging the call bell. I nodded politely but didn't ask where he was from because, well, he looked like another city native, like myself. I jotted down his card information and saw the note in my mom's loopy scrawl, indicating he'd reserved his usual room—the master suite upstairs. I handed him the keys with a smile and wished him a happy stay.

Easy enough.

But the demands that followed . . .

Every time I was finally in a rhythm, balancing finances at the desk or replenishing the homemade biscuits—which looked decent, if I do say so myself—some guest needed yet another accommodation, almost on cue, like they had a running checklist to test me. They wanted a window opened, or extra blankets, or even a recommendation for the best route to the fall festival in the square.

Down the sidewalk, I wanted to snap, but I instead cordially walked them to the front porch and pointed them in the direction of town with a polite "Can't miss it."

They gave a half-hearted wave in thanks.

I have a full day to unwind until my next guest arrives. I can only hope they will be kinder than the last checkout, where the parents wouldn't stop their kids from constantly petting Rocket. I shut the front door before their minivan was even done puttering down the driveway.

There's a lot to like about being an innkeeper. I don't mind the cleaning all that much. The accounting aspect is comfortable for me, and I already have advertisements lined up for the next month.

But there's also the discontented guests. And the crushing quiet of not being in a city. The distinct lack of another person. The simple fact that I'm *alone*.

It's not that I miss Allen. He slept in the guest room for months; we discussed separating once or twice. I should have known what was coming.

But even so, when I walk into the kitchen, it's devoid of the sound of his newspaper crinkling or the smell of our steaming morning coffee. I don't hear about his scheduled surgeries for the day.

Just endless ladder commercials.

The Burke family is my only reprieve from silence despite not talking to them since the dinner. I know their schedule. Emily roams past their open kitchen window, laughing on the phone, at around seven o'clock every night. Brittany wanders through the bushes into our parking lot after school, peering near our windows, as if seeking out Rocket. And then there's Cliff, arriving home from work late, mid-laugh as he steps out of his truck, like a crack of lightning in the empty sky.

They seem like fun, which is so different from the household I grew up in.

Regardless, I told the Burke family I didn't need help, and I don't. I'm not going to renege on that now. Things are going fine.

I spend the rest of my evening cleaning to the low hum of the radio. When I jerk open the creaking kitchen cabinets for an early dinner, only a half-empty bag of sugar and a tin of coffee stare back.

Right. I went through food quickly this week.

I might as well restock supplies while I'm at it, so I flip through Mom's binder, and—jackpot—she has a list of essentials. Releasing it from the sheet protector, I grab my mom's purse and Rocket's leash, slung on the kitchen hook, then head out the front door.

Now firmly in the middle of September, Copper Run's trees are a watercolor wash of golds and russet reds. Leaves wither and float to the ground, creating crunchy piles for Rocket to sniff through.

He shoots me a pointed glare. *These leaves aren't from the city, Shelly. They smell different. I don't like different.*

"I don't either," I whisper.

When are we leaving?

I sigh. "Not for a while."

The town square is packed with bustling families overwhelming every sidewalk. Kids run across the street without looking both ways. There's the video store, the post office, and . . . a pizzeria / coffee shop combo? I don't want to know.

Mom romanticized this town so much that it started to feel untouchable. It's like a little pocket of the universe that existed only in her imagination. A place with the best pumpkin pies in the world, festivals for every holiday, and perfectly breezy autumn weather.

I pull my cropped cardigan closer to my chest.

The square smells like apple pies and hay. Crunching leaves and maple syrup. A banner slung between two lampposts reads COPPER RUN HARVEST FESTIVAL. It's packed with people. Teenagers laugh under the park gazebo, corded with orange lights. A child toddles through the haystacks. And near the pumpkin patch's wooden fence are the only familiar faces I know.

The Burke family.

Cliff walks hand in hand with Brittany. She jumps, and Cliff swings her with one arm a couple of inches in the air for a moment before placing her back down. They repeat the game a second time, and she giggles so loud that I can hear it from here.

He looks around, as if searching for someone. I stiffen and pick up my walking pace toward the corner grocer. I tie Rocket's leash around the lamppost.

"Stay," I command.

His butt plops on the ground. *You've got five minutes.*

"Five minutes," I agree in a whisper.

I slip through the door and grab a plastic basket before haphazardly tossing in items from Mom's list. Baking powder, butter, milk . . .

Like scratching an itch, I finally cave and peer out the store's floor-to-ceiling window. In the park, Brittany, Emily, and Cliff walk down an aisle of pumpkins. He's beaming down at Brittany with that lopsided grin of his. I can't decide whether he's charming or . . . I don't know . . . *cocky*. It's like a whole comedy routine is permanently at his lips, ready to be unleashed without request.

Someone walks up to Cliff, and they exchange words. The woman is laughing, clutching her stomach, basically bent over.

Okay, Cliff's not that *funny.*

But then he talks to another person—a man with a thick mustache and a small gut—and the two of them grin from ear to ear. The man lightly hits him on the shoulder. Cliff loops an arm around the man in return.

Once again . . . charming . . . or cocky?

Finally, Cliff pinches the fabric of his pants to squat down to Brittany's level. She points out a booth behind him. He nods over and over with a grin, rolling his finger in the air, as if saying, *Yeah, yeah, sure, sure, sure.*

Emily looks in the same direction that Brittany did. Cliff stands up, gesturing two fingers from his eyes to theirs before walking off with the mustached man.

I don't realize I'm frozen in the narrow soup aisle until someone bumps into me. We collide, and an apple atop their grocery basket topples out.

"Oh, I'm sorry." I shake my head and bend to pick it up.

An older female voice responds shakily, "Oh, don't you worry . . ." She pauses and gasps. "Oh my goodness, Michelle?"

I look up to find a woman I don't recognize at all. She blinks down at me, crouched on the floor with my hand wrapped around the apple. Her cropped white hair is soft along her jaw, but her oversize glasses drown her eyes into pinpricks.

I straighten up. "Do I know you?"

"George!" she calls into the air. "George, it's Shelly!" I raise a single eyebrow as she yells again, "George!"

The aisle is already tight, but when a man shuffles around

the corner with glasses as large as this woman's and pants tugged up to his ribs, it suddenly feels too cramped.

"Christ," he grunts. "What is it, woman?"

"It's Shelly!" She holds her palm up to present me. "Birdie's girl."

George squints. "I thought Sara was—"

"Hi," I interrupt. "I'm Michelle. It's nice to meet you."

I extend my hand, but when I realize I'm holding the apple, I drop it back into her basket. Her smile is wide.

"I'm Lisa. This is my husband, George. We're really close friends with your parents. You must have heard all about us."

"Yes," I lie.

I only know them from Cliff. The man's helping, even when I don't want him to.

"We didn't know when you'd make it," Lisa says. She elbows George. "From what Paulie said, it should have been a month ago, but I haven't been able to get in touch with him since then. I assumed he was busy . . . well, you know . . ."

Grieving.

"Dad's in California now," I explain. "He's staying with my sister temporarily."

She gapes. "So it's just you?"

"Just me."

The two words settle in my stomach. I came to terms with the fact that it'd be *just me* after the divorce. Honestly, it felt more comfortable than *me and Allen*. But having it said out loud again pinches my chest. My thumb twitches against my bare ring finger.

I glance out the window again—suddenly wanting to be anywhere but here—and I spot Emily talking to a teen boy. Her cheeks are flushed as she leans closer. Brittany runs through the pumpkin patch behind her.

"Oh goodness, you poor thing," Lisa coos, her palm wrapping around my wrist, snagging my attention back. "George, did you hear that? She needs help."

My face falls. "Oh, no—"

George grunts, "I can hear fine."

"No," I repeat quickly. "No, thank you. I've got a list." I flash it with a forced smile. "Mom left instructions, so I'm set."

Lisa's lips turn down, and I wish they hadn't. Lately, that expression forebodes tears, and I can't handle any more emotions.

"We miss her, you know," she says, her hand tightening on my arm.

Yeah, I definitely can't do this.

"She was the best lady," Lisa continues. "Volunteered at the festival. Drove the mayor's Fourth of July float. Hosted Thanksgiving for the neighborhood last year . . ."

"A real class act," George finishes.

"She was," I respond, except I was never close with this version of my mother—the one who belongs to Copper Run. The bed-and-breakfast mother hen. The town sweetheart.

Sara knows her, but I only know the woman who kept a garden with my little sister and tried—tried so hard—to do the same with me.

Rocket barks. I jerk my eyes to the window to see he's tugging against the leash, eyes locked on Brittany, who stands in the pumpkin patch by herself.

Wait, where did Emily go?

Lisa pats my arm. "We'll stop by the inn soon, okay?"

I shake my head. "You really don't have to."

A boy approaches Brittany in the pumpkin patch. Rocket whines, tugging against his leash restraint.

"No, we help each other around here," Lisa insists. "Now,

here. I've got coupons," she announces, splaying them out like a magic card trick. "Take them. Please."

"Thanks, but I should go."

"Dear—"

"I've got to—"

"If you would—"

"I'm all set," I snap.

George's head jerks back.

And then I hear Allen's words cycling through my head once more. *"You deserve to be alone."*

Outside, there's a high-pitched wail. I look to the window. Brittany is sprawled on the ground between two pumpkins. And that same boy stands over her.

Maybe I do deserve to be alone. I could spend the next few months running the inn by myself and do fine. Apparently, *alone* is my specialty. But my blood boils at the sight of a little girl getting knocked down. She doesn't deserve that.

I push through the corner market's door with my basket discarded and without a single goodbye on my lips, untying Rocket's leash and running toward the park with him by my side.

Chapter 5

CLIFF

I don't have eyes on Brittany, but I'd recognize my daughter's cries anywhere.

"You forgot your change, Cliff!" Betty calls as both I and my buddy Lars bolt from her stand, empty-handed, apple cider abandoned.

I don't turn around. I'm already hopping over the fence toward the pumpkin patch, where I left Brittany with Emily.

I dart around the low wire fence housing the fishing booth, sidestep the pony for children's horseback rides, and pivot through a crowd, where Winston chortles from his face-painting booth, "Whoa, Cliff!" and, "Got somewhere to be?"

Skidding around the corner of the haystacks, Lars points. "Cliff, there."

I finally spot Brittany.

On the ground.

Crying.

I rush over, crouch down, and inspect her from head to toe for injuries. I swipe a thumb across her cheek, wiping away a single tear. My heart aches. Something about when kids cry a single tear makes it infinitely sadder. And it's worse when it's *my* daughter.

"Britt, hey, look at me."

Another tear falls.

"Britt Britt. Hey."

I continue checking over her arms and knees for bruises, and once I realize she's fine, the ridiculousness of this scene finally washes over me. Brittany is plopped on the ground beside a pumpkin—like she's a Cabbage Patch Kid emerging from the vegetable birth canal.

I chuckle. "You all right?"

Brittany tries to smile through her choked tears.

That's the secret thing about raising a kid—if it doesn't look like a big deal to you, it's not a big deal to them.

Lars chuckles beside me. He's standing, hands tucked into his pockets and shaking his head. "You gave this guy a fright, little lady."

Lars has been my best friend since high school. He's had a mustache since the eighties, when he adored *Magnum, P.I.*, and his pizzeria is so good that his belt notches have steadily risen since then as well.

From behind me, I hear a nasally "She pushed me first!"

Lars and I turn our heads and find some kid standing a few feet away, pointing his finger accusingly at my little girl.

I close my eyes and sigh, barely managing a "Where are your parents?"

At the same moment I ask, there's a bark across the street. A flash of black-and-white fur zooms under the park's iron archway. As of a week ago, there's only one border collie in our town, which means a stern woman is close behind.

And there she is.

Michelle crosses the street in a half jog. She looks intense. Her brown hair is a teased mess, and that maroon lipstick of hers could kill a man. Or a child, in this case.

The kid freezes on the spot as Rocket leaps over the pumpkin patch fence and beelines to Brittany.

"Hey, hey, hey." I leap to grab his collar, but Brittany scoots closer and wraps her arms around his neck, burying her cheek in his fur. My anxiety skips to my throat. "Britt, let's back up. We still don't know this dog that well, all right?"

Rocket's head jerks toward the boy, and if I didn't know any better, I'd say his eyes narrow.

"Hey," Michelle says through heavy breaths, her slender hand splayed over her ribs. "How's everything going over here?" It's not a question though.

My lips tip up at her authoritative tone. The kind that says, *I know everything is not okay, but I'm asking to be polite*.

"Mostly all right," I answer, watching as her eyes dart between Brittany and her dog.

Lars's eyebrows rise as he gives her a sly grin. "Don't think we've met." He reaches out to shake her hand. "I'm Lars."

"Michelle," she answers, now focused on the boy and missing my buddy's extended hand.

Lars tongues his cheek with a grin, running his eyes up and down her figure. He likes out-of-towners, and they like the mysterious local reminiscence of Tom Selleck. The moment he finds out she's living here, his interest will flitter away.

I jerk my chin at the boy. "Hey, kid. Parents? Are they here?"

Brittany rubs the back of her fingers across her snotty nose. "He's grounded."

"I am *not*," he retorts, taking a step closer.

"Watch it," I warn at the same time Michelle takes a tentative step forward. My eyes roam over her. I can't help but grin at her bulldog nature, which is, surprisingly, not the actual dog in this situation.

"*Are* you grounded?" I ask the boy.

His lips curl in as his cheeks redden.

I sigh again, exhausted by this whole event. "Fantastic. Then why are you here?"

He opens his mouth and closes it.

In the silence, Brittany yells, "He's mad Steve won!"

Oh. That's when I finally recognize him. *Luke.* Steve Austin–hating Luke. Luke, who finally got that mop of his cut. His mom has been pushing for a haircut for months now. I barely recognized him.

Lars snorts and shakes his head. "Oh jeez . . ."

"He didn't *deserve* to win!" Luke snaps back.

I grip my nose between my thumb and forefinger. "Christ almighty."

"Who is Steve?" Michelle asks.

"Steve Austin," I clarify, but the little scrunch above her eyebrows says this explanation means nothing. "A wrestler. Eh, never mind."

This situation must seem ridiculous to her. It's ridiculous *to me*. Two elementary-aged children fighting over a grown man's winning streak.

Sighing, I say, "Go home, Luke."

"But—"

"And, yes, I'm calling your parents when we get home to let them know you were out while grounded."

His face is red, but at least the boy has enough sense not to shout back. Surprisingly.

Michelle's eyes slowly grow wider. "Cliff, she's bleeding."

"She's *what*?" I roam my hand over Brittany's legs once more, panic rising. I look at her calf, and sure enough, there's a small scratch along the back.

How did I miss that?

I gather Brittany in my arms. My daughter is all that matters right now. And potentially killing that other kid, but I'll leave that for another day.

"I can get Band-Aids at the corner store," Michelle offers.

"Nah, we'll go to the shop," I say. "I've got first aid there."

"But she's fine!" Luke pleads.

In that moment, Brittany's bottom lip sticks out, and another tear trickles down one of her flushed cheeks.

I tilt my head toward Luke. "Listen here. If I see my girl on the ground in front of you again, I'll be having a more serious talk with someone. Your mom. The mayor. Bill Clinton. And next time Steve wins—which he will—and you get upset about it, know that I'm training her to wrestle."

"You are?" he stammers.

"You are?" Lars asks, an eyebrow raised.

"Uh-huh," I confirm.

"Oh," Luke breathes.

"Yeah, *oh*. Now, go home."

I don't stick around to see if he does. I turn on the spot and stride across the street.

"Mind finding Emily for me?" I ask Lars.

He salutes and jogs off, back into the hay-riding, pumpkin-filled fray of the Harvest Festival.

"Are we really gonna wrestle, Daddy?" Brittany whispers through sniffles.

"When you can bicep-curl one hundred pounds, sure."

"Yes," she says on a silent celebration.

Behind us, Michelle follows, clenching and unclenching her fists, heavy sighs rushing out of her nose. If she could breathe fire, I might see plumes of smoke.

"You all right back there?" I call to her.

She blinks up at me, as if broken from a trance, shaking out her hands and nodding.

The jangling of a collar alerts me to her dog, now loyally following by my side. Well, not *my* side. Brittany's.

Our little crew continues down the block until we reach the bakery door. I jangle the door and exhale. Carol must have closed for the day. I knock on the glass, praying she's still inside, but after a couple of seconds, with Brittany continuing to sniffle in my arms, my patience wears thin quickly.

I shift on the spot, trying to pat for keys in my pocket, but Brittany is too heavy in my arms. I move to set her down, but she whines pitifully.

"Can you stand for me, Britt?"

She fervently shakes her head and whines, "No."

I sigh. "Okay, well, can you—"

"What do you need?" Michelle asks, stepping forward.

I blink. "My keys. They're in my pocket."

To my surprise, Michelle says, "I don't have a problem getting them for you."

My beautiful new neighbor—a woman who seems to roll her eyes at most things I do—is offering to dig around in my pocket. I lean my head back and blink at the sky. The big man upstairs really decided to test me today.

"Front left pocket," I instruct.

I bounce Brittany higher in my arms to give Michelle room.

Michelle's shoes snap on the sidewalk as she gets closer. She smells like amber and cloves, like she did the other night. No, it's not crème brûlée. Maybe a coffee cake.

Slowly, gently, Michelle sneaks her hand into my pocket. I hiss as her cold fingers radiate across my thigh.

"Your hand is like ice."

She pauses. "Sorry, is my help too inconvenient for you?"

I bite my lip to stifle a laugh. *She's funny.* "Worried about your blood flow, is all."

I can't see her expression, but she doesn't respond.

Michelle tucks her fingers closer to the outside, probably making sure to not brush against my inner thigh. Each movement zips through my veins. I haven't had a hand . . . well, *that* close in years. I try to think of anything else. Dennis Rodman kicking that cameraman in the balls. That pig in *Toy Story*. "Candle in the Wind."

I'm almost at peace, but as Michelle finally grips the key ring and tugs, the sharp ends of the keys trail over me anyway.

I clear my throat and shake my head.

Getting action with my own keys. Pathetic.

"Which one?" she asks.

"The bronze one with the dent on the top," I say on a strained breath.

She strides to the front door, inserts the correct key, and twists the lock, pushing the door open.

I nudge my shoulder on the light switch, turning the main lights on, then place Brittany on the front counter. Her legs dangle and kick the counter. I observe the back of her calf with the cut, which is very surface level, but probably enough to be shocking for a kid. Can't blame her for crying.

I turn and find Michelle lingering in the corner of the shop, arms crossed as she observes the cupcake painting on the wall. I wonder if she also sees how crookedly hung it is. I smile to myself. At least she's not saying it out loud, and thankfully, Carol isn't here to notice either.

"I'm gonna get the first aid kit," I say. "Mind watching her?"

"Of course not."

I journey to my office, grab my kit buried under a stack of paperwork, and walk back. I catch the tail end of a conversation.

"He can sit too," Michelle says. "Try it."

"Sit," Brittany whispers.

"More intention. *Rocket, sit.*"

"Rocket, sit," Brittany echoes, and, boy, does that dog drop on the ground quickly.

I grin right as the bell above the door dings. Lars holds the door open, and Emily ducks under his arm, rushing through the threshold with her eyes the size of dinner plates.

She gasps, palms covering her mouth. "Oh my God, Dad, I couldn't find you."

"Where were you?"

"I . . . I was going to be right back. But Josh . . ."

Yeah, good mood gone.

Lars slowly, awkwardly walks back out the door.

"You were supposed to be watching your sister," I say to Emily. "And you went off with that boy?"

I pop open the kit and shake my head.

"It was only two seconds," Emily stammers out.

I crouch in front of Brittany with a cotton ball and antiseptic.

"You don't leave Brittany like that." I tip the bottle upside down on the cotton ball. I hold up the soaked cotton to Brittany. "Big-girl time, all right?"

She nods, gripping the counter harder as I press it against the scratch. She wails. Fixing wounds is the worst part of this whole dad thing.

"Dad, I'm so sorry," Emily pleads again.

"Em—" The phone starts to ring, and I swear it's like nails on a chalkboard in this moment. "I don't have time for this right now. Just—" The phone rings again. "Can you get the phone?"

She doesn't budge.

I know she feels bad. And of course, I was a teenager once. I snuck around with my crush, like she did. But that's the problem. That crush resulted in a fourteen-year marriage. I won't allow Emily to get in the same trouble her mom and I did. I can guarantee the last thing she wants is to be tied to freakin' *Josh* forever.

Michelle strides to the phone on the wall. "I've got it." She lifts it to her ear. "This is the . . . uh . . . local . . . bakery? How can I help you?"

I hold up a Band-Aid in each hand to Brittany. "Unicorn or dog?" I wave the rainbow-colored bandages back and forth.

Brittany cuts her eyes to Rocket, then back up. "Dog."

I sigh. If I gotta worry about Emily with boys, then I'll need to worry about Brittany with dogs.

"Dog it is," I say, fastening it to her skin and pulling each side to stick it down. "And, hey, next time you wanna play between pumpkins, let me know, and we'll work it out. And maybe we'll even throw your sister in there too."

That gets me both a giggle from her and a slight twitch at the edge of Emily's mouth.

I reach out for Emily's hand. "It's fine, kiddo. We'll talk about it later, okay?"

"Okay," she murmurs.

"Nothing a good ol' yelling match can't solve," I tease.

"Can I throw a pillow at your head?"

"Only if I do it first. We'll put on Metallica."

Emily grins. "Cool."

"Cliff?" Michelle asks, covering the phone with her palm. "Someone named Tracy wants to talk to you."

Almost instantly, it's like a bucket of cold water empties over my head.

"Mommy!" Brittany calls, swinging her feet back and forth more.

I stand, walking over to the phone. Michelle places the receiver in my hand. Her fingers graze mine, and my chest tightens. Her hand is so soft compared to my calloused ones. But any fire I feel disappears when I raise the phone to my ear.

"Cliff?"

"Hey, Trace."

"I called the house, and you weren't there."

No niceties today. Got it.

"We were at the Harvest Festival," I explain. Then I turn the corner and murmur, "You're a week late. Everything okay?"

"I've been busy," she says. Then, with slight hesitation, she adds, "Thanks for asking."

There's a moment of silence between us—a moment that didn't exist until a few years ago. After she permanently moved away, her feelings toward me have oscillated between irritation and guilt.

I respond with a sigh. "It's all right."

"Can I talk to Britt?"

"Sure." I hold the phone out. "Hey, Britt Britt. Wanna talk to Mom?"

She hops off the counter easily, like the cut never happened —sly girl—and snatches the phone.

"Hi, Mommy!" she says, rising onto the balls of her feet and back down.

Emily leans against the counter with her arms crossed, pulling in a deep inhale. I clap my palm onto her shoulder. Tracy always wants to talk to Brittany first.

Emily shrugs my hand off her shoulder and walks to the

kitchen, whispering to Brittany in passing, "Let me know when she deigns to talk to me."

Brittany scrunches her nose. "What's *dang* mean?"

"Never mind."

Brittany throws me a confused look, but I give an assuring thumbs-up. She smiles and goes back to talking with Tracy.

Michelle stands in the corner with her arms crossed, eyeing the empty display cases and the chalkboard menu over the counter. I finally catch her gaze and raise my eyebrows. I feel bad she's here for this, so I throw her a lopsided smile. She lifts a single eyebrow in question. Chuckling, I nod my chin toward the door. In unspoken agreement, we both walk outside. Lars is nowhere to be seen. He'll call later to ask how everything went. He doesn't like to interfere with family things. Michelle, on the other hand . . .

Leaning against the lamppost, I run a palm through my hair. Neither of us says anything, and I almost appreciate the silence after the last ten minutes. Almost.

"Thank you," I finally say, "for helping. You didn't have to."

She shrugs. "I don't like seeing people get bullied and hurt."

A smile slides over my face as I nod to myself.

Inside the shop, Rocket sits stiffly beside Brittany as she swings side to side, getting out energy.

"He makes a decent guard dog," I observe.

Michelle sighs. "He has a mind of his own."

"He seems well trained enough."

"Because he likes Brittany," she responds with a shake of her head. "He only listened to my ex. He prefers anyone but me."

"The ex or the dog?"

She snorts. "Both."

"How do you know Rocket doesn't like you?" I ask.

"The same way I know he's not a drug dog."

I smile even wider when her full lips tug in the corners.

I click my tongue. "So, you *can* joke around."

"Sometimes."

"What times?"

She checks her watch. "Two o'clock on Sundays."

Her smile rises a little, and I can't help but grin in return.

But then her smile fades. "Do people normally sign guest books?"

Taken aback, I run a palm through my hair again. "Uh, sure, I would imagine."

"Hmm." She stares off in the distance.

I hesitate to respond. It's the first time I've seen a crack in her doorway, almost like she's letting me slip a foot through.

"Daddy!" Brittany yells, standing in the bakery's threshold. "Mommy wants to talk to you!"

I look from Michelle to the open bakery door and back again. I point a finger at her. "Talk later?"

"Sure."

"Thanks again."

She nods and pats her thigh, calling out, "Come on, Rocket."

And as Michelle predicted, he barely listens to her. She repeats herself, and after a lingering moment, the dog finally saunters out of the shop, like some reluctant adolescent. Maybe she's onto something.

I walk inside and take the phone from Brittany. "Hey, Trace."

"I don't talk to her for a week, and this happens?"

It's funny; both Michelle and Tracy get straight to the

point. But the difference between their tones is so distinct, like Tracy is a viper and Michelle is a garden snake that wants peace. I can't help but laugh a little.

"Cliff, this isn't funny. She said some boy pushed her."

"I'm working on kicking his ass; don't worry."

"I swear, if—"

"Everything is fine over here. I promise. Kids get knocked down. It happens."

"Maybe . . . maybe I should visit more."

My chest tightens. Every time anything dangerous happens with the girls, she second-guesses her decision to leave. And I get it—I do. But moving was the best decision for Tracy and us. She'd been in Copper Run her entire life, glued to me since we were sixteen and through a teen pregnancy neither of us could have predicted. Six years ago, she insisted we should try for another child. That maybe a planned pregnancy would be different. But in the end, when she grew distant, irritated with us, when I ended up on the couch each night, I wasn't surprised she had drawn up divorce papers.

A few months after that, she wanted to go start a career in the city. She considered bringing the kids, but after I argued that they were settled here—that Copper Run was a good community—she left. I encouraged her to go. I had my bakery; she needed to find her dreams too. Unfortunately, it didn't take much convincing.

"You're fine, Trace," I reassure her.

"She said Emily left her alone. She should at least *try* to be a good role model."

I grit my teeth as a spark of irritation skitters through me. "She is."

"Not good enough. Listen, if something like this happens again, I want to consider . . . I don't know . . . something."

The sudden tension in my chest almost cuts off air. "Something? What do you mean?"

"Maybe Brittany can . . . I don't know . . . stay with me."

Tracy does this every so often. She feels guilty and considers adjusting our custody agreement. It scares me every time. She makes good money. It would be too easy for her to change her mind.

I force a laugh. "Trace—"

"The schools here are good. I think."

"The schools here are good too. They're settled here. She likes it."

"Being raised there and liking it are two totally different things."

The words feel like a knife stabbing through my chest. First, my parents moved, then hers, then Tracy. Some people view Copper Run as a prison. I can't understand why.

I bite my lip and nod to myself. "Yeah, well, let's put a pin in that thought. School just started back."

She sighs. "Fine. But . . . I'm serious," she repeats, but it's hesitant, as if maybe she didn't convince herself the first time. "I'll call next week."

"Can't wait." It's probably more sarcastic than it should be because Tracy doesn't say goodbye; I only hear a click and then the dull dial tone moaning back at me. I slowly place the phone back.

Emily strolls out from the kitchen, arms folded over her chest and staring at a blank spot on the wall. "She didn't ask to talk to me," she murmurs.

My heart sinks, plummeting deeper and deeper with each passing second.

"She was running behind, kiddo," I manage to say. "I think she's been really busy out there with work."

"Sure," she mumbles.

I squeeze her shoulder. "She didn't forget."

Emily nods, then strides right past me, taking Brittany's hand and walking her back to the Harvest Festival.

It infuriates me how Tracy treats Emily. I try as hard as I can to shield Emily from her mother's resentment. It's not Emily's fault we didn't use protection at sixteen. But Tracy plays favorites, and it sends my blood pressure skyrocketing every time.

Deep down, Tracy didn't want a family. She was forced into that role, and being a mom felt like a burden. *I* was a burden with my stupid jokes and sarcastic comments—an enlightening statement that came out in the divorce proceedings, which I'll be mulling over for years.

But while I understand her motivation to leave, I can't fathom genuinely *wanting* to.

I love my girls so much it hurts. The idea of leaving them would never cross my mind. But that was Tracy's prerogative. Not mine.

Through the bakery windows, I spot Michelle leaving the corner store across the street and untying Rocket's leash from the light pole. I'll need to properly thank her for her help today. I'm just not sure how.

Chapter 6

MICHELLE

The guest book is no longer empty, but I wish it were.

> *Copper Run is an idyllic town.*
> *The autumn leaves and cozy fall festival were perfect.*
> *New management was fine.*

Fine?

I flip back a page, where every entry complimented the bed-and-breakfast experience, complete with a few sentences on the host herself. My mother's stunning breakfast, the compelling conversation, the overall homey feeling.

I swallow and shut the book, blowing out a breath and closing my eyes. It's been another week of guests lifting their noses in my direction.

After setting up breakfast this morning, I received a weak smile from the mother in the small family—a condescending *please leave us alone* smile—so I walked off. I'm leaving them be. I followed every guest around last week, and that didn't work either. I keep trying different things, and none of it is clicking. But that's okay. This is another focus group, like in advertising. Another problem to be solved.

But this problem's solution isn't clicking. Something *always* clicks eventually, and the fact that it hasn't is irritating. I'm better than this. I'm an advertising manager for a *reason*.

"Oh, it's beautiful," a voice coos.

I look up. Lisa waltzes through the front door, peeking around the foyer in awe. George follows. I stiffen behind the front desk. After I left our conversation at the corner store, I didn't expect to see them again.

"Wow, you even washed the doilies!" Lisa picks one up from the entryway table and grins.

I can't tell if she's genuinely beaming or if her cheeks are over-blushed with powder.

"How are things going?" George asks.

"Oh, and the flowers!" Lisa interrupts on a gasp. "And you restocked the newspapers! I always told Birdie she needed to stay on top of that, but, oh, she was never concerned about the news. George, that reminds me; we need to get the paper this morning."

"You can take one," I say.

Her hand rests over her heart. "So sweet."

George lifts an eyebrow, circling back to "Things are going well?"

"It's been good," I answer, eyeing the guest book and tucking it aside. "Running like a dream."

Lisa sniffs the air. "Have you been making some of Birdie's biscuits?"

"Yes. They're in the—" My sentence is barely out before Lisa shuffles past me, down the hall, and into the kitchen, past the STAFF ONLY plaque.

George clears his throat, giving me a pointed look. I'm not sure *what* look, but it's enough to make me leave to follow Lisa. The creaking floorboards indicate he's close behind.

I swing open the kitchen door, and Lisa already has a biscuit to her mouth.

"I used to love these."

But when she crunches down, her face twists. Bugged-out eyes, scrunched nose, and pursed lips. Her *mmm* is so forced it's embarrassing.

My heart sinks. "What is it?" I ask. "Are they not good?"

She grabs a napkin and spits it out.

Oh no.

"Dear," she says, pushing up her glasses, "they're terrible. Is this what you're feeding guests?"

She says it so loud that I walk to the kitchen door connected to the dining room and ensure nobody is out there. But a family is at breakfast. And their biscuits are untouched. With a grimace, I shut the door.

"But nobody's complained so far," I whisper to Lisa.

"Are there guests in there right now?" she asks.

"Yes," I answer more quietly.

Lisa peers over my shoulder at the dining room door. "And you're not eating breakfast with them?"

"Am I supposed to?" I thought they didn't want that. What am I *missing*?

"Oh dear . . ."

The phone on the kitchen counter rings, and I instantly grab it. Anything to get away from this conversation.

"Bird & Breakfast. How can I help you?"

Lisa hands the biscuit to George, who shakes his head in refusal.

Oh, come on. They can't be that bad.

"Shellfish!" My sister's peppy voice rings through the phone.

"Hi," I exhale.

The tension in my chest releases. I didn't realize my shoulders were hiked so high up.

"I thought you'd call!"

I smile grimly. "You didn't give me your new number."

"Oh. Right." She laughs. "How are things?"

"Good. How's Dad?" I realize I'm changing the subject, but the last thing I want to discuss is how terribly I'm running this place.

"Dad's moved on to reruns of *Cheers*," Sara answers.

"Improvement from *M*A*S*H*, I guess."

"For me at least."

I catch eyes with Lisa and point to the phone. *Sorry*, I mouth.

She waves me on, as if to say, *Take it*.

The front door creaks open down the hall.

Lisa gives me a thumbs-up. "I'll handle it," she says.

"Wait—"

But she's already shuffling out of the kitchen, leaving the door propped open behind her. I groan. I miss when people actually listened to me.

George follows his wife, giving a final look at that crusty biscuit as if it committed a war crime.

Seriously?

"Shells?"

"Yeah, still here," I answer Sara, squatting down to sit on a small step stool.

"How are you?" she asks.

"I'm doing fine. The guests are nice. The place is immaculate. Mom left it in great condition."

"Good! Ooh, have you met Lisa and George yet?"

"Yeah." I snort. "I can't get rid of them actually."

"Trust me, you don't want to. They helped Mom all the

time. They know that place inside and out. Also, how's the hot neighbor?"

My stomach drops. *Oh, you mean the neighbor whose pocket I was digging through? The neighbor with toned thighs?*

I pick up the pen on the kitchen counter and start to doodle on the blank paper meant for messages. "He's—"

"Lisa!" a friendly voice booms from the foyer. I know that low tone.

I lean to the side on my stool, trying to peer out into the hall, but I can't get a good line of sight past the coat rack filled with jackets.

"Oh, Cliff!" Lisa coos. "What are you doing here?"

I swallow.

Knew it.

"Shelly, stop zoning out!" Sara whines.

"Sorry. I missed what you said."

"Hot neighbor?"

I swallow. "I can't get rid of him either actually."

Sara laughs. "I love that town. They're all so friendly."

Too friendly, is what I want to say.

Seattle was somehow both loud and quiet; people were all around, sure, yet nobody was dropping by your house unannounced. I miss it.

Instead, I mumble, "He and I really don't talk that much."

I lean back on my stool again and finally catch a glimpse of Cliff. He's resting forward on the front desk, running a hand through his hair even though it instantly flops back down. His wrists are so . . . *defined*. His leather watch band, buckled around one wrist, slides up and down his arm with each movement, and I can't understand why that adds to his appeal.

No. He's not appealing.

"I saw your car here and thought I'd come to apologize," Cliff's distant voice says from the front desk. "I know Emily left work earlier than she should have . . . again." He shakes his head.

Lisa waves her hand. "Oh, she went to see Josh, didn't she? I was a teen once."

Cliff snorts. "So was I. And now, at thirty-three, I have a sixteen-year-old."

There are two sides to Cliff Burke. The goofy town local with a worry-free crooked smile. And the single father—a man who carried his daughter in his arms when she got a cut on her leg. A man who's protective of his girls. Stressed. Uncomfortable. Clenched jaw.

"Anyway," he continues, "this is for you."

I can't see what he hands her, but Lisa immediately gushes, "Oh, Cliff!"

"Snickerdoodle, right?"

She tsks. "Oh gosh, yes. My favorite."

"So, how about guests?" Sara asks in my ear. "Have you met any cool guests?"

I return to scribbling on my notepad. "No, not really. I let them do their own thing."

"What? Why? That's, like, the best part about that place. People travel and have amazing stories!"

"I tried talking. They're on vacation," I say. "I don't want to bother them."

From the foyer, I hear Lisa again. "Oh, delicious, as always." Then she lowers her voice. "Might I suggest teaching Birdie's girl how to bake? Her biscuits—"

"Atrocious," George blurts, and if I didn't know better, I'd say he purposefully growled it louder so I'd hear.

Really?!

"Is that right?" Cliff says. I can almost picture that crooked smile.

Sara's voice chimes in again. "Shell, you're not bothering guests. If they wanted to vacation alone, they'd go to a motel outside of town. They like the whole experience. They want to talk to you."

"No, they don't."

"Yes, they do!" she answers with a laugh. "That's the whole point. Dad was telling me the other day that Hot Neighbor—"

"Not his name."

"Always brought over baked goods and talked with the guests too. Does he do that with you? Maybe that'll help."

I hear Cliff's distant laughter, low and rising straight from his chest. Genuine, like everything else he does.

"No," I admit. "I might have explicitly told him not to help actually."

Sara gasps. "What did you say to him?"

"I said I could do this on my own. That's all." Saying it out loud sends guilt sliding over my skin, like I'm getting secondhand embarrassment for myself.

I lean back on my stool again and catch a glimpse of Cliff. The stool groans the further I lean. Cliff's forearms relax on the front desk as he leans close to Lisa. I snort. I'm not surprised he's invading someone's personal space.

"Shelly," Sara snaps, "listen to me."

"What?"

"Make friends!" she pleads on almost a laughing whine. "You're gonna be there for three more months. And you're not even talking to guests? Aren't you lonely?"

"You deserve to—"

I shake Allen's words away.

I look around. The place is clean. Dishes are done, and

coffee is waiting to be taken out to guests. I even made extra biscuits. Though I guess those no longer matter.

I'm doing everything right. And whatever isn't working—the biscuits, apparently?—needs to be adjusted. It's trial and error, like most problems.

I look over at Rocket with his nose pressed to the back window. I wonder if he's waiting for Brittany to appear.

There's a hiss of a whisper from the foyer.

I push the linoleum with my boot and lean back on the step stool again.

I watch Cliff. His brown hair with loose strands hanging over his ear. That smooth, curved jaw. His typical smile with the full bottom lip crooked up more on one side than the other. That same thick flannel, like he's one second away from cutting down a whole forest or preserving it.

Lisa leans closer to Cliff to whisper.

My back molars grind. What are they saying? What other possible critique can they make about my stupid hard biscuits?

"Shelly?" Sara asks.

I give an extra little push, rising to only two stool legs. Cliff's eyes dart over, catching mine in the process. My heart drops, and the toe of my shoe suddenly leaves the ground.

No, no, no!

I fall backward. The breath whooshes out of my lungs. I hit the kitchen floor hard. The phone clatters across the floor. Rocket scrambles up onto scraping nails, darting down the hall like some Wile E. Coyote cartoon.

There's a stool rung broken beside me, and as I analyze the damage—my aching tailbone and racing heart, which I can feel down to my fingertips—footsteps rush into the kitchen. A hand hooks in the crook of my elbow to help me up. I stand and am suddenly eye to eye with Cliff.

"Are you all right?" he asks.

"I'm fine. I'm fine."

After his eyes dart over my clothes, down to my legs, and back up—the same dad-like look he gave Brittany when she fell, as if assessing for bruises—he finally finds my gaze once more.

I'm not accustomed to being this close to a man who isn't Allen. I can feel Cliff's breath on my lips. I see every little line beside his eyes and that faded scar above his mouth. He smells like cinnamon and vanilla—the organic cologne of a working baker.

Slowly, that crease beside his lips deepens. My chest feels so hot; it's like lava boiling up into my neck.

"Were you eavesdropping?" he teases in a whisper that sends goose bumps rolling over my arms and chest.

"I wasn't eavesdropping," I lie.

"I've gotta say, you're awfully defensive."

"And you're quick to draw conclusions."

"I'm not the one who fell off a stool."

My heart hammers as one corner of his lips slides up.

"Shelly?!" I jump as Sara's tinny voice echoes from the phone on the floor across the kitchen. "What's going on?"

I notice Cliff's hand holding my arm, his rough thumb catching the sleeve over my elbow. I pull away. His eyes flick to me, and he lowers his hand as well.

I dust my skirt off with any potential dignity I have left and bend to grab the phone.

"Hang on, Sara."

"Are you okay?" she asks.

"I fell. I'm fine. Hang on," I repeat. I push the mute button and set the phone on the counter.

"Goodness, are you okay?" Lisa asks by the doorway, her palm over her mouth and a snickerdoodle cookie held in the other hand. George appears behind her with furrowed eyebrows.

"I'm fine," I answer. "Really."

"Are you sure?" Lisa asks.

"Yes." My response is stiff and probably too stilted.

Rocket slinks around the corner, giving me a once-over. I can't tell if he's checking if I'm okay or if he's making sure there are no more loud noises. He eyes Cliff tentatively.

"Gonna be nice to me today?" Cliff asks, bending down and extending his hand.

Rocket sniffs it for a second, then walks away.

"Guess not."

"Give me one second," I say, picking up the phone once more.

Lisa and George leave with indecipherable murmurs. Cliff is last, lingering at the doorway. I wave goodbye, and he chuckles. I don't know what to make of it.

I unmute the phone. "Hey, Sara."

"God, what happened?"

"I fell. I'm fine."

"Did I hear other voices?"

I sigh. "Yeah. My neighbor was here."

"I thought you said you didn't talk to him."

"It's impossible to *not* talk to him."

There's a pause, and I swear she's grinning on the other end. "Well then, he's the perfect candidate to be your first friend."

My body tenses. "Sara—"

I hear slurping and a clank of a bowl. Mouth likely full of cereal, she says, "Please try to be happy there. I'm so jealous of you! I bet the leaves are so gorgeous this time of year."

"Yeah," I admit, "they are."

"Then enjoy it. And accept some help. And stop being off-putting."

"Hey."

She giggles. "Do it for me."

I let out a frustrated groan. I pace the kitchen and watch Cliff cross toward the front door.

"Do you want to come over for dinner?" Lisa asks him before he's all the way out. "We'll make enough meat loaf for the whole family."

As if he can sense me looking, Cliff's eyes dart to mine, sending waves of flames over my chest and up my neck. He inhales before turning his gaze back to Lisa.

"No," he says, letting out an exhale and laughing. "But thank you. I should get back before the house explodes. Emily is finishing her volcano science project."

George smiles, and it's so much kinder than any he's ever given me. "We'll keep a lookout for an explosion."

Cliff gives Lisa a final hug, and the door shuts behind him.

"Promise me you'll make a friend," Sara says in my ear. "Talk to guests. Something." Then she swallows. "If not for me, then for Mom."

I sigh, looking down at Rocket, whose nose is pushed against the window again, looking out in the backyard for the little girl next door.

"Yeah," I answer. "Yeah, I'll try."

"Promise?"

"Promise."

Chapter 7

MICHELLE

My shoes squeak over Bird & Breakfast's cobblestones in the front yard as I flex my fingers out, then back in. As much as I want to turn heel and storm back to the inn, I've procrastinated having this conversation for as long as I can.

All three rooms at the inn are fully booked for the first time since I arrived. I tried smiling more this afternoon—thinking, *I can do this on my own*—but my first attempt at small talk didn't go over well.

"Love your dress! Might have to find it later," I said to a woman as she unloaded her suitcase.

In retrospect, her disgusted expression was valid. She must have thought I was threatening to steal the worn clothes from her room. I walked away, beating my head against my hallway wall.

I'm bad at useless conversation, but I know one person who isn't. And that neighbor is who I'm going to convince to be my friend.

God help me.

I walk across my driveway, cross on crunching fallen leaves, and stop short of Cliff Burke's fence.

I can do this. I can make nice with the snarky man next door.

I take a deep breath, eyeing his open window. Plates clatter together as the sound of running water flows from the kitchen.

They're busy. They probably had dinner. It's a bad time.

I turn, but Rocket's tail whacks my calf.

Shelly, don't be scared.

"I'm not scared," I whisper back.

You're being a scaredy-cat.

"Fine. I'll do it."

I unhook the white fence to his property. Rocket walks through the open gate with me, nipping at my heels, as if herding me through.

There's commotion from their house before I even step onto the porch. Someone inside barrels upstairs. A muffled television plays the local news.

I raise my fist and clang their door knocker twice. The sound reminds me of hammered nails in a coffin. My own coffin. I stand on the porch awkwardly for either one second or one minute—I don't know; I'm agonizingly stuck in time—until the door finally whips open.

When Cliff sees me, his eyebrows rise. He holds a book in one hand while his eyes roam from my lips down to my tucked-in white shirt, black leather belt, jeans, and white sneakers, then back up. A crooked smile slowly slides up the corner of his mouth. It sends a zip of anxiety through me. He never fails to make me feel exposed.

"Michelle. This is a surprise."

He places the book on an entryway table, then leans an arm and his hip against the doorjamb. His loose cable-knit sweater is rolled up his forearms. He looks so casual. Effortless. Confident.

I clear my throat and gesture by my side.

"Rocket wanted to see Brittany," I explain.

Cliff blinks down at Rocket. His tail beats ferociously on the porch. I haven't seen Rocket this excited since we moved. Either he genuinely likes Brittany or he's a master manipulator, working for my side. It's likely the former. He's never been on my team.

Cliff chuckles. "You're here because your dog asked for a playdate?"

"Yes."

With another quick assessment of the two of us, Cliff finally turns at the waist and calls through the house, "Britt! Rocket's here for you!"

Footsteps pound down the stairs. I wish I could bottle the expression on Brittany's face the moment she sees us. Her grin couldn't be any wider. She bounces on her toes, practically thrumming with excitement in her black-and-white-spotted nightgown.

"You've got ten minutes because we're already past your bedtime," Cliff says.

"Really, Daddy?"

"Really, really. Be very careful. Don't hug him. Don't spook him. Just . . . throw sticks or something. Okay?"

Brittany zooms into the yard so fast that she practically falls down the porch stairs. The moment she passes Rocket, he's right behind her, chasing her through the grass.

Cliff tucks his hands into his pockets, watching in silence.

I squeeze an outside fold in my jeans and release, finally saying into the quiet, "Mind if I talk to you, Cliff?"

His eyebrows rise once more in surprise. I must be throwing him too many curveballs. I don't blame him; I can barely keep up with them myself.

"Sure, Michelle," he says, laughing through my name, mimicking my formality.

He takes a seat on the top porch stair, and I squat down to join him.

I draw in a big breath. He grins in anticipation.

"Yes?" he coaxes.

"I need help," I blurt out.

"You . . . need help," he clarifies slowly.

"Yes. I mean, I'm good at running the inn. I'm great at advertising—a professional actually—and the finances are no problem. I have excellent instructions for the day-to-day and—"

"So, why do you need help?"

I grip my hands together. "My bedside manner is apparently . . . not pleasant."

Cliff barks out a laugh. I jump, and the heat in my cheeks is from either embarrassment or anger. Or both.

"Well, it's not *that* funny," I say with a sneer.

"No, no. Sorry, sorry." He waves his hands and tries to stifle his chuckle by biting his bottom lip. "I . . . well . . ."

"It's obvious, isn't it?"

"The fact that you question it at all is almost charming."

"I know my strengths. I'm willing to accept when I'm wrong."

He looks at me like he doesn't believe me. "So, you're asking for my help? To . . . what? Make you more hospitable?"

"Yes," I answer.

"All right . . . uh . . . well, I'm not sure how to—"

I close my eyes tight and let out a strained "Please."

"What was that?"

"Don't make me say it again."

"God, asking for help hurts so bad for you, doesn't it?" he teases. "All right. So, how can I help this . . . problem of yours?"

"I need to be"—I click my tongue—"warmer, I think."

"Warmer?" he asks with a smile.

"I accidentally told a woman I wanted to steal her clothes today."

Boyish laughter bubbles out of him, and some of the tension in my shoulders releases.

I choke on a laugh. "It was awful."

"How can I help though?"

"People seem to like you around here."

"They seem to," he muses, leaning his forearms on his knees and linking his hands together. He tilts his head to me. "But I think—and feel free to disagree—but I *think* I might annoy you."

I scoff. "Oh, please. I barely know you."

"C'mon. Be honest."

"You're definitely . . . *different* from people I normally talk to."

His palm slaps his chest. "Ouch."

"Hey, you said—"

"Well, I say a lot of things," he teases.

I try to bite back the smile growing on my face, which only has his grin widening as well.

"Well"—he stretches his arms out—"I don't know. This is sure asking a lot."

"I'm not asking for it for free," I counter. "Anything you need, I'm right next door."

He squints. "I have a sneaking suspicion you're trying to be my friend." When I don't answer, he says, "Uh-huh." Cliff leans closer, his shoulder touching mine as he whispers, "Of course I'll help, Shelly."

"Just Michelle," I correct him, shifting away from his touch. "If that's all right."

It's not that I don't like being called Shelly. But that was

Allen's nickname. Rocket's. My mom's. And I don't know Cliff well enough to be Shells or Shellfish. Those belong to my dad and Sara.

"Honestly, I don't even like nicknames," I admit.

"All right then. You're Michelle," Cliff says. "But only if I'm Cliff. Not Clifford."

"Not the big red dog?"

He shakes his head. "I'm cursed with that joke. I swear it's the universe laughing at me."

"Why would it laugh at you?"

He points out the scar above his lip. "I was bitten by a dog as a kid. Three stitches and a fear to last forever. Dogs seem to like me though. I think they're all conspiring to make me uncomfortable."

"You're telling me he's not cute?" I ask, nodding out to Rocket with his tongue lolling out.

"Dog propaganda."

"How?"

"Ehh," he muses uneasily. "I don't trust them."

"True. Rocket is manipulative."

"Isn't he supposed to be man's best friend?"

"Yes. *Man's* best friend. Not woman."

Cliff squints. "There's a story there."

"It's complicated."

"Your relationship with your dog is complicated?"

"Isn't your relationship with your family complicated?"

"You're saying he's family?" Cliff counters.

"Close enough." *He's all I have here.*

Cliff gives a weak smile, a cough, and repositions himself on the porch. "Fair."

"There is." I side-eye him, and he's already smiling. "A story, I mean. I guess."

"You gonna share it?"

"I don't know."

"Sharing is normally how friendship works."

I chew on my bottom lip and sigh. "Rocket belonged to my ex. So our relationship is tumultuous at best."

"What happened?" he asks. "With . . ."

"Allen," I supply. "He found someone younger."

He winces. "Damn."

"She called me."

"Damn," he repeats.

"She said she didn't know he was married. That I deserved to know."

"Do you wish you didn't?"

"No. It was for the best."

He hisses in a sharp breath, letting it out with a final "Damn."

I nod, and then we're in silence once more. Wind rustles the trees, sending brown leaves waving to the ground. Across the street, kids cycle past on the sidewalk with playing cards tucked in the spokes, making them sound like puttering motorcycles.

"Well," Cliff finally says, "if it makes you feel better, I'm in the divorcé club too. Saw it coming for years."

"Can't tell if that would hurt more or less."

"Me neither," he admits.

I swallow. "Must be rough. Two girls. Running a bakery."

"Carol closes the bakery without me most days." His broad chest rises and falls as he stares off. I wonder if that's the last thing he wishes were happening. "And Emily has after-school stuff. She's in a work-study program."

"Are you sure she's not sneaking around with that boy?"

"No," he says on a laugh. "Thanks a lot for that." He leans

his head to the side, watching Rocket and Brittany, in her pj's, roll in a pile of leaves. He sighs in exhaustion. "It's hard sometimes. But we get by fine, even if it is a little hectic."

He smiles at me, and I don't know if I've seen such a genuine smile in my life. Maybe on my sister, but never like this.

I think for a moment, then straighten up. "If you're helping me, let me help you."

He laughs. "How?"

"I'm at the bed-and-breakfast all day. I can watch Brittany after school. Lighten the load a little for you if you want to stay late to bake." I bet that's what he wants.

He stiffens, mouth opening and closing. I guessed correctly.

"No, I couldn't ask that of you," he says.

"You didn't. I offered."

"I'm not going to burden you," he says.

"You're not a burden," I say softly.

Cliff doesn't respond. I didn't know this man was capable of being speechless, as he is now.

He exhales, winding his hands together. "Yeah, I don't know . . ."

"She can sit in the living room and watch TV," I say. "I'll make sure she does her homework. Plays outside. Things kids do."

He side-eyes me with a smirk. "You've never been around kids, have you?"

"Only my sister."

He chuckles. "I don't know. Maybe. Birdie used to watch her, so Britt *does* know the place."

My chest tightens. Sometimes people in Copper Run drop hints about my mother, and it's always jarring. But they're like precious shimmers. I want to grab each one.

"She did?" I ask.

"Yeah. She was always there when we needed. Good woman. Didn't even have to ask." He smiles to himself. "She'd simply show up."

It's quiet for a moment, only the skittering of leaves across the concrete. Distant child laughter down the street. The *thunk-whine* of a dribbled basketball.

"So, what exactly is your plan here, Michelle?"

I tug at my earring and pull my knees up to my chest. "I'm here to keep this place running," I answer honestly. "If I can make it until December with this place intact, then I'll be happy."

"What happens in December?"

"I go back to Seattle. Back to my job. My life. Dad and Sara will move back and take over."

He flicks his nose with his thumb. "Why is it that every woman needs the city life?"

"*Friends* makes it seem fun," I joke.

That earns me a huge grin, and my fingers twitch at the sight.

"You already know how to be—what did you call it?— oh, *warm*." He nudges my elbow with his. "You should tell more jokes. Be yourself. It's charming."

"Charming?"

"You've charmed me."

I roll my eyes.

"See?" he says. "Your scowl, for one, is gorgeous."

"Very funny."

His gentle smile doesn't fade. "Jokes aside, I'll help you. Then you can go take taxis and drink at coffee shops or whatever you city people do."

"That was still a joke," I observe.

He shrugs. "I can't help myself."

I shake my head. "I'm sure my mom would *love* to hear I'm asking for help. Or that I butchered her biscuit recipe."

"Did you?"

"You heard George. They were—and I quote—'atrocious.'"

He chuckles, and for the first time tonight, he doesn't respond with a loose-cannon comment. He seems genuine when he says, "Birdie would've thought that was funny."

"Would she?"

"Oh, very much so." He gives another smile. "Want some advice?"

"Signed up for it, didn't I?"

"Make friends with Lisa and George. Make friends in general."

"I hate people."

He barks out a laugh. "Okay, well, Lisa and George mean well. Keep the phone line open for them, all right?"

"That won't be a problem. Nobody else will be calling. Besides guests, I mean. And maybe my sister."

He stares at me, and as before, I feel completely disarmed by it. How he can switch from goofing around to sincere in a heartbeat is a magic trick I don't understand.

Cliff hums and asks, "Nobody else will call because they don't want to or because *you* don't want them to?"

I hesitate, then admit, "Both."

He nods sagely. "Well, you came to the right town. Copper Run is a great place to disappear to." He sighs. "We should start over, I think."

"What do you mean?"

He holds out his palm. "Hi, I'm Cliff."

I gingerly reach out to shake it, his large hand engulfing my own. His index finger presses on the inside of my wrist. My pinkie grazes the outside of his rough palm.

"Nice to meet you. I'm Michelle."

Shake.

"I'm your next-door neighbor," he says. "I have two girls. They're both total snots."

I laugh despite myself. "I have a dog. He's also a bit of a . . . snot."

Shake.

Cliff smiles, and the handsome crease beside his mouth deepens. "This is the start of a very weird friendship."

I return the smile. "Agreed."

"Agreed."

October
1997

Chapter 8

CLIFF

"I get to play with Rocky after school?"

"Since when are you on nickname terms with him?" I tease. "And, yes, I told the driver to drop you off at the bus stop instead of at the bakery. Make sure you remember, okay?"

Brittany barely says, "Okay!" before running onto the bus with her backpack jostling back and forth. Metal zippers whack against the Tamagotchi, whose health no longer stands a chance now that Rocket's in the picture.

I wave as the bus leaves with its groans and whines toward the elementary school. Walking back to the house, I grab my own bag, drop it in the truck, and cross through the bushes in the backyard to Bird & Breakfast's parking lot.

Through the back-door window, I can see Michelle pacing like a madwoman through the kitchen—clicking a button on the coffeepot, wiping her hands on a small black apron, and tucking on quilted mitts.

I open the back door right as she pulls a pan from the oven.

I wave. "Morning."

Michelle yelps at my voice, fumbles the pan, and drops it on the open oven door.

My face falls. "Shit."

With a loud hiss, Michelle backs against the counter, her chest rising and falling as she shakes out her arm and tenses her hand into a fist.

I snatch a hand towel from the counter and pick up the hot, abandoned pan. I plop it onto the stovetop. When I take a look at her arm, there's a bright red burn line glimmering in the space right above her inner elbow. I join her hissing sound.

"Why didn't you *knock*?" she snaps, eyes closed tight.

"I'm sorry. Force of habit," I quickly say. "Okay, you got a little burn—"

"You think?!"

"Easy fix." I gently wrap my palm around her forearm and guide her to the sink.

She's not looking, as if she's afraid of looking at the burn, should it appear worse than it actually is. Or maybe she doesn't want to see me because she'd spit fire my way. The thought alone makes a single laugh slip out.

"What is so funny?" she says with a sneer.

"Only my imagination." I turn on the sink.

"Keep your imagination to yourself, then."

This time, I fully laugh out loud as I run my fingers under the water until it turns warm.

"All right, dip your arm under."

I guide her arm under the faucet. She pulls in another breath when the water hits her burn, but nods, as if encouraging herself through it.

"There we go," I assist, stroking the inside of her arm to calm her. "Good. Hold it there for a moment."

"Shouldn't this be cold?"

"From one baker to another, trust me, warm is good."

"I'm not a baker," she adds, strained.

"You're doing great," I say, ignoring her jab. "Got coffee ready?"

Her eyes finally open, and she narrows them. "Yes . . ." The word drags.

I take down a chipped mug from the cabinet.

"Make yourself at home," she says sarcastically.

"Thank you. I've been at the bakery since four this morning. I'm beat."

She watches me tip the coffeepot over the cup. "Are you always this . . . invasive?"

I lean against the sink with my coffee mug poised at my lips. "Yes."

I look around the kitchen. The counter—normally stacked with mail or newspapers and countless coffee cups—is spotless. I wonder if they were wiped down with the tea towel folded next to the sink. The only mess—if you can call it that—is a neat stack of papers with hole punches on both sides. A logo on top shows an advertising agency. I wonder if this is work from Seattle.

"Why are you here again?" Michelle asks.

I casually shrug, sipping the coffee. "I wanted to touch base about Brittany."

"Oh." She shakes her head, as if trying to eliminate the snappiness from her voice. "Right. That's today. Sorry."

"Please." I wave her away. "If I could count the number of times someone got irritated with me . . . Anyway, the bus will drop Brittany off at the stop down the road around three. She knows to come here, so you don't have to wait outside for her, but—"

"I can wait outside," she interjects. "If that's what you're most comfortable with."

I pause, kick my foot, then nod. "Are you sure?"

"Yes."

"Then yeah, actually, I'd like that, if you don't mind."

She nods, looking back down at her burn. "Not at all."

I tongue my cheek. "Sorry about the surprise. And the coffee, I guess." I run a hand through my hair. "I'm used to walking in whenever. Birdie was—" Her eyebrows turn in, and I laugh awkwardly. "Y'know what?" I hold my palm in the air. "Doesn't matter."

"What were you gonna say?"

"Mind if I try one?"

She blinks. "What?"

I throw my thumb over my shoulder toward the jumbled biscuits on the pan. "The biscuits," I clarify. "Mind if I try one?"

Michelle stares at me for a few seconds in confusion. I know it was a whiplash-like change in conversation, but the last thing she needs is a constant reminder of her mom, especially after I've caused enough havoc this morning.

She swallows and nods. "Sure." Then adds, "Don't burn yourself on the pan."

"Ha. Funny." I wag my finger at her. "You're funny, Michelle."

"It's to ease the pain," she jokes.

I love it when she has a sense of humor.

I stroll across the kitchen to the abandoned pan. The biscuits are far too put together, which, after a drop like that, likely means they're hard as rocks. Not to mention, the brown tint is too dark, and the tops are lacking any sort of butter yellow I'd expect.

Michelle watches as I pick one up and take a bite. It cracks against my teeth. There's no flavor. It crumbles apart over my tongue in jagged little pieces. Brittany could make better biscuits than these. I wince.

"Oh, don't do that," Michelle breathes. "Are they that bad?"

"Christ, we've got to do something about these," I say.

"You're playing it up."

I hold out the remainder of the cracked monstrosity in my palm. "Do you want to try it?"

"No." She slouches against the sink, bent over and resting her head on the edge. "No," she repeats on a dragging groan. "I know they're bad."

I laugh. "I'll see you after work, Michelle. Don't forget the bus."

She tosses a weak thumbs-up without looking away from the sink.

"Three o'clock," I repeat.

She shakes her thumb higher in irritation.

I laugh. "*So* happy we're friends now."

"Don't make me show you a different finger, Cliff."

MICHELLE

I wait outside the inn at two fifty-five with Rocket by my side. A cooler breeze is picking up as each day passes, and while it's only the first week of October, the Halloween spirit is already in full swing. I saw my neighbor two doors down hoisting up spiderwebs on their front porch this past weekend. The house beside them buried tombstones in their yard.

And both owners said hi to me.

People *love* saying hi here. I'm accustomed to strangers who generally don't talk to me unless there's a coffee in hand or in special circumstances, like if I cut them off in traffic. Apparently, every circumstance is special in Copper Run.

"Spooky, huh?" I ask Rocket, nodding to the bouncing ghosts hanging from tree branches.

He huffs out through his nose. *If one of those things moves, I'm going back inside, Shelly.*

A yellow school bus lurches around the corner, stopping at a storm drain down the street. When the door creaks open, a slew of kids is released from the bus. One boy grips a skateboard and kicks himself down the sidewalk. Two girls giggle over a magazine with the face of Jonathan Taylor Thomas plastered on the cover. And finally, Brittany emerges with bright pink pants and an oversize Spice Girls tee.

She instantly makes a beeline for Rocket. He perks up, wagging his tail over and over until she finally barrels into him, wrapping his neck in a hug.

"Hi, Brittany," I say, but she's too buried in Rocket to notice. I pat her back. "Come on. Let's get you a snack."

"Can Rocky come in the house?" she asks.

"Of course. He's a good dog."

Rocket peers up at me, as if to say, *Since when?*

I ignore him.

"Your hair is cute today," I say to Brittany, trailing my fingers over her zigzag headband.

"Emily did it," she answers. "She's really good with hair."

"Really? What's your favorite style she does for you?"

"I really like pigtails, and, uh . . ." She tries to find the words in the way only kids do. "Sometimes, she uses this thing that gives me waves and stuff."

"That sounds really neat."

"It is," she says, tilting her chin up proudly.

When we reach the kitchen, her hand hasn't left Rocket's back, and he hasn't stopped walking loyally beside her.

I open the top cabinet. "I picked up some apples and peanut butter. How's that sound?"

Brittany hops up onto a breakfast nook chair, swinging her legs back and forth. "Mrs. Birdie used to have Pop-Tarts."

I turn around, popping my hip and leaning it against the counter. "Pop-Tarts? Really?"

My mother gave her Pop-Tarts?

This was the same woman who said TV dinners weren't nutritious enough.

Brittany nods affirmatively. I have a pretty good eye for when people are lying, and she's so distracted by petting Rocket anyway that I bet she's telling the truth.

"What else did she let you do?" I ask, crossing my arms.

Brittany looks up at the ceiling, thinking, then shrugs. "We'd play outside."

I blink to myself, opening my mouth, then shutting it. "Did she ever make you do homework?"

She giggles. "No. Daddy would get *so* mad."

"She was funny, huh?"

"Mm-hmm. Daddy says she's in a better place now."

My stomach coils, and I force a smile. "She is. But unfortunately, I don't have Pop-Tarts." Brittany frowns, but before her bottom lip can start wobbling, I add, "We'll play outside for an hour first. Then you have to do homework."

She wiggles in her seat, jumps down, and rips open the back door into the fenced yard.

Rocket looks at me. *Since when do you bend the rules?*

I roll my eyes. "Hush."

I close the door behind her and search the cabinets for an apple corer, but instead find myself face-to-face with the mug cabinet. In the back, I find a white one with multiple tiny handprints across the surface in a colorful mess. I swivel it around, and smudged in messy black finger paint are the words THANK YOU, BIRDIE.

I set it down and stare. My fingers drum on the counter.

My mom was so involved here. It's not that she wasn't present in my life as I was growing up, but it was different when I was younger. She was detached. She spent a lot of time in bed alone. She was kind but flawed. Copper Run never saw that. Maybe that was for the best.

When Sara was born, things looked up. Mom got out of bed. Dad told me later that she'd started going to a therapist. Mom worked hard to make up my childhood to me, but we never really had the same connection she and Sara did. I was always closer with Dad.

After a couple of moments, I gather myself and cut up the apple, staring blankly at the cutting board. I'm trying not to stew, but I can feel my mind racing as quick as my heart.

I wish she could see me now. I'm running her inn. I'm doing fine with my career in Seattle. People listen to me. I sell dreams and make them happen. No, I'm not just fine—I'm thriving. I'll make her inn thrive too.

Dear Sara.

I slice the knife down. Pain sparks up my finger in an instant. I yell and jerk my hand close to my chest.

"Shit," I hiss, a line of blood drooling down my finger. "Shit, shit."

Striding to the sink, I turn on cool water to soothe it. But right before dipping it under the faucet, I stop.

Cliff said warm water.

I don't know if it's only for burns, but I spend a few more seconds letting the water adjust to a warmer temperature, and then I dip my finger underneath. The cut stings as tendrils of red dilute to pink, dribbling down to the steel surface.

Maybe Mom was right, leaving this place to Sara. Or maybe Sara was right about me asking for help. I've lived here for one month, and I've already gotten injured in this kitchen three times.

I normally know what I'm doing. What the *hell* is happening to me?

"How's it going in here?"

Lisa's voice startles me. I almost hit my palm on the faucet. She stands in the doorway, tiny eyes blinking behind massive glasses. They dart to the cut, then back to me.

"Terribly," I answer honestly.

Slowly, she nods. Her red lips purse together with little lines pinching under her nose.

"Okay, well, go find a Band-Aid. I'll finish up the apple."

I nod stiffly. "Thanks."

"You're welcome."

I walk back to the bedroom, sifting through the bathroom medicine cabinet behind the mirror for a Band-Aid. When I close it, I stare at myself. I look like the same Michelle—soft hair with forced volume from a blowout, perfectly plucked eyebrows, wearing my favorite mauve lipliner and a black vest over denim jeans. Professional yet approachable Michelle. Michelle who has everything together.

But there's a burn on my inner arm and a cut on my finger. And I feel *tired*.

I pull the Band-Aid over my cut and click off the bathroom light, darkening the pink tiled walls once more. When I walk past my window, I notice someone outside. Emily traipses by with her backpack on, away from their house and hand in hand with a boy her age.

How long has she been at home? School let out within the past hour.

They're mid-laugh when our gazes catch. She halts. The boy does too. The three of us stare like we're some weird herd of spooked deer.

The boy looks like he leaped out from the image of Kurt Cobain on Emily's tee. His shoulder-length dirty-blond hair is partially tucked behind an ear that's pierced with a single hoop. Brown hairs wisp over his upper lip, and irritated little red dots gather in clusters near his forehead and cheeks. I have to assume this is the fabled Josh. The very-disliked-by-her-father Josh.

Emily's eyebrows cinch inward. A silent plea.

I consider saying something. But eventually, I turn away from the window and walk back down the hall without a word.

I don't know what I saw, but I definitely know it isn't my business.

Chapter 10

CLIFF

"George, if you place one more last-minute catering order, I'm going to ban you."

The older man gruffs out something that might have been a curse word as I carry the box full of bear claws, cinnamon pecan Danish, and almond croissants down the sidewalk to his parked car.

"I'm serious," I continue. "Maybe even death or something. First-degree murder. Premeditated. Same with your bingo group."

He ignores me, keying open the door. I slide the box into his passenger seat.

"Thanks again, Cliff," he grunts.

I wave my hand in the air. "Yeah, yeah, you're welcome."

"You'll forgive me tomorrow."

"I won't because I've already forgiven you now, you old coot."

I'm giving him a hard time, and he knows it.

With a final wave and a smirk, he lowers into his car, backs out of the spot with the type of lead foot the confident elderly love, and putters down the street toward the community center for evening bingo.

"Why is there a mess?" Carol asks when I get back to the bakery.

"George had a fire drill again. I had to improvise."

I take my blue apron from its hook beside the prep table and tie it back around me. My trusty apron is old, scarred by burns and multiple stitched-up rips. But Emily's little kindergarten handprints, smacked on the front in faded red and white paint, are visible beneath it all.

"Brittany didn't get off the bus today," Carol observes.

"I know." I shift a pan of croissants to the left of the steel table to make room.

"I haven't seen Emily either."

"Probably at work. I'll call Lisa later."

She narrows her eyes. "What are you doing?"

"Baking."

"Why?"

"Because it's what I do here."

"Okay," she says slowly. "But aren't you worried about where your daughters are?"

"No."

Carol shakes her head, pinching her eyes closed. "I'm confused."

"There are some leftover cannoli in the case if you want some."

"Don't change the subject. I mean, yes, I'll get one, but"—she waves her hands—"not the point! You're here. You're never here past three. At least not since Birdie passed. And your girls aren't running around here either."

The bell above the front door dings, but before either of us can go to the front, heavy footfalls grow louder and Lars appears in the kitchen.

"Whoa, what's with the mess?" he asks. "Shouldn't you be heading out soon?"

I narrow my eyes. "Why are you here?"

"I always pick up a doughnut before opening shop," he says.

"Every day?"

"Every weekday lately," Carol says with a sneer. "Freeloader."

Lars tosses her a wink. "You let it happen."

He crosses in front of her to grab an already set-aside doughnut on a square napkin. I was wondering why that was there.

"So, what's going on, Cliff?"

I clear my throat. "Michelle is watching Brittany."

Carol gasps, her palm flying to her chest. "Really?"

"It's not that big a deal."

A slow smirk curls onto Lars's mouth. "It's driving you insane, isn't it?"

Carol shakes her head. "God, how'd you trick her into watching Britt?"

I scoff out a laugh. "I don't trick people. Ever stopped to think that maybe I'm naturally charming?"

"No," they both say.

I click my tongue. "All right. Well, other people think so."

"I know, and it's *so* annoying," Lars teases, taking a bite of his doughnut. That's been Lars's favorite pastry since we were kids. Specifically, he likes the plain glazed kind. He's a simple guy.

Carol groans, slouching against the wall. "I swear, Betty asks me weekly if you're ready to get back on the market. She said she has a niece or a distant cousin or something. I don't know."

My stomach clenches. "Definitely not ready for that."

I've been divorced for two years, and Copper Run has been waiting for the gun at the starting line ever since. It's not that I'm *not* ready to date. I'm ready for a lot of things—Michelle digging into my pocket last month proved that. The real concern is that I'm not sure who would *want* to date me. Copper Run wants to set me up, but they don't know what it's like to be with me all the time. Tracy wasn't shy about telling me when I irritated her. I don't need someone else voicing that again.

Lars talks through a mouthful of doughnut. "You know what? You need to get laid, man. You made two kids, so I know you can do it."

"Gross," Carol says, folding her arms over her chest.

"I'm not gonna sleep with just anyone," I murmur.

"And why not?" he asks.

"Because . . . I'm not." I shake my head.

"Because you've only slept with Trace?"

Carol groans. "Can we *not* talk about my brother having sex, please?"

Lars grins wolfishly and takes another bite of his doughnut.

"Anyway, yes," I continue, "Michelle offered to watch Britt. I didn't trick her into anything."

"And why would she offer?" Carol asks.

"I'm giving her hospitality lessons."

"Why does she need those?" Lars says through a laugh. "Is Michelle not a nice person? She seemed nice to me. And pretty." He raises his eyebrows and lowers them.

"You've got doughnut in your mustache," Carol says.

I shoot him a look. "Michelle's not your type. She'll be here for three months."

"Oh. Never mind."

For some reason, relief washes through me. It's probably

because I know the last thing Michelle needs is Lars and his crumb-filled mustache.

"Of course she's nice," I say. "But . . . she's nice with many walls up." I smile to myself. "But even brick houses have charm. So, I'm helping."

"So, you annoyed her into submission, is what I'm hearing," Carol says.

I snort in response.

Carol nods at the prep table, now smeared with watery flour, which is building up to a sticky substance becoming dough. "And what's with the mess?"

Wisps of cinnamon litter parts of the table. They smell a bit like Michelle, but not quite. I have to start somewhere though. Birdie's favorite pastry was cinnamon rolls. I'm determined to know Michelle's too. It's like an itch I need to scratch.

"I'm making cinnamon rolls," I explain.

"Are they for your new friend, Michelle?" Lars asks.

I squint. "Why are you up my ass today?"

"You could use a smoke," Carol adds.

"And when did you say you're quitting again?" I ask.

She purses her lips. "Don't turn this back on me. You're a mess right now."

"I'm making rolls, Carol. It's not a big deal."

Then Lars smirks. "You can't relax for a second, not knowing how it's going with Britt."

He's right. He's been right about most things since we were kids, and I hate it. He was right about Tracy too—repeatedly asking on my wedding day if I was sure—but he's too good a guy to hold that over my head.

"I'm fine," I say. "I'm great even. I have so much time to do extra things now."

Carol gasps. "Oh my God, I've rubbed off on you. You're a basket case too."

I pause mid–dough roll and lean my forearms on the prep table. "Are you always this pleasant in the afternoons?"

Carol smiles. "No, this is only for you."

"Well, get used to seeing more of this face around this time of day."

"What face?" she asks. "The Basket Case's face?"

"Yeah, we don't want him," Lars throws in.

"No, I—" I pinch my nose. "*My* face, you two."

"I don't like your face," Carol says.

"Too bad. I'm getting my life together. Baking more for this place. We'll stay open later. Make more money. It's good. I'm turning over a new leaf."

Carol tsks. "Pretty sure the leaves outside are dead."

My face falls. She shrugs innocently, pulling out her pack of cigarettes and walking out to the front. Lars licks the remaining glaze off the tips of his fingers and grins.

"Have fun," he singsongs, leaving the kitchen and disappearing out the door too.

I glance through the large windows, watching the trees lean in the fall breeze. Below, curled—and very dead—leaves gather in a pile.

"Looks like turned leaves to me," I grumble, throwing a balled-up rag like a basketball to the laundry basket in the corner and completely missing, the rag instead slapping on the tiled floor, as if taunting me.

∽

Two hours later, I walk across Bird & Breakfast's front yard with a box of cinnamon rolls balanced in my palm. Brittany sits in the grass with two teacups nestled in bare patches.

Rocket stoically sits across from her as she tucks a teacup between his stiff paws.

"Drink!" she commands.

He doesn't move, but his tail wags.

"Britt, I don't think he understands," I say, causing her to jump.

"Daddy!" she squeals.

I bend down, set the box on the grass, and capture Brittany in my arms.

"How was your day?" I ask.

"Rocket and I are having teatime!"

I peer over her shoulder. The dog blinks at me, blank-faced and bored.

"That's . . . sweet," I say. "How was school?"

"We made pumpkins!"

"Real pumpkins?" I gawk. "No way."

"No! Paper pumpkins!" she says with a giggle.

"Ohh," I say, feigning surprise. "And how was the afternoon with Miss Michelle?"

"Miss Shell gave me apple slices, and I got to talk to some lady from Michigan!"

I swivel my gaze over to the porch. Michelle sits on the hanging swing bench with her legs tucked under her. I grin. She always presents herself so pristinely.

"That's exciting," I say to Brittany. "Well, you keep playing for five more minutes." I pat her shoulder. "Then we've gotta eat dinner, okay?" She reaches for the box, and I swoop it in my arms. "Pastries later."

"Ahh." Brittany pouts in an over-the-top way.

I ruffle her hair. "Yeah, yeah," I mock. "Dad sucks."

She pokes out her bottom lip and reluctantly goes back to pouring invisible tea.

I crunch over fallen leaves, walk up the squeaking front porch steps, then fall down on the opposite side of the bench swing. My momentum has us swinging back wildly before evening out again. Michelle eyes the box in my lap.

"Brought you something," I say, tipping open the box to reveal a row of cinnamon rolls, the icing I drizzled over them seconds before leaving the bakery still dripping.

"Are these leftovers from today?" she asks.

"Try one."

She narrows her eyes, and I laugh.

"Come on. Try it."

She takes a cinnamon roll from the box, slowly raises it to her full lips, and bites down. Maybe it's a baker thing, but I love watching people eat pastries. More specifically, I like how Michelle looks when she eats one of mine. Her eyes flutter closed. The corner of her lips quirks into a smile. And her thin eyebrows cinch together in the middle.

"These are amazing," she moans.

Christ. My heart is pounding.

"That's a noise I like to hear," I say.

Her eyes snap open. I chuckle.

"I'm a baker. We live for others' enjoyment."

Except, immediately after, she puts the roll back in the box.

Huh.

I know when a treat *belongs* to someone—when it captures them so well that they can't put it down. Cinnamon rolls are not her favorite. Noted.

She assesses me for a moment before asking, "So, why did you want to show me these?"

"Because they're good."

"Very cocky."

"And," I say, leaning in, "because they're easy to make. You're gonna start baking these instead of biscuits."

She huffs out a laugh through her nose. "I can't make cinnamon rolls."

"Sure you can. Because I'll teach you."

She shakes her head. "We haven't even started the People Lessons we agreed to."

"*People Lessons*," I muse. "Love that."

"Baking lessons too?" she continues without acknowledging my side comment. "It's too much, Cliff."

"Being able to bake a decent breakfast for your guests goes hand in hand with People Lessons. Trust me. Also, I can decide what's too much, all right?" Before she can protest again, I nod my chin to Brittany. "How'd this work out today?"

"Good. She's a good kid."

"Good."

"She likes Rocket a lot."

I nod. "I can see that."

"I'm surprised you're not more nervous," Michelle observes. "Given the scar and bite. All the trauma you carry," she finishes with a sly grin.

"Just because I had a bad moment with a dog doesn't mean Brittany needs to. I always want better things for her and Emily. Thankfully, Brittany is already far braver than I was at her age."

"She tried sliding down the banister earlier," Michelle says. "And she carried on a whole conversation with some woman who probably wanted to read the paper in peace."

I bark out a laugh. "She wasn't too much work today, was she?"

"No, the woman adored her by the end of it," she says before adding, "And I'll decide what's too much."

I smile as she lifts a teasing eyebrow.

"Funny." I think Michelle's subtlety in her humor is what I like best.

She reaches up to twirl her earring between her fingers. I wonder if it's a nervous thing. But below her nail polish, I spot a small Band-Aid wrapped around her finger.

"Whoa, what's this?" I reach out and trace my finger along hers.

She draws in a breath. "I cut myself slicing an apple."

"Christ, you're gonna accidentally kill yourself in that kitchen."

"I'm not entirely helpless."

I grin. "This"—I touch her Band-Aid—"and this"—I brush my thumb over the pink burn on her inner arm—"are not helping your case."

Michelle blinks at my fingers tracing over her arm. Her spine is as stiff as a board. Her eyes meet mine, and I feel my brow furrow.

I chuckle. "Everything all right?"

But then I realize I'm touching her.

Shoelaces snapping on concrete interrupt us, drawing my attention over to my house as I jerk my hand away. Emily marches up the driveway. Her headphones rest over her ears, and the Discman is held in a fist by her side.

"Em!" I yell. She doesn't look up at first, so I cup my palms over my mouth. "Emily!"

She jerks her head up and slides down the headphones.

"How was school, kiddo?"

"Good," she says, tucking her CD player and her palms into her jean jacket pockets.

I narrow my eyes at the short answer because it's all too familiar. "Seeing Josh at the video store again?"

"No," she says defensively. "I worked. After school. I went straight there."

"That doesn't sound suspicious at all."

"I worked," she repeats, but she's notably kicking a curled-up leaf on the ground. Her eyes dart to Michelle's, then back to me.

"So, if I checked your bag, you wouldn't have a movie in there?"

"Yeah, but it's from, like, two days ago."

"What movie?" Michelle calls over.

Emily plays with a loose string on her jacket. "*Nightmare on Elm Street.*"

"You're gonna have nightmares," I say.

"No, I'm not."

"Don't let your sister watch it either. So, how's Josh?" I ask.

She darts her eyes to Michelle again. Almost nervously. Then she looks back at me. "He's fine."

"So, you *were* at the video store today."

She groans. "God, you're so *insufferable* about him."

"Doing my dad-ly duty," I call, but she's already ripping open the screen door to our house and clunking through the threshold.

"'*Insufferable*,'" I mimic with two finger quotations. "She's gonna ace the SAT with words like that."

Michelle's gaze lingers on the closed door before swiveling to me. "You don't like Josh?"

"I don't have many opinions about the guy. But he's a teenage boy. And he thinks teenage-boy things." I laugh under my breath and lightly kick the porch, sending our bench rocking back. "Her mom and I got together at that age. And, well, sex education didn't exactly exist for us. So, Emily was our surprise."

"You don't want her to get pregnant," Michelle detects, but it's not a question.

"I want her to do whatever she wants to do," I answer. "But I want her to be smart about it. I wouldn't trade Emily for the world, but parenting was hard. *Teenagers* trying to parent is *hard*. We were so young. I don't want hormones to make the decision for her."

The front door of my house squeaks open again, and Emily holds out our phone. One hand covers the receiver as she yells, "Brittany, it's Mom!"

I swallow. The heart-jerking moment of my ex calling never ceases to darken my good day like a light switch.

Brittany scrambles up from the grass and across the yard, saying goodbye to only Rocket and not me or Michelle. I shake my head with a grin, but Michelle stares at the front door for a second or two after it closes.

Behind us, the inn's door creaks open, and a guest pokes her head out.

"Hi," she says, looking at Michelle but lingering on me when I smile back at her politely. "Do you have any flyers for the Harvest Festival?"

"It ended last week," Michelle answers quickly. It's short. To the point. Not exactly irritated. Factual. No hint of a smile.

The woman's eyebrows pinch together, and she nods. "Oh. Right. Well, thank you."

Michelle nods, then turns back to me as the guest ducks back into the inn. The door snaps shut behind her.

I blink at Michelle, choking out a laugh.

"What?" she asks defensively.

I chuckle. "I'll drop by for lunch tomorrow."

"What? Why?"

"Trust me."

"You're inviting yourself over?"

"Pretty much." I rise from the bench to stretch.

"Why?"

"Because we've *got* to kick-start those People Lessons." I pocket my hands. "I didn't realize it was that bad."

"It's not that bad."

"That"—I point to the door—"was sad."

Her face falls. "Really?"

"Oh. It was terrible, Michelle."

"What did I do? I gave her the information she'd asked for."

I tilt my head to the side and mutter a teasing "And you don't even know what you did wrong."

Michelle purses her lips and twists the corner of her mouth. "Fine," she spits out. "Lunch tomorrow."

"Attagirl."

I head toward the stairs, but she stops me with, "And, Cliff?"

"Hmm?"

"You're insufferable."

I give a full-blown grin. I can't help myself. "So I've heard."

Chapter 11

MICHELLE

"Okay, them. Right there," Cliff whispers.

"Why them?"

"Look at them," he murmurs into my ear, his voice low.

Cliff and I are crouched at the top of the stairs, peering through the spindles of the banister that overlook Bird & Breakfast's main parlor. A couple sits on the floral chaise below, rotating a floppy map of Copper Run and the surrounding Vermont area.

Cliff leans closer, resting his forearm on his knee and pointing. "They need help."

"They have a map. They're fine. They don't need me bothering them."

At work, I let my employees figure things out on their own unless they ask for help. Anything more makes it seem like I don't trust them. How is hospitality any different?

He raises both eyebrows at me. "Are you serious?" He holds out a palm. "They clearly need advice."

"No, they're figuring it out," I say. Of course, that's the moment when the couple flips the map sideways. I cringe. "Maybe."

"So, as their host, wouldn't you love to offer some assistance?"

"I don't know this town either."

He chuckles. "Then you would figure it out together. How fun."

Walking around this town is on my very long list of research to do. I love finding exactly what makes something so appealing that you can't ignore it. It's why I'm good at what I do. But I don't mention that.

I snort. "That's ridiculous."

"Or endearing."

"I'm not endearing."

"*I'm* endeared by you."

"Ha ha." I fake laugh, moving my attention back to the couple and not letting the compliment linger between us more than it already is. They're tapping an area on the map now. "See? They don't need help."

"Yes, they do," Cliff says through a barely stifled laugh. "You gotta go down there, enough to be present, but not enough to be overwhelming."

"Then *you* help."

"You."

"No."

"Yes," Cliff mocks back.

The two guests whip their heads to the stairwell, and Cliff and I quickly stumble back, my shoes fumbling into his legs and his palm landing on my back to steady me as we scramble up the stairs.

We reach the second-floor landing, and my face is hot.

"That was embarrassing." My hands shake, and I stretch them out.

Cliff stares at my fidgeting hands. "Are you okay?"

"I'm fine."

"You sure?"

I give a pointed look.

"I don't like being bad at things," I explain. "I don't know the last time I was bad at anything."

He chuckles, threading a hand through his floppy hair, which somehow never seems to land in a place he's comfortable with. "Michelle, if you want my help, you've got to listen to me once in a while."

"I like things a certain way."

The line near his mouth stretches and deepens as he lifts his lips to one side. It's the cocky smile I've gotten accustomed to throughout the afternoon.

"You asked me to be here," he reminds me.

"I know; I know."

He takes a step forward, placing large, heavy palms on my shoulders. I hiss in a breath. That's the thing about Cliff—he touches everyone, and it's always warm.

"Why do you think I own a bakery?" he asks.

I tilt my head to the side. "Because no company would put up with you."

He grins. "Because I like being my own boss. But sometimes, even I need help, which is why I hired Carol. And"—he squeezes my shoulders once before letting go—"yes, being an employee somewhere sounds like torture."

"Did you ever work a job?" I ask curiously.

He scratches behind his head. "In another life. Before the bakery."

"Why'd you quit?"

He shrugs and simply says, "Freedom."

I twist my lips to the side, and he laughs.

"Also, I'm damn good at baking. So, let's move on to that next. Maybe we'll have more luck there."

I groan.

"God, you're worse than Emily sometimes—you know that?"

"Are you calling me a teenager?" I ask.

He lowers his gaze down to my black clogs and back up. "If the shoe fits."

I grimace. "Funny."

We walk down the stairwell. I exhale a breath upon seeing the map couple gone. With them and the other guest out sightseeing, the house is empty for the first time all morning.

We enter the kitchen. The strong scent of cinnamon filters from the oven.

"Mmm." Cliff rubs his palms together. "Smells promising."

Good.

I expected Cliff to be irritated that I'd started without him, but instead, he laughs at my proactiveness. I'm quickly realizing that not much bothers Cliff Burke. It's such a contrast to Allen, who would have given up teaching me altogether had I pulled a stunt like that. Part of me wonders if that's what I wanted to happen.

These are *my* cinnamon rolls. I started baking last night and have made three terrible batches since then. I wanted to prove I can do whatever he can. Maybe I'm not good with people, but I don't need baking lessons on top of it. And I can feel it—*this* is the batch that will prove it.

Cliff squeaks open the oven. I stand on my toes to look over his shoulder, and my face falls. The rolls are a dark brown, and even I can see that's probably *too* brown.

Cliff's eyes widen before swiveling over to me. "How long have these been in here?"

"My mom's recipe said thirty-five minutes."

He snorts. "No, it didn't."

"I think I know what it said. I read it this morning."

"Not closely enough," he says, crossing the kitchen to a drawer.

I fold my arms over my chest. "Oh, really? And how do you know?"

He grins. "Because I wrote it for her."

Of course he gave my mom this recipe.

I curl my lips in to silence myself as embarrassment slides down my spine like a freezing ice cube.

Cliff snatches mittens from the first drawer he finds. He seems to know where everything is in this kitchen.

When Cliff's back is facing me, I slip my finger into the bookmarked section of Mom's black binder and reread her cinnamon roll recipe. I grumble. Cliff was right. They were only supposed to be in there for *twenty*-five minutes. Tonguing my cheek, I look back, and Cliff is already smiling.

"Was I right?" he asks.

"You were right."

The familiar cocky smile spreads across his face, and he looks at the ceiling, as if praying to heaven. "I love it when that happens."

He slides on the mittens, opens the oven, and takes out the deep dish of rolls, placing the pan on the spare towel on the counter. He drops the gloves and pulls out a fork from yet another drawer he instinctively knows will contain flatware and unceremoniously cuts into a roll, spearing it at the end of the tongs.

Cliff blows on it first, then slowly takes a bite. I watch the metal tips disappear between his lips and stare as the fork steadily slides back out, tugging part of his bottom lip with it. His tongue flicks to the corner of his mouth, licking a smidgen of leftover cinnamon. Why does it feel like slow motion?

"That's terrible."

I blink back to the present and shake my head. "Terrible?"

"Terrible," he repeats. "The worst roll I've ever tasted. Toss it out."

I open and close my mouth, trying to find words, until I see a sly, lopsided smile. My lips straighten into a line. "You're messing with me."

He chuckles. "It was in there too long, so it's a little stiff. It's not bad though." He raises his eyebrows and lowers them. "But you can do better."

Cliff digs in a brown grocery bag set on the floor and pulls out flour. Rocket's head lifts from the rug as he sniffs the air.

"You brought more ingredients?" I ask as he removes sugar next. I sigh. "You knew we'd have to remake it."

"Thought I'd let you try first," he says with a little wink. A wink so casual that my heart stutters.

I don't know the last time anyone winked at me.

"And, yes," Cliff says, leaning in closer like we're sharing a secret, "I had a feeling you'd try before I got here, so I brought extra."

I drop my shoulders and roll my head back. His low laugh rumbles in his throat as he dips both arms into the bag again. He emerges with two sandwiches in clear zipped bags, presenting them to me in his palms.

"Ham or turkey?"

"You made lunch for me too?" I ask, almost whining. "Cliff, please . . ."

"I'm not gonna invite myself over, then ask you to make me a sandwich. I got them from Betty's sandwich shop. Ham or turkey?"

"Cliff, you're already helping me—"

"Ham or turkey, Michelle."

I hold out my palm and sigh. "Turkey, then."

"Good. Ham is my favorite." Even though Cliff smiles when he says it, it doesn't reach his eyes. That crease beside his lips isn't as deep as it could go.

He sets his sandwich aside. I wonder if he's lying.

"I also brought"—he reaches into the bag and pulls out a small box, opening it to reveal a doughy, sugar-crusted blue triangle—"a blueberry scone."

"Oh. Thank you."

"Try it?"

"Now?"

"Yes."

I squint. "Is this a weird baker thing?"

He chuckles. "Try it."

I remove it from the box, side-eyeing him with a *fine, whatever* smile as I take a bite.

Oh God.

I cup a palm under my mouth to catch any falling pieces. It's good—too good—with a thin layer of sugary, hardened crust but a soft, fluffy inside. The blueberries taste almost fresh. I wonder if this is what having a baker friend is like. Constant, unimaginably tasty food.

"It's really good," I say, but weirdly enough, Cliff doesn't seem satisfied.

Instead, he lets out a low hum as he crosses the kitchen to rip open another drawer to pull out parchment paper.

"What?" I ask. "It *is* good."

"But it's not there yet."

"What are you talking about?"

"It's a weird baker thing," he says with a smile, mocking my words from earlier. He knocks his chin toward a cabinet behind me. "Mind grabbing a bowl for me?"

I set the remainder of my scone back in the box and open the cabinet to find a set of stacked bowls nested inside each other.

"Do you know where everything is?" I ask.

He nods. "I've spent more time here than in my own house this past year."

"I can't believe you were so close to my mom."

"She was a good lady. Better to my girls than their own mom." He chuckles. "Funny how that works out."

I hum noncommittally, but my mind is stuck, like a snagged sweater, slowly unraveling the thoughts of my own mom. Our complications.

I set down the bowl, and within moments, he's whisking sugar and flour. He explains the baking steps as he fills another bowl with wet ingredients. He says he uses whole milk so it's richer and this brand of yeast because it's quicker for my specific needs.

His secret is a bit more butter because, "Well, it's butter," he answers with a shrug.

Cliff then rolls up his loose cable-knit sweater sleeves, slaps the dough onto flour-coated parchment paper, and starts kneading the mix with his palms. Spreading and pulling, sending puffs of white over his pulsing forearms. I find myself breathing heavier, swallowing deeper, and tapping incessantly on the counter beside him.

I didn't realize baking was . . . *this*. Strong forearms and deft hands.

Cliff looks toward me, and I hold his gaze. I know I'm overcompensating with how hard I'm staring because this man *cannot* know I was watching him work like that.

"Birdie talked about you," he says. "A lot."

My heart drops. "She did?"

"You and Sara."

"Probably more about Sara. She's more exciting."

"Mmm," he muses again, returning to the steadily forming dough. "No. Both of you. You were . . ."

"The more serious one?"

He chuckles. "The responsible one. She worried about you sometimes."

I look down at my feet and inhale. But my eyes travel to the binder like they have a mind of their own.

Dear Sara.

Cliff stares at me with his eyebrows stitched in the middle, like he can hear the circles I was running through in my head.

"Everyone here saw pieces of Mom I didn't," I murmur on a breath, and one look at Cliff's attentive face has me adding, "Or . . . didn't want to maybe." I part my lips, in shock that I even said that, and I quickly close them again. "Just . . . if I'm being honest."

"You want to talk about it?"

"No."

"Fair enough." He clears his throat. "You know, your relationship with Birdie reminds me a lot of Emily and her mom."

"What do you mean?" I ask.

"Emily and Tracy are . . . tumultuous together, to say the least. You seem that way with Birdie."

I swallow and don't address it. "Emily's a teenager. Of course they're tumultuous."

"It's more than that. Tracy makes it obvious that Emily was unplanned. That she's the reason we're tied together."

My mouth drops open. "Do *you* think that?"

"Hell no," he snaps so quickly that I almost jump back. "Emily was a surprise. And, sure, I'm now tied to Tracy in some way for the rest of our lives. But that's not Emily's burden. And it's unfair that Tracy puts that on her." He looks into the flour as his smile tugs his mouth to the side, like whatever thoughts are going through his brain soothe him. "For all we've put her through, Emily's such a great kid. I feel like I blinked, and suddenly, she has opinions and interests. And it's weird that she's into boys—and not just boys, but . . . boys with hormones and peach fuzz." He shakes his head with a breathy laugh.

"Do you miss when she was Brittany's age?" I ask.

"Yes. And no." He shrugs with another smile. "Every phase gets better and better. She's a little bit of a jerk sometimes, but, God, I love that about her. She'll probably kill Josh if he ever hurts her." He chuffs out a laugh. "If I don't get to him first." He clears his throat. "Anyway, thanks for that."

"For what?"

"Listening."

"You talk so much; it's hard not to."

He smirks. "I know."

"And you're very open about your ex."

"There's no point in keeping any of it to myself now. Don't you feel the same?"

"No," I admit.

"No?"

"Just because you don't have anything to be ashamed of from your marriage doesn't mean I don't."

Removing his hands from the dough, he tilts his head to the side with a smile. I can already tell I've presented a challenge he can't resist.

"Tell me one single secret, Michelle."

"A secret?"

"That's what I said."

"No."

I distract myself by grabbing my turkey sandwich. He eyes it before quickly averting his gaze. When he looks away, I switch it out for the ham.

"Aren't we friends?" he teases. "I told you about Tracy. Tell me about what's-his-face."

"Allen," I correct.

"Right. The loser."

"He's not a loser. He's . . . well, he's a doctor actually." I give a pointed stare. "*Not* a loser."

"He's a loser," Cliff repeats, moving back to kneading dough. "Why else would he cheat on you? You're stunning."

My heart skips as I stammer, "Wh-what?"

"That's not an opinion. That's a fact. You are. Even when you scowl at me."

Then, slowly, Cliff peers up through hooded eyes, scanning from my lips down to my waist and back up. Goose bumps press into the fabric of my shirt.

"You're stunning. And he's a bonehead."

I click my tongue and nod. "That's . . . well . . . thank you."

"You're welcome."

I shift from one foot to the other, eyeing his moving arms . . . the little popping veins and—

"You mentioned another life," I say.

"When?"

"Upstairs. Before the bakery. What did you do?"

"Sales."

"That's not bad," I say. "I work in advertising."

"And do you like it?" he asks.

"I love it."

He smiles to himself. "Well . . . I didn't. It's what Tracy wanted." He nods to the stack of paperwork on the counter.

They're faxed papers from Mark. The logo for Topsy's Travel Agency—our biggest client in Washington—is displayed on the first page. "Are you working your Seattle job, even out here?"

"I can't help myself."

"Love it that much, huh? Why?"

"I don't know . . . I do. It's hard to describe."

"I assume that's not the juicy secret I'll be getting today," he says with a side smile.

Cliff is so unabashedly honest. So himself.

"Fine," I say. "You want a secret?"

"The best one you got," he confirms.

"I . . ." I tilt up my chin. "I hated when Allen snored."

Guilt roils through me. Like I shouldn't be talking about my husband—*ex*-husband—like that.

Cliff opens his mouth in a mocking gasp. "Whoa, tone it down over there. That's hard-hitting. I can't handle that level of cruelty."

Cliff relaxes into a teasing, lopsided grin, and that little piece of me—the one that felt guilty for even bringing up a silly annoyance—breaks apart and flits down to the ground. Because my answer wasn't that serious and Cliff's question wasn't either.

I choke out a laugh and step forward to push his shoulder. "Hey! You asked for a secret, and I gave you one."

He stares at the small spot where I touched him, then grins. "Barely."

"That was big for me."

He chuckles in sync with me, as he darts his eyes down to my lips. Similar to his lack of personal space, Cliff also has no issues lingering with his gaze either. My smile quickly fades, descending into a defensive frown.

He flicks his eyes up to meet mine once more. "See? I was right. You're beautiful, even when you scowl."

I roll my eyes. "Oh, shut up, Cliff."

But the simple moment has me smiling, and I can't wipe it off my face.

He glances at the sandwich next to me, then at the switched one closer to him on the counter.

"Change your mind?" he asks.

"I could tell turkey is actually your favorite."

"You said you wanted it though," he says. "I was trying to be nice."

"And I'm trying too."

We exchange another small smile, and he goes back to kneading the dough.

Cliff can be frustrating.

But I also kinda like him.

A little bit.

Chapter 12

MICHELLE

"The bathroom towels are in your dresser, and I have a little binder on top with some things to do in Copper Run. The fall festival is over now, and Halloween decorations are around town. There's a man two blocks down, named Winston—you can't miss his house—and he sits on his porch every night to watch people look at his decorations. He's really proud."

"Wow, and are they good?"

I have no idea. This information was fed to me by Cliff, even though he won't let me walk past Winston's house myself yet.

Cliff says Winston's an artist. He makes murals around town, but he also decorates for every holiday. He transforms his house into an erected haunted maze on Halloween, and Cliff doesn't want to ruin the surprise for me until it's finished.

But Miss Margaret and her single suitcase won't be staying long enough to see it, so I smile and answer, "They're the perfect amount of spooky."

The woman grins from ear to ear.

"Well"—I clap my hands together—"I won't keep you. Make yourself at home. And please let me know if there's anything else I can help you with. I'm heading to lunch, but I'll be back after one to make some extra coffee."

She beams. "Thank you."

"Of course."

Cliff's words echo in my ears. *"Enough to be present, but not enough to be overwhelming."*

As she sits on the end of her freshly made bed, complete with a welcome letter on the pillow, I discreetly drop a wrapped toffee on the dresser. Lisa says leaving little breadcrumbs are the thoughtful things guests will remember.

I take the stairs down to the foyer and grab Mom's purse from its hook in the kitchen. I take Rocket's leash beside it. The rattling sound makes Rocket shoot out from the bedroom. I clip it to his collar, and we head out the front door, down the cobblestone walkway, and to the mailbox, where I gather mail, tuck it under my arm for later, and head toward Copper Run's square.

The details I left for Miss Margaret are correct; Copper Run has exploded with decorations the past two weeks. Spiderwebs stretch across front doors, porches, and gates. Pumpkins with carved Cheshire cat grins line fences, and plastic skeletons claw up from rough dirt graves throughout grassy yards. Every time we pass the house with dangling linen ghosts swaying from tree branches, Rocket lets out a low growl.

"They're not gonna hurt you."

He huffs out through his nose. *Liar.*

We hit the square, and I drop by the sandwich shop first, smiling as nice as I can to the owner, Betty, who always insists I try new ingredients.

"The turkey and ham sandwiches, as usual," I say.

"Oh, you must try the new secret sauce!"

"No, thank you."

"You'll never guess what's in it, but I promise it's good." She spreads the sauce on the bread as if she didn't hear me.

"Thanks, Betty."

"Anytime, Shells!"

People in Copper Run love calling me by whatever they like, even though I don't think I've given the impression that I like it even once. But the familiarity—the sweet little smile Betty gives me as she hands me the bag of sandwiches—makes the insult not so bad.

In the square, scarecrows lie abandoned beside the walkway. A giant felt spider is belly up beside stacked cardboard boxes with labels like LIGHTS and GHOULS and . . . FAKE BLOOD?

Cliff's friend Lars is across the park, plunging stakes into the soft grass. He tosses me a friendly wave, as does the local florist, Sandra, who walks across the stone steps with her arms full of fall-colored bouquets.

I'm realizing quickly that it's difficult to be alone in this town. I lived a quiet, efficient life in Seattle. Nothing here works like that.

Cliff stands at the top of a tall ladder beside the gazebo, stringing spiderwebs between the poles. His cheeks are red with exhaustion, even with the cool breeze whipping up. I smile a little at the sight of Cliff flushed.

"They roped you into decorating?" I ask.

He looks down at me, eyeing my white-knuckled fist around the bag of sandwiches. I hold the ladder steady while Cliff takes wobbling steps down.

"Betty call you Shells again?" he asks.

"Yes," I mumble.

"The nerve!"

I flatten my lips in a line at his subsequent grin, and then I dig in the bag.

"Turkey for you," I say, handing him the sandwich. "Topped with Betty's new secret sauce she insists is good."

"Oh no," he moans.

We both sit on the bench inside the gazebo—Cliff on my left and a deflated blow-up ghost on my right.

"By the way, your booklet seemed to go over well," I say.

His eyebrows rise. "Oh yeah? So, you made the pitch about—"

"The yard and decorations and all that," I finish for him.

"Fantastic. See?" He waves his sandwich around because the man is incapable of not talking with his hands. "You're getting the hang of things."

"People smile around me more."

"You're a good person to smile around," Cliff says, taking a bite.

He does things like that—giving casual compliments like they're Halloween candy. I never know how to react, and I used to think that was his intention. Shock and awe. But now . . . now, Cliff throws out nice things without any pause for recognition.

"Betty was right," he says, gesturing with his sandwich. "The sauce is good. Try it."

I take a bite, and my face must contort because he chuckles.

"What's wrong?"

I shake my head and wince, barely getting out a muffled, "I think the secret sauce is mustard."

"You hate mustard?"

I nod, then reluctantly swallow.

Cliff laughs and takes another bite of his own sandwich with an exaggerated "*Mmm*."

I point the sandwich toward Rocket. "Want it?"

Even Rocket sniffs at the yellow sauce staining the bread. He turns his head away. *Filth.*

"Agree."

Cliff throws a thumb over his shoulder. "I have some leftover croissants from this morning if you want one."

"Please."

"Good, and if you're not gonna eat that . . ." He reaches out for the sandwich.

"All yours."

I smack my hands together to dust off the breadcrumbs. I sigh.

"Yes?" Cliff asks through a smile.

"Well, there's still no glowing guest book notes."

"Did you expect someone to call it the Taj Mahal?"

"Maybe."

He squints with a smirk. "You never fail, do you?"

I straighten my posture and scoff, "Of course I do."

"When?"

I tilt my head to the side, as if to say, *You're being ridiculous*, which happens a lot around Cliff.

"It'll take time," he says, leaning in.

The sandwiches in his hands almost touch my shoulder as he waves them around. I bat the bread away. He laughs.

"You'll get a guest who appreciates all these changes. I'm not worried about it, Michelle."

The corner of my mouth twitches. I like that he says my full name, mostly because I know it's intentional. Cliff might lean too close or ask too many personal questions that catch me off guard, but he knows how to make people feel seen. Sometimes *too* seen.

He's so different from me. If I'm autumn, he's spring.

He's all smiles and glowing warmth. His blue eyes are so deep, like the first beautiful clear sky of the season. He likes to rest them on my breeze-blown hair, drift them down to my painted lips or to the cardigan falling off my shoulder.

He looks down at my stack of mail on the bench, then gasps. "Michelle, is this a birthday card?"

"What?"

Cliff places his sandwiches down and holds up a pink envelope. "It's addressed specifically to you and says *Happy Birthday*."

There, in his hand, is my sister's loopy writing with a doodled cake underneath.

My face burns as I snatch it from him. "No."

"It is," he says on a laugh.

"I don't want to talk about it."

"I do."

"I hate my birthday." I tuck the card underneath the rest of the mail.

His mouth opens mid-laugh, like he's surprised. "Why?"

Sourly, I confess, "It gets lost in the mix of other holidays."

"Oh, you poor soul. When is it?"

I purse my lips. "It's at the end of this month."

"Halloween?"

I roll my head back and groan, "Cliff—"

"Is it?"

I sigh. "A few days before."

"Well, lucky for you, I love birthdays. I love birthday *parties* even more."

My eyes widen. "Cliff, don't you dare plan something."

"I would never." He spreads his palm over his chest. "Who do you think I am?"

"The pushiest person on earth."

He tilts his head side to side, but I don't miss how his lips turn down almost imperceptibly. I wonder if I offended him.

He points to the spiders hanging from the gazebo ceiling. "How do you think they turned out?"

That's the magic of Cliff. He knows when to change the subject, and he does it without warning. Sometimes it's jarring, but sometimes it's my favorite thing about him. It only makes me worry more that I said something to upset him.

I trail a hand over the one spider dangling near my head. "Not bad actually."

He nods his chin to Rocket. "What do you think, Rocky?"

Rocket turns up his nose. *How dare you speak to me?*

"The attitude," Cliff says under his breath.

"Testy, isn't he?" I joke, smiling to myself.

We finish lunch together and I watch Cliff return to work, pushing his flannel sleeves up his forearms—his watch shifting down his protruding wrist and back up with the motion—to pull more items from an open brown box.

He ascends the ladder again, and I stand to lean on the side of the gazebo. My face flushes red hot as he climbs each rung. His jeans fit well.

"Cliff!" Carol calls, making me jump. She strides down the path toward us.

Cliff twists on the spot, and my hand shoots out to steady the ladder.

Carol finally sees me and waves. "Oh, hi, Shells."

I close my eyes in frustration at the nickname, and Cliff snickers.

"So . . ." Carol says slowly. "Don't kill the messenger."

Instantly, his grin slides down his face. "Why?" His word drags out almost as slow as hers.

She winces. "Lisa said Emily skipped work today."

"She what?" In two seconds, Cliff is off the ladder. "Do we know where she is?"

"No. But . . . I have a feeling . . ." Another sentence lost to the unspoken abyss.

Cliff's jaw grinds back and forth. Then his eyes dart across the square—directly to the video store.

Oh no.

Suddenly, he's striding through the haystacks and pumpkin-lined walkway.

I exchange a wide-eyed glance with Carol and then Lars staring from across the park before rushing after him with Rocket by my side.

"Cliff, where are you going?" I ask.

He doesn't answer me. I know where he's going. Anyone in town would know where he's going.

I groan in frustration. "Cliff!"

"I gotta check," he growls.

"She's probably not there."

"But she might be."

I hurry into a walk-jog—Rocket trotting beside me on the leash—and finally catch up to him before he crosses the street. He places a hand on the small of my back, escorting us until we're on the other side, then rips open the door to the video store. The dinging bell is so loud that I wonder if he knocked it from its screws.

I wrap Rocket's leash around the light pole and push my way inside too.

I instantly sigh.

Leaning over the checkout counter, hinged at the waist with her chin poised in her palm, is Emily. And clicking at the keyboard behind the counter is the same pimpled teen I saw sneaking around with her two weeks ago—Josh.

Damn it, Emily.

"What movie are we renting today, Em?" Cliff calls out. "*Rebel Without a Cause*? *Dazed and Confused*? 'Cause that's sure me right now. Or how about *Ferris Bueller's Day Off*? That seems the most applicable, kiddo."

Emily turns, and any tint of red she had while batting her eyelashes at Josh drains from her cheeks. "Dad—"

"Did the post office explode?" Cliff asks.

"Wh-what?" Emily stammers out.

"Well, that's the only explanation for why you're not there, working with Lisa. But considering I haven't seen a single mushroom cloud all morning, I'm a hair confused."

The only other time I've seen him this frustrated was when he found Brittany after she was pushed in the pumpkin patch at the Harvest Festival. But even that pales in comparison to now.

His cheeks are flushed. The curved jaw is somehow clearly defined, ticking and denting near his molars as he grinds them in irritation. His forearms flex—corded veins under a dusting of brown hair—with each extension of his defined fingers. And suddenly, I'm very out of breath at the sight of it all.

"I finished work," Emily fumbles out.

She's a terrible liar.

"Is this the first time you've skipped out on Lisa?" he asks. "Or are we about to have more uncomfortable conversations than I'd like?"

I freeze. Of course it isn't the first time Emily's skipped work. I saw her leave the house earlier this month. I know that. *She* knows I know that. Emily's eyes desperately catch mine.

Josh takes a step closer to the swinging half door behind the register, holding out his palm. "Hey, dude. I'm—"

Cliff stiffly points a single finger. "I wouldn't finish that thought, *dude*."

To his credit, Josh clams up and lowers his hand. But then none of us speak, all looking cautiously at the on-edge dad in the middle of the video store. Somehow, it's worse that the only accompaniment is the high-pitched notes of Mariah Carey ringing out from the store speakers.

Cliff threads a hand through his hair, messing up his brown strands and leaving them to hang on his forehead. It's very grunge rocker of him, making me tense up more—which I don't think is his intent, but he's too frustrated to care.

"Emily, go home," he says. "And call Lisa the moment you get back."

"Dad—"

"You're going to apologize. And then we'll talk later."

"But—"

"Unless you want to talk now? But I'd really hate to embarrass you in front of—" Cliff snaps his fingers. "What's your name again?"

I curl my bottom lip in. He obviously knows Josh's name. Even so, the poor teen opens his mouth to supply it to him but is overpowered by Emily's huffing groan. She swings a single backpack strap over her shoulder. Her shoelaces snap on the blue carpet, and the key chains rattle on her bag as she steps toward us like she's going to war.

"God, you're *so* annoying sometimes," she grumbles under her breath as she sidesteps past us and pushes through the door, straining the bell over the door almost as much as Cliff did.

"Hey—" Josh starts.

I shoot him a look because he's truly playing with fire right now. Thankfully, the boy is smart and shuts his mouth again.

Clenching his fists and releasing them, Cliff finally turns on his boot and pushes through the door. The bell screams again. Josh and I meet eyes.

"I didn't know she was skipping," he pleads. "She said some days she didn't have school."

His eyebrows are tilted in so close that they might as well be a unibrow.

I sigh. "You do know that school is five days a week, right?"

"She's smart though. I thought maybe they let her go early or something." He shrugs so matter-of-factly, so innocently, that it almost makes me smile.

"She's a smart girl," I agree. "But don't let her skip anymore, okay?"

"I'll try." He lifts his shoulder again, but the way his lips twist to the side tells me controlling Emily might be a futile effort.

I walk toward the door, then twist back around. "Oh, and word of advice? Maybe next time, don't introduce yourself to your girlfriend's dad with *hey, dude*."

Color drains from his face. "I freaked." He wipes a hand down his face. "He hates me."

I manage a smile, making his shoulders relax a little.

"He'll get over it," I say.

I leave the store with the lightest *ding* that poor doorbell has seen all afternoon and find Cliff sitting on the curb. I squat down and join him. His forearms rest on his knees, hanging limply.

"I forget how exciting it is to be a teenager," he muses. "There's nothing quite like skipping when you know you shouldn't," he jokes with a forced laugh and a weak smile. Even now, with residual anger beating in his heart like a steady drum, he's trying to be optimistic. Cliff is always trying.

"Everything's fine," I assure him. "She's just a kid."

"I know," he says, wiping his palm over his face. "I know. She's such a good kid. I feel like we didn't start arguing until all this boy stuff."

"I think that's a common bridge for dads to cross."

"I get worried. She's smarter than this."

"She also has a lot of hormones."

He lifts an eyebrow. "Don't I know it."

And I know that wasn't directed at me, but the low tone and the amusing nature of it all have me looking away and tapping my shoes on the sidewalk.

"Also," I whisper, "you know his name."

"Who? James?"

I knock my elbow into his ribs. He chuckles.

"It's Josh. And you're a menace. But you're a good dad."

His eyebrows rise.

Is he surprised?

"You are," I repeat, then discreetly check my watch. "I've gotta head back. Want me to swing by your house this afternoon and check on her?"

"No. You don't have to."

"I want to," I insist.

Cliff nods to himself silently. And then his palm lands on my knee. I freeze. Cliff isn't shy to touch. His touch is always gentle. It's not greedy or wanting or even carrying implications. But he's also never touched me *here*. The warmth of his heavy hand and lengthy fingers spans across my entire knee and part of my thigh. It radiates through me in waves of fire. The palm is gone as quick as it landed, but I'm breathless.

He smiles at me, weak and exhausted from the day. "Thanks, Michelle."

"Yeah," I answer quickly. "Of course."

I know I'm flushed. My heart is racing.

I stand, untying Rocket's leash from the pole and wrapping it around my wrist. I barrel down the sidewalk.

"Bye?" Cliff calls through a husky chuckle.

"Bye!" I yell back to him.

The buzzing through my knee tickles the whole trek back. Even Rocket glances at me, as if saying, *You're walking funny, Shelly.*

"Shut up," I hiss.

I'm flustered. Flustered by *Cliff*.

I know Cliff likes physical touch. Little knee touches mean absolutely nothing for him. I've seen him wrap an arm around Lisa for no reason or high-five Lars for something as simple as complimenting a croissant. A pat on the back is his standard greeting. But it's been probably a year since I've felt a man's palm so close to my thigh. And it's been almost seven years since I've been touched by any man except my husband.

Ex-husband.

Cliff is sarcastic and shameless and cocky and . . . attractive.

I roll my eyes and groan at my own admission.

Obviously. I'd be blind not to notice, of course. He's got that baker charm. The broad shoulders, built from lugging heavy bags of flour; the thick forearms, strong from molding dough; and the smile of a man well practiced in swaying people to indulge in icing-covered delicacies.

Cliff is attractive when he runs a palm through his hair. He's attractive when he huffs out frustrated breaths in defense of his daughters. He's attractive when he smiles, and he's attractive when he gives that half smirk and the little line beside his lips creases.

But Cliff is so far from my type. Two months ago, I was in a brick brownstone and dressed for dates at white-tablecloth restaurants. That's who I am. I'm not the kind of woman to lie on a quilted bed and dress down for dinner at the combination pizzeria / coffee shop—which is a monstrosity I have yet to get an explanation for.

I barrel into the bed-and-breakfast, out of breath and gritting my teeth, unhooking Rocket in a hurry, as if I can *run* from these intrusive thoughts about Cliff. But they're torn from me when I find Emily sitting on my kitchen floor.

Her knees are pulled up to her chest. Her Converses, stained and ripped, tilt in. Her blond hair hangs in two curtains beside her face.

"You didn't rat me out," she states. "Why?"

I cross my arms, trying to calm my heavy breathing from my walk here. "I don't know."

"You don't know?"

I swallow. "It didn't feel like my business to tell."

"But you're my dad's friend," she says.

I bite my bottom lip. *Friend.* Cliff Burke is my friend. My funny friend. Not my attractive friend.

"Sure," I agree. "But I know what it's like to be a teenager. And, believe it or not, so does your dad."

"No, he doesn't get it," she grumbles. "Not him or Carol or Mom."

"Your mom doesn't?"

Emily barks out a laugh. "Oh, sure, she *totally* gets it."

I feel borderline assaulted by her over-the-top sarcasm. My lips stretch into a straight line.

She blows out a breath. "Whatever."

"Is it complicated?" I ask.

"Totally."

"You know..." I turn and take down coffee grounds and a filter. "I had a complicated relationship with my mom too."

"With Birdie? As if."

"I did."

Emily scoffs. "I would *kill* for a mom like Birdie." She rests her chin on her knees. "God, you don't get it either."

"Maybe not," I agree. "Nobody can know what you're going through, except you."

She peers up at me through her lashes.

I shrug. "But you're not the first teen with parent issues—I'll tell you that."

She blinks to herself. "Josh is a good guy," she mumbles more to herself than to me.

I flick on the coffee maker and lean against the counter. I fold my arms over my chest.

"He seems all right," I say. I tilt my head to the side. "Dumb." That grants me a small snort of laughter from her. "But pretty all right."

We exchange a small smile.

"I like him a lot," she whispers.

"Then let your dad see that," I say.

"He doesn't take us seriously."

"He takes it more seriously than you think."

"Dad doesn't want me to end up like him and Mom. But I'm not gonna get knocked up. I'm not that stupid."

Ouch.

"Don't judge your parents too harshly," I say. "Love makes you do crazy things."

"How do you know? Have you ever been in love?"

"Yes," I answer, but my lurching stomach wants to fight back.

My feelings on storybook love suddenly feel dull and unnatural. For the life of me, I can't seem to remember the fire I had with Allen. Allen and I were so serious all the time. We were two stubborn people who found their stubborn puzzle piece.

I can't recall passion—at least not the kind of all-encompassing obsession that clouds all judgment and keeps you up at night. I don't remember whether I felt like Emily, desperately needing to see a guy at every waking moment. I can't remember the last time I had a zip in my stomach, like when Cliff's palm was on my knee.

Christ, I *don't like* Cliff. He's too . . . he's too . . .

"How are your grades?" I ask, pulling down mugs from the cabinets.

"I'm acing everything," Emily grumbles into her legs.

"And you're caught up? No late assignments or anything?"

She pulls her knees closer and suspiciously drawls, "Yes, I'm caught up."

"Then I'll talk to him about you and Josh."

Emily straightens up with wide eyes, like a spring uncoiling. "You will?"

"Stop sneaking out, okay? And go to your work-study. Stop skipping school. I don't wanna lie to your dad."

Except about how attractive I find him.

Emily grins, and I can see little inklings of Cliff in the twinkle of her blue eyes. They beam with hope, just like his.

"Swear," she says. "Won't sneak out again."

"Or skip school or work."

"Or skip," she confirms.

I lift the pot from the coffee maker and cross the kitchen, kicking through the swinging door to the dining room. I lean my shoulder against it, gesturing toward the counter with my elbow.

"Grab those mugs, will you? If you're gonna be here, I'm putting you to work."

Chapter 13

CLIFF

I pace the house, trailing down the hallway, with my phone in hand. My fingers hover over the numbers, but I don't press them. I dread this call.

I pass Emily's room. The door is shut, as it's been all afternoon, with a lined piece of paper taped crookedly on the front. Written in block lettering with a black Sharpie is a mishmash of pretty, angry poetry. Probably song lyrics discreetly implying *go away*.

I descend the stairs. Carol sits on the couch in the living room. Brittany leans her head on her shoulder in rainbow pajamas, her hair wet from a shower. They're watching two grown men fake punch in a ring, like they do every Monday night.

I sit at the wooden table in the kitchen, absentmindedly moving around the frilly place mat before standing once more. Inhaling, exhaling, I finally dial Tracy's number.

It rings once, twice . . .

"Hello?"

"Trace. Hi."

"Cliff?" Her voice already sounds tired. "Is there a problem?"

I scratch behind my head. "I don't only call when there's a problem."

"Yes, you do."

"Right. Well . . ." I clear my throat and pocket my hand, pacing to and from the sink before fiddling with the faucet. "Thought I'd update you on some things."

"What did Emily do this time." It's not a question.

My chest feels itchy at the insinuation. I'm irritated, and we're less than a minute into the conversation.

"Well"—I force out a laugh—"she didn't kill someone or jump off a tall building."

"Then why are you calling? Does Brittany need something?"

Her words always snap at my insides like rubber bands, stinging when they land and leaving bruises in their wake.

"No," I say, dragging out the word. "But your firstborn has a boyfriend."

The exhale through the phone whistles in my ear. "Are you serious right now?"

"Wish I weren't, but . . ." I kick the rug, then fix it back after, biting my lip and staring at the ceiling. I can't stand still. "She skipped school to see him."

"Cliff, you're joking me."

"Hey, she's a headstrong kid," I say with a laugh. "Like her parents."

Tracy sighs, and it's a breath punctuated with a growl. I never know if what I'm saying is the right thing or if it makes her any less annoyed with me, but I'm guessing by that reaction that it was a check mark in the *bad* column.

She sighs again. "We're gonna have a teen pregnancy on our hands if we're not careful."

"Emily's smart."

"Well, I should hope so. Is that all?"

"Yeah. Thought you'd want to hear it from me instead of Brittany. Kid talks about everything," I say with a chuckle.

"Well, thanks." She sighs. "This boy isn't going to be around Brittany though, is he?"

I bark out a laugh, but she doesn't return it. I can feel heat rising up my neck and to my cheeks.

I lower my voice and walk to the window. "Emily isn't a delinquent—you know that, right? She's a kid. And he's just some teen guy. He works at the video store, Trace. Brittany is fine."

"I worry about Emily," she admits. "We had no idea what we were doing."

"They're both being raised right. *Both* of them," I emphasize.

"I'm sorry. Yes. I . . ." She groans.

The girl I once knew—the perky blond cheerleader with the sunny smile and cheeky eye rolls—feels so distant now. Sure, Tracy wasn't bound to be that girl forever. She became a woman. Protective of her children. Strong. Bold. But, God, it only made me love her more. As parents, we had so many sleepless nights, school events, arguments on how to raise them together. Sure, we got into fights, but what couple doesn't?

Then it's like everything got turned on its head all at once. This idea of a perfect home, a perfect family, a perfect life. Our marriage wasn't perfect, but it was us. I loved us. I loved *her*.

"Emily brought home a report card," I say. "She got all As."

"Really?"

"Better than you or I ever did, huh?" I respond with a laugh.

She sniffs dismissively. I hear bangles rattling in the background. She always wore stacks of them on her arms before going out. She must be getting ready. I look at the clock—nine p.m.

"Is that boy still bothering Brittany?" she asks.

"I've got him buried six feet underground so—"

"Clifford."

"I called his parents. They grounded Luke for eternity. Kids do dumb stuff. It happens."

Keys rattle in the background.

"Where are you headed to this late?" I ask.

"There's a work dinner in Chelsea."

"Chelsea. She sounds fun," I joke.

"It's a place, Cliff."

I mouth to myself, *I know*, because saying it aloud isn't worth the fight.

"Well, that sounds fun," I say. "Have a great time."

She scoffs. "Okay, well, you don't have to sound pissed about it."

"I'm not—" I shut my eyes. "I'm not pissed, Trace."

Tracy doesn't respond to me, and the longer she doesn't speak, the more I realize she's playing chicken with me. She wants me to speak first. But what is there to even say? What can I say that won't be taken the wrong way?

I glance out the kitchen window at Bird & Breakfast. Across the dark yard and over the white fence is Michelle's bedroom. I wonder if she fought with her ex like this. The idea of *Allen*—I roll my eyes—saying anything snappy to Michelle makes my fingers twitchy. I don't like it.

Michelle has walls. A lot of them. And I don't know when they were built—whether it was with Birdie or her ex—but they've closed her off to everyone. They've made her tough though. Confident. And I kinda like her *screw everyone* attitude.

But she's also funny. Kind. Gentle even. More generous

than she lets on or probably wants anyone to see. I don't want to remove her walls because that'd destroy her strength, but I'd kill for more peeks into the other side.

I blink at the darkened bedroom when, suddenly, it lights up. Behind the sheer white curtains walks a silhouette. Michelle's silhouette.

She's a shadow, delicately floating across the room. Her arms rise, with small fingers releasing her hair from its ponytail holder. The thick locks cascade over her shoulders, swaying side to side as she runs fingers through it, shaking it out like she's relieving the stress from the day.

Michelle's been stressed a lot. Hell, she's been stressed since she arrived in Copper Run. I'm sure I'm not helping either. Not even a little. I barge into her house, make her eat lunch with me, and run into video stores like a caveman, ready to wring the neck of some teenage boy with her having to hold me back. It wasn't until after Michelle rushed away with barely a goodbye that I realized how overbearing I'd been.

Though, selfishly, it's been nice, hanging out with her recently. I've been happier. Like my smiles aren't as forced as usual. It's become a game to see how often I can make her laugh. Michelle won't laugh out of pity, so when I do get one, I know it's real. I know I've cracked through yet another brick in her wall.

She clicks on a lamp before turning off the overhead light. She's now a partial blur in a dim orange glow, an outline of a narrow waist and long legs. I swallow. I've noticed the length of them before, but it isn't until I see her now that I see exactly how far those slender legs stretch.

Michelle moves around, doing indiscernible things. Maybe

picking up a book. Moving the pillows. Pushing back the sheets. But then her shadowy palms reach across her waist, and the fabric of her shirt slinks up, up, up—

I turn on my heel and stride away from the window.

Shit.

I'm not that kind of guy. I'm not gonna peep on the woman next door like that.

"Cliff?" Tracy asks.

I jump, my hand tightening on the phone. I forgot we were talking, and my ex's voice is like a bucket of ice water dumping over my head.

"Sorry. Yes?"

"I asked if you had anything else to say. I've really got somewhere to be."

"Yeah, no, sure," I say quickly, running my palm over my hair. "That makes sense."

There's an awkward silence before she asks, "Are you okay? You're acting weird."

I chuckle. "I'm always weird."

Tracy hums in agreement, which I knew she might. My self-deprecating humor is her favorite type of humor.

"I'll talk to the girls tomorrow," she says.

I don't miss the implication of *Don't call me before then.*

I nod to myself. "Yeah. Talk then, Trace."

I don't get a goodbye, but I don't care. I set down the phone after the dull dial tone blares, walking back to the window. Michelle's bedroom is darkened once more.

Good.

I shouldn't have been looking at anything anyway.

MICHELLE

One week before Halloween, I meet Brittany at the bus stop—waving to the few other parents I see each day, who love saying hi—and within seconds, she unloads costume ideas onto me like confetti shooting from a cannon. It isn't until her third utterance of "we" that I ask who she expects to make these over-the-top creations.

"You," is her answer.

I laugh. "Excuse me?"

"Birdie made my Halloween costume last year. Emily normally makes it, but I liked it better when Birdie did."

My chest twinges. "Oh really?"

I wasn't aware I'd signed up for all of my mom's local duties on top of running the bed-and-breakfast. Yet, two hours later, Brittany's somehow suckered me into sitting on the floor in the parlor, cutting black bedsheets into pieces to the sound of Backstreet Boys on the stereo.

Emily walks in with her backpack slung over one shoulder, and Cliff trails behind her—a stack of letters in one hand and a box with Burke's Bakery's logo in the other. His eyes widen, taking in the fabric spread on the floor and the cut pieces and strings scattered in piles.

"It'll look better than it does now," I say.

"Do you sew?" Cliff asks.

"No."

"Well then . . ."

"I'm trying my best."

Emily, finally broken from her stunned state, bursts out laughing. "Oh, it looks *bitchin'*, Michelle."

Cliff nudges her elbow with his. "Emily, come on. Language. We're in her place of business."

I smile at Emily as she raises her shoulders with a cheeky, "Oops."

"Can you even tell what it is?" I ask.

"Not even a little," Emily says.

"Miss Shell, can I get a snack?" Brittany asks, lying on the floor, feet swinging behind her and a crayon poised over punched paper, where she's drawn a halfway-decent wrestling ring.

I nod. "Pop-Tarts are in the top cabinet."

"Yay!" she yells.

"Em—" Cliff starts.

"I'll get it for her," Emily says, walking through the kitchen door.

I distantly hear the two sisters fighting over which flavor to get, then instantly dropping the argument to play with Rocket. It reminds me of Sara and me. What is a sisterly relationship if not tumultuous with immediate forgetfulness?

I look at the destroyed sheets on the floor, then to Cliff. He's casually splayed out in the floral armchair near the fireplace. Cliff is the kind of guy who really relaxes into a chair, like he's getting comfortable for hours to come, even if he's only going to sit for five minutes. He parts his thighs momentarily before resting one ankle over the other knee and grinning with the box in his lap and mail on top.

While Cliff is cocky to a degree, I think I initially mistook it for arrogance. The lazy, lopsided grin. The raised eyebrows. The cheery lines beside his eyes. The natural confidence.

Allen was arrogant; Cliff doesn't need to be.

He extends his hand out with the letters. "Mail?"

"It's a federal crime to grab someone else's mail."

"Want me to stop?"

"No."

I take the stack of envelopes and curl my legs under me on the ruffled floor cushion.

I eye the white pastry box. "Is that also for me?" I ask.

His grin only gets wider. "Why, yes, it is."

"More weird baker things?"

"Absolutely." He leans forward to hand it to me.

I open the box, and inside is a square cut of a layered pastry with a single plastic fork nestled beside it. It smells like honey.

I lift an eyebrow. "I'm assuming you want me to try it?"

"If you'd be so kind."

I slide the fork through and take a small bite.

God, he's so good at this.

It's sticky and sweet against my tongue with almost a nutty flavor to it. Light flakes break between my lips, and when I swallow, I'm left with the lingering scent of cinnamon.

"It's delicious," I say, setting the box down.

However, Cliff looks disappointed, like he always does when I eat something of his.

"What is it?"

"Baklava," he answers as if unimpressed with every crumb of it. He leans back in the chair with his chin propped in the palm of his hand. He stares at the box intently. "Too sweet, you think?" he asks.

"I think everything you make is delicious."

"Hmm," is all he says in return. He taps his finger on the chair's arm, then finally refocuses on me. "Oh, I like your sweater today. Brings out your eyes."

My face flushes as I scoff out a laugh. The man loves when his compliments disarm me because his smile always reaches the little wrinkles beside his eyes. I tug at the sleeves, which suddenly feel too tight against my skin.

"You know, I was thinking—" he continues.

"Oh no," I interrupt with a bubbling laugh, trying to break myself out of my spiraling thoughts about his smile.

He throws me a smirk.

I chew my bottom lip, biting back another laugh. "Okay, what were you thinking, Cliff?"

"What if I got a camera?"

"Like a camcorder?"

"Or maybe even a disposable."

"Why?" I ask, slicing open an envelope with my finger. I set it in a separate pile for bills.

"So organized," he observes in awe.

"Finish your previous thought."

"Oh. Right." He adjusts in the seat, leaning further into his elbow. "Well, I barely have any home videos of Emily when she was Brittany's age. I want to make more memories. I'm not good about that."

"Aw. That's cute."

"We couldn't afford a camera back then. But I can now."

"Then do it."

I sort through piece after piece of mail, placing each with bills or junk.

"Yeah, let's say I get a camera though," he continues. "What if I don't use it?"

"Then the girls can."

He grits his teeth. "Well, then I'd get pictures of Josh though, wouldn't I?"

He looks at me as if expecting laughter, but I shrug.

His eyes widen. "What? Are we not making fun of the kid anymore?"

"Maybe—"

Cliff gasps. "She got to you. You're a double agent. You've been compromised."

I tongue my cheek to hold in a laugh. "You know . . . maybe we should give him a chance. Let him come over for dinner or something. Don't you trust her?"

He pulls in a breath and sighs. "Yes."

"At least spend an evening with him."

Cliff hums for a second, then nods. "Fine. But you have to endure it too."

"Don't drag me down with you," I say with a twitching smile as I sift through another letter.

"Oh, I'm dragging you," he teases. "You're coming with me, Michelle."

My breath catches when I reach an envelope with fancy lettering. Very fancy, barely legible lettering. The type of illegible cursive only a doctor can achieve. My heart sinks.

"Michelle?" Cliff asks.

"Sorry . . ." I shake my head, closing my eyes and opening them again. But the loopy scrawl hasn't disappeared. "Another birthday card."

Cliff's brow furrows, and for some inexplicable reason, when he holds out his hand, I place the card in his palm. I'm on autopilot now, and apparently, my default is to trust Cliff.

He tucks one long finger into the open gap and slides it through, ripping the envelope open and pulling out the card.

He stares for a moment, then opens it. The front illustration faces me. It's a bunny hopping over a lit cake.

Hopping You Have a Very Good Birthday.

Cliff, with his jaw tightened, flips the card around so I can see the inside too. There's printed writing that reads a generic *Happy Birthday!* message, and the only written piece is a signature. The most I can make out is a very familiar *A*.

That's all I received from my ex-husband for my thirtieth birthday. A messy signature, similar to every piece of paperwork I've seen him sign as a doctor.

I turn my face away. If the man loves anything, he loves cards.

"His secretary has a Rolodex of birthdays and anniversaries," I murmur. "And she always sends presigned cards to his patients. He must have hired someone new. I guess I haven't been taken off the list."

I can't believe this is what we've come to. An impersonal Hallmark card he probably snapped up at a grocery store in the checkout line, unaware it'd go to me. I feel humiliated. And angry.

I sniff back the burning behind my eyes.

"Whoa, hey now." Cliff slides down from the armchair to the floor. He settles himself with one leg extended behind my back and the other knee bent beside my thigh. "You all right?"

"Yeah," I whisper. "Yeah, I'm fine."

Except I'm not. My hands are shaking.

He peers down at them, and slowly, gently, he takes one hand into his. It's not intimate. He doesn't thread his fingers between the grooves of my own. He simply holds it between his palms. But my heart still misses a beat. It does it again when I look at the set-aside birthday card.

"Talk to me," he insists.

"It's so frustrating that . . ." I exhale.

"Breathe."

I swallow. "That I'm a stupid, impersonal card now. Everything meant . . . nothing."

Cliff doesn't ask me to clarify what "everything" is, which is good because I wouldn't even know what to say. "Everything" could be our marriage. Our life. Me.

I meant nothing to him.

I'm entering a new decade without the man I spent most of the previous one with. And it feels . . . aimless.

The kitchen door swings open to the dining room, and Emily halts in place when she sees us sitting on the floor, holding hands. Brittany bursts through after, but Emily palms her face and pushes her back into the kitchen.

Brittany's muffled "What are you—" is overshadowed by the squeaking of her sneakers on the hardwood.

Emily walks her back. "I want another Pop-Tart, Britt Britt. Move it or lose it."

"Emily!" she whines.

"Move, or I'll read your diary."

"It's locked!"

"It's plastic."

Through a cacophony of arguing as both girls disappear back into the kitchen, Cliff's hands don't leave mine.

"Hey," he whispers.

I look up. A smile waits for me—the one with delicate creases beside his eyes.

"I've never met the guy or anything, but . . . your ex is a jackass. You know that, right?"

I manage a small laugh, looking down at the card. "He's . . . yeah, he really is."

"You deserve more than a birthday card from someone you were married to for years," he says.

"Five years," I clarify.

"Five years," he echoes.

"I wasted most of my twenties on him. And he gets to . . . move on. Like it never happened." I slap the card against my palm. "Is it that hard to make sure I'm not on the recipient list?"

"Easy really."

"I can't believe I'm starting over. I'm in my thirties. No guy wants a thirty-year-old."

Cliff grins. "I *love* women in their thirties."

I tsk and tug at the end of my hair. "You know I saw a gray hair for the first time the other morning?"

"Join the party," he says with a chuckle. "I've got a mess of them." He runs a finger through his hair, lifting the longer strands to reveal a smattering of salt and pepper along his temple.

I gasp. "How did I never notice that?"

"It's my secret stash."

I tilt my head to the side. "See? But that's attractive."

"It's attractive?"

"Men don't have to worry about getting older. You get more . . . refined with age. And we women get cast as witches and hags."

"A reliable Halloween costume, if you ask me."

I shoot him a glare, and he gently smiles.

"Well, I'll let you in on a secret. Men? We want women. Period. Over thirty. Forty. Hell, over sixty. Short, tall, brunette, blond—doesn't matter. We like them all. *Especially* women over thirty."

I snort, and he smiles wider, leaning in.

"And especially women with gray hair."

The nerves in my fingers pulse with him this close. I can smell the vanilla and cinnamon from the bakery. And a hint of something else . . . citrus?

"Don't let Lisa hear you," I joke, my voice a little shaky. "With the gray-hair thing."

"Oh, she wishes," Cliff drawls with a grin.

I look away, fiddling with the card in my lap again, but then our gazes snag in place. They always do. His blue eyes dart between mine. The world narrows in on us—only us.

"It gets better out there, I promise," he whispers.

I sheepishly confess, "Men don't want women like me."

"Like what?"

Unfun, too serious, workaholics.

"I don't know," I mumble.

He gives a devilish, absolutely wicked smile. "I think men secretly want women *just* like you," he growls, leaning even closer. "And the men who don't are cowards."

I swallow, the resonating crack of the *c* in his last word pumping to the beat of my pounding heart—so hard that I can barely breathe.

"Let me help you this afternoon."

"What?" I ask, blinking back.

Suddenly, all the noise surrounding us returns. A hum of a distant TV. The girls talking in the kitchen. Hardwood creaking from footsteps upstairs.

"Around the inn," Cliff says.

"Why?"

"Because," he says with a shrug, "you need to relax. I can check the reservations or make beds. Birdie used to keep a list—"

"Do you know everything about this place?" I ask.

He tilts his head side to side. Then his lips quirk up into a lazy smile. "Yes. So let me help you."

I nod. "Okay."

Cliff stands, then holds out a hand for me. He jerks me up, and I stumble into him, my palms splayed over his chest. It's harder than I expected. Larger. I step away, blinking through the sudden touch. He doesn't seem to notice. Or maybe he pretends not to.

He bends to the ground and picks up the card, extending it to me. "Want it?"

I swallow. "Yes."

I expect him to be disappointed in me for caving in to nostalgia, but he hands me the card without judgment.

"Do you want to come over for dinner tonight?" he asks.

"I . . . actually, I need to do things for the project at work."

"Seattle work?"

I nod, and he gives an almost pitying smile.

"Workaholic," he teases. "Even when I take over one thing, you have something else."

My stomach drops, and I simply reply, "Yes."

He reaches out and squeezes my shoulder, sending sparks running through my chest again.

"Go do what you've gotta do."

"Thanks, Cliff."

"Anytime," he says, but when his hand leaves me, I want it back.

That evening, I lie in bed until the sunset beams through my sheer curtains, leaving a haze across the room in muted shades of bronze and gold and a white glow so bright that I have to shut my eyes while they disappear below the horizon.

I looked over documents all night, but the papers blurred together until the only clear thing in my room was Allen's birthday card resting on my side table. I fell down on the bed and stared at the ceiling, and now it's too dark to see anything. I never bothered to turn on my lamp, and the sun has been going down earlier and earlier lately.

The Burke kitchen window is open, as usual. Brittany whines about dinner, then laughs at something else. Carol yells something across the house, making Emily reply equally loudly, and below it all is Cliff's husky laughter.

I close my eyes, but I can't sleep, so I lie in the dark with the sounds of Rocket's lazy snoring and the leaves tumbling together in occasional gusts of wind.

He invited me to dinner, and I said no. What if he never invites me again?

For the first time in almost a month, I feel alone. Me and the heartless birthday card. I would cry if I wasn't so angry. If my blood wasn't overflowing from my heart like lava and dripping down to my stomach in hissing drops of disdain. It's so loud in my ears that I can hear each drop *plunk*.

Plunk.
Plunk.
Plunk!
My eyes flash open.
Plunk!

I rise in bed and peer out the window, jumping at the sight of Cliff silhouetted in his kitchen window. He waves. I return it. With his other hand, he tosses something at my window. I flinch when it hits the glass with another *plunk!*

Creaking forward on my mattress, I spot six large cherries in the grass below my windowsill.

Across our yards and in his kitchen, Cliff curls a single finger, gesturing for me to come over. The motion snags on me, coaxing my chest forward, like his finger has a string tied to my body.

But when I don't noticeably budge, Cliff mouths, *Please.*

I fight a wide smile, holding up my index finger, indicating that I'll be there in a minute. He disappears from the window before I can second-guess my decision. I slip into house shoes and throw on a loose sweater over my dress.

Rocket's head rises from his dog bed. *Where are you sneaking off to?*

"Next door," I whisper.

I thought you didn't like him.

I hesitate. "We're friends."

Rocket huffs out a sleepy grunt and rests his head on the cushion.

I walk down the hall and push out the kitchen's back door, crossing through the rosebushes and into Cliff's yard, trailing the three steps to his kitchen's back door. The screen door creaks open before I can knock, and I'm greeted by Cliff's body in the threshold, blocking my entrance.

He holds up a silk tie and snaps it. "Turn around."

He's gonna give me a heart attack one of these days.

I laugh awkwardly. "Why?"

"Because I said so."

"What are you gonna do?"

He lowers the tie and leans his head to the side. "Can you not be suspicious for once?"

"Well, you're acting very suspicious, Cliff."

He gently holds up the fabric again, slipping it between his fingers, as if showing me how harmless it is. The tie is frayed in places, the raised stitches fuzzy and pilled. I vaguely recognize it as his wake outfit. This was worn by a more serious, unfamiliar, salesy Cliff. Not my baker Cliff.

"Do you trust me?" he asks.

"No." *Yes.*

He barks out a laugh. "Turn around. Let me put it over your eyes."

I turn on my heel and face the dark backyard. The last things I see before the fabric slips over my eyes are the orange Halloween lights from a house on the opposite side of the fence.

Cliff's fingers trace over my cheeks as he ties the soft silk behind my head. I can feel his breath tickling the hair at my neck. Swishes of fabric rustle against my ears. His hand ghosts over my hair, like he's fixing strands he messed up in the process.

"All right," he whispers. "Now we're heading to my bedroom."

My heart rises into my throat. "Cliff," I warn out loud.

"Shh, the girls are asleep," he admonishes on a chuckle, winding his palm up my forearm to tug my inner elbow.

He walks us into the house and gingerly shuts the kitchen door behind us. I stumble as he guides me down the hall, occasionally pulling me closer or coaxing me around a corner with a palm on my lower back.

"Couldn't you have only covered my eyes?" I whisper.

"And have you peek and spoil the surprise? No."

"So, it's a surprise," I guess.

"Why else would I blindfold you, Michelle?"

I can think of a few reasons echoes in my head, and my cheeks instantly heat.

His low, husky laugh acknowledges my silence. "Naughty. But we're not *those* types of friends."

It's funny though; my heart tightens at his instant denial.

I swallow. "I wasn't thinking that."

"Of course not," Cliff whispers.

I stumble into a wall. He laughs, but it's instantly muffled, like he covered his own mouth.

"And you were worried about *me* being the rambunctious one," I say.

"Shush," he teases.

I can't help but grin.

We turn another corner, and I enter what feels like a smaller space that smells like Thanksgiving. A door snicks closed behind me. Cliff places his palms on either side of my arms.

"Okay, stay here," he whispers.

When his hands leave, I suddenly feel the chill in the room. Distantly, Cliff's footsteps creak on the wooden floor. I don't like standing here like this. My fists shake, but then warm palms wrap around them once more.

"Okay, nervous woman," he murmurs. "Ready?"

I choke out a laugh. "You've got a chain saw, don't you?"

He chuckles. "Nah, I'll save that for trick-or-treating next week."

Cliff's fingers twist through my hair, untangling the tie's knot behind my head. I inhale, and there's that hint of citrus again. Normally, he smells like vanilla and cinnamon—a working baker. But beneath that, there's now something else.

A cologne that's uniquely Cliff. A person beneath the charismatic baker he wants everyone else to see. I wonder how many people get this close to him to know.

The tie slides off my eyes, softly slipping over my cheeks and disappearing.

"Open your eyes."

I blink a few times and let myself take in Cliff's room. The overhead light is off, and the room is lit by the orange glow of a lamp in the corner and dancing shadows on the cream wallpaper. Pictures of him and the girls hang in wooden frames around the room. Low bookshelves line the walls, some with stacks of books on top—mystery novels and a few by Stephen King. A desk sits in the corner with a lamp, scribbled notes on yellow legal paper, and a square TV. A brown alarm clock blinks red numbers on his bedside table. It's almost eleven thirty. His bed takes up most of the room, and placed precariously on a wooden cutting board is a chicken potpie with three lit candles stuck in the center, a line of wax dribbling slowly down one side.

"Happy birthday," Cliff says. "You said you don't like big celebrations. And there's no way you ate dinner tonight. Also"—he picks up the remote to the TV—"I checked what's on TV tonight, and you're in time for *Saturday Night Live*."

My mouth opens and closes. "Cliff . . ."

"I hear Chris Farley is hosting—"

A laugh bubbles out of me. "Cliff . . . this is—"

"All right?" he finishes for me with an unsure lilt to his words. "Is it all right?"

"It's all right," I agree, but *all right* comes out more like *perfect*, and I can tell he knows. I reach up to twist my earring. "This, uh . . . this isn't because of the card today, is it?"

His face scrunches up. "I've been planning this since you

first told me about your birthday." Cliff waggles his eyebrows. "Alex made it easier for me to look good doing it."

"His name is Allen," I correct.

"I know," he says, a wicked smile dancing on his face.

I laugh again, taking in the flickering birthday candles and moving shadows.

"You're really something, Clifford Burke."

He chuckles. "I'll let myself imagine what that *something* is." He inhales, then lets it out. "All right, well . . ."

Cliff steps toward the door, as if taking his leave. I shoot my hand out before I think about it. My fingers linger on the outside of his palm. His eyes widen, drifting from my fingers up to meet my stare. His lips part in surprise. His chest expands like he's holding his breath, and his blue eyes dart between mine. I don't say anything for a moment because this expression is so new to me. I didn't know it was possible to throw Cliff off guard like this.

"Don't go," I say.

"I figured you'd want some quiet alone time outside the inn."

"You're not gonna leave me on my birthday though, are you?"

He blinks down to my hand, twisting his palm around to squeeze mine.

"I guess that would be unfair," he says.

"Very."

A grin slides up the corner of his mouth. He releases my hand and picks up the pie from the bed.

"It's on channel three," he instructs.

I scoot back on the bed until I can rest against the headboard. Kicking off my house shoes, I extend my feet out, my toes wiggling underneath my sheer black tights.

As I click through the channels, Cliff cuts out two slices—one for each of us—and places them on plates. He leans across the mattress to hand me mine.

Once he has his own, Cliff crawls on the opposite side, shuffling over the fluffy tan comforter until he's situated beside me. His legs stretch out, too, though his black socks extend well past my own feet. We wiggle our toes side by side.

And together, with our plates of potpie, we eat with tiny forks beside the dim lamp and the cool glow of the TV.

Chapter 15

CLIFF

"Pillow?"

"Pillow." Michelle tosses the inn's guest room pillow over, as requested, but instead, the pillow smacks me right in the face. She covers her mouth to halt a laugh. "I thought you were looking."

I pick the pillow up and toss it back at her. It lightly knocks her in the face, but she gasps.

"Clifford Burke—" Michelle picks up the pillow from the hardwood and pummels me with it.

I hold up my arms, laughing as I protect myself from the second blow. Her bottom lip is tucked in as she tries not to laugh, but when I wrestle the pillow from her and hold it above her head, she folds her arms over her chest and exhales.

I lean closer. "You can't stay mad at me."

"Untrue," she says, snatching the pillow from me and adding it to the other three already plopped on the bed. She gives a teasing smirk. "I'm always mad at you."

"Touché."

Each pink sham on the mattress is either frilly or lacy. It feels like we're in one of Lisa's rooms with too many dolls. The rain outside makes it extra unsettling.

"Who would want this on their honeymoon?" I ask, leaning against the doorway. "Yuck."

"Are you *yucking* my honeymoon setup?" Michelle asks.

"I'm *yucking* Birdie's honeymoon setup."

Michelle hip-checks me on her way out the door, then flicks off the light behind her. "The pink quilt was specifically labeled for the honeymoon package, so that's what they're getting."

Cliff hmms. "I can't tell if having a honeymoon on Halloween is cool or creepy."

"Creepy," Michelle responds right before I say, "Cool."

She lifts an eyebrow.

We descend the stairs together, taking the last few steps quicker. She hits the main level first.

"That's three to two," she declares.

"Okay, see, the last time, you jumped though. I don't count that."

"Sore loser."

I roll my eyes with a grin as we turn the corner to the parlor. A bloodcurdling, high-pitched scream erupts from the TV, and Michelle's hand shoots to her chest.

"Really?!" she admonishes on a heavy exhale, her lips straightening into a line at both Emily and Josh. They sit exactly two feet apart on the couch, as instructed by yours truly. "A horror movie in the middle of the day?"

"You said nobody was checking in today," Emily says with an innocent shrug.

I laugh. "I thought you two were gonna watch *Charlie Brown's Big Pumpkin* or whatever."

"That's not what it's called," Michelle interjects.

"Josh didn't have a copy at the store," Emily continues. "So, we got *Scream* instead."

"At least it's true to its name," Michelle muses.

"Dad, you'd love this one."

"Seen it."

"When? You saw it without me?"

"It's when you were with your mom last year."

Emily grumbles to herself.

"Sorry, kiddo."

Michelle crosses in front of the TV toward the kitchen, and Emily shimmies in her seat.

"Oh, wait, Michelle! Watch, watch, watch!"

Michelle turns on her heel.

I walk in front of the TV behind her, and of course I get a "Dad, move!" instead.

"The attitude, jeez," I say on a chuckle, taking a spot beside Michelle by the dining room threshold.

I pretend to watch the screen, but from the corner of my eye, I'm peering at Michelle. I've seen this movie before. Killer in a mask goes after teenagers with a knife. But with each passing moment, Michelle's face slowly changes. Her lips part, her nose scrunches up, and tiny lines deepen between her brows.

"Oh God, this is brutal, Em," she says.

"No, no, the garage door is about to—"

"Sick," Josh says, making my own nose scrunch.

I wasn't exactly *thrilled* about having Josh in my life, but he makes Emily happy for some reason. I've never seen her more excited than when I said they could have a date, as long as it was in the house and everyone was home. I'll have to deal with Mr. Fig Roll for now.

Rocket lies on the couch beside them, nuzzling his nose into the couch cushion, like he's trying to shield his own eyes from the horror movie gore.

Michelle pats his hind leg. "Rocket, you all right?"

The dog's tail beats on the couch in acknowledgment.

"Dad, can you get the light?" Emily asks, pointing to the switch near the kitchen.

I snap it off right when Michelle pets Rocket and murmurs, "Good boy."

My head jerks back, and she grins, looking from Rocket to me.

"Not you, Cliff."

Emily snickers at me.

"Keep it down in here," I say, opening the kitchen door for Michelle. She ducks under my arm to pass through. "And hands where Rocket can see them at all times," I add, pointing between them, then gesturing to Rocket with his muzzle buried in the cushions.

He's not doing his job at all.

"Hey, and if your sister comes in, you kick her out immediately, okay?"

"Okay. Bye!" The last word is a little too pushy, but I wave them off and join Michelle in the kitchen.

She takes the other door right back into the foyer. She does this a lot—circling the house to double-check things she's already done.

In the entryway, she adjusts the fresh-cut flowers. Fanned around the vase are brochures for Copper Run's annual Halloween party in the square. It's kid-friendly and not nearly as scary as the haunted maze Winston creates for his yard each year, but Brittany is spooked by both events, so we'll be keeping to the houses and sidewalks.

The front door is propped open, letting in the hiss of quiet afternoon rain. Water thunks through the gutters above the porch, and kids outside cycle through splashing puddles. Brittany is at a friend's birthday party down the cul-de-sac. She'll probably come back covered in mud.

I lean my forearms on the front desk, looking at the delicately arranged paperwork and three cubbies with keys for each room. I reach out to ring the front-desk call bell, but Michelle slaps my palm away before I can. She peers at me under her lashes and smiles.

"All right. Well, I've got to head back before Carol kills me," I say. "But what are you doing tonight?"

"I don't know. What *am* I doing, Cliff?"

I sputter out a laugh. "What do you mean?"

Michelle tilts her head to the side. "You're my social planner."

"Since when?" I ask on a chuckle.

"You make the plans; I show up. And if I don't, you always seem to find me anyway. So, what are we doing?"

"Emily's making spaghetti for dinner. Want to come over?"

"Yes, sir, social planner," Michelle teases, which does something to me I can't explain.

I huff out a laugh, then add, "Is it that bad? Me always bugging you with things?"

She shrugs. "You keep me busy."

"Well, good." I shift on my feet. "But I'm not too . . . I don't know . . . overwhelming?"

"Are you kidding?" she asks, darting her eyes to meet mine even though her head stays pointed down at the papers. "You're *so* overwhelming."

I bite my bottom lip and attempt a smile. "Right."

She shrugs again and keeps writing. "But I'm *under*-whelming, so it's fine. We balance out."

I've never had someone be so blunt yet so unintentionally

kind at the same time. But that's the kind of woman Michelle is.

"You're not underwhelming," I say, smiling.

The side of her lip twitches up, but she doesn't acknowledge my compliment. I let it slide. I'm too busy watching as she shifts papers to the side, tucks envelopes into cubbies, and slides out the guest book. She places her pen in the coffee cup, which has little handprints along the sides, reading THANK YOU, BIRDIE.

I smile at the mug, touching some of the pens circling the edges. "I remember this."

She blinks up at me. "Really?"

"Yeah."

When she doesn't go back to working, I lean back. Michelle rarely wants to talk about her mom, but she's been more open about it lately. She's taking small crumbs, like maybe the crumbs will lead her somewhere. Where, I'm not sure, but I'll leave behind any she needs.

"Yeah," I repeat. "She hosted Thanksgiving last year. We got all the neighbor kids to make this for her after. She loved it."

Michelle stares at the mug while she reaches up to play with her ball earring. Maybe she's considering something to say in response, but nothing comes out.

"All right, then." I knock on the desk. "Well, I'll leave you to it."

"Hmm," she muses before pulling open the guest book. "Thanks."

"Anytime."

I'm almost to the door when her sudden yelp stops me. I turn on my heel. Michelle stands behind the desk with both hands pulled up to her mouth. Her eyebrows are raised up to her hairline, and she's breathing heavy. My heart sinks.

"What?" I ask, walking over. "What happened?"

"I got my first good review," she says. "I got— Cliff, look!" She exhales a laugh, hoisting up the guest book and attempting to hold it in my face.

I take it from her. "No kidding."

"Read it!"

I clear my throat and read, "This is by far the best bed-and-breakfast in Vermont, if not all of New England. Michelle is a darling to talk to and is perfect company while having an already excellent breakfast."

Michelle waves her hands. "Keep going!"

I read the next line to myself first, then laugh and announce, "The morning cinnamon rolls were divine."

"Di-vine," Michelle repeats, punctuating each syllable with a pump of her hand in the air.

"Divine," I repeat, setting the book down.

"Divine!" she squeals, rounding the desk and barreling into my arms.

The breath rushes out of me on impact. Her hands loop around my neck. I let my palms settle on her waist, squeezing her sides, inhaling the soft burnt-sugar perfume. The hints of rosemary—*rosemary*—in her hair. The soft strands that fall over my nose.

She bounces in my arms before pulling away. I reluctantly let go, watching with a wide grin as she circles back to look at the guest book entry again. She's beautiful like this—thrilled and entirely *over*whelmed. I don't know what lies she tells herself; there's no way she could be underwhelming.

The phone on the counter rings, and I rush around the side to pick it up.

"Cliff, no!" she says through a laugh.

I hold out my free palm to keep her away, tucking the phone between my ear and shoulder.

"Thank you for calling Bird & Breakfast, where the morning cinnamon rolls are *divine*. This is Clifford. How may I help you?"

"Cliff," Michelle whines between laughs, bouncing next to me and reaching to grab the phone.

I keep twisting out of her grasp. But the farther I move away, the closer she gets, until her breasts are pushing against my chest and ribs, and then her waist is in my palm and—

Hissing in a breath, I quickly hand the phone back to her.

She's all smiles—maybe oblivious to what happened, who knows—as she takes the call. But I'm out of breath.

I aimlessly pace out from behind the desk, running a palm through my hair, letting it fall back onto my forehead as I watch the rain trickle off the front porch's lip. I swallow down the heartbeat soaring into my throat and finally turn around to see Michelle nodding against the phone and tucking the end of her pen between her teeth. The glow of the small lamp on the front desk reflects on her pink cheeks, casting her eyes in a dark shadow, where she peers at me with a grin.

The world tilts. It suddenly feels like I'm falling through the ground, straight to the center of the earth.

God, she's breathtaking.

As she asks the person on the other end of the line question after question, I could stare at her plump lips all day. They're full. Dark. Parting only slightly to reveal slivers of straight white teeth.

How the hell did I get privileged enough to see this side of her?

Michelle is a smart woman. A powerful woman. The kind of woman who struts down city streets, holding a thick agenda, filled with high-end events spanning the next two to five months, at a minimum. Meanwhile, my only plans each night are with my two daughters and sister. Maybe drinks with Lars or bingo night with George, if the old man invites me.

We're so different. Michelle wears polished belts, tailored shirts, and fifty different flavors of designer shoes. I wear flannel and sneakers, and half the time, I've got some wisp of flour or sugar somewhere on my skin.

But . . .

I like her.

My stomach tightens into a hard knot.

I like Michelle.

I'm *attracted* to Michelle, which isn't news to me at all, but this heart-pounding affection . . . it's foreign yet so oddly familiar, all at once. It's something I haven't felt since I was sixteen. Michelle is funny when she wants to be and sometimes when she doesn't. She's gorgeous. She's kind. And most of all, she's not afraid to tell me when I'm being an ass.

I swallow audibly, then look away from her.

I have a crush on my very unattainable friend.

Maybe in another world, it could work out. I don't know what world that would be, but it sure isn't this one, where I'm a walking tornado and she's beautiful, out of my league, and leaving in two months.

Michelle looks up and grins as I linger in the threshold.

She waves me off and mouths, *Get out of here.*

I chuckle.

Yeah, I need to get the hell out of here.

I rush back to the bakery, where a small line files out, wrapping by the window painted with pumpkins and a cartoonish mural of Dracula.

"Sorry, sorry," I say, holding up my palms.

Carol gives me the biggest stink eye imaginable.

"Cliff! You have more muffins back there?" Sandra asks, peering to the side with her arms full of flowers as I stroll back to the kitchen. She must have made a pit stop before another delivery.

"For you? Absolutely," I answer.

Someone else rubs their palms together, as if they anticipated it.

Vultures, these people, I swear.

I get to work immediately, making my second batch of everything for the day. The food prepped at four this morning has already dwindled down to scraps, so I take out all the prepped food from the fridge and plop those into the oven, one right after the other.

Once the post-lunch rush dies down—including a few extra items, gifted on the house for the long wait—I finally tuck a small batch of new puff pastries in the oven. They're layered with a jam mix of raspberry and rosemary. I haven't made them in a while—they're not exactly a town favorite. But maybe some people will like them this time around. Maybe Michelle will.

Carol finally joins me in the kitchen, leaning her hip against the prep table. "And where were you this afternoon?" she asks.

"The inn."

"With Michelle again?"

I chuckle. "Yes," I say slowly.

"Doing what?"

"What's with the third degree?"

"No reason," she answers, but it's said in a faux nonchalant, *yes, there is obviously a reason* kind of way.

I can't hide the heat rising up my neck. "She's my friend—you know that."

"Your friend?"

I scoff. "Yes."

"This is the first *friend* you've ever had."

"Lars is my friend."

"A non-mustachioed, non-pizza-and-doughnut-obsessed female friend."

I tilt my head to the side, leaning the heels of my palms along the side of the curved prep table. "Got something to say, Carol?"

She bends at the waist and whines, "Come on. She's not just a friend. She's gorgeous."

My heart sinks.

"Well, of course she's gorgeous. But, yes," I whisper sarcastically, "also *just* a friend."

Carol grits her teeth. "What's so wrong about liking her?"

"I *do* like her."

"You know what I mean." She purses her lips. "Is it because you're hung up on Tracy?"

"No," I say on a rushed-out breath, shaking my head and exhaling as nerves zip through me. "God, no."

"Good," someone answers, but it isn't Carol.

Lars rounds the corner, already wearing his buttoned-up white shirt and red tie with little pizzas repeating over the fabric.

"Lars, do you ever work?" I ask.

He shrugs. "Pizzeria opens late. I own the place. I can show up whenever." He glances at Carol. "Doughnut?"

She hands him a set-aside napkin with one glazed doughnut, as she does most afternoons. But her eyes don't divert from me.

"We're talking about Trace?" Lars asks. "Or is it Michelle?"

"No," I say at the same time Carol answers, "Yes."

"Hey, drop it," I say pointedly.

"No, because I haven't seen you look this happy in years, and I want to know why you're pretending like it means nothing."

"Oh yeah, everyone can see it," Lars interjects with little flecks of crumbs shooting from his lips.

I rub a palm down my face. "Are there conversations I'm being left out of?"

"We talk about you all the time," Lars says. "Betty and I were saying the other day how if you wanna find Michelle, you might as well look for Cliff too. You two are always in the same spot."

Carol's eyes widen, as if to say, *See?*

"We're friends," I repeat. I sound like a skipping CD, and I'm almost annoyed with myself at this point.

Carol crosses her arms. "No, I'm not doing this anymore."

"Doing *what*?"

"Seeing sad-sack Clifford."

Lars laughs so suddenly that he coughs through his bite of doughnut.

"I mean it," Carol says, absentmindedly clapping my best friend's back. "You were sad with Tracy for years. And she was awful—"

"Hey, that's the mother of my children."

"So?" Carol snorts. "She's also your ex-wife, who nobody liked."

I swallow, my chest tightening. "What are you talking about?"

"Come on," Carol groans. "We put up with her because she was Trace. But, God, we all knew she didn't deserve you. We all watched it happen. I got a front-row seat, and I hated every moment. But you're my brother, and you said you were happy, so I went with it."

"We all knew though," Lars says, punching a fist against his chest as he coughs once more.

Carol sighs. "I understand the scenario you were in, but you were fighting for your life, trying to get people to like her. You were her only redeeming quality."

"Carol, let's not—"

"No. I'm gonna say my piece, and you can shut up for once, *big brother*."

It's quiet. Deadly quiet in the otherwise noisy kitchen, which is filled with the sounds of the Smashing Pumpkins on the radio and a lone cough from Lars.

Lars looks between us. "Uh, am I . . . should I go . . ."

Carol barrels on. "You deserve better. And Michelle's a total knockout. She's the kind of woman Tracy *wanted* to be. Except this woman likes you. For you."

I scoff. "In no reality would she ever like me."

Lars coughs, "Bullshit," into his fist.

"Do you need some *water*?" I ask.

Carol groans. "You're very likable, Cliff. And Tracy sucked and made you think you weren't. And if I could punch her for it, I would."

Another quiet moment follows, where Lars rolls up the

napkin in his fist and smacks his lips. "Well, I guess I'm gonna go run a restaurant now. This wasn't relaxing at all."

"I'm sorry for getting heated," Carol says, but she's not talking to Lars. She's lifting an eyebrow at me. "But I'm not sorry for what I said."

Around then is when the oven dings, alerting us to the new rosemary-scented pastries.

Carol darts her eyes to the oven window. "Puff pastries? Who are those for?"

I tongue my cheek, at a loss for words, and she immediately grins.

"Just a friend, my ass."

Chapter 16

MICHELLE

The inn is packed. With two days before Halloween, people were bound to travel here. And not only the honeymoon couple, but two other families as well. There are only three guest rooms in the whole house, but they're at the most capacity we can manage.

"Okay, I've got the blow-up mattress ready to go," I say to a mother who looks run ragged. "And I put Power Rangers bedsheets on it, so there's no question about who's sleeping on it." I nod to her twin boys zooming through the parlor with an action figure held high. "You'll get the main bed."

She exhales. "You're a saint, Birdie."

Chills skitter across my arms when she shakes my hand.

"Oh." I freeze. "Birdie is my mother actually. I'm Michelle."

The woman runs a palm down her cheek, pulling the skin around her eye with it. "Oh God, I'm so sorry. I've barely slept in days."

"Don't worry about it," I say, forcing a laugh.

The mistake was bound to happen. We haven't updated all the signage and innkeeper information. Maybe it's a good thing it happened so late in the month, when I've been here long enough to be okay with it. But it doesn't ease the squeezing in my chest.

The phone in the kitchen rings, so I shove through the swinging door.

Emily and Brittany sit at the breakfast nook with papers scattered around them—Brittany with a Lisa Frank coloring page and Emily with her homework. I trip over Rocket's dog bed, basically stumbling to the phone. Emily looks up. Dark circles run under her eyes.

"Are you okay?" I ask her, the phone blaring beside me.

"Yeah."

"Em?"

She slouches. "Josh hasn't called today."

"Oh, I'm so—" The phone rings again, and I groan. "One second." I pluck the phone from its cradle. "Thank you for calling Bird & Breakfast. This is—"

"Shells!"

My sister's voice sends my heart flying into my throat, followed immediately by guilt. I cannot remember the last time we talked.

"Sara," I say on a breath. It's funny how the distraction of the inn made me completely forget about everything else.

"Is this a bad time?" she asks.

"No, no, it's a perfect time," I lie.

Emily lays down her pencil and raises a judging eyebrow. I raise both of mine in return.

"It's a full house over here," I amend. "Halloween, you know."

"Oh, cool," Sara says.

I hear a leather couch squeaking on her end of the line. She's settling in, which means this might be an hour-long phone call if I'm not careful. Normally, it wouldn't be a problem—we haven't spoken in a week or two—but my back is aching, and the arches of my feet are screaming from hurrying around the house all day.

"Yeah, it's pretty packed, Sara," I say.

Emily's eyes widen.

I cover the phone with my palm and whisper, "It's my sister."

"Your sister?"

"Who is that?" Sara asks.

I fiddle with my earring and squeeze my eyes shut. "Sorry, that's Cliff's daughter."

"Hot Neighbor?"

"Is she from Seattle too?" Emily asks.

"Yes," I answer both of them.

"*Ooh.* Shells, so you *do* think he's hot?"

"Sara. He's not—" But I don't finish because, well, that's not exactly a bridge I want to cross.

Sara gasps at my silence. "Oh snap."

"Can I ask her why boys suck?" Emily chimes in with a scowl.

"You can ask *me* that," I say.

Sara laughs. "Ask you what? If you think he's hot?"

"Sara," I warn again, "he's only a friend."

Emily gasps this time. "Are you talking about my dad?"

I point a finger at her. "Hang on a second."

"Me?" Sara asks.

"No, not you."

"Not me?" Emily asks.

"Stop being difficult."

Sara laughs. "Me?"

"No!"

I slouch against the wall right as the kitchen door swings in. One of the guest's twin boys sneaks in for a snack.

Thankfully, Emily stands, gives me a thumbs-up, and silently nudges him back into the parlor with a "Where's your mommy?"

Beyond the door, a hum of indiscernible conversation continues, but it's muffled enough for me to take in a breath.

"Sorry," I say into the phone with an exhale. "It's a little chaotic here."

"Sounds like you're chillin' though."

"I guess. The place is running at least."

Emily pokes her head in the door. "Can you ask her—"

"Em!" I snap with a laugh. "Give me a second!"

Emily grins, knowing she's hamming it up. She disappears on the other side of the door.

"That teen is gonna kill me," I murmur to Sara, sighing and rolling my head back against the wall. My sister is quiet for a moment on the other end of the line, to the point that I have to ask, "Sara, you there?"

"You sound happy, Shells."

I let out a strained laugh. "Do I? Because I feel stressed."

"You like being busy and stuff. And you sound like you've got friends."

"Right. Who wouldn't want a sixteen-year-old friend?" I deadpan.

"No, you called her dad your friend."

I slide the pendant over my necklace chain. "Oh. Well . . . because he is."

"I can't wait to meet him!"

"Are you guys coming to town?"

"Yeah, Dad's talked about it."

I freeze on the spot, licking my bottom lip and squeaking

my shoes together. I haven't asked about Dad once. I disappeared into Copper Run, like I'd intended. But now I've gotten lost in the woods, so enraptured by making the inn thrive, immersing myself in Copper Run, and getting tangled in work, like I always do.

"How is he?" I ask.

"Better. No more show reruns. He's going on walks."

I let out a breath. "That's amazing."

"It's been great," she says. "So, I was thinking I could come over when my school is on Thanksgiving break."

"That would be great."

"And I could meet Hot Dad Neighbor."

I laugh, but it fades off. "You know what? You'd probably really get along with him. He's funny. I think he might like blondes." I don't know why that left my mouth. It was so quick, like a jumble of words I basically tripped over.

Cliff is my friend. He hasn't dated since he divorced two years ago. My sister is like bottled sunbeam. He needs a bit more sunshine.

"Really?" Sara asks. "Nothing is going on between you two?"

My chest tightens. "No. Seriously, nothing is going on."

"I mean, if he's cute," Sara says on a giggle, "I wouldn't say no."

"I'll ask him about it, then."

I've never set up a friend with my sister before. I've never had a guy friend available to even consider it. Maybe that's why my stomach is churning. Because of my lack of matchmaking skills. I don't want my sister to get hurt, and I don't want Cliff to get hurt either.

The kitchen door swings open, and Carol pokes her head in.

"God, it's too loud out there," she says, already removing her pack of smokes from her pocket.

"Where's Cliff?" I ask.

"At the bakery," she says, fumbling the pack open and frowning. "We closed early. He has lots of last-minute Halloween party orders."

I smirk. "Can't help himself."

"No, but"—Carol tosses the empty pack in the trash and settles at the table with Brittany—"I'm here to relieve you of your babysitting duties."

The door bursts in again, and this time it's the woman with the two boys.

"I'm so sorry. What was your name again? It wasn't Birdie, but—"

"Michelle," I say quickly.

"I'm so sorry, Michelle. Are there towels upstairs?"

"Yes—"

"I've got it," Carol chimes in, walking through the door before I can argue.

"I'm gonna call you back in a couple of days," Sara says on the phone.

I blink back to our conversation. "No, wait—"

"Yes. You're busy. I'm hanging up now. Don't argue. I love you."

I nod even though she can't see me. The tight coil in my chest is pulling taut with heat springing all the way down to my fingertips.

"Love you," I answer, and the moment I do, I hear the dial tone.

I hang up the phone right as Carol walks in with Lisa and Emily on her heels.

Lisa touches my shoulder, her eyes like tiny marbles behind her thick glasses. "How's it been today?"

"Hectic," I answer.

"Big families?"

"*Big* families," I echo. My stomach rumbles, and I place a hand over it. "Ugh. I think I forgot to eat lunch."

Carol's eyes shift from my stomach, to me, then to Lisa. She and Lisa exchange a knowing nod.

"Get out of here," Lisa demands.

I lift an eyebrow. "What?"

"Go," Carol throws in. "Get a sandwich at Betty's or something."

I snort. "I can't leave."

"Yes, you can," she says. "Get away from this house for an hour. We've got this. Emily too."

Emily gawks. "Wait, I'm working? But what if Josh calls?"

Carol nudges her and nods to me. "Go, Michelle. I'm kicking you out. How about this? You'll be helping me because"—she digs in her pocket and pulls out a five-dollar bill—"you can buy me another pack. See? Helping."

Lisa sniffs. "Carol, dear, that's a terrible habit."

I lift an eyebrow. "I'm not supporting it either."

"You both sound like Cliff," she says dully. But she waves the five at me anyway. "Go. Now."

My feet knew where to go before I did. Ten minutes after leaving the inn, I knock on the locked glass door to Burke's Bakery.

I tuck my hands in my leather jacket pockets and look out at the square while I wait. The park is prepped for trick-or-treaters this Friday. Black wrought iron fences line the sidewalk with speared pumpkins, and plastic skeletons lounge in the gazebo rocking chairs. Papier-mâché ghosts glide from tree branches, bumping into the sparse leaves of maroon and gold.

Seattle Halloween and Copper Run Halloween couldn't be more different. Instead of honking cars, there are whistling breezes. There aren't secret, invite-only spooky parties, but instead, the entire town is a celebration, complete with yard themes and businesses covering their glass windows from top to bottom in Frankensteins or witches.

I'm not accustomed to feeling the holiday spirit like this.

The bakery's glass door swings out with a *ding*. Cliff leans on the doorframe. His hair is wild. Its usual color of fallen autumn leaves is now flaked with specks of powdered sugar—probably from the same incident that caused the hand resting on the doorjamb to be coated as well. His apron is stained with what I assume is orange and white icing. Beneath it, he wears only a white T-shirt. I'm not sure I've ever seen him in anything less than long sleeves. Somewhere in the back, a radio blasts some Billboard Hot 100 alt rock song I hear too often but can never name.

The crease beside Cliff's mouth deepens, and a half smile slinks onto his lips. "What a pleasant surprise."

I duck under his arm and walk inside. "I got kicked out by your sister."

Cliff chuckles, snicking the door shut behind us and securing the dead bolt. The overhead lights in the bakery lobby are turned off. Only beams of fluorescents bleed out from the back. The place smells incredible, like vanilla and cinnamon spice and cakes. It smells like Cliff.

"What did you do this time?" he asks.

"My job."

"Ah, don't you know that Carol hates people who work?"

He follows me to the kitchen, where I halt on sight. It's a disorganized *mess*. The steel prep table is overwhelmed by thrown-aside icing piping bags, used cookie cutters, an explosion of sugar, and trays of cupcakes with heat rising from their puffed tops.

"Impressed by my disaster?" Cliff asks. "If Carol could kick me out of this bakery, I guarantee she would."

"Why can't she?"

He leans closer and growls out, "Because nobody bakes like I do."

His cocky smile lifts at the edge of his mouth as he bypasses me with his hard chest brushing against my back. I stiffen in place. His ability to *say things* and have them be confident like that is pure talent.

"You look busy," I say.

"It doesn't only *look* that way," he responds. "I am."

"How can I help?"

"You work addict," he teases right as the oven beeps. He nods his chin toward it. "Wanna get that?"

I do as he said. I notice him watching, leaning against the table with his arms crossed as his eyes rove over my shoulders and arms.

"I like your hair like that."

"O-oh," I stammer out. "Uh, with my hair pulled back?"

"Yeah, you look good."

"It's just my hair."

"That and the way you're pulling the pan out of the oven," he says. "You look like a natural. You're not burning yourself at least."

"As far as you know."

He absentmindedly points out a rack I can set the tray on

as he pushes off the prep table. Cliff stalks closer, reaching out to trace his hand over my elbow. His thumb strokes over the faint burn above the crease in my arm. Goose bumps roll over me as I swallow.

"It's mostly faded," he observes.

"It's gonna be red for a while, isn't it?" I ask.

"Maybe forever. It's a battle scar. We all get them."

I roll my eyes. "You? The professional baker?"

"Professional? Please."

He rolls up the short sleeves of his T-shirt and holds out his arms, flipping the undersides out for display. I've never noticed the faded imperfections along his skin. His arms have always been hidden beneath sweaters or partially rolled-up flannel, but now I see a line or two along his upper arms—curving with strong biceps I've also never seen—and one faded scar close to his muscled shoulder.

"Wow. I'm truly in the baker club," I say.

He scoffs out a laugh. "I'll get you a membership card. They're edible."

I grin and roll my eyes.

Cliff jerks his sleeves back down. He grabs a new sheet of parchment paper and tosses flour on top before taking whatever he recently rolled and spreading it out again. I watch his hands knead and stroke. His wrist twists when he reaches for one of the abandoned icing containers. It's funny how Cliff's chaotic energy seems to get laser-focused when he's working on a prep table.

"Yes?" Cliff asks.

I jump. "What?"

"You think very loud. Has anyone ever told you that?"

"You have."

"Ah," he says, throwing me a knowing smirk. "By the

way, see the little box over there? I've got a new weird baker thing for you."

I grin. I'm starting to look forward to his weird baker things.

I open the box. Inside is a diamond-shaped pastry, folded in the middle over a thin layer of what looks like jam. Powdered sugar is sprinkled on top. It looks delectable. Cliff doesn't need to instruct me to taste; I already have it halfway to my mouth.

One bite is enough to likely rival any food that could exist in heaven. I inhale and exhale.

"Cliff—"

"Good?" he asks.

"One of your best."

I gently place it back in the box, but that only makes him sigh.

I wipe my lips with a spare napkin. "You seem like you're never satisfied."

"Because I'm not," he answers matter-of-factly. "So, how was your day?"

"You're gonna change the subject like that?"

"I am. Busy day?"

I know there's no redirecting once Cliff has his mind set, so instead, I nod and follow his lead. "Yeah. I got a call from my sister."

"Bad news?"

"No. She and my dad will be here for Thanksgiving."

"Paulie!" Cliff calls out to nobody. "Miss that guy."

Paulie. Birdie.

I close my eyes. God, that woman called me by my mom's name.

Why did that feel so . . . *weird*?

The radio's song changes to some other vague popular rock ballad. I cross one of my boots over the other and continue watching him roll dough. I sigh.

Cliff randomly laughs and squints at me. "So, do you want to talk about what's bothering you?"

My head jerks up. "Hmm? No."

He pops his lips. "Fair enough, then."

"That's it?"

He pushes the heel of his palm into the dough and shrugs. "Well, if you want to keep it to yourself, that's your business. Not mine."

I open my mouth, then shut it, trying to process this new logic.

This is so different from how Allen insisted I talk. Now, when I tell Cliff that I don't want to, he lets me exist in the way that makes sense for me. I don't know how to handle that type of understanding. Ironically, it makes me want to talk more. Maybe that's what Cliff wants. Maybe it's reverse psychology. But something tells me it isn't.

"Actually, yes." I change my answer. "I want to talk about what's bothering me."

Cliff stops working and slaps his palms together, sending flour up in a cloud. He smiles. "My attention is all yours, Michelle."

I roll my head to the side, inhale, and say, "Someone called me Birdie today."

His face falls. "Oh."

"It's fine."

"How did you feel about it?"

I shrug. "I think it reminded me that I'm managing *her* inn."

"Is that a bad thing?" he asks.

"No," I admit. "I've been running on autopilot. I forgot that a world exists outside of this one. I've been"—my eyes catch on his forearms and how they pop out from being folded over his broad chest before looking away—"distracted." Quickly, I add, "It was weird, hearing about her again."

Even though I bounce my eyes to every place possible, clenching and unclenching my grip on my elbows, Cliff's eyes remain steady on me.

"I wish I knew more about her life here," I continue. "That I had more of the memories of her that you have. Maybe more pictures."

"Don't tell Brittany that." He snorts. "I already told her about the camera idea."

"Now she won't stop talking about it?" I ask.

"All the time," he groans. "So, what do you want to know about Birdie?"

The question guts me. It's like I snuck out of the serious conversation, and now I'm being nudged back in.

I hesitate before asking, "Was she kind?"

"Incredibly."

"She looked after Brittany?"

"Like she was her own grandkid."

I smile. "I used to love seeing her with Sara."

"Oh yeah?"

"Yeah," I muse. I rest my hip on the wall beside me. "They'd run around the yard together all the time. Mom always had rosebushes, even at the house we grew up in. Sara would pluck them out, and Mom would get *so* angry. But it was all pretend, you know? Nobody actually stays angry with Sara," I admit with a smile.

"And where were you?" Cliff asks.

My eyes jerk to his. "What do you mean?"

"While they were playing outside with roses, where were you?"

I shrug. "I don't know. Inside. Reading maybe."

"You didn't want to go outside?"

My face falls, and I swallow. "I never really felt invited."

"That doesn't sound like Birdie."

"It was complicated. She was sad a lot when I was little. But when Sara came, it all seemed to make sense again. She was a breath of life into our family. I can't explain it."

"I like how you talk about your sister," he says.

"She's my favorite person in the world," I admit.

The gentle smile that spreads over his lips sends a warmth trailing over me, rising up my neck to my cheeks.

"I think that's enough feelings talk from me right now," I murmur.

He nods. "Fair enough."

"Your turn," I say, nudging my boot out, as if prompting him. "You have enough feelings for the both of us."

He barks out a laugh. "Do I?"

"Oh yes. I bet you'd cry at the drop of a hat."

"Maybe I would," he admits. "Let's see . . . what do you want to know?"

"How are you?"

"How am I?" he asks back. "Huh. I don't know. The bakery is exploding. Emily has a boyfriend. And Brittany keeps telling me she wants to be a wrestler. So, you could say I'm a little more stressed than usual. And Trace is . . ." He pauses. "I don't know. Concerned, I guess. Typical mom stuff."

I slide my pendant across the necklace, twisting and trying to think of what to say to that. I never know how to react when he brings up Tracy. They were together for so long that anything I might say feels inappropriate. How could my five years of marriage compare to his fourteen?

"She's a good person," he continues. "Things are"—he sighs—"complicated." Cliff throws me a weak smile. "But, hey"—he huffs a laugh—"I have no room to talk. I'm exhausting."

My face falls. "No, you're not."

He shoots me a look, and I shrug.

"I mean, yes, but . . . it's an exhausting that makes you, *you*. I think most people like it."

He lets out a heavy exhale. "Listen, I've been told most of my life that there's *a lot* of me to go around. You don't need to be nice about it."

"Well, if you're exhausting, so am I," I say. "High-maintenance. Argumentative. Abrasive. According to my ex, boring." I scoff.

"First off, never call yourself that," he says sternly with a pointed finger. "And second, what I'm hearing are other words. Classy. Opinionated. And intimidating to people who can't handle strong women. Which I really like about you."

I roll my eyes. "I'm closed off."

"You open up to people you like."

"I don't like anyone."

"Yes, you do. You like me."

My chest stutters, and I curl my lips in. "Sometimes," I tease.

"Sometimes is better than not at all."

The song changes on the radio again. I recognize it this time. It's not difficult to place Eddie Vedder's mumbled crooning. I sway to it a little, but I instantly freeze when I catch Cliff gazing at me with the corner of his mouth tilted up.

"What?"

"Want to dance?" he asks.

"To what? Pearl Jam?"

The rest of Cliff's smile spreads over his face. "Yes."

I scoff. "We are *not* going to slow dance to Pearl Jam."

"Oh, yes, we are."

He slowly walks over to where I lurk. He tucks a palm into my elbow so that I release my crossed arms, sliding one of my hands into his and wrapping the other around my lower back. I suck in a breath when he tugs me closer and lowers his cheek down to meet the side of mine.

And then we sway.

Eventually, he takes a step forward, and I take one back. He steps to the side, and I follow. I'm being guided through a dance. I hate being guided. But with Cliff, it doesn't feel like he's taking control. He's moving with me in tandem. It's a dance that takes two—not the overwhelming power of one.

"I remember the first time I heard this song," he murmurs, his warm breath tickling my ear. I can feel it down to my neck. "I was driving Emily to the doctor. She was coughing up a storm. Poor kid was miserable, and I was at the end of my rope. Hadn't slept in days. But when this came on the radio, it was like her coughing suddenly stopped. I don't know how to explain it. She says she remembers that night too. Or maybe I've told the story so many times that it feels real to her."

"I like that story," I whisper.

"Mmm. It's a great song and all, but that kind of memory should have been associated with . . . I don't know . . . something other than Eddie Vedder."

I snicker. "Want to know a secret?"

"A Michelle secret? Finally."

"I actually love this song." He chuckles against my neck, and I continue. "Allen hated this song."

"Who could possibly hate this song?"

"It's funny; we met when I was twenty-three, and it didn't matter what it was . . . if I liked it, it was *too young* for him. Too childish."

"You? Childish?"

"He also hated *Pretty in Pink*. Don't even get me started on that."

"How old was this guy?"

"Allen is twelve years older than me." Cliff remains silent, and a little part of me is embarrassed. "I think I liked that he was . . . an adult, you know? That I didn't have to take care of him like I did my mom or my sister. That maybe *I* could be taken care of." I breathe out a laugh. "Is that stupid?"

Cliff squeezes me closer to him. "Not even a little bit. You deserve to be taken care of, Michelle."

I swallow down his words. "And the woman who called me . . . she couldn't have been more than twenty-two either. Maybe he didn't like that I'd gotten older. I don't know."

Cliff laughs again, but it doesn't feel like it's at my expense. The sound rumbles through me, over my shoulders and down my spine, where it settles into his palm, like he's holding my nerves close. Protecting them.

"I don't . . . I don't think I was surprised when I learned he'd cheated," I admit. "And honestly, I don't even miss him all that much. I miss . . . noise. It's so quiet, being alone."

Cliff gently sets his thumb and forefinger on my chin, slowly rotating me to face him.

"It goes away," he says.

My lips part as I whisper out a breathy "I hope so."

"Tell me another secret," he murmurs, the question humming in my ear.

"I've got too many," I admit. "I don't know where to start."

"I'll take any I can get."

"I want to know more about you."

He chuckles. "Your secret is that you want to know about me?"

"Why didn't it work out between you and Tracy?"

Cliff is suddenly silent.

I cringe. My face burns red hot.

I wheeze out a laugh. "See? I'm abrasive."

He removes my hand from his, but instead of walking away, he pushes my elbows up so my arms wrap over his shoulders. He pulls me closer to his chest. "Don't say that," he demands.

I link my hands behind his neck, and all I can think to say is "Okay," because the shakiness in his tone felt painful. Like he's angry the word left my mouth.

"What happened is that, one day, Tracy decided she didn't want to be here anymore," he confesses. "Simple as that. Said she'd been thinking about it a long time. Even before we had Brittany."

"How old was Brittany when you split?"

"Three," he answers. "I was surprised when she said she wanted to try for another, especially since Emily was getting old enough that we could do more things. Have a bit more freedom we hadn't gotten as teen parents. But Trace said she wanted to try for a kid that was planned this time. And who was I to say no? I loved being a dad.

"But after Brittany, it was like whatever she was looking for still wasn't there. Then she sat me down one day and said she didn't like me anymore. Not *love*—I distinctly remember that. She didn't *like* me. I asked how long she knew she didn't like me, and she said maybe she never did."

I feel a prick in my heart. An uneasiness. *Who could say that to a person? Who could say that to* Cliff?

"I'm so sorry," I murmur.

He lets out a sardonic laugh. "You didn't say it. I know I talk in jokes. I'm sarcastic and generally not serious. I'm difficult to like."

The sentence doesn't feel like they're his words. They're Tracy's. These thoughts were planted years ago with time to sprout, and now they're rooted in him.

"You're very easy to like, Cliff," I say. "I was serious. I don't like most people. But you were right; I do like you. So, don't apologize for your jokes now. I enjoy them."

He snorts. "Don't go soft on me."

"Fine. No compliments for your jokes ever again as long as you keep telling them."

He chuckles. "Deal."

I let my head fall to his shoulder. His palm cradles the back of my head, his fingers massaging through my hair. Warm. Gentle.

"I can't believe we're dancing to this stupid song," I say on an exhale.

"I can't believe I actually got you to do it."

I laugh a little, and then he does. He hugs me tighter, and I bury my head into the crook of his neck more. I can smell the vanilla and cinnamon on him, but also that unique citrus cologne underneath—the secret Cliff hides behind all his walls.

He strokes my back. I know Cliff is only touching me out

of habit. That's how he operates, no matter who the person is. But part of me wants Cliff to touch me because I'm me.

I lift my head slightly, and he leans his cheek against mine.

"You should get back to work," I whisper.

"I should," he murmurs back.

"Thanks for the secrets."

"Thanks for the company."

I lean back, but my arms don't fall from his neck. His hands drift down to my waist, his thumbs running a circle over my ribs. My index finger finds its way to the hair at the nape of his neck. His eyes dart to my lips and back up. I can't calm my nerves when he looks at me like that. My heart is beating erratically, and with my chest pressed against his, I can feel his pulse thundering too.

I hear myself swallow. I can see every shimmer in his blue eyes, every small speck of hazel within. I feel how deeply they see *through* me, rattling me to my core, pinning my feet exactly where they stand. My heart claws its way up my throat, and maybe . . . maybe . . .

A loud knock booms on the bakery door. I jump, but Cliff doesn't move. His hand pauses on my waist. His eyes search mine, but I'm not sure what he's looking for.

A fist knocks against the glass again.

I blink and step out of his arms. "You might want to—"

"Yeah," he interrupts, running a palm through his hair and striding out of the kitchen to the front.

The bell above the door dings as Cliff rips it open.

"Mr. Burke—"

"Josh," Cliff announces.

I walk to the bakery's lobby, watching the color slowly drain from Josh's face as his eyes dart between the two of us.

"How *wonderful* to see you," Cliff continues through gritted teeth. "How can I help you?"

"I didn't know if Emily was here. She didn't stop by like she usually does."

"She's at the inn," I interject, somehow out of breath. "She's been waiting on your call."

"Crap, I knew it," he whines. "My mom has been hogging the phone. She got some radio sweepstakes thing."

"Shame," Cliff says, but he seems disconnected from the conversation as much as I am.

I'm so lost in what happened. Whatever it was. If it was anything at all. One minute, we were dancing, and the next, I'm so nervous. I've never been this nervous around Cliff.

"I'll go find her at the inn," Josh says.

"Front door is unlocked," I say.

"Thanks. Oh, and, Mr. Burke?"

Cliff's eyes squeeze shut. "Yes, Josh?"

"Can I . . . can you tell me what her favorite dessert is? I figure . . . I don't know . . . I'd like to find out how to make it or something."

Cliff's shoulders deflate, and he nods, breathing out, "Apple fritter."

"Apple fritter, apple fritter . . ." Josh repeats.

"I'll give you my recipe."

"Thanks, dude. I mean, Mr.—"

"Call me Cliff."

I swear the boy's grin gets so big and energized that it could power the entire town of Copper Run.

"Thanks, Cliff. I'll, uh, be seeing you."

The bakery door shuts, and Cliff slowly turns on his squeaking boots. He tucks his hands in his pockets as his gaze trails from my hair, down to my lips, and back up. He's taking me in, and even though he's always looked at me like that—with a stare that sees *through* me—I've never felt more exposed than I do in this moment.

My face flushes red, and I can feel heat everywhere. Not in my cheeks or my chest, but down to my stomach and dangerously lower.

"I've got to get back," I blurt out. "Lisa and Carol are probably overwhelmed." I dig in my pocket and hold up Carol's five-dollar bill. "She gave me money to get her a pack."

He swallows and forces out a laugh, looking down at his shoes instead of at me. "Oh. Well, definitely don't do that."

"Didn't plan on it," I respond. I place it on the counter. "I'll tell her I lost it."

Cliff grins. "I'll sneak it back into her purse tomorrow."

"Thanks."

I bypass him without another word and push out the door. Behind me, the dead bolt locks.

I don't want to turn around. I don't want to know if he's watching me walk away. I don't want to potentially see his subtle smile rise up the corner of his mouth. I don't need to feel my heart beating faster. And I definitely don't need to confirm my newest secret.

I like Cliff Burke. *Like* like, as Emily might say.

I like his deadpan humor and his messy, complicated life. I like the fact that he needs touch as much as he needs oxygen. I like that he says what he wants and takes what he wants and doesn't apologize for either. I like that, at the end of the day, he's my friend.

I like Cliff Burke. And this charming guy who has the entire small town wrapped around his finger? I know he could never like an abrasive woman like me.

Chapter 17

CLIFF

Halloween is the biggest holiday in Copper Run. Sure, we love Christmas too, with the snowflakes hanging on bare branches and hot chocolate stands, but if you want to get Copper Run hyped up, place a few crusty skeletons in the yards and blast the "Monster Mash." If you live here, it's expected that you celebrate ghouls and slasher films like the good resident that you are and you *always* wear a costume.

I look at myself between the stickers on Emily's long mirror and sigh.

"Remember when you used to make me a ghost?" I say. "Or Batman. Why not make me Batman again?"

"Because Ghostface is what's cool right now," Emily answers nonchalantly.

Emily has been either choosing my outfits or making them since she was little. And this year, she chose the most popular costume of the season from the biggest slasher movie of the past year.

I hold out my arm. Black fabric slithers down and hangs in a large open sleeve, revealing the cuff of my red flannel underneath. Only an inch of skin shows between that and my black gloves.

She bends at the waist to stroke more black nail polish

onto her toes. "It was the last one at the mall, Dad. You *have* to wear it."

I pick up the white mask from Emily's dresser and place it over my face. Through the thin black mesh, I can see drooping eye holes and a yawning mouth staring back.

I take it off. "I'm gonna scare your sister."

"I showed it to her beforehand. I told her it's from an old kids show," Emily says. "She thinks it's funny."

"Em, that is incredibly irresponsible." I straighten the black robe on my shoulders. "But also genius. You're ungrounded."

"Her head jerks up. "Wait, I wasn't grounded."

"I was debating it."

I flip up the lanky hood, then put on the mask again. It's difficult to breathe under the plastic and mesh.

When I tsk to myself, Emily laughs. "Trust me, you're gonna be the *coolest* guy out there."

"I'm already cool."

"As if. You could use more coolness."

"I'm not trying to impress anyone."

"Not *Michelle*?" she taunts under her breath.

A rope lassos around my chest so tight that I almost cough. I rip off my mask and nervously fiddle with my black glove, pulling it farther up my wrist.

"She's already intimidated by how cool I am," I joke. "Why make it worse for her?"

Emily blows on her nails. "No, you're not *nearly* cool enough for Michelle."

"Why does it matter?"

She gives me that slack-jawed expression that is normally followed by a *duh*. Instead, she sighs, silently puts on her cat ears, and rises from the end of her bed.

"Oh, Dad," she finally says on a pitying sigh.

"I'm considering grounding you again."

"Dad!" Brittany runs into the room with her unicorn pillowcase gripped in her fist. "Look!"

I look down at her, and my jaw drops. Without hesitation, Emily bursts out laughing.

My six-year-old daughter is wearing a bald cap. It's not even a *well-placed* bald cap, or maybe she pulled at it too much. The top of her head looks like an overgrown mushroom. Strands of hair stick out underneath. Scribbled under her nose and along her chin is a black goatee. She's wearing jeans and a black vest I vaguely recognize as the black bedsheets that were on Bird & Breakfast's floor last week.

"Wow," I breathe. "Em, have you seen Brittany? Because I think"—I lower my voice to a guttural tone—"*Steve Austin just entered the room!*"

I flex my arms, dip down, and throw her over my shoulder. Brittany screams through uncontrollable giggles as I run to Emily's bed and toss her onto the mattress.

"Wait, Dad, Steve always wins!" Brittany pouts—or at least she might if she wasn't laughing so hard.

"Oh, right." I smack my palm on my forehead. "My bad." I fall backward on the bed and lie still as Brittany pushes down on my shoulders.

Emily smacks her hand on the sheets. "One, two, three! And Steve Austin wins!"

Brittany raises her arms in victory.

I pick her up again, swinging her in the air as Emily and I chant, "Undefeated champion! Undefeated champion!"

"Oh, wait!" Brittany squirms in my arms until I set her down. She runs out the door. "I forgot something!" Her voice is a distant echo as she scrambles down the hall to her bedroom.

I look back at the mirror and find Emily already staring at me.

I jump. "What?"

"I could talk to Michelle if you want," Emily says.

My heart does that stuttering thing again. "I can talk to Michelle on my own."

"Yeah, but what about—"

Brittany runs back into the room. There's a click and then a flash of light. Black darkens my vision, followed by tiny bubble-like spots. I rub my eyes and blink the room back into sight. That's when I see the yellow disposable camera in Brittany's tiny palms.

I laugh. "Where'd you get that?"

"Miss Shell gave it to me!"

If my heart jumps into my throat one more time tonight, I swear I'm gonna pass out. I don't know the last time I felt this disoriented. It's so unnerving to be taken off guard by the mention of a single person—a person I have no business getting nervous over.

"That was really nice of her," I say. "Did you tell her thank you?"

"Oh." She lowers the camera. "No."

I pat Brittany on the back. "Let's make sure we do when we see her. All right, trick-or-treat time. Before it gets crowded out there."

Emily's clear purple phone rings on her dresser, and she instantly picks it up.

I groan. "Em—"

"One second," she whines.

"Make it quick," I instruct. "We gotta move."

But I don't think she hears me past her giddy, "Hi, Josh."

I grab my Ghostface mask and nudge Brittany along,

murmuring, "We're giving her five minutes, and then we scare her."

Brittany giggles in agreement.

We take the stairs down to the living room. The front door swings open, bringing in the booming music, screams, and childish laughter from the sidewalks, where kids dressed as ghosts, mummies, and devils run by. Carol crosses over the threshold in a black wig and pointed hat before slamming the door shut behind her. The busy trick-or-treaters are muffled once more.

"You're a witch again?" I ask.

"It's the only costume I have," Carol says, plopping on the couch and clicking the TV remote. "I almost ran over a few kids to get here." She quickly flicks through channels until she stops on a familiar slasher movie. "I've never seen this one." She settles into the cushions.

I clutch Brittany's shoulders and rotate her toward the kitchen.

"What is that?" she asks, peering around my legs at the TV, where a man is now raising a revving chain saw.

"Something not for little-girl eyes," I say, nudging her to the other room and covering her ears with my palms.

The kitchen back door swings open the moment our feet hit the tiles. Rocket barrels through, immediately circling around Brittany in a mad rush. Michelle stands in the doorway, tucking a strand of hair behind her ear as she closes the door behind her.

"Is there no courtesy knocking anymore?" I tease as I attempt to pocket my hands, but my palms slide down my thin, pocketless robe instead. It only makes me uneasy.

God, I'm *uneasy* around Michelle. And it's not because she's in a cute costume—she didn't dress up, which I'm definitely gonna rag her about. Or because Michelle is any more stunning than usual—impossible. It's because she's here and it's her.

I don't know what would have happened if Josh hadn't stopped by the bakery when he did. The rational part of me knows she would have likely gone back to the inn and I would have continued baking. But there's another part of me that wonders if we would have crossed an unspoken line.

Michelle, the confident woman from the city, and me, some random small-town baker. My closest friend right now and I . . . crossing a line.

Her hooded eyes, surrounded by her dark lashes, were staring at me with an intensity I'd never seen before. My hands were threaded through her hair. Her lips were parted, and her warm breath tickled my own. My heart was hammering.

Then Josh happened.

I've plotted at least five different ways to kill him since then.

"I should have dressed up," Michelle says, her lips in a fine line.

"You definitely should have dressed up," I agree with a grin. "But I like it. It's casual. Looks good on you."

"You didn't dress up?" Brittany asks Michelle, her face falling.

"I didn't want to take away from your amazing costume," Michelle responds, crouching down and tucking a few errant hairs back into Brittany's haphazard bald cap.

My chest stings. She's so good with Brittany.

"Too cool for costumes?" I tease under my breath.

Michelle pushes my arm. "Not cool *enough*."

We both laugh, but her gaze sticks to me, and I swear we

inhale at the same time because I think we both realize what happened. Michelle never touches me playfully.

"Who are you again?" she asks.

I hold out my palm. "Ghostface. Pleasure to meet you . . ."

Her bottom lip tucks between her teeth as she shakes my palm. My large gloved hand engulfs hers.

"Michelle," she answers.

Shake.

"Well, Michelle, I'll be your guide for Halloween in Copper Run tonight."

Shake.

"Thank you very much, Mr. Ghostface."

Shake.

Our hands linger.

I slide my hand from hers. "All right, let's get moving out there." I squeeze Brittany's shoulder. "Ready?"

"Yep," Brittany says, lifting her camera and taking another picture of me.

I blink through starry eyes.

"Britt, be careful with that thing," I say, fumbling to pick up the kitchen phone. I bring it to my ear and hear Josh's voice saying something about how the drummer for R.E.M. left the band.

I tuck the phone closer to my lips and channel my best Ghostface impression to growl, "Do you like scary movies?"

From the floor above, Emily screams, and Josh squeals even louder over the phone.

"O-oh my God," Josh stutters through the phone.

"Don't do that, Dad!" Emily screeches.

"You gave me the costume, Em. I have the power to do the voice. Get off the phone."

"What*ever*," she whines through a terrified exhale. "You're such a buzzkill."

"You'll see each other in two seconds anyway."

"Y-yes, Mr. Burke."

Emily groans. "Josh, he said you can call him—" But I don't hear the end because I put the phone back on its base, letting them sort out their goodbyes themselves.

I clap my palms together. "Let's get this show on the road."

I peer over at Michelle, and she's paused and staring directly at my lips. My heart does that terrible thing again, flip-flopping like a fish out of water. I clear my throat, and she flicks her eyes to mine.

"Ready?" I ask with a chuckle, trying to keep my words steady when I am anything but.

"Ready when you are," she answers quickly, walking past me to the living room with her thumb and forefinger dragging her mom's pendant over the chain.

She only does that when she's nervous.

Is she nervous?

Emily barrels down the stairwell with an empty pillowcase flying over her head. "Let's go get candy!"

"Yeah!" Brittany yells in the lowest, most wrestler-like voice a six-year-old girl could muster.

I swing open the front door. Brittany skips out first, followed by Emily ducking under my arm to run out too.

I tilt my chin, signaling Michelle to pass. Without looking at me, she crouches to cross under my arm. Her hair slides against my hanging robe, adding static to some loose strands. Instinctively, I chuckle and stroke them back into place.

I swear she stares at my lips again, then smiles, as if trying to cover up how obvious it was, before turning on her heel and clicking down the sidewalk after my girls.

"Have fun trick-or-treating!" Carol calls to me. "And don't get too spooked!"

I swallow. "Sure thing."

Though I fear there is something much scarier than ghosts tonight.

Chapter 18

MICHELLE

The streets are overtaken with running children, clusters of preteen kids, and parents chatting behind them in either no costume or one that matches their child's. Leave it to the Burke family to have an eclectic variety of a horror movie villain, an inappropriate wrestler, and a cat.

"I've never seen a town so excited about any holiday," I say.

Cliff grins. "We take Halloween very seriously. Lars has this whole pizza competition in the square. If you can eat the whole ghost-shaped pizza, you get free slices for a year."

"And you deprived me of that?" I ask with a gasp.

"You think you could win?"

"Maybe."

"I'd like to see you try. Oh, we're going this way," he interjects, placing a palm on my lower back to direct me down another street than the way we were going.

I'm already lost in the mix of things, and I've jumped twice after a group of boys ran past with a fake chain saw. But all that doesn't compare to the thrumming in my chest when Cliff touches my lower back.

Up ahead, Josh and Emily hold hands. Her cat tail bobs

behind her, right next to his paper dog tail. She nudges her shoulder against his. He returns it.

"Thanks for telling me to give him a chance," Cliff says. "He's not the worst kid she could like."

I snort. "Is that a compliment for Josh?"

"It's not an insult."

"You're growing, Cliff."

He rolls his eyes. "I think having another teen daughter would give me an early heart attack."

"Hate to break it to you, but . . ." I point at Brittany, who's racing down a driveway with her floppy pillowcase partially weighed down by a small collection of candy.

Beside her is Luke—the boy who supposedly hates Steve Austin—dressed as the Undertaker. He asks her to race him to the next house, and they bolt off with Rocket in tow, carried by the leash attached to Brittany's wrist.

"I'm doomed," Cliff says with a grin.

I bite my bottom lip, staring at his smile again. I can't help myself. I like the little line beside his mouth and the fan of check marks beside his eyes.

I keep trying to pinpoint the last time I felt this anxious. I was so nervous on my first date with Allen that I could barely eat. But for the past five years, with our steadily declining communication, with all the times he got home late from the hospital, with how he chose to take the guest room so he wouldn't wake me up, eventually taking up permanent residence for no other reason . . . the only nerves I've felt were bad.

Are these butterflies around Cliff bad?

Are they butterflies or moths?

And in what world am I having potential butterflies at all?

I'm having them in this one—this world, where we're

walking down busy streets and trick-or-treaters disregard sidewalks and cars putter through the crowds at a snail's pace. I have butterflies for this small-town baker nestled in Vermont. For this man—a friend—I would have never met in any lifetime except this one, with my divorce and without my mom. But I'm not sure I'd want to be in any other place right now, and that's the scariest part.

"Dad, Rocket got candy too!" Brittany says mid-run back to us with an open pillowcase. She tilts it to show a small doggy treat among the wrapped candy.

"Wow, good for him," Cliff says, peering down at Rocket, whose tail is wagging up a storm.

I haven't seen him this happy since we got to Copper Run. That makes two of us.

"Next house!" Brittany yells, running off again, toward the house blasting groaning ghoul sounds and a fog machine.

Cliff leans down and whispers in my ear, "Discreetly look to your left."

A shiver rolls down my spine at his proximity, but I do as he said. In a yard nearby, Betty and Lisa sway back and forth. They each hold a bright orange flask with black stickers plastered on one side to resemble a jack-o'-lantern grin.

I gasp. "Are they drinking?"

"We can't be held accountable for our actions on Halloween," he says with a grin.

"I can't believe my mom lived here. This is so . . . different."

Cliff blows out a breath, then laughs. "Oh yeah. She and Lisa were little heathens together."

"Really?"

"I've never seen Lisa and Birdie party as hard as they did at the haunted house last year."

I bust out laughing. "Wow."

"Have I told you the story about when she tripped over a grave?"

"No," I breathe.

"Best part? It wasn't even Halloween."

I laugh again, and the joy feels so foreign. But it's there, releasing from me through a collapsed dam. I hold my hand over my mouth to stop myself from laughing louder. Cliff smiles down at me, almost like he doesn't want to see anything else *but* me.

A bright light flashes through the darkness, and I blink through the stars.

"Oh God—"

"Britt, you gotta warn us," Cliff says with a laugh, rubbing his own eyes and shaking his head in shock.

Brittany giggles with her fists curled around the camera I gave her. She runs off, and another bright light blasts off across the street without a single warning.

"She's gonna blind someone, if she hasn't already," he says.

"Or wrestle them."

"Did you get that for her?"

"The camera?" I ask.

"Yeah."

"Mm-hmm. If she ever needed one, it was for tonight."

He smiles. "Thanks."

"Who was I to say no to *Steve Austin*, Cliff?"

"I would have caved too."

Up ahead, Emily turns around, looks at us, bites her bottom lip, then turns back to whisper something in Josh's ear. My smile fades, and I stiffen, feeling *too* seen in that moment, realizing that Cliff's arm is nearly touching mine and the space between us is minimal compared to everyone else walking by.

"I hate it when teenagers whisper," Cliff murmurs. "I feel like I'm getting bullied."

"Were you ever bullied?" I ask.

"Of course I was. I was the class clown. But anything they said about me was something I'd already said about myself. Oh, wait." He quickly slings an arm around my shoulders, directing me to the left. "You have to see Winston's house."

Down the street, a shuffling line of people walk toward erected, shrouded walls. Fog coats the ground as they cautiously disappear through a black curtain. Screams and chain saws echo inside, almost as loud as the sound of ghouls moaning through the speakers at the house next to us.

"A haunted maze?"

"A haunted maze," Cliff confirms.

"Am I ready for that?" I ask with a grimace.

"Probably not. But whether you're ready or not, we're doing it."

"We are?"

"Trust me," he says. "Social planner, remember?"

"I'm trusting you," I murmur.

The sentence lingers between us for a moment, and when I turn to Cliff, his eyes dart between mine on a deep exhale.

"I promise it's worth the wait." My stomach smarts as he turns to call, "Hey, Em! Can you watch Brittany and Rocket for a second?"

Emily, down the street with a heavy pillowcase full of candy, looks between us with a half smirk that is all too similar to her dad's mischievous grin. I narrow my eyes, and it only grows bigger.

"Sure!" she yells to Cliff. "Have fun."

A warm glove slides into my palm, and when I look at Cliff again, he's wearing the white mask. I jump on the spot and squeal.

His husky laugh is muffled behind the mask as he gently leads me by the hand down the road toward the haunted maze. He twists his palm in mine and threads our fingers together, nestling our hands comfortably between us. A shiver trickles down my spine, and I start to shake.

"You're more skittish than I thought you'd be," he says once we're in line. He leans closer to my ear and whispers, "Does the unshakable Michelle get scared?"

The sad part is, when I gulp and lie, "Absolutely not," I'm not sure if it's in response to the dark tunnel ahead of us or Cliff's hand entwined with mine.

I'm so scared.

Winston's wife stands at the entrance, moving her hips side to side to a joyful tune from the boom box next to her, which I bet is trying to drown out the bloodcurdling screams ahead.

"You ready?" she asks with a grin, pumping her arms side to side, dancing the twist.

I tilt my chin up with a defiant, "I'm ready."

Cliff chuckles. "Attagirl."

I grip his hand, and he tightens his hold as we duck between the heavy curtains, made from black tablecloths, into the haunted maze.

Grass crunches under our boots. We slowly make our way down the narrow hall. Streetlights attempt to break through the black folds of the makeshift walls, but the only way ahead is shrouded in darkness.

There's a scream. I pause, my back colliding with Cliff's hard chest. He snickers.

"We can go back if you want," he says.

"Never."

"Good, because that would make you a quitter."

"Shut up," I hiss-whisper.

He barks out a laugh, placing his palm on my shoulder and stroking in reassurance. But if anything, it puts me more on edge. Especially when he languidly slides his hand down my arm and over my wrist to slip our fingers together once more.

We turn the corner, and a masked clown leaps out. I scream but immediately laugh when Cliff does as well.

"Oh, are *you* scared, Clifford?" I tease with a grin.

"Whatever," he drawls.

A skeleton drops from the mesh ceiling.

"Winston!" I yell.

Cliff laughs behind me, and I swear I hear a little kid's laughter beyond the blackened walls. It's most likely Winston's family, getting their kicks.

"Keep walking," Cliff says, rubbing a thumb in the middle of my spine.

Slowly, his palm opens fully, splaying out across my back, tangling in the folds of my dress. I walk slower, frozen by his touch.

"You gotta keep walking," he repeats, and the husky murmur brushes against the nape of my neck.

My body heats. I reluctantly take more steps forward.

Another turn reveals a man in a leather mask. The one after that is a werewolf. Then a devil. But my jumps are smaller. Maybe I'm getting desensitized. Or maybe my focus is solidly on the man behind me, spreading his fingers wider around my waist.

His chest is against my back. His breath is in my hair. I never realized how tall Cliff was until now, as he towers behind me like a shield. I gingerly reach back and entwine my opposite fingers with his. His thumb makes gentle circles around my wrist.

This man—this charming man—is so close. To me. Why me?

The maze empties out on the side of Winston's house. A man darts toward us with a chain saw extended over his head. Cliff and I bolt away from the exit, our synchronous laughter echoing in the night.

We run down the grassy yard until we reach an impasse. To the right, leaves raked on either side of a pathway lead back to the neighborhood sidewalk. On the left is a tall row of bushes, coated in fake spiderwebs, with a small sliver in the middle to sneak through.

My feet halt at the fork in the road.

I hate that they do.

I hate that I consider the what-if of turning left. Of being alone—hidden in the bushes—with Cliff. What would happen? Do I want something to happen?

I turn around, and I'm met with a white mask staring back. I scream so loud that Cliff bursts out laughing and places his palm over my mouth.

"I forgot about your stupid mask," I say, partially muffled against his gloved hand.

But our laughs lessen, and then we're standing there, frozen together, with his palm cupped over my lips. My stomach twists into knots.

And then I make the decision. I don't know when my mind decided to, but I'm already stepping backward toward the bushes. Cliff walks forward after me.

I walk backward.

He paces forward.

Step by heart-pounding step, Cliff and I disappear into the bushes. We take the quiet, alone, away-from-the-world path.

Beyond the bushes, the bramble-filled dirt is pitch-black under our feet. My backside hits the paneling of Winston's house. The distant streetlamps and house decorations trickle through the bushes, leaving only a sliver of light. Cliff lifts his mask up. His eyes hide under the shadow of the long white mask, but I can feel them on me.

He removes his hand from my mouth, tracing the back of his knuckles over my cheek, down the column of my neck, and to my shoulder. His thumb dips into my collarbone as we both draw in a shaky breath.

The air around us changes. The autumn breeze that's been still all night suddenly rustles the leaves. A single leaf catches on Cliff's hood. I reach up to pick it off, and he sucks in a breath as my arm brushes over his cheek.

He leans closer, resting a palm on the wall beside my head, caging me against the paneled siding. His other hand ghosts up my arm, tickling the fabric of my shirt with the back of his gloved fingers. Shivers prickle over my skin despite the layers of clothing between us. I'm trying to breathe normally, but my inhales keep catching.

I want to kiss him.

I want to kiss Cliff so bad it hurts. But he's so cautious. So careful.

I wonder if it's because he's unsure. I don't blame him.

"Don't do something you think you'll regret," I whisper.

He shakes his head without hesitation. "I wouldn't regret this."

His hand finds the column of my neck, running up the side. I pull in a breathy gasp.

"Do you think you would?"

I don't know what answer to give. My heart is beating out of my chest.

What would this mean for us? Is he looking for an autumn fling? Am I? Or is this more? He's my friend. My best friend. I've never had a best friend outside my sister.

In my extended silence, Cliff finally lets out a choked laugh. He removes his hand from beside my head and pushes away. My heart pounds at the loss of his warmth. Anxiety courses through me as he steps back.

He pulls his mask back down and tilts his head to the side. "Do you have a favorite scary movie?" he teases, his voice carrying a sinister, raspy timbre beneath the mask as he quotes the movie from his costume.

Cliff laughs at himself, and then I'm laughing too.

Leave it to him to break the tension.

"Come on, Michelle," he says in his normal voice. I can hear the smile on his face. "Let's get you back."

And that—that right there—is the exact moment I know I *need* to kiss him. Because, despite Cliff taking a risk, he immediately backtracks when he thinks I'm uncomfortable. Because he's that kind of friend. He's that kind of man.

I don't know what our kiss might lead to. I don't know if my leaving in two months will matter. Maybe we won't stay in touch, or maybe we will. Maybe this will be something we can laugh about. There's a lot of uncertainties, but one thing is for sure: I'm not uncertain about Cliff. He's sarcastic and loud and open. He's not buttoned-up, like Allen. But Cliff is more of a man than any of the self-proclaimed kind and altruistic men I've dated before. He's more of a man than Allen ever was.

Cliff turns to walk away, but I shoot my hand out and grasp his elbow. He stiffens, twisting back to look at me. His mask—no, *Cliff*—suddenly rips fear through my heart, but I tug the crook of his arm anyway, coaxing him back. Leaves crunch beneath his boots as he stalks back to me again. This time closer. Chest to chest.

I push the bottom of his mask up with my thumb, high enough to finally see his sky-blue eyes in the moonlight. His eyebrows are pulled closer. I can feel his heart pounding against mine.

"I wouldn't regret this," I whisper.

Cliff blinks at me, eyes darting between mine. "You wouldn't?"

I shake my head side to side. "No."

Cliff slowly traces his fingers along my jaw. The glove's fabric is rough, catching in my hair as he cups the back of my neck.

I close my eyes when he purses his lips on my forehead, lingering for a moment before trailing a kiss to my temple. My cheek. My jaw. Cliff is slow with action, like he's savoring every piece of me I'm allowing him to touch.

He leans back. I open my eyes to find Cliff's lips are less than an inch away. The warmth of his breath sizzles over me.

"Michelle," he breathes, tilting his head to the side, "we can't."

An anvil slams down to my stomach. "Oh," is all I can get out.

He immediately chuckles. "Not right now, I mean." Then he leans closer, flashing the most wicked smile. "I don't want to start something I can't finish."

"Oh," I repeat, but this time, my cheeks grow hot.

He exhales with a hum, tucking hair behind my ear. "I think doing . . . *things* . . . in Winston's bushes probably isn't the best call. We'd never live it down."

"Right," I agree, shaking my head. "That makes sense."

Cliff stares at me with a solemn smile. I return it, but my heart won't stop pounding. My body is buzzing with energy. And with each passing second, I can see his smile fading. The crinkles beside his eyes disappear. His lips straighten into a line. And finally, he exhales.

"Ah, screw it."

Cliff sinks his hand into my hair, cups my head, and collides his lips with mine.

It takes the breath out of me. I stumble, but his other hand steadies my waist. The flame in my chest licks up to my throat. It's fire. *He* is fire. My fingers slide up his robe, tangling in the fabric, tugging him closer. And when his hard chest hits mine, I melt into it.

He opens his mouth in tandem with mine. An embarrassing whine leaves me. But my sound has him groaning in response too. I've never heard such a desperate sound coming from Cliff. I'd never have imagined I'd be so desperate to hear it again.

I bite his bottom lip. His tongue sinks into my mouth. I tug on his hood, knocking his mask to the dirt. He pushes me backward. My spine is firm against the house behind me. His hips tilt against mine. My breath catches.

We're eager, sliding hands over each other's neck, jaw, and hair. I can feel his heartbeat through his wrist on my cheek. He can probably feel my heart through my palm at the base of his neck. I exhale into him.

But then our feverish lips transform into something slower. Sweeter. Gentler. His thumb strokes over my cheek. My hand releases his fabric. His palm on my waist ghosts up my ribs and back down. The kisses start to linger.

He finally places what feels like the last kiss on my lips

and pulls back. But when I lean in, he steals what he can get again—pressing his lips against mine over and over until we extend the little moments in between. I can't get enough. I could kiss him forever.

We finally part, and when we open our eyes, we both start laughing. We laugh to get the nerves out. We laugh when we notice that my hair is tangled and that his cheeks are flushed.

I reach up and trace my fingers over that little scar above his lip and the deep crease beside his mouth. He chuckles again, kissing the tip of each finger as it passes by.

I feel safe. I'm content for the first time in I don't know how long.

That is until, in the distance, someone calls out, "Cliff! Where's Cliff?"

Another person yells, "Go find Cliff!"

But the final thing that has Cliff jerking away is a screeching "Dad!"

We immediately bolt.

Chapter 19

CLIFF

Hand in hand with Michelle, I shimmy through the scratchy bushes and run down the leaf-filled yard in search of my daughter, who's calling my name. My heart is pounding, my pulse beating into Michelle's palm.

One second, I was in bliss, holding this beautiful woman by the waist. And now . . . now . . .

I'm terrified.

It doesn't take us long to find the source of the call.

A collection of people stands in a circle near a storm drain. George sees me and solemnly waves me over. The crowd parts when I run up, and Michelle drops my hand when there's only enough space for me to break through. On the concrete, Brittany is holding her knee through sobs. My stomach plummets.

Maybe it's like the pumpkin patch. She took a simple fall.

One knee looks scratched, but the other . . . it's not as lucky. The wide cut looks like it penetrated deep. My heart leaps into my throat as I squat down beside her.

"Hey, Britt." I hold her cheeks in my palms. "Tell me what happened."

Snot slides down her upper lip. She's sniffling too much

to get out words. They're jumbles of "uh" and "he" and "scary." With a single finger, she points at Rocket.

The dog slinks next to Emily, his body crouching low to the ground, whining with his tail tucked between his legs. Emily's fist is tangled in Rocket's leash.

"What happened?" I ask Emily.

"One of the yard ghosts scared Rocket," she says. "When Brittany went to pet him, he freaked out and tried to run. She had the leash, so it dragged her with him."

My first instinct is to get angry with Rocket. But once the fuel in my veins runs its quick course, I'm sad. I'm sad because Brittany is looking at him like she's been betrayed.

Brittany sniffles, choking through another outburst of tears. She tries to wipe them with the heel of her hand, but there are rough road marks there too, where she must have caught her fall. I move her hands away and stroke my thumbs over the tears myself.

Michelle—*Michelle*—takes the leash from Emily's hand. Rocket scurries behind Michelle's legs, trailing his belly low to the ground and continuing to whine. Michelle crouches to pet his fur, but the dog only stiffens up more, managing a small warning growl of discomfort.

He's scared.

And then I realize the small Clifford who was bitten isn't the same man staring at this dog now.

I know it isn't Rocket's fault. It's Halloween, and any dog would be uneasy around skeletons and ghouls and devils. But I don't like that my daughter was collateral damage or that he's taking it out on Michelle too. He's an animal; expecting rationality from him is ridiculous, but I'm too fueled by irritation. Every extra moment I look at him, the more upset I get.

Brittany squirms in place. She's overwhelmed with tears. I glance at her knee. The skin is split; the cut is deeper than a Band-Aid can probably handle. I wonder if she'll need stitches.

I can't slow down my racing heartbeat.

We need to leave.

I tuck my hands beneath Brittany's back and knees, then swing her into my arms.

"We're heading to the ER," I announce. "Emily, stay here. Tell Carol what's going on."

Her worried expression follows my footsteps. "You sure you don't need—"

"We've got to get going, kiddo," I say. "We'll be fine."

"I can help, Dad."

Brittany's tears pick up again.

"Em, not right now, okay? I'm sorry."

Emily's jaw clenches. Josh rubs a palm over her back, but she furrows her brow, rolling her shoulder to get his hand off her.

"Let me come with you," she insists.

"I can't handle two things right now, kiddo."

She freezes. "Things? I'm a *thing*?"

My stomach drops. I pinch my eyes shut. "That's not—"

"Whatever," she snaps.

Emily tightens her fists, then storms off.

"Emily!" Now I'm reeling, my thoughts spiraling as I consider how to fix everything all at once. But there's too much, and I have a six-year-old wailing in my arms.

I stop next to Michelle.

I don't know what to say. I wish I could tell her that everything about tonight was so new to me, that it was the first time in nearly twenty years that I felt *alive* again.

I wonder if she regrets it. If seeing me here with my little girl in my arms is too much. And if it is, there's nothing I can do because my girls are my girls and they're the center of my world.

Is Michelle rethinking this? Did I push too hard?

I don't have time for those questions. My mind is too crowded with other concerns surrounding my girl.

How quickly can I get to my car?
Will there be traffic getting out of town since it's Halloween?
How many stitches will Brittany need?
What do I say to Emily?

"I'll check in on Emily," Michelle says, as if reading my mind.

I want to hug her.

I want to tell her that she knows me more intimately than anyone has in years.

I want to touch Michelle in any way that will reassure her I meant every word I said outside of Winston's house. I don't regret kissing her, and I hate that our night has turned out like this.

But "Thank you" is all I can muster before picking up my walk to a jog to get back to my house and truck.

The last question on my mind makes my ears ring with anxiety.

The question I wish wasn't going through my mind so soon after pinning Michelle against a wall and disappearing into her lips. A person I wish wasn't interrupting the heart-pounding thrill I'd experienced from kissing someone else for the first time.

And it's not because she needs to know.

And it's not because I need approval.

But it's because I'm carrying our girl in my arms and I know this phone call won't be the one she wants to hear on Halloween. Because it's the last call I want to make. It's the last question I want to think about right now.

What the hell do I tell Tracy?

MICHELLE

"Em—"

"I don't want to talk to anyone."

"Emily," I sigh.

"Leave me *alone*!"

Our small crew scrambles through the house behind her—me with Rocket hoisted in my arms, Josh with his crooked puppy-dog tail bouncing by his side, and Carol now rousing from the couch. Her orange bowl of candy drops and empties onto the carpet.

"What happened?" she asks.

"Too many things," I say stiffly.

So much.

I can't begin to wrap my head around tonight. The scary house. Brittany's cut. Emily. Cliff.

Cliff.

His hands gripping my waist. His hard, desperate lips. My heart beating at an erratic rate, so high above normal range that I'm worried it might explode.

And now I'm chasing his daughter through his house, barreling up the stairs, only to have the teenage girl's door slammed in my face.

My, Josh's, and Carol's heads all jerk back in unison. We exchange glances. Carol's intensely wide eyes. Josh's borderline scared expression. And me, determined and clutching Rocket to my chest.

He squirms, and I set him on the carpet. He lowers to his belly between my legs.

"Brittany fell on the ground," I explain to Carol, pulling my hair up and tying it back. It needs to get off my sticky neck, coated in overheated attraction and sweat from running down the street after Emily.

"Where is she?" Carol asks.

"Cliff took her to the ER."

"Oh my *God*, is she okay?"

"She probably needs stitches," I say, the words hurrying out of me before I swallow them down.

She needs *stitches*.

I had Cliff pulled in the bushes, making out with him behind Winston's house, while my dog dragged his six-year-old daughter across the concrete.

I glance down at Rocket. He won't look at me. His nose is buried in his paws.

After a full month of us taking alternate routes in the neighborhood to avoid those ghosts, I should have known better than to leave him alone. I should have looked out for him. I should have looked out for Cliff's daughter.

I kept Cliff from his girls. I was selfish—wanting more, more, more, like I always do. More things for *me*. It comes barreling in like a tidal wave, pushing me against the wall, and I pinch my eyes closed.

"You okay, Miss Michelle?" Josh asks.

I peer at him and tongue my cheek. I nod silently, then rush forward and rap my knuckles on Emily's door.

"Hey, open up, Em."

"No!" Her voice is sharp.

Josh curls his lips in, taking small steps forward. "Sunshine—"

"Don't *sunshine* me, Joshua."

He cringes, and so do I.

I knock again. "Emily—"

"No." This time, her protest is shakier.

"I promised your dad I'd talk to you."

Carol steps forward beside me, palming the door. "Hey, Em—"

"Shut *up*, Carol!"

Carol recoils and nods to herself, murmuring, "Yeah, about what I expected."

I can already see her patting her pocket for smokes.

I huff out a breath and grit my teeth, pounding my fist on the door.

"Emily, I'm talking to you either way. Do you want it in front of everyone or alone?"

There's a beat of awkward silence, followed by the squeaking of a mattress and then the clicking of a lock turning.

The door creaks open a sliver, and my heart sinks.

Her painted-on cat whiskers are bleeding down her cheeks through streaks of tears. Her eyes are red. Everywhere around them is pink and blotchy.

I soften. "Can I come in?"

She sniffs, darting her eyes to the side and opening the door to let me in. "You're going to anyway."

I shrug because, well, she's not wrong.

I catch Carol's and Josh's eyes. He leans against the wall. His paper puppy ears, attached to a headband, flop over his long hair. Carol folds her arms over her chest and nods solemnly. Rocket lies on the floor, his snout between his paws.

I cross the threshold, and immediately Emily slams the door closed behind me.

I glance around. I've never been in Emily's room. It's a scrapbook of girlhood phases. The walls are painted baby pink. Stuffed animals are scattered across the floor and on the unmade bed. The ceiling is coated in glow-in-the-dark stars, along with a yellow smiley face poster and another one of Leonardo DiCaprio from *Romeo + Juliet*. Scribbled notes on scrap pieces of paper layer the walls with torn-out pages from album booklets between them. Bookcases, filled with Goosebumps and The Baby-Sitters Club, line either side of the doorframe.

Emily sniffs. "What did my *dad* want you to tell me?" she asks, her tone oozing disdain.

"He didn't tell me to say anything. I told him I'd check on you."

"Well, I'm here. I'm alive," she says with a sneer. "Happy?"

"Don't take your anger out on me," I say, leaning my head to the side and crossing my arms. "Tell me what's wrong."

"You wouldn't understand."

"Make me understand."

She scoffs so gutturally that I wonder if it hurts. "I wasn't picked. Again. I was pushed to the side. Again. Dad didn't trust me. Again."

"Your dad trusts you, but he was overwhelmed."

She stares at me. "Brittany is more important."

I can hear the same words leaving my lips when I was her age. The angry whine breathed in my dad's face as I watched Mom outside with Sara, lying in the grass together as I sulked in my room.

Dear Sara.

It was never Sara's fault though. I know it wasn't Mom's either, but it still stings.

"Brittany is younger," I say. "She can't drive herself to the hospital."

Emily blinks. "I *know* that, *Mom*."

My body stiffens. I'm at a loss for words, and somewhere in the silence, Emily looks up with worried eyebrows.

"I'm sorry," she whispers.

I shake my head. "It's fine."

"I don't want to be second pick anymore," she says. "I'm tired of it."

My stomach drops.

I took Cliff for myself.

And why? Only to leave in two months? To disrupt the precarious balance of this family?

I sit next to her on the bed. "He would never pick favorites, all right?"

"Mom does," she mumbles.

"Your dad wouldn't. That's not the kind of man he is."

She sniffles, blinking at me through watery eyes. Then, suddenly, she buries her face in my shirt. I freeze. I'm not sure what to do. I've never been hugged like this by anyone except my sister. My arms hang in the air, and slowly, I let them fall around her back, holding her close.

The door creaks open, and Carol pokes her head in. Emily loosens her arms around me. I expect Emily to yell at Carol again, but with her bottom lip poked out, she gives a silent nod to her aunt. Carol crosses the threshold, and Emily gets up and barrels into her arms.

My head swims as Cliff's daughter cries while her aunt holds her. I swallow back a lump in my throat. I feel like an intruder on this moment. I want to leave.

This is what Emily needs—what Cliff's daughters need. I have a life I've worked for in Seattle. A good life that I love. Why am I here, stepping into the shoes of a motherly role with these girls? It's irresponsible. It's selfish when I know I'll be leaving.

"Your dad's not the bad guy," Carol whispers. "Promise."

Emily sniffles and quietly nods against her chest.

Copper Run is a fleeting moment for me, but for the Burke family, this is real.

I'm indulging in temporary happiness at the inn. I can't distract Cliff from what really matters. I haven't had many close friends in my life, but I imagine that's not what friends do.

Chapter 21

CLIFF

The drive home from the ER feels longer than the drive there. Brittany is conked out in the passenger seat with a large bandage covering her knee and the few stitches beneath. Three, to be exact. A number I won't forget anytime soon either.

"Three stitches," Tracy repeated over the phone.

My heart was in my throat at that point. I wished I'd had time to cool down, but I wasn't sure how long we'd be in the emergency room, and I'd already deposited the quarter, so a quarter's worth of scolding would be my punishment until the pay phone inevitably cut us off.

"I'd like them to spend Thanksgiving with me this year," she said.

I almost stumbled in place. "What? You already come over for Christmas."

"I want them."

"Trace," I breathed, pinching my nose as I parsed through the logic. "You can't be serious."

"Clifford, I . . . I think I need to."

I could tell she was nervous. Scared. Uncomfortable with everything, and I understood that, but it felt like the rug was getting ripped out from under me.

"I mean, you're letting her play with random dogs by herself."

"The dog didn't do anything to her. It got scared."

"And where was Emily in all this?"

"She was there," I said. "There's nothing anyone could have done."

"You could have not let our daughter be *friends* with an *animal*."

I rested my head against the cold phone box.

"Trace, please don't take them for Thanksgiving." I hated how it'd sounded like I was begging, but the words had slipped out. "It's their favorite holiday. We always have a big dinner with neighborhood people."

"But they can see the Macy's Thanksgiving Day Parade in person. Wouldn't they love that?"

Of course Brittany would love seeing it. Even Emily might get a kick out of the spectacle. But that meant they'd be gone. I didn't want them gone.

"Yes. But . . ." I'd never sounded so desperate in my life, but I couldn't find a single argument that wasn't selfish.

"I want to spend the holiday with them," Tracy said. "You think I don't think about my babies every day?"

I didn't.

But she couldn't hear that. So I didn't argue.

I said, "Yes, that makes sense," and, "Yes, they'd love the parade," and, "As long as they're back the day after," which was met with zero resistance.

I look over at Brittany, with her head lolling against her seat belt and her lips parted with puppy-like, breathy snores.

How in the world am I supposed to tell the girls I won't have them for Thanksgiving?

My truck rumbles past the lattice Copper Run sign, under the covered bridge, through the square, and down the couple of blocks to our house. The porch light of Bird & Breakfast glows orange and gold, illuminating the swinging bench with Michelle and Carol.

My foot shakes on the pedal. I haven't been more than a block or two away from Michelle this past month, and after what happened between us tonight, I can't help but feel uncomfortable with the distance. I don't know what that says about me, but I'm sure it's not a good thing.

I turn into the driveway, gently unbuckle Brittany's seat belt, and carry her up to her bedroom. She only whines a little when I take off her shoes before tucking her into bed. She snatches her stuffed unicorn closer and snuggles under the covers without opening an eye.

I pass by Emily's room. Her door is shut, and the light is off. I lightly knock but hear nothing in response.

The house is abnormally quiet, especially compared to how loud the streets were hours ago. It makes me uneasy.

I walk downstairs. A note by the phone says Lars called, along with George, Betty, and Sandra. I assume the whole town has heard about the incident by now.

I push through the back door, letting the screen snap closed behind me. My boots crunch across the leaf-filled driveway and snap over the cobblestone into Michelle's yard. Carol and Michelle pause talking. I know I should say something, but I'm too distracted by Michelle's worried eyebrows and parted lips.

Somewhere in the last month, we've become inseparable, and I don't know when it started. It's like how, one day, the leaves are bright and green, and then, suddenly, they're flittering to the ground in dull browns and oranges. The seasons of our relationship changed without my consent. Now I don't know what to make of us.

We kissed, but what does that mean?

I can imagine the smell of rosemary in her hair and taste the cinnamon on her lips, and I want to relive those kisses over and over. She's leaving in two months—*two months*—which adds a wrinkle to everything.

A long-term plan doesn't seem possible with Michelle's job waiting for her across the country. It feels too optimistic. Irresponsible.

She loves Seattle. I won't hold another person to Copper Run. I can't.

"Well?" Carol asks. "Is Brittany okay?"

"She's good. Three stitches." The two words ring in my head again like a gong.

Michelle sighs. "Poor girl."

I run a palm through my hair. "Yeah, she slept the whole way home."

Carol pulls her bottom lip between her teeth and snickers. "Did you know you're still dressed up?"

I look down at the massive black robe clinging to my chest, pooling over my boots, and flowing on the porch steps.

"I didn't," I answer, managing a laugh because I can't imagine how I must have looked, rolling into the emergency room with my daughter in a bald cap and me dressed as 1997's scariest serial killer. At least I didn't have my mask. Michelle had knocked it off while we were . . .

I swallow. "Emily'll get a kick out of that."

Michelle and Carol exchange looks. I lean against the porch railing and cross my arms.

"How's Emily?" I ask. "Is she okay?"

Both women cringe. I might laugh at the twin looks if it were under different circumstances.

"That bad?" I ask.

"She felt like she was being ignored," Carol explains. "You know how sensitive she is with that."

I groan and thread fingers through my hair again. Everything feels uncomfortable. This loose robe. My eldest daughter's loneliness. The terrible truth I'll have to tell my girls tomorrow, which will only make things worse. And then there's the memory of kissing Michelle, which hangs over my head like an axe.

Carol slaps her knees. "Well, I should get going. I'm full with candy and drama." She stands, saying goodbye to Michelle and clapping me on the shoulder. "I'll see you bright and early tomorrow, Cliff."

I place my palm on her hand and pat it. "Yeah, see you."

Carol crosses the yard, back to our driveway, revs up her beater, and starts down the few blocks back to her house, leaving me and Michelle on the porch alone.

I scuff my boot on a porch plank and clear my throat. "Hey—"

"I—"

"No, you go first," I say. I hop onto the railing, leaning forward with my hands clasped between my spread knees.

Michelle sits up straighter, crossing one knee over the other and setting her delicate hands in her lap. Always so pretty and composed.

She exhales. "I'm sorry."

"Why are you sorry?" I ask.

"What isn't there to be sorry about?" she says. "Sorry I distracted you from your daughters—"

"I chose that—"

"Sorry that Rocket scared Brittany—"

"He was spooked—"

"Sorry that I kissed you."

Our overlapping words halt in that moment.

"You're sorry that we kissed?" I ask.

"I've been thinking about it," she says, not meeting my eyes for once.

"Me too."

"And"—she twists her skirt between her fingers—"I'm only going to be in Copper Run for two more months. I have a life in Seattle, and you have your life in Vermont."

"True—"

"And I like you, Cliff." She lets out a disbelieving laugh.

I chuckle. "I like you too, Michelle."

"But . . ."

"But we're only friends," I finish for her.

"Yeah. You're my friend," she confirms.

I can't tell if I'm relieved or not. She's thinking exactly what I was—because of course we're on the same page—but I can't help how my heart sinks at the reality of hearing it out loud.

I jump down, sitting next to her on the swinging bench, sending the whole thing creaking on its chains.

"We're probably just"—she rolls her eyes with a smile—"super-horny divorcés, and I don't want to ruin the good memories we've created so far with some fling."

I chuckle. She's not wrong. At least about the latter. And, sure, maybe a little of the former. I'd love to sink my hands into her hair and kiss her more. I'd love to dip my fingers beneath her skirt, too, but I also want to laugh with her.

The last thing I want is to lose her for the two months I

have her. I have to forget the kiss if it means I get to keep her. And I need to keep her while I can.

"You're right," I say. "It was only a kiss anyway, huh?"

She reaches up to twist her earring. "Right." Her face is crestfallen. "This whole thing is complicated."

"Hey," I say, reaching out to cup her face in my palms.

She freezes under my touch.

"I'm with you on this, okay?"

I'm surprised, warmed, when she tilts her head to the side, leaning a cheek into my hand.

"I like you, Cliff. Someone needs to tell you that."

And that alone has me smiling. "Thank you for telling me."

"I'll tell you anytime you need."

I manage a low chuckle. "I'll hold you to that."

She rolls her eyes. "You deserve to get back out there, you know," she murmurs.

"So I hear."

I swallow, stroking my thumb over her cheek, and kiss her forehead, closing my eyes. My heart pounds in my chest as I linger. Her breath tickles against my neck. Then I slowly pull away, catching her eyes with mine.

"Friends?" I ask.

I see her swallow. "Friends."

A slight Halloween breeze blows past, sending a shiver down my spine. Because even though she's here and we're okay, I know a piece of my heart—the piece she captured so quickly—flitted away like a leaf on the wind.

"Well," I say, breaking the silence, "that's that, then."

I place my palm on her knee and squeeze like I normally do to give her reassurance. But it feels different now. Inappropriate.

"I should get to bed," she says, shifting on the bench. "It's late."

I nod and fake a yawn, but I know I'll be up all night.

"Me too," I agree.

"Thank you," she says. "For a really fun night."

Fun.

"I do what I can," I tease.

She's right; it was fun. That's all.

Two lonely, divorced friends, having fun.

November 1997

Chapter 22

MICHELLE

Brittany doesn't come over anymore. Days that were once filled with child laughter now only have the dull monotony of a humming television with daytime game shows.

Rocket lies by the back door, waiting for her, every day around three o'clock, as if the school bus will drop her off at any minute. I've told him a few times that it won't, but I don't think he hears me—or at least he pretends he doesn't.

Breezy October weather has been replaced by a harsh November chill. The days are rainier, tearing the remaining leaves from the trees, sending them flying into sopping piles on the yard that squish under boots and are impossible to rake.

My job in Seattle has been reaching out to me less and less, and it's making me anxious. I faxed some reports and ideas, but I haven't heard anything back. I'm not desperate enough to call, so I dive into advertising for the inn instead. Something to distract my mind—to feel a sense of home again.

Every evening, I sip coffee with my sweater and blanket and paperwork. I watch Cliff pull in the driveway with Brittany, and every day, I wonder if she'll run over, but the moment she sees Rocket lying next to me, leash tied to a porch spindle, she scrambles into their house.

Cliff comes over most nights once the girls are asleep, sighing into the swinging bench seat and taking my papers from me.

"You're done for today," he announces, and I let him.

"Any updates with Brittany?" I ask.

"Rocket is still enemy number one."

I bend down to pet him. "Sorry, bud."

Rocket ducks from my palm, walking the max length his leash allows, then plopping back down. He's not happy with anyone.

Bird & Breakfast guests join us on the porch sometimes, and we regale them with every detail of the amazing Halloween that passed—everything except for the haunted maze, which we both now pretend never happened.

I'm happy we agreed to move on. My relationship with Cliff means more to me than anything else in Copper Run, which is a sentence I never thought would cross my mind weeks ago. I'll miss him. I'll miss the whole Burke family.

But that's a problem for 1998. Not now, when I'm sitting next to my silly small-town crush I'm sure I'll laugh about later because a crush is all Cliff ever can be. A crush where I smile at his low laughter and the handsome fans of lines beside his eyes. A crush where I imagine tracing my fingers over the small scar above his lip.

My laughter-filled nights are very different from my somber afternoons. Emily slouches on the parlor couch almost every day after work, flicking through channels and settling on some flashy, high-octane MTV music video.

Today is no different. Emily lounges on the sofa, one cheek smooshed into her palm, an oversize red flannel layered over a cropped tee, staring at the TV. Rain beats on the windows, making the whole scene that much more depressing.

"Still mad at your dad?" I ask, leaning against the wooden hutch with my arms crossed.

"Yes," she mumbles.

"It's been a week."

"So?"

"Your sister is over it. And she got stitches."

"She didn't get told to fuck off."

I flick my eyes to the one lone guest sitting on the pillowed bench seat in the bay window. She peers out at a rainy yard, seemingly unbothered by the mouthy, lethargic girl on the sofa.

"Number one," I whisper to Emily, "no cursing around guests, please."

She cringes. "Sorry."

"Number two, Cliff didn't say that, and you know it."

Emily groans. "He *basically* said it without saying it. He's just like Mom. And now he's sending me off on Thanksgiving too? He doesn't want me either. I'm like a giant game of hot potato."

I would laugh if it didn't make me so sad. Cliff said Brittany was ecstatic to be in New York for Thanksgiving, but Emily . . . not so much. And she's made it everyone's problem.

"That's not true," I say. "Your mom wants to see you for Thanksgiving."

She rolls her eyes so hard that I worry for a moment if they're stuck.

"I can see through it," she mumbles.

The woman at the padded window seat raises her hand like she's in a classroom.

I smile. "Hi, Marge. How can I help you?"

"Do you have any afternoon coffee?"

"Of course. I'll get that started. And I'll also make cookies soon, if you'd like."

Marge nods, satisfied, then goes back to peering outside. She's one of my quieter guests. And even though she asks a lot of questions, I'll take requests from her over loud families any day.

On my way to the kitchen, I pause in front of Emily, blocking her sight line to the TV. She leans her head to the side, trying to look around me.

"Your dad didn't mean anything by it," I say again. "It was a tough Halloween."

She shifts higher on the groaning sofa.

I place my hands on my hips. "If you're gonna keep moping, I'm not gonna let you meet my sister."

That gets her attention.

"What?" she asks, scrambling to sit up. "The cool art sister from California?"

I almost take offense, but my sister *is* the cool sister. She's bubbly and wonderful, and she'll charm every person in this town way faster than I ever could. I still haven't spoken to the bulky man who runs the hardware store, and I think it'd be too awkward to start now.

"Yes," I answer. "But if you're gonna be sulking the whole time like this"—I wave my finger in front of her—"I'll be forced to tell her you're always this way. A dull, uncool—"

"I'm smiling! See? I'm smiling." A big, toothy, over-the-top grin stretches over Emily's face. "I've got so many things to ask her. Like, what is California like? Is it as perfect as it looks?"

I hold my palms up and huff out a laugh. "Okay, you've been watching too much TV."

"I'll be happy," Emily says, cheesing from ear to ear again.

I snort. "I'm gonna go make cookies."

"Save me some!"

I push into the kitchen, sifting through the cabinets, only to realize I never restocked on chocolate chips. I sigh, but the truth is, I'm not upset to make a trip to the square.

Why make cookies when I'm friends with the local baker?

I step back into the parlor and unhook Mom's purse from the wall, making Rocket turn around from his sentry role at the window, always seeking out his lost playmate.

"I'll be back," I announce to Emily. "Mind starting the coffee for me?"

"I thought you were making cookies."

"I'm out of chocolate chips."

She nods slowly. "Are you going to visit my dad?"

"He makes the best cookies, doesn't he?"

"Mm-hmm."

Her face falls, as if my visiting Cliff is a betrayal. I don't point out that she's wearing her dad's flannel.

"I'll be back," I say. "And I'll see if he can throw in a muffin too."

"Apple fritter," Emily corrects.

I side-eye her and smirk. "Apple fritter."

Rocket scrambles from his bed, halting at the door and waiting for his leash.

"It's too rainy."

He snorts. *I don't care.*

He's been testy since Halloween—more than usual anyway. He's eager to get out of the house.

Maybe it'll be best for both of us when we leave. He won't be heartbroken over Brittany, and I won't be desperately grasping for every moment I can with the charming local baker.

It's pathetic. Selfish.

In two months, Rocket and I can get back to our comfortable, less confusing version of happy.

Chapter 23

CLIFF

"Brittany, off the counter. Sorry, George."

George waves his hand with a smile. Brittany kicks her legs out, then back in on the bakery's front counter. Her heels bang against the hanging sign below.

"Britt Britt, head to the kitchen." I pat her back, coaxing her down. "I bet Aunt Carol would love to hear a detailed breakdown of Steve's fight last night."

Brittany's lips form a big O as she hops down and rushes to the kitchen.

I exhale and run a palm through my hair.

"Wasn't she staying at the inn after school?" George asks.

I rest my palms on the counter. "Would you like doughnuts or not, George?"

"Yes."

"Good. Then no questions, please."

"Is it because of Halloween?"

"George . . ." I seethe.

He holds his hands up in the air.

"I'll bring them to your car in a second."

He gives a grumbling affirmation, then exits through the dinging door.

I stride back to the kitchen and find Carol nodding

intently with wide eyes as Brittany regales her with the most recent wrestling match.

"Is that so? *Wow*," Carol says, feigning interest.

I lean my hip beside Brittany sitting on the prep table.

"He also does this thing where—"

"Do you have any homework?" I interrupt.

She's mid-sentence but nods. "Uh-huh."

"Perfect. Go to my office, start it, and then I'll lock the door behind you and throw away the key."

"Dad," she says through giggles.

"Come on. You're all over the place today," I say, pushing my hands under her armpits and lifting her. "Did they give you crack at school?"

"Pixy Stix," she answers as I carry her on my hip.

"Close enough," I murmur, kicking open my office door.

My desk is a mess. Papers that are, admittedly, never organized are now haphazard, flopping over the corner and fluttering to the floor in the wind from the open door. Order receipts overflow from their Tupperware, and some of the typed numbers are blurry from streaks of icing. Nothing is where it should be. I've been distracted, to say the least.

I unceremoniously swipe an arm over my desk and shove everything to one side. A pen or two clatters to the floor.

"Got your backpack in here?" I ask.

"Yep!" Brittany points to the corner.

She swivels around in my office chair while I unzip it and dig out her folder, placing it on the desk. I grip the back of the chair and halt it.

"Pencils are here." I prop a cup full of pens and pencils in front of her. "Water bottles are behind you. Coffee machine is in the corner—I know you can't live without it."

She giggles. "I don't drink coffee."

I kiss her on the forehead. "I'll check back in an hour, okay? Clock is up there if you wanna keep track," I say, pointing to the wall clock, which is ticking loud enough to feel like a metronome in my cluttered brain.

"Got it," she replies, rattling a pencil out of the cup.

I go to close the door, but she yells, "Dad!"

"Yes?"

"You aren't really gonna lock it, are you?"

I roll my eyes with a smile. "Of course not."

Shutting the door behind me, I trudge back to the kitchen with a sigh. It's been a long week since Halloween. Brittany won't go near the inn, in fear of Rocket, so now she hangs out at the bakery after school. Emily barely talks to me. And everything that happened between Michelle and me is shoved under the rug.

It's absolutely fantastic.

Not. Emily's teen voice runs through my head.

The other night, I dreamed about Halloween again. For a fleeting moment, I felt like I was there, palms splayed over Michelle's back, across her ribs, cupping her cheek. But I woke up, and all I saw was my circling ceiling fan.

I can't get her flavor out of my mouth. I realize everything I've been trying to bake for her is nothing like the real thing. She isn't cinnamon. She's honey all the way through, and I need to taste it again.

"Sorry you lost your free babysitting," Carol says.

I run a palm through my hair, but it does nothing to keep it out of my eyes.

"We can't help that Brittany is scared of Rocket," I respond with an exhale. "It's understandable. But a little less chaos in the bakery would be nice."

The bell above the door chimes again.

"Be there in a minute, George," I call.

I rush to grab the doughnuts cooling on the rack. Carol strides past me.

"I'll stall him."

"Thanks." I chuckle, patting her on the shoulder as she passes.

But as I'm loading up the doughnuts from the tray to the box, Carol returns.

"It's Michelle," she says. "She wants three peach pies."

Her name alone has my heart leaping into my throat.

"Three?" A laugh bubbles up. "She's worse than George."

I round the corner to the front of the store. It's raining outside, beating down on the sidewalk and splattering against the glass windows. But in the center of the lobby is the only woman who could make a rainy day seem not half bad. Maybe it's because she's a bigger storm cloud, and I like that about her. At her feet, Rocket sits, his nose wiggling, no doubt smelling the last croissants of the day finishing in the oven.

"Three peach pies?" I ask Michelle. "Really?"

She lifts a single shoulder. "No, only cookies. And an apple fritter."

"You wanted to get my attention?"

"Yes."

"I assume an apple fritter for Emily?"

"You're too good."

"I know my girl."

I flick through order form sheets and click a pen with my thumb. I almost fumble it. I can't help but feel on edge. We're doing fine as friends, but there's a tightening in my chest whenever she's around now. Erasing the taste of her isn't something I can do overnight—or in seven days for that matter.

"So, ol' Paulie's coming back to town?" I ask, forcing conversation.

I don't like the lingering silences between us anymore, and when I add a grin too, it feels unnatural.

"Ol' Paulie," Michelle muses with a smile. "Yeah, my dad and my sister will be here next week."

"Excited?"

"Yes," she says on a breath. "My dad sounds like he's doing a bit better. And my sister is excited to travel out here. She loves going anywhere. She's a hippie at heart."

"We should get her a van."

"Sara wishes."

I chuckle. "Well, I'm excited to meet your sister. If she's half as blunt as you, I'll learn many new things about myself by the end of the month."

"No, Sara's nicer than me," she says. "She's total sunshine. Kind. Generous."

"So are you. You gave up a lot to be here for her," I say.

Suddenly, she's quiet, blinking to herself, as if maybe she's never considered it a sacrifice before. Of course she wouldn't.

"Well," she says quietly, "she means the world to me."

The way her eyes glass over when she says it makes the corner of my mouth tip up. Her smile is a mix of admiration and contentment. It feels like I'm watching something I shouldn't.

Rocket sniffs the seat near the door but stands solidly next to it. Always so statuesque.

Michelle catches me looking.

"Rocket misses her," she says.

"Does he?"

I don't blame him for Halloween. He's a dog after all. Man's best friend . . . more like a little girl's best friend.

I pull open the display case and pull out a biscuit. I tear off part of it and step out from behind the counter. Rocket watches with cautious eyes as I bend down and hold it out. Sniffing, he walks closer, gingerly looking from it to me before nibbling the bread from my fingers.

I'm on edge, more than I should be as a grown man. But when I pat his head and he leans into my palm, it's not as bad as I thought it'd be.

"He waits by the back door for her every day," Michelle says.

"Like how you wait on the front porch for me?" I ask.

She scoffs, her mouth gaping open with a twitching smile. "I do *not*."

"Hey, you can admit it. I won't get a big head. And I'm sure you'd bring me back down to earth if I did anyway."

"You're so annoying."

"See?" I point out.

She slides her pendant over the delicate chain, holding back a laugh.

I rise and walk back behind the counter. "So, what can I do to help with your family coming into town?"

"I don't know," she says. "How can I help Brittany get comfortable with Rocket again?"

"Ah, so neither of us has answers." I smile.

"What's new?" Michelle says.

"Not a thing."

And then, the moment I have a permanent smile on my face from our banter, logging her cookie order, Michelle says,

"I meant what I said on Halloween. I . . . I think you should get back out there."

My pen cuts across the page.

I don't look away from the paper when I attempt to casually ask, "Get out where?"

"Dating."

"Should I?" I add stiffly.

"You should," she confirms. "It's been two years for you. You deserve a second shot at happiness."

I huff out a weak laugh. "Yeah, maybe. I don't know." I rub the back of my neck, and I still can't look at her. "I've never dated anyone except Tracy. What do you even say over dinner? *Do you like the chicken? I got the pork; it's fine. But don't try the wine; it's not divine.*"

"You'd rhyme the whole time?"

"Now you're doing it. See? It's contagious."

She laughs. "Seriously. Go on a date. See what happens. And be yourself."

"'Cause that worked out so well the first time."

Finally, I look at her. Her eyebrows are pulled in the middle.

"I want you to be happy, Cliff."

I don't want to date anyone. And it's not because I'm nervous. It's because I want the storm cloud of a woman in front of me. I want the unattainable. Problem is, I can't say no to this woman either way.

"Fine, I'll get out there," I concede.

She smiles. "I'll put out feelers. Lisa has the hots for you."

"Not into married women," I tease back with an eye roll. But it doesn't stifle the tugging in my chest.

Two months.

She's leaving in two months.

From behind me, tiny footfalls echo out from the kitchen. Brittany peeks from behind the counter at Rocket. When he finally sees her, she pops her head away again.

"It'll take time," I say to him.

Unfortunately, time is what we both need more of.

Chapter 24

MICHELLE

My sister's umbrella blooms open like a flower, pink and beautiful, matching her massive grin.

"Shellfish!" Sara breaks out in a run. She bypasses going down the driveway or the cobblestone path, instead opting to slap through the muddy yard, kicking up patches of grass under her rain boots.

"Wait, get off the grass!" I call over the pounding rain.

Sara either doesn't hear me or doesn't care because she runs the rest of the way, ducks under the porch awning, and tosses her open umbrella to the side before pulling me into a bone-crushing hug.

"Oh, I missed you," she exhales into me.

Sara is shorter than me—five two to my five nine—which is why she nuzzles closer, burying her face into my breasts like a burrowing rabbit.

"Stop," I groan through an exhausted laugh.

"I didn't realize this was a customary greeting," Cliff says, leaning away with his hands in his pockets. "I've been saying hello wrong for months."

I elbow him, and he gives a grinning *oof*.

"How was the drive?" I ask her.

"Terrible," Sara groans. "Our rental car was seconds away from breaking down. I was scared the entire last *hour*."

"Sometimes I think they do it for fun," Cliff comments. "Like a survival game. See who can cut it in the wild. Or on the highway."

Sara's eyes slowly swivel to Cliff, but they very quickly shadow over. I stiffen, following her gaze to him.

Cliff looks like he always does. He's wearing his go-to flannel, double layered under a cable-knit sweater. His boots are the rustic brown kind with little love marks from the bakery. Sara lifts one curious eyebrow as she scans from his grinning smile down to the defined wrists peeking out from his pants pockets.

I thought only I noticed his wrists.

Sara extends her hand out to him. "Hi. Sara."

She shamelessly bites her lower lip, giving one stunning, dimpled smile.

Cliff untucks a hand from his pocket and shakes hers. Sara looks down to his large, veiny hand.

"Cliff. I live next door."

"I've heard."

"Have you, now?" Holding her hand, Cliff swivels his eyes to me with a crooked grin before landing back on her.

Shake.

They aren't letting go. It feels so similar to our handshakes. My stomach coils.

"Well, it's great to finally meet you," he says to her.

Shake.

Sara smiles, giving another shake of his hand as she bares her dimples at their full capacity. Adorable. "Pleasure is all mine, Cliff."

Whoever said it was a chilly rain today was a liar because, suddenly, I'm heating up from the inside out.

I clear my throat and walk off the porch without an umbrella. "I'll go check on Dad."

"Need help?" Cliff calls after me.

"I'm fine."

I use my arms to shield myself from the rain until I reach the rental car. I tug the handle once, then twice, and the door finally pops open. I slide in on the squeaking brown leather and shut it behind me.

Dad sits in the driver's seat, letting out a slow exhale. The only other sounds are plunking raindrops on the roof and the low hum of Bob Dylan on the radio.

"Hey, Dad."

He smiles, but it doesn't reach his eyes. "Hi, Shellfish."

Dad looks better than he did months ago. He's gained a bit of weight. He's shampooed the few remaining wisps of hair on his bald head. But he hasn't lost that distant, thousand-yard stare. I follow his gaze to the parked car at the end of the driveway. Mom's car, covered in wet leaves.

"How was the drive?" I ask, changing the unspoken subject.

"Good. A little rainy."

"The whole way?"

"The last half."

"Cliff is here," I offer. "He's excited to see you. He's staying for dinner, along with his daughters and Carol."

"Oh, Cliff," he says, finally looking over at me with a lopsided smile. "What a character. He's a good boy though."

"I've told him the same thing. Well, I called Rocket a good boy, and then Cliff thought—" I smile and wave my hands in the air. "You know what? Doesn't matter."

I feel so silly with my stories from this town, especially ones with Cliff that never sound quite as funny as they did during the moment.

The little time Dad spent thinking about happy things is slowly replaced with melancholy as he sees the baby angel statue near the porch—the one with tiny wings, thick ankles, and a mischievous smile.

"Your mom loved that guy," he says. "Did you know his name is Stu?"

"I didn't. Cliff calls him Chunky Charles." One of too many inside jokes with Cliff.

Dad snorts out a laugh. It's half-hearted, but I'll take anything I can get. He sighs. I place a hand on his forearm.

"Are you okay, being here?" I ask.

He pats my knee. "I wouldn't want to be anywhere else for Thanksgiving."

"I'm sure Lisa and George will be thrilled that you're in town too."

"How are they doing?"

"They're good. Nosy, as always," I say with a light smile. "But good."

"And the inn?" he asks, his tone changing with worry. "It's doing well?"

"It's doing great," I say confidently. "In fact, I made cinnamon rolls. They're fresh. I've been told they're *divine*."

Dad nods. "Good, Shells. Good."

"Let's head inside, all right?"

But before I get out of the car, Dad reaches out to stop me.

I look to his hand on my forearm and back up. "Are you all right?" I ask.

"I like that you're smiling again."

My heart skips a beat, and I choke out a laugh. "Well, it's hard not to when you and Sara are here."

"It's not me," he says, giving me a pointed stare. "You've caught the bug of this town. I can tell."

For some reason, a lump catches in my throat.

"Come on," I respond with a weak smile. "Let's get inside."

That night, the Bird & Breakfast dining room is more crowded than I've ever seen. On one side of the long table are me, Emily, my dad, and George. Across from us are Sara, Cliff, Carol, and Lisa. At the head of the table, far away from Rocket lying at my feet, sits Brittany. She fluctuates between sitting proud and cautiously squirming as she keeps a very suspicious eye on Rocket.

"This pot roast is fantastic," Cliff says, raising his forkful. "Really good stuff, Michelle."

It's objectively not good.

Emily walked me through how to make pot roast earlier that afternoon. It's painfully dry, but Cliff keeps complimenting it loudly, almost like he's prompting the cacophony of assent from the rest of the table.

I tear off a piece and bend down to let Rocket sniff it. He turns his head away.

Don't poison me, Shelly.

I can always count on Rocket's honesty. But when Cliff reaches under the table with a piece of the bread, Rocket trots closer and nibbles it from his fingers. Since Halloween, I think he might like Cliff a little more.

See? He likes it, Cliff mouths to me, tossing me a wink.

Air catches in my throat, and I start coughing, having to take gulps of water to stop. Emily claps my back as my heart thrums in my chest so hard that I'm worried it will burst out. That wink should be illegal.

"So," Cliff says, scooting out his plate and steepling his fingers, "how's California been, Paulie? Catch any rays?"

Dad smiles. "It's gorgeous every single day out there." But his words are quick and closed off with no room left for discussion. He tips back his wineglass.

George pats his arm.

"That's great," Cliff says slowly, with an unnatural grin.

He flashes me wide eyes, as if to say, *What now?*

I clear my throat. "Sara, how's school? Emily has been dying to hear about it."

Emily nervously laughs. "I haven't been, like, *dying*."

She's maintaining her cool. I curl my lips in, and Cliff shakes his head with a partial eye roll and smile.

"I saw that, Dad," Emily shoots over with a snarl.

"You saw nothing," he counters.

Sara leans in toward Emily. "You would *love* art school. Drawing at all hours of the night to meet deadlines. Waking up early for critiques."

Emily scrunches her nose. "That sounds not fun at all."

Cliff glances at me, and I feel that taut tether between us. The line of rope where I find him and he finds me, and we exchange a knowing look that nobody else notices.

"There's nothing better than late-night sessions, even if everyone is tired in the morning. There's always someone in the studio, so it's constantly buzzing with creative energy. And sometimes we sneak in drinks."

Emily sits up. "That's what I'm talking about. Pass the wine, please?"

"Em," Cliff says, "you're sixteen."

"You're sixteen," Brittany echoes with a giggle, wanting to be part of the argument.

"That's not far off from twenty-one," Emily argues.

"That's five years," Cliff counters. "Five years ago, you were eleven."

Carol sips her own glass of wine. "Yeah, but she's not asking to drink at eleven."

Cliff tosses his hands up. "Okay, you two are being difficult to be difficult."

"Daddy, can I drink?" Brittany asks.

"See what you did?" Cliff says to them.

Emily holds up her index finger and thumb to make the shape of an L on her forehead.

I lay down my fork. "All right, let's bring the conversation back from the Burke comedy hour."

"Hey!" Cliff says with a laugh, picking up a piece of broccoli and tossing it at my plate.

"I'm only speaking the truth."

Sara looks between us, blinking at the quick exchange, and laughs. "If I knew what I was missing, I might have visited sooner," she says, playfully leaning in to bump her shoulder against Cliff's.

Cliff being Cliff, he grins at her and nudges back. My spine stiffens. I avert my eyes and shove another forkful of the terrible pot roast into my mouth.

"So, are you excited about taking over the inn?" Cliff asks.

Sara straightens up and nods. "Yeah! Of course. I already have ideas for painting the main hall."

"Really?" he says, intrigued. "Big reno plans, huh?"

She shrugs, but it's more to herself. "Nah, probably painting on the weekends or something."

"I bet the guests would love your paintings throughout the house," I encourage her.

Sara beams, sipping more of her wine. "Yeah, maybe."

Over dinner, we talk about Copper Run's decorations for Thanksgiving. Dad mentions they're repeating old favorites, and the square is full of orange and brown bunting, cornucopias, and a sheet of poster board under the gazebo with hand turkeys, made from all the palms of the elementary kids in town. Cliff proudly says Brittany's is front and center, at which Emily grumbles into her fork.

I nudge my elbow against hers. She side-eyes me.

Sara regales us with tales from art school, and Cliff keeps inserting his funny one-liners. Sara cackles at every one, touching his forearm as she does. My molars grind. *I* think Cliff is funny. But he's an acquired-taste type of funny. Sara hasn't had time to acquire it yet. Or maybe I didn't understand him when we met. Maybe I judged him too harshly.

I swallow uncomfortably and offer to take the dishes, mostly full with food people have sufficiently pretended to like. I push into the kitchen. Rocket follows me, curling into his dog bed and burying his snout into the cushion crease.

I sigh. "Are you upset Britt isn't saying hi?" I whisper.

He exhales through his nose.

"I'm sorry."

The door swings in, and Sara stumbles through with her wineglass.

"Got another bottle?" she asks, shaking her glass through giggles.

My sister is cute when she's tipsy. Her pink cheeks and dimpled smile are the human embodiment of champagne. Bubbly and sweet and always served at fun events.

"This might be the most I've seen you drink," I comment with a smile.

"*You* should be drinking more."

"I'm not much of a drinker," I answer. Fact is, I don't like being out of control of my own body.

"Art school made me one."

"How do you have any time to paint?" I ask.

"Don't be a stick-in-the-mud." She pouts. "Do we have more wine?"

I reach up to the cabinet, past the row of tattered, used cookbooks and fake hanging vines, to Mom's collection of wine. I pull one down.

"Whoa, Mom had a *stash*?" Sara gawks.

"I was as surprised as you."

Sara raises her empty glass. "To Mom. She would be happy we're here together."

Sara pulls me in for a side hug. She smells like raspberries and bubble gum. Up close, I see she added glitter to her cheeks. I haven't seen Sara in this kitchen yet. The floral wallpaper matches her pastel top. She fits in well.

"Maybe Mom's here in spirit," she says.

My stomach twists.

"I don't believe in ghosts."

"You're so boring," Sara teases.

I smile, twisting the screw into the cork and tugging.

"By the way," she says, pulling back and pointing a finger at me, "you were right."

"About?"

She darts her eyes to the closed door and leans in. "Cliff is *so cute*."

My stomach drops right as the cork pops out.

"Yeah," I quickly agree. "Yeah, he's . . . handsome, I guess."

I set the cork beside the wine, reaching out my hand for her glass. She almost drops the stem through my fingers. I catch it with both hands, and Sara covers her giggle.

I start to pour as she coyly says, "So . . ."

"So . . ."

She kicks her cute little boot over at me. "Anything there?"

"Where?"

"Between you and Cliff. I know you said there wasn't, but something feels like it's changed or whatever."

The wine bottle clatters against the glass from my shaking hands. "Us? No. Oh. No. Not at all."

"Really?"

"Yeah. Why?"

"He looks at you weird sometimes."

"He's a weird guy," I joke, and I instantly feel bad about the insult. It's one thing to call Cliff weird to his face; it's another to do it when he's not around.

"Hmm . . ." She clicks her tongue in thought. "Then I don't know . . . do you think you could set me up with him?"

It's like my heart stops, starts again, then takes an Olympic leap into my throat. I keep emptying wine from the bottle into her glass, but my fist is tightened around the neck of the bottle. I swear I can hear my blood pressure in my ears.

"Aren't you a bit young for him?" I ask.

She snorts again, though I'm not sure if it's from derision or too much wine. "No way. I've dated older."

"You have?" I ask with wide eyes.

She grins, placing her index finger in front of her plush lips with a "Shh."

"How old?" I ask.

"I don't know. Forties."

"Sara!"

She giggles. "Don't tell Dad."

"That could basically be one of Dad's friends."

"Whatever," Sara says, pushing my arm. "Anyway, Cliff's into blondes, right?"

"Is he?"

"You're the one who said that." She laughs. "Oh my God, Shells, are you *trying* to get me drunk?"

I notice I've filled her wineglass nearly to the rim.

"Sorry." I got distracted. "Anyway, when did I say he was into blondes?"

I slowly hand her the glass, and the wine sloshes dangerously close to the lip.

"Oh, Cliff! Right. Yeah, over the phone. You said we'd get along and that blondes are his thing, and *thank God* because he's *so* cute."

I did say that, didn't I? But that was before Halloween. That was before . . . well, nothing, I guess. According to both me and Cliff, nothing happened or would happen again. And that's a good thing. That's how it should be.

"So, think you could talk to him for me?" Sara asks. "Please, please, please?"

Sara and Cliff. Cliff and Sara. My sister and my charming neighbor. My best friend and my sister.

Sara narrows her eyes. "Unless . . . you *are* into him," she says, setting down her glass and holding up both hands. "I'm not gonna step on your toes."

I realize too late that my brow is furrowed.

"No," I say quickly, blowing out air and shaking my head as I pour myself wine. "God, no. No, it's Cliff. He's . . . no."

She squints more. "You two seem close."

I set the wine bottle on the counter with a definitive plunk. "I'm honestly closer with his daughters," I lie.

"Hmm. Well . . . think you could . . ." Her words fade off as she playfully chews her bottom lip and knocks the toe of her shoe against mine.

I should hook them up. It makes sense. *I'm* not going to date Cliff, so why would I steal potential happiness from both of them? After all, Sara will be his neighbor after the New Year, and I won't. If it works out, then my two favorite people will be happy.

She's sunshine. Cliff deserves sunshine after all he's been through.

I squeak the cork back into the bottle. "If you really like him, I'll talk to him for you."

She gasps, hopping toward me. "Really?"

"Sure."

Sara grabs my hands between her palms. "Thank you! Thank you, thank you!"

I force a smile and push her toward the dining room. She grabs her glass and slyly snatches the entire bottle of wine before disappearing through the swinging door.

The moment she leaves the kitchen, I slump against the counter. From the floor, I hear a low woof. I lean my head on my own shoulder to glare at Rocket.

"Yes?" I ask.

He blinks slowly, darting his eyes to the door, then back. *Do you really want her with Funny Guy?*

"He's not that funny," I grumble.

I've laughed once or twice.

"Oh, what do you know about humor?" I scoff, sipping my own wine and pushing through the door and back to the dining room.

Chapter 25

MICHELLE

By the time I slink over to Cliff's house, it's nearly ten o'clock.

I tucked my very drunk sister into my bed. Dad stared at the nightly news until finally shuffling up to the free guest room. I cleaned the dishes, staring down at the soapsuds popping and fizzing while my mind whirled. I tried to look over the budget, but I couldn't focus. No faxes have come in from work either. I feel in the dark about too many things.

After turning off all the lights, I slipped on my house shoes, grabbed Rocket's leash, and traipsed through the bushes between my house and Cliff's. The rosebushes are where he finds me.

"Michelle?" Cliff asks with that familiar laugh.

"Hey," I whisper. "Are you awake?"

He crunches through the brush until he grabs the crook of my elbow and tugs me out.

"Clearly," he answers. "What are you doing?"

"Coming over to talk." I look at him for a moment. "Wait, why are you out here?"

He looks so different this late. In the glow of his porch light, his hair is messier. He wears checkered pajama pants and a baggy, faded Chicago Bulls tee. There are small dips under his eyes, but over them are round, wire-rimmed glasses.

I bite my bottom lip to hold in my laughter. "You wear glasses?"

He takes the glasses off, examines them, then puts them back on. "I do?"

"Ha ha."

He smirks. "My vision is terrible."

"I didn't know that."

"I didn't need you to know I was imperfect," he teases.

I roll my eyes. "Why are you up?"

He shrugs. "Couldn't sleep. You?"

"Finding you. Want to go on a walk?" I ask.

He examines my now-muddy blue slippers and chuckles. "Sure. I'll go on a walk with you."

He wraps an arm around my waist and coaxes me back to the driveway and down to the sidewalk. Rocket trails beside us, bopping down the street with his nose wiggling into each plant.

"So, be honest with me—how was dinner?" I ask.

"It was—"

"Terrible? Terrible, right?"

"Terrible?" he echoes in mock surprise. "No, absolutely not."

I shove his shoulder, and he laughs.

"Oh, watch out for that branch there. God, you're gonna hurt yourself." He shifts me closer to the yard and himself to the outside of the sidewalk. "This is worse than when you cook."

"You said I'd gotten better," I counter, louder than I should in a sleepy neighborhood.

His palm covers my mouth as he quietly chuckles with a "Shh."

The last time he cupped my mouth was on Halloween, and he had gloves on. I've never felt his bare skin against my lips. His hands are warm. Rough, working hands. Large and spanning between both sides of my jaw. My chest burns.

He removes it, and I finally feel like I can breathe.

"Your baking is good," he says, his voice low and husky, attempting to be quiet among the crickets and near-silent wind. "The roast?" He holds out his palm and moves it side to side. "Questionable."

"Rude."

"Honest." He narrows his eyes. "I thought you appreciated honesty."

"I do."

He kicks an errant rock and looks up at the sky. It's pitch-black. The streetlamps are spread out, illuminating every ten feet with blurry golden circles of light. When we pass beneath one, it casts his face into contrast. High cheekbones. The little checks beside his eyes when he smiles. The crease beside his lips. We keep walking and are again plunged into the darkness of night.

"It's weird, isn't it?" he says.

"What?"

"Seeing your sister here. I'm sure it's like seeing the light at the end of the tunnel or something. You're probably itching to go back."

I swallow. "Yeah. A little." I laugh. "I want to be back in my corner office. I miss my morning runs. I miss my coffee shop down the street. I miss how loud the city is."

"Still can't sleep?"

"No. And, God"—I let out a frustrated groan—"I want to know what the hell is going on with my client because I know Mark is messing it up out there."

"Damn Mark," Cliff says with a grin.

I sigh. "I miss it all. But . . . I knew what I was doing, coming out here."

"What were you doing exactly?"

I shrug. "You don't take a leave of absence as long as mine and expect to come back to the same job. But I did what needed to be done, and I'll do what needs to be done when I get back too."

"Bet you'll love every minute of it too, huh?"

"Of course I will. It'll be tough, but I've always liked a challenge."

"I know you do."

Cliff chuckles, scuffing his sneakers on the ground. I'll miss his occasional bashfulness. I'll miss the events in the square. I'll even miss Winston's yard, now decorated with a giant turkey standee smack-dab in the middle. But these feelings will all pass—everything does—like the seasons do.

"So, uh, what were you coming over to talk about?" Cliff asks in the silence.

I freeze. "Oh. I was . . ." And suddenly, this conversation feels more fitting. I *am* leaving, aren't I? "I was gonna talk to you about my sister actually."

"What about her?"

"She thinks you're cute," I say matter-of-factly, sliding my pendant down the thin chain.

"That's nice of her." He says it so quickly that we both laugh before fading into quiet once more.

"I, uh . . ." I tilt my head to the side and twist my lips. I'm pulling so hard on my chain that it's cutting into my neck. "Well, I told her I'd set you two up."

Cliff's steps slow down significantly, coming to almost a lull before picking up again. It's so dark that I can't see his expression.

Finally, he murmurs, "Why?"

"I think it'd be good for you."

"Huh."

We slowly walk back into the circle of light, and I watch his face come into view. No lines. Not a smile in sight.

"We were talking about you getting back out there," I quickly explain. "This would be perfect. I know you. I know my sister. You're both really happy people."

He snorts. "Is that the recipe for a good date?"

"Maybe. You're the baker, aren't you?"

He huffs out a half laugh. His sneakers scratch on the concrete as he lingers in the last bit of darkness before the next lamppost. I stop a few paces ahead of him. My fingers won't leave my necklace.

I hear him sigh. "Why are you pushing this whole *getting out there* thing, Michelle?"

My lips part as I think, but I can't find the proper words. I must take too long because what starts as a pause in the conversation turns into awkward silence, and Cliff isn't covering it like he usually might. He wants an answer.

"Because you deserve a chance at happiness," I finally breathe out.

His palms shift in his pockets. His foot scuffs on the concrete.

It's painfully quiet, so I finally add, "She's your type."

Cliff hisses in a breath, and slowly he starts taking steps

toward me. One. Then another. I'm breathless as he stalks closer, crossing into the beam of light above us. I can finally see him again. His eyebrows are tilted inward. His chest is suddenly only inches from mine.

"Uh-huh," he muses, his voice low as his blue eyes flick between mine. "And what is my type, Michelle?"

I straighten my spine. "Blond. Bubbly."

He tongues his cheek. He looks irritated, but that only makes me stand taller. He's never been like this with me, and I don't know what to do with it.

"Yeah," he says slowly. "Yeah, I guess you're right. Blond. Bubbly. That pretty perfectly describes the woman I divorced."

The words ooze with disdain. It's like getting shot in the chest, puncturing my heart so swiftly that I didn't see it coming.

"Are you mad at me now?" I ask sharply.

Cliff exhales, some of the tension in his shoulders releasing, as if he just realized he was stressed at all. He threads his fingers through his hair, letting the strands drop back into place. "I don't think this is a great idea. I barely know her."

"That's the point of a date, isn't it?"

His jaw ticks as he looks off to the side. "I don't know, Michelle . . ."

"Don't you want to finally move on?" I ask.

He blinks, staring at me. Staring *through* me.

"I'll think about it," he murmurs.

"Good."

"Good."

Rocket tugs on the leash, pacing ahead like he wants out of this conversation as much as I do.

We continue our walk, and Cliff is only tense for half a

block before we're talking normally again. Sort of laughing. Pretending like the conversation didn't happen. But there's a small edge to every word. A sharp cut.

I don't address his attitude because there's no point.

I know what I did, and it isn't worth it to start an argument I know I'd lose.

Chapter 26

CLIFF

I don't want to go on a date with Michelle's sister.

It's not that Sara isn't cute. She's very pretty—perky, I guess would be the best descriptor. Smiley with dimples that I could tuck my thumbs into and blue eyes that would make any man with half a brain, or even none at all, completely obsessed with her.

Unfortunately, I've developed this irritating attraction to sour, controlling brunettes. I can't say *no* to Michelle. And that is why I'm five minutes away from picking up this woman's sister for a date.

"I'll reserve you a table," Lars says over the phone.

I groan. "Don't make it a big deal."

"But it is a big deal."

"It's really not."

"I set out flowers."

"*Lars.*"

I hear the dial tone before I can argue more.

I sigh. We're set to have dinner at Lars's pizzeria in the square. Inevitably, all of Copper Run will see, gossip, and ask questions for the next three to five business days.

I should have anticipated this, but when I asked Sara on a date, all I thought was, *If this will make Michelle happy . . .*

I throw on my best sweater, khakis, and a loose sports coat. I look at myself in the mirror, running a hand through my hair and shaking it out.

"Christ," I murmur, threading fingers through it again and again but stopping because The Flop™ will never go away unless I get a different haircut.

I've only been on two first dates in my entire life. The first was at sixteen, when my parents drove me and Tracy to the theater. I paid for popcorn with my birthday money. And then we conceived Emily a couple of weeks later.

The second date was one month after I signed my divorce papers. Carol told me there was *passion* out there and that I needed to find it. I looked into ads and called a woman who said she loved kids. I drove into Burlington too early, realizing at the hostess stand that I hadn't made reservations for the restaurant. We went to a sandwich shop down the road instead, talked about our jobs and the future—she wanted three of her "own kids," then, "no, maybe five"—and then decided not to get dessert. I never called her back, and she never called me either.

I take the stairs down to the living room. Emily and Carol sit in front of the TV, watching some rom-com with Meg Ryan. She's pretty, but I *do not* have a thing for blondes. I don't.

"Be back later," I call.

I don't expect them to look—I'm getting Emily's cold shoulder, and she's taken sudden solace in her aunt—but they both turn at the same time.

"Whoa," Emily breathes. "Where are *you* going tonight, Dad?"

Carol's surprise is similar, but with an exaggerated gasp. "Hot date?"

I adjust my sleeve cuffs. "Actually, yes."

Emily's jaw drops. "Shut up. Really?"

"Yes."

"You've never dated though," Emily says.

"I did once. Sort of."

After a second, a cool smile slides onto Emily's lips. "Oh. Oh, I see." She shoots out a palm toward Carol. "Cough it up."

Carol digs in her pocket. "You were right."

I narrow my eyes and point between them. "What's going on here?"

"I called it," Emily says with a grin.

"Called what?" I ask.

"That you and Michelle were *totally* doing it."

It feels like a cold bucket of ice—not water because water would hurt less—is thrown in my face.

"Emily. Burke."

She startles, and I wonder if my tone was sharper than intended. Though I think my blood pressure wanted it to be.

"Ugh," she groans, rolling her eyes. "I meant *dating*."

"I'm not going on a date with Michelle."

"What?!" Carol asks.

"Shh, Brittany is asleep," I whisper.

"What do you *mean*, it's not Michelle?" Carol hisses back.

"Who are you going on a date with?" Emily asks.

"Sara."

"Michelle's *sister*?!" they ask at the same time.

"Shh! Yes."

Carol scrunches up her nose, finally looking at my outfit. "God, you've *got* to change your shoes, then."

"What? Why?" I kick out my brown boots.

"They're Classic Cliff," Carol says. "Classic Cliff is the person you show *after* a few dates."

"But you weren't gonna say anything if I was on a date with Michelle?"

Carol shrugs. "Well, yeah, she already knows you and likes you for who you are."

I suck in a breath, and an awkward silence follows when Carol's sentence washes over all three of us. I don't like it.

Emily pops her lips. "They don't match your jacket, Dad. You need to make a good first impression."

I clap my hands together and gesture between them. "I didn't ask for your opinion, but thank you anyway."

I'm halfway through the back door when Carol calls, "Change your shoes if you want her to like you!"

I hesitate for a moment on the threshold, and then I shut the door behind me, wearing my same brown shoes.

I knock on the door to Bird & Breakfast. I shake my head and bite my cheek. I'm embarrassed for myself.

When was the last time I knocked *on any door in Copper Run?*

I feel uneasy, like I'm missing something. Maybe I forgot to turn off the stove. Or maybe I forgot my wallet. I am patting my pockets to double-check that my wallet is there when the door rips open. I don't know why I expected it to be Michelle—force of habit—but Sara's cheery face answers instead.

"Hi," she says on an exhale.

"Oh. Hey." It's awkward. *I'm* awkward.

Sara's dressed very differently from me. I feel like an outdated old man in my sports coat. She's cute. *Too* cute. Too young. Too much like a bubbly version of my own daughter, which sends a chill down my spine.

Her hair is parted into multiple intricately braided strands, pulled back to a sudden burst of spikes in some sort of updo. I don't understand how any of it works. Around her neck, she wears one of those braided chokers that Emily has, and her shirt and skirt have enough space between them to show her belly button.

And I'm in *khakis*.

Before I can speak, she says, "Let me get my purse real quick!"

Sara hurries up the stairwell. She must be occupying one of the guest rooms. I stand on the threshold. I've never *not* casually walked into Bird & Breakfast, but it suddenly feels inappropriate, considering I'm on a date. It's like walking into her parents' house.

Instead, I lean to the side to see if I can spot—

There she is.

Michelle sits in the parlor with her legs tucked under her on the couch. A notebook lies open in her lap. She's working.

I smile. *Typical.*

In one hand is a pen, and in the other is a steaming mug. Knowing her, I'm guessing there's probably coffee in there.

I manage a low whistle. Her head pops up, and she bends forward to peer around the corner.

"Hi. I'm Cliff. Nice to meet you, Ms. Cadell."

I hold out my hand in the air. With a twitching smile, Michelle holds hers out too. We shake hands through the air, twenty feet apart.

"Call me Michelle. Nice to meet you, Cliff."

I keep my hand moving.

"Lovely home you have here."

Shake.

"Thank you," she responds.

Shake.

I tip my chin at her coffee. "You're gonna be up until midnight."

"I can drink a cup and go to bed seconds later," she says.

My mouth tilts up at the corners. "I know you can."

Michelle twists her lips to the side, then stops moving her hand. I let mine fall too. She leans back to hide from my sight again. My smile disappears.

Sara barrels back down the stairs, taking them two at a time with her hand on the railing, rings on almost every finger skidding along the surface. She's rubbing her lips together. A pink gloss shimmers on them.

"I'm ready!" she says, adjusting the purse strap on her shoulder. "What do ya think?" She spins.

I manage a smile. "You look very pretty."

"Thank you." She bats her eyelashes in an over-the-top way that makes me laugh.

"Want to head out?" I ask, throwing a thumb over my shoulder.

"Sure," she says, raising her shoulders and dropping them, as if motioning, *Yeah, whatever. It's cool.*

I place a hand on the small of her back and guide her through the door.

"I won't stay out too late, Shells!" Sara calls behind us.

But before I follow Sara out the door, I turn back around to look at the parlor. Michelle peers around the corner. When our gazes catch, she squirrels away.

༄

"Two, Lars."

His eyes are so big that I can see the whites along every edge. I sigh. I know what it looks like. I, Clifford Burke, town celibate divorcé, am on a date. Not just a date, but a date with someone like Sara. Young. Cute.

"Two," Lars echoes.

"Two," I confirm, straightening my lips into a line and raising my eyebrows.

Lars quietly grabs two menus with a suppressed grin on his face. As he walks us to a table with a red-and-white-checkered tablecloth, I see Betty at dinner with Sandra. Luke is across from his parents. All eyes are on us. I'm going to be news tomorrow, if not in the next five minutes.

I pull out Sara's chair for her with a whining screech on the hardwood and scoot it back in once she's sitting. I take the chair across from her. Lars twiddles his thumbs.

"You're serving us?" I ask.

"Of course."

"You own the place."

"I lead by example. Wine?"

I throw him a pointed look.

They don't even have *wine here.*

"We're all set, Lars. Two waters for now."

"Of course," he says, eyes darting between us. He doesn't budge.

"Lars?"

He startles. "Yeah. Be back."

Lars scuttles off, but when he gets behind Sara—out of her sight—he throws me a thumbs-up. I roll my eyes and prop up my menu.

"What do they have here?" Sara asks.

"Pizza," I answer. "Cheese. Meats. Veg. Coffee."

"Coffee?" she asks.

I smile. "It's a combo pizzeria-slash-coffeehouse. Trust me, none of us understand Lars's mind either."

"Oh. Any pasta?" she asks hopefully.

"No, that would make too much sense."

She giggles. "Then pizza it is. Any recommendations?"

"The meat lovers. I could only eat that for the rest of my life, and I'd never get sick of it."

We look at the menu for a moment in silence. The loud, blaring sounds from the bright arcade machines in the corner are battling against Third Eye Blind over the speakers. I peer over at Sara. She's pretty. Peppy. And definitely out of place, being on a date with me.

"What about the cheeseburger pizza?" she asks, then murmurs, "God, why do I feel like Michelle would love that?"

I feel my lips turn up in a smile. "Nah, she hates mustard."

Sara flicks her eyes to mine, blinks for a moment, then smiles.

"I'm going with meat lovers," she announces, gingerly setting down her menu.

"Good choice."

"I hear it's the best."

I chuckle. She's sweet; a colorful macaron would suit her.

"So," I say, lowering my menu as well. "Art school, huh? That's really neat."

"Yes!" Immediately, her expression changes. It's like light beams through to her very soul at the mention of art. "I have this dream of opening my own studio. Like something with installations that rotate through each month, you know?"

"That sounds ambitious."

"What can I say? We're an ambitious family."

I snort. "You're right. Michelle can't cut away from work if she tried."

"She's admittedly a bit more ambitious than me."

I try not to act too interested when I ask, "Is she? How so?"

"Well"—she tilts her head to the side—"she moved to the city in her early twenties—which I would *never* have done—and she . . . did it, y'know? Found a job. Moved her way up. Did she tell you she was the first woman exec at her company?"

I smile. "Really?"

"Yeah. And now, God"—her eyes widen and she shakes her head—"she took over the B and B so easily." She blows out a breath. "She's my superhero. And I can't even imagine how much she's had to learn about this place in such a short amount of time."

"She's a quick learner," I say, a laugh tickling up my throat. "Very quick."

Sara exhales shakily. "It's a lot to learn."

I peer up at her as her eyes bore a hole through the table's wood. "Hey, I'm sure you'll do great."

"Yeah." She readjusts in her seat and waves a nonchalant hand in the air. "Ugh, anyway, enough about me. What about you? How'd you get to be a baker?"

"Uh . . ." I rap my knuckles on the table. "Well, it was a dream forever. Home ec in high school really resonated with me. And there was a storefront that went vacant—a block away actually—right after my divorce, and . . . I guess you look at life a little differently after everything you thought was real suddenly isn't. You embrace silly dreams a bit more."

Sara blinks at me, nodding slowly, as if really soaking in my words.

"I love that," she says. "I mean, not the whole *divorce* thing. That didn't work out. But I like that you went for it and made your dream come true."

It's always weird when people who aren't divorced discuss divorce. *That didn't work out* feels like such an oversimplification of it all. I manage a wan smile anyway.

"How old are you?" she blurts out.

"Thirty-three."

"Twenty-four," she counters.

"Oof," I grunt out, shaking my head and tonguing the inside of my cheek with a hesitant laugh.

She grins. "Too young?"

I don't know a nice way to say, *Yes, because you're less than ten years older than my daughter*, so instead, I tilt my head to the side. "Question for you, Sara."

"Okay," she says, giddy.

"Why aren't you dating someone at school?"

"Is this your dad side coming out?"

I chuckle. "Maybe."

Sara sits taller. "I'm not interested in boys out there. They like to surf and smoke and listen to dumb music. And . . . I don't know . . . they're not my type."

"What is your type?" I ask.

"Older dads."

A laugh bubbles out of me. I pinch the bridge of my nose and close my eyes. "You're very confident—I'll give you that."

Sara grins, shimmying her shoulders as she settles into her seat. "Thank you."

"Michelle talks really highly of you. It's nice to see you match what I imagined."

She blinks. "Wait, what? She did?"

"Yeah. You're her favorite person in the world."

Her posture falters more. "She said that?"

"Yes, a ball of sunshine . . ." I say slowly, then laugh. "Why? You sound like that's weird to hear."

"It is."

"Nah, come on. She'd do anything for you. This should show it."

"What should?"

"Taking over the inn. She wouldn't sacrifice her job for anyone else."

"Did she . . . I mean, she . . ." Sara shakes her head. "Yeah. Sure. I guess she doesn't talk about her emotions much. Not with me."

I can't help but smile. "It almost feels rewarding when she does, doesn't it?"

Sara opens her mouth, then closes it, but Lars comes back to the table before she can answer. We place our orders, and when he leaves again, he looks between us, curls his lips in like he has a secret, then rushes toward the back of the house.

"Don't be weird, Lars!" I call after him.

Sara's eyes dart between mine and the door he escaped through. "What does that mean?"

I lean across the table. "Well, just so you know," I whisper, "this entire town will know about our date by the end of the evening."

"Really?" she asks.

"Really. They're vultures, all of them." I look around, and a few people are staring our way. I wave at Betty until she has enough tact to look back at her pizza slice.

Sara bites her lip. "Well, we should give them something to talk about then."

I raise my eyebrows, but my heart instantly starts racing.

"Uh, maybe," I respond.

"I'll come up with something; don't worry," Sara says.

"Come up with what?"

"Something to talk about," she answers with a playful wink.

All I can manage is an amused laugh. "Man, you two are very different, aren't you?"

"Who?"

"You and Michelle."

"Oh. Yeah. Mom always said that too," she replies. "Two sides of the same coin. Sun and moon. Blonde and brunette. Sagittarius and Scorpio."

I chuckle. "I never understood the sign thing."

"Okay, well, Scorpios are intense. That's Michelle."

"She's definitely that," I agree. "It took me forever to get a reaction out of her that wasn't hate. But, eh"—I lean in like I'm sharing a conspiracy—"pretty sure she still hates me."

Sara laughs, but it peters out. She curls her lips in.

"Well, Michelle only says what she means," she says.

I smile. "That's what I like most about her."

Sara's eyes flicker between mine for an uncomfortable moment before she leans forward on her elbows and threads her fingers together.

"Question for you now, Clifford," she says, mocking my tone from earlier.

I chuckle and raise my glass. "Shoot."

"Do you know you're in love with my sister?"

I sputter into my water, spilling it over the table. I grab the napkin and wipe down the tabletop.

"Yeah," she says through smacking lips. "That's what I thought."

"That's not . . ." I laugh through growing nerves. "We're friends."

Sara narrows her eyes. "She tells you things she won't even tell me."

"Okay, we're *close* friends," I amend.

"She's in love with you too, isn't she?"

"No, it's not like that."

She toys with her napkin and fork. "Did you *want* to go on this date?" She peers up at me through her lashes.

My heart sinks.

I exhale. "You're very nice."

"But . . ."

"Michelle wanted me to get back out there, *and* she really loves you, so it made sense. She really does talk highly of you, and you're nothing but lovely. But . . . I also haven't been on a date in a long time. So, no, I didn't. But that has nothing to do with you."

She smiles. "Well, good. Because I *am* lovely. And I'm happy Michelle has a friend like you."

I nod. "She means a lot to me. And she's leaving in two months, and I'm . . ." I blink for a moment. "I'm happy to have been her friend for this short amount of time. That's all." I shrug. "She's special to me."

Sara's mouth gapes open. "Oh my *God*, you are *so* obsessed with her."

I shake my head, continuing to let out uncomfortable laughter. "I'm not."

"It's so crazy too. She said nothing was going on between you two."

My heart skips. "Oh . . . oh yeah?"

"Yeah. I mean . . ." Sara blinks, widening her palms beside her head like she's trying to comprehend too many things at once. "God, she even *joked* about it."

Joked.

I clear my throat. "Did she really?" Suddenly, my chair is very uncomfortable. It's too hard. I shift my position and click my tongue. "Huh."

Sara's eyes widen. "Oh, I didn't—"

"No, it's okay," I say, managing a laugh. "Yeah." I inhale and let it out. "Well, like you said, she doesn't say things she doesn't mean."

"She . . . I mean, it's hard to know what she's really thinking," Sara says.

"I know," I agree. "Yeah, that's true."

Of course, it's at that exact moment that Lars comes over with two palms balancing the pizzas. He sets them down, grinning between us again.

"Anything I can get for you?" he asks. "A candle?"

I shake my head. "We're good, Lars."

And for the first time, my precious meat lovers pizza tastes like shit.

Absolute shit.

Chapter 27

MICHELLE

My coffee has been cold for hours. I glance at the clock. It's a little after ten, so I can't reheat it or I'll be up all night. Though I'll be awake anyway with how my mind is racing.

Rocket grumbles on the other side of the sofa. I realize I've been tapping my feet, making the cushions bounce under his head.

Shelly, calm down.

I grip my cold mug closer. "Sorry."

Are you apologizing to me?

"I'm capable of apologizing," I counter, irritably sipping, then scrunching my nose. Cold coffee again.

I've been in the same position on this sofa for hours, reliving every second before Sara and Cliff left for their date.

I didn't like how Cliff looked when he left. Sure, he was handsome in his sports coat—I didn't know he was capable of dressing up outside of funerals—but I didn't like how softly he cooed when he called Sara pretty.

My sister is gorgeous, so he's honestly blind if he thinks *pretty* is a good enough word for her, but I shift uncomfortably on the cushion when I remember that he complimented her at all. I can't forget that Cliff is only a man—and he's a nice one at that. Of course he noticed her looks, and of course he told her.

But . . .

It was also the way he touched her lower back. I know Cliff touches everyone—if his hand isn't resting on someone for any length of time, he might shrivel up and die—but I didn't know I'd feel a heart-aching stab while watching.

There are footsteps on the porch. Rocket's head lifts. I shush him, and he lets out that irritated whine of his.

I didn't even bark, Shelly.

I barely decipher murmurs through the front door, but nothing discernible except a laugh or two.

They're having a good time.

Are they dancing around the good-night kiss?

Is Cliff slowly walking her back against the side of a house, like he did to me on Halloween?

I stand from the sofa and push through the kitchen door at the same time the front door keys open and Sara walks inside.

I freeze, and there's a moment or two of awkward silence with the clock in the kitchen ticking and Rocket's tapping claws on the linoleum.

"Michelle?" Sara whispers. "Are you awake?"

I nonchalantly set my coffee cup down, clear my throat, and whisper back, "Yeah. Hey. I'm in the kitchen. I got caught up with work. Lost track of time."

The kitchen door swings inward. I notice that her updo looks intact. Her pink lip gloss doesn't look smeared either.

"How'd it go?" I ask, swirling the bottom of the mug on the counter.

She glances at the empty counter. "You got caught up with work?" she asks with an edge of suspicion.

I also eye the noticeably paperless counter. "Yes," I lie.

She narrows her eyes. "Were you waiting up for me?"

I attempt a casual laugh. "No. Of course not. You're an adult—"

"And I'm also on a date with your friend." She takes a seat at the breakfast nook and brings both legs up to cross in the chair.

"Oh yeah, how'd it go?"

She pulls her bottom lip between her teeth and eyes me from top to bottom. Staring. Squinting.

"You know, it went really well actually," she drawls with a satisfied smile, sinking deeper into her seat. "Like"—she closes her eyes and sighs—"*really* well."

A knot tightens in my stomach.

"Oh yeah?" I ask shakily, taking another sip of the cold coffee and grimacing. "That's great."

"It wasn't simply great," she says. "It was *spectacular*. He's . . . well . . ." She looks at the floor and exhales a heavy breath before snapping her eyes to mine again. "He's a really good kisser."

Without my consent, my butt lands in the chair across from her. The gut punch is harder than I thought. My vision is blurred at the edges.

"Oh . . . oh, really?" I ask weakly, but I can barely register my own words.

"Yep," Sara continues with a grin, blinking up at the ceiling like she's thanking God for such a night. "We tried to wait until we were out of the restaurant, but he couldn't help himself. Cliff is *not* the gentleman you think he is."

The walls are closing in on me.

"That's great," I whisper.

I think I'm getting tunnel vision. Sara is all I can see, but I swear I can hear the distant, joyful laughter of Cliff next door—the laugh of a man who had an amazing date. I wanted that for him.

Didn't I?

I force a smile, but I need to lie down. I did this to myself. I told him to date her. And now they're gonna be together and—

Sara suddenly slings her purse across the table. It skids to the opposite side, bumping into my arm before plunking on the floor.

I flinch back. "What the hell are you—"

"God, I'm so *pissed* at you," she hisses.

"Pissed at *me*?"

"You like him!"

I blink. "What are you talking—"

"We didn't do anything!" she whines, throwing a defeated hand in the air. "I lied. Because I needed to see you squirm for a teensy second." She leans forward with her forearms on the table. "Shells, he talked about you all night. All. Night."

"No, he didn't," I breathe in disbelief.

"Yes, he did."

"So, you didn't kiss?"

"Are you joking me?" she asks with a laugh. "He didn't even look at my cleavage, which, for the record, is incredible. I put glitter on the girls."

I stifle a laugh. "He didn't look at your sparkly boobs?"

"He didn't," she says with a flat stare. She smacks my arm. "Cliff likes you, Shelly. What are you doing?"

"I don't understand the question."

"What. Are. You. Doing?" she says, enunciating every single word. "That man would jump off a bridge if you told him to, except, whoops, he's already jumped, and he's now down the river, waiting for you to tell him what to do next."

I scoff out a laugh. "Sara—"

"He's hot. He's nice. He's funny. He opened doors for me. He heard me blab on about art school and actually *listened*. Guys don't do that. Trust me."

"Sara . . ."

"Do me a favor," she snaps.

"What?"

"Go get laid."

I blink to myself and sit taller. "What are you talking about?"

She slides her arms across the table and grasps my hands. "Be happy with the stupid, amazing man next door who is stupidly *obsessed* with you."

Cliff is *obsessed* with me?

The thought feels so ridiculous. He likes me—or liked me at some point. But that's it. A crush. Nothing more. But the knot in my stomach grips tighter, and I feel like I'm lying to myself.

Sara snaps her fingers in my face. "Stop thinking," she says irritably. "Tell me what's on your mind. Out loud."

"I'm not doing that."

"Oh, but you tell Cliff everything?"

I roll my eyes. "I don't tell him every—"

"Yes, you do. I had to find out through him how you feel about me."

I disentangle my forearms from her grasp and cross them over my chest, leaning back in my chair. "What are you even talking about?"

"You never tell me how much you love me."

I stiffen. "I say it all the time," I say breathlessly.

"Three words is nothing compared to what he told me. He said that you think I'm . . . a ball of sunshine? Which I had *no* idea you even could think something like that." She scoots her chair closer to mine. "He even said that I'm your favorite person in the world. Though"—she tsks—"I think I've got stiff competition with Cliff now."

I laugh and shake my head.

"He also said . . . well . . . how were you able to get here? Stay at the inn, I mean. Your job let you, right?"

I swallow. "Of course they did."

"It didn't . . . set you back or anything?" I can't find words fast enough before Sara slouches. "Why did you do that?"

"You need to graduate. Mom needed this."

"And you have a life you've *worked* for."

"And I love you more than any of that."

Sara shakes her head, her eyebrows turning in. "You deserve to be happy. You should talk to Cliff."

"It would never work," I answer.

"You don't even wanna try?"

I reach up and twirl my earring. "We live on opposite sides of the country . . ."

"So?"

"I just got divorced."

"*So?*" she repeats with more emphasis.

"He's not a guy I'd normally go for."

"Because marrying a fancy doctor worked out so well for you."

I shoot her a warning look, and she groans.

"You're so difficult. But whatever." Sara flings her hands in the air. "Do what you want. It's your life. What do I know?"

"You know a lot."

"I know; it's terrible being smart *and* pretty," she says with a teasing smile.

We're silent in the kitchen with only the sound of the humming refrigerator and my tapping nails on the table.

"I don't know," I mumble.

"Don't know what?"

"Anything. I . . ." I clear my throat. "Cliff appeared in my life and never seemed to go away. And at first, I hated it. He's . . . so *frustrating*. But he doesn't make me be someone I'm not."

"So . . . you like him," she says.

"Yes."

"So . . ." She rotates her palm in a circle, as if coaxing me on.

I side-eye her, then exhale. "Yes, he means a lot to me, if that's what you're implying."

"God, you can't say anything out loud, can you? Say you've got feelings for him, Shells."

I can't. Because saying that I have a crush on Cliff—not simply thinking it—will only put something out there that I can't take back. What would it accomplish anyway?

"Well, for what it's worth," Sara says, "*I* think you'd be good together."

"That's very sweet."

"I mean it."

A little smile breaks onto my lips. "Thanks."

"Can we have a sleepover?" she asks. "Like old times?"

I laugh. "I'm thirty."

"So? We can even get Rocket in on it."

His eyes look between us. *Absolutely not.*

I laugh. "I don't think he's into it."

Sara's nose scrunches. "He's really vocal for a dog that doesn't talk, isn't he?"

"Very," I agree. "He's not half bad though."

And I think, from the corner of my eye, I see Rocket wag his tail.

"Shells?" Sara whispers.

"Hmm?"

"If you say it, I won't tell anyone." She holds out her pinkie. "I promise."

I can feel the strings of my heart pulling taut. My arms want to tuck closer to my chest, like I'm protecting myself. The truth is, I've tried to keep a small piece of me locked away from everyone.

Exhaling, I turn the key and whisper back, "I really like him, Sara. And I don't know what to do."

MICHELLE

"All three of us can't fit in a bed."

"Ooh, but we could sing campfire songs while we're going to sleep!" Sara teases.

Dad peers over the *Wall Street Journal*. "Could be fun."

I close my eyes and pinch the bridge of my nose. Sara laughs, loudly slurping her coffee. I'm not laughing at all.

We overbooked the inn. I had a feeling it would get crowded for Thanksgiving, but part of me assumed people would want to celebrate with their families in the comfort of their own home. Turns out, at least three people didn't care to discuss politics or religion with their crazy uncle or abrasive grandma. Now all three guest rooms are full, which leaves only my king-size bed for me, my sister, and my dad with a bad back.

"Okay"—I walk to the hall closet and heave out the heavy, deflated rubber air mattress—"I've got this I can sleep on."

Dad folds down his paper. "You're not sleeping on a cot, Shellfish. I'll take the—"

"No," Sara and I both snap at the same time.

"You're definitely taking the bed," I demand, and Sara nods firmly in agreement.

"You have to run this place," he argues. "You need good sleep."

"I can run on no sleep."

That's wrong. I'm actually a high-maintenance sleeper. I always wear an eye mask and earplugs. One time, I accidentally popped one out at three in the morning, and the next day, I stumbled down the sidewalk to work through bleary eyes, clutching a massive coffee. But my dad doesn't need to know that.

The back door opens, and Emily strides in with a backpack over her shoulders. Cold air sweeps in behind her until the door shuts, blinds snapping against the window.

"Getting coffee before school," she says without looking at us. "I'll be quick. Britt's outside."

I lean to the side to find a teeth-chattering six-year-old in a color-block windbreaker, gripping the straps of her pink backpack for dear life.

"Doesn't Brittany want to come inside?" Sara asks.

Emily groans. "She's still afraid of Rocket. But"—she grabs a to-go mug from the cabinet and shrugs—"she's at least in your yard. That's progress."

As if on cue, Rocket's ears perk up from his dog bed, and he taps to the window, jumping to rest his paws on the windowsill. His tail cautiously wags as he presses his nose against the glass, sending pulsing puffs of heat on the surface.

Brittany stares at him for a moment, then slowly raises her mitten in a small wave. Rocket's tail shakes more.

"Oh my God, I didn't even think about Rocket!" Sara says, leaning back in her chair more. "So, we've got three adults and a *dog* in one room for a couple days?"

"What?" Emily asks.

"It's nothing," I say. "We overbooked the inn. It's not a big deal."

"It's sort of a big deal," Sara interjects.

"I can take the air mattress," Dad mumbles to himself.

"Dad," I warn.

"You should stay with us," Emily blurts out.

My family goes dead quiet, like a gust of November wind blew through and chilled us to the bone. But when I look around, my sister and Dad are nodding, as if considering this idea.

So, maybe I'm the only one who's shocked.

The inn is fully booked the night before Thanksgiving and the night of. That's two nights. *Two nights* where Emily expects me to sleep under the same roof as Cliff?

As if reading my mind, Sara flashes me a devilish grin.

I slide my clammy hands over my skirt. "Em, shouldn't you talk to your dad first?"

She blows air through her lips. "Psht, he won't have a say. He's trying to get on my good side."

"Well, you can't surprise your dad with this."

The back door swings open again, bringing with it another gust of near-winter chill and Cliff himself. He's wearing a dark brown corduroy jacket with the cuffs of his long-sleeved maroon shirt peeking through the ends. His freshly shaven jaw scratches against the collar when he turns.

"Em, why is your sister outside?" he asks, throwing a thumb over his shoulder.

"Rocket," Emily says, spinning the cap of her mug to secure it. "I'm heading back out now."

He blows out a breath. "Coffee's a good idea. I've got the truck already running."

"I'll get the heat going. Oh, and I invited Michelle to stay with you for a couple of days." Emily throws that in like a tossed grenade. As the back door closes, she quickly says, "Okay, bye. See you."

Cliff's eyes catch mine, then quickly dart to Sara. It feels so sudden, like he didn't want to look at me to begin with.

My brow furrows.

"Emily was being funny," I say.

"Why would she say that though?"

Cliff looks between Sara and Dad. *Not me.*

"We're overbooked for Thanksgiving," my dad says behind the paper, indicating he never left the conversation fully.

"Huh," Cliff considers, then says, "Well, yeah, Michelle can take my bed."

Leave it to Cliff to be unfazed by this news.

"That's not—" I shake my head. "No, we're not doing that."

"And I'm not asking," he says quickly. It's weird how he's somehow both balancing a generous offer while also looking like he's one step away from never allowing me near his house again.

Is he upset with me?

"This is perfect," Sara says.

I shake my head. "No, I don't think—"

"It's not a problem," Cliff finishes.

"Maybe we should—"

Then Rocket barks. *Why are you so nervous about this, Shelly?*

I close my eyes. "Can you people quit interrupting me for two seconds?"

The room goes quiet again.

I open my eyes and find Cliff staring. His mouth is in a straight line. I hate that I can read Cliff like a book. And while I've never seen him like this, process of elimination tells me this is a new type of irritation, aimed directly at me.

But why?

"Stay with me," he insists.

I let out a frustrated exhale, peering over at Sara with her bottom lip pulled in and her shoulders raised to her ears. She gives the cheekiest grin imaginable.

"It *does* make the most sense," she agrees innocently. "I don't know Cliff as well as you do."

I narrow my eyes. She knows what she's doing.

"Perfect," Cliff says.

His words don't sound *perfect* at all. Not even a little bit.

"Got more coffee for me?" he asks Sara.

Sara—not me.

Why isn't he talking to me?

"Half a pot. Have at it," she says.

He smiles at her, patting her back when he passes by her.

Her. Not me.

Cliff makes his coffee with the same familiarity as his daughter. My chest strains when he walks past me to leave, a quick bit of warmth and cinnamon following. It's like I'm both drawing closer and also being kept at arm's length. The same ends of a magnet, pushing when we've been pulled together for so long.

"Bye, Cliff!" Sara says with a wave.

"Bye, guys."

He leaves through the door without even a second glance.

Oh, screw this.

In only my jeans and tucked-in button-up, I rip open the back door and walk out barefoot onto the stone steps. The door snaps shut behind me as the cold surface freezes my toes. I clutch the outside of my arms, now prickled with chills, and stride forward.

"Cliff!"

He turns on the spot with the coffee mug halfway to his lips. His eyes scour over my shivering body.

"Hey, Michelle." The sentence feels almost exhausted.

My face drops, along with my mouth. "I . . . well, I just . . ." I hate when I stumble over my words like this. I hate feeling out of control in a conversation, and I feel at a loss for words more than ever. This isn't my Cliff. Not even a little. "You seem irritated."

"I am," he confirms without hesitation, making my head jerk back. His words are so matter-of-fact. Transactional.

"Why?" I ask stiffly, mirroring his tone.

He looks back to his truck idling in his driveway, hazy puffs from the exhaust warming the chilly air. Loud music from the radio blasts inside. Brittany taps Emily on the shoulder, and Emily looks like she's seconds away from murdering her little sister.

Cliff faces me again, resting his eyes on my lips before looking back up.

"Because I'm really confused about us and I'm trying to sort through it," he confesses.

My body heats. Goose bumps skitter over my arms. For once, I'm not sure I like how honest Cliff is.

"Us?" I ask.

"Us," he echoes. "We agreed it was fine if we were friends, but . . . then you set me up on a date with your sister. And . . . it's not . . . I don't know. I said yes, so it's my fault too."

"If you felt weird about it, why'd you agree?" I ask.

"Because you told me I needed to move on. And, listen,

you're right, but . . ." He groans, as if upset with himself now. "But then I found out you never really felt the same about it as I did. And that . . ." He shakes his head. "That wasn't fun to hear. Especially since it didn't come from you."

I'm speechless, my mouth opening and closing like a gutted fish. And part of me *is* gutted, torn in two because . . . not having feelings for Cliff? I snort, crossing my arms at my own thoughts. Quite frankly, I have *too many* feelings for this man. And right now, they're bordering on frustration.

"Cliff—"

"It's fine," he says. "Really. I'll get over it."

"No, it's not fine at all. Let's talk about this."

"Later."

"Why not now? I didn't say that. And it's not true."

He pinches his nose. "Michelle, it's seven in the morning. I've already been up since four to prep the bakery, and I'm about to be late driving my daughters to their last day of school before break." He holds his palm out. "And you're standing there, freezing your ass off. I mean"—he laughs sardonically—"what type of conversation do you want to have right now?"

My blood pressure rises up to my ears.

"I don't know," I admit sharply. I repeat on a haughty breath, "I don't know, Cliff. But I did have feelings. I do. I . . ." I shake my head. "I don't know. You're right. We can't talk about it right now."

He nods understandingly, the small bit of the Cliff I know seeping through. "All right." He turns to walk toward the car, then whirls back around with a sigh. "And, for the record, of course it's okay if you stay with us. Don't think my irritation has any bearing on our friendship."

"How can it not?" I say on a disbelieving laugh.

"Because you mean more to me than just a simple, confusing kiss."

The quiet around us is deafening. The wind whips past my ears, but suddenly, I don't feel so cold.

He runs his free palm through his hair. A little strand sticks out. "Stay with me."

"What?"

"For Thanksgiving. I'll take one of the girls' beds since they'll be gone anyway."

I'm frozen on the spot, shivering in the whipping wind.

Cliff eyes my arms, then lurches forward for half a second, like maybe he wants to rub the chill from me, but instead pauses and grits his teeth. "And, for God's sake, go inside. You're gonna catch a cold or something."

I don't move from my spot as Cliff tightens his fist, then stretches it out. He turns on his heel, and his boots thump on the stone walkway. He crunches through the hard, dying grass between our yards and gets in his truck. He shuts the door, turns down the loud radio, and putters out of his driveway with Brittany and Emily blinking back at me through the window.

Chapter 29

CLIFF

I slap down a bag of canned food on the folding table outside Brittany's elementary school.

"You're a thief," I joke. "You swindle me out of cans every year."

Brittany's elementary school principal—and my former kindergarten teacher—shakes her head with a smile. "Hi, Cliff."

"Hi, Debra."

Debra scribbles on her clipboard, then peers up at me through her lashes. She smiles sweetly, chewing on her bottom lip.

I narrow my eyes suspiciously, the twitch of a smile at the edge of my lips. "What?"

"Well, you see, my cousin, she's got a thing for bakers and . . ."

Every fiber in me recoils.

"Deb . . ."

This is the fifth person to pitch their loved one to me today, and it's only noon. George and Lisa parked outside the bakery with Polaroids of their cute granddaughter. Sandra rushed over after with a handful of photos tucked beside flowers. Divorce proceedings almost feel like a cakewalk compared to hearing, *Oh, my aunt's best friend's daughter is single* . . .

I force a smile at Debra. The last thing I want is for my neighbors to think I'm ungrateful for their matchmaking, even if it makes me want to stab my eyes out.

"I'm not dating, Deb."

Her face falls. "What? But Lars said he saw you with Michelle's sister."

The knife twists.

"It was a onetime thing."

I cringe, thinking about how much we brought up Michelle, but Sara wanted to know everything about our relationship, and talking about Michelle felt comfortable. I don't know how to date, but the thought of Michelle relaxed me.

The smile on Sara's face grew wider and wider further into the night, until she finally touched me on the arm and said, "You've got to tell her."

All I could respond was, "It wouldn't work."

If I'd been asked a few weeks ago whether I should date Michelle, I would have said it didn't matter. That we were friends and I was going to enjoy every moment with her while I could. But after my date with Sara, things shifted in me, like a craggy, yawning hole opened up in my heart.

I don't want to go on more dates. I want Michelle. Not as a friend. Not as a fling. I *want* her. But I know who I am, and I know what our situation is. Michelle loves her life in Seattle. She wants nothing more than to go back. Life after divorce isn't easy, and any sense of normalcy is so vital. I want her to heal. I would be a selfish man to steal that from her. The last thing I want is to take what's not mine to begin with.

I clear my throat, coming back to the here and now with another bag of canned food in the crook of my arm and a pastry box in the other.

"Doughnut?" I set it on the table and unfold the top. "Take as many as you want."

Her eyes light up. "Thanks," she says, taking out a lemon-filled doughnut.

I figured out Debra's doughnut preference a long time ago. A sweet, bright, lemon-filled doughnut to match her kind, elementary-school-teacher interior. Some people are easy to guess. Michelle, on the other hand . . .

"If you change your mind, my other cousin is a dentist and really pretty."

I huff out a laugh. "I'll keep that in mind, Deb."

"Boy, you've got a lot on your hands lately, huh? You know Luke has a crush on Brittany, right?"

"Luke? *The boy who pushed my daughter* Luke?"

"Yep. Two little wrestling-loving lovebirds."

"Good grief," I sarcastically murmur to myself. "Not in my house."

I recently got accustomed to Josh. Now, I've gotta worry about Luke? How did the whole Burke clan go from having zero relationship issues to being saddled with every single one?

Debra sets the pastry aside on a spare sheet of paper, licks the glaze from her thumb, then slides over a piece of paper.

"Hand turkey?" she offers.

"Can't the school come up with any other crafts to send home?"

Her face turns to unamused stone. "My other cousin—"

I snatch the paper turkey and wave it in the air. "It's perfect. Thanks for the turkey."

She waves. "Have a happy Thanksgiving, Cliff."

I pick up my doughnut box, slap some random kid's hand turkey on the top, and stroll toward the high school and the second food drive of the day.

It's cold. It's overcast. And the fall leaves have mostly disintegrated into a piecemeal mess beside gutters and cracks in the sidewalk. Thanksgiving is only a few days away, but the weather and I aren't exactly in the turkey-and-cranberry-sauce spirit this year.

My girls are leaving for New York in three days, and then they'll be gone for three more. I've never spent this holiday without them. We have traditions. How am I supposed to run down the hallway the morning of Thanksgiving, gobbling like a lunatic turkey, without them?

I keep telling myself that I'll be all right. It isn't the end of the world, even if it feels like it.

Outside the high school is another table with a brown tablecloth and stacks of cans piled in a corner. I plop my grocery bag on the tabletop.

"Hanging in there, Terri?" The high school math teacher gives a sly smile, and before she can open her mouth, I add, "I'm not dating. Doughnut?"

I open the lid and turn the box around. She twists her lips to the side.

"Fine, but I have the perfect woman for you," she argues anyway while snatching a cruller. Her hand hovers over a glazed one, and she peers up at me. I nod solemnly with permission, and she steals that one too. "She's a blonde. You like blondes, right?"

What is with this weird assumption that I like blondes? Didn't I divorce a blonde?

I snap the box closed. "And to think, I was gonna offer a third one."

"Ah, Cliff, don't be so dramatic. But I'm glad you're—"

"Getting back out there?" I finish. "I'm not."

"Oh, but you deserve to! You're such a catch."

I narrow my eyes. "Are you buttering me up for a third doughnut?"

"No, I'm being sincere," she counters. "You're a kind man with a great personality."

"People only say that about ugly people."

"You didn't give me time to say that you're handsome as well."

I pop open the lid again, and she draws out a third doughnut while shimmying for joy in her chair.

"Good luck with the food drive," I say, nodding toward my dropped-off bag.

"Thanks. And, Cliff, you know my granddaughter is—"

I hold up my hands with a half smile. "I'm good, Terri, but thanks."

"Let me know, and I can give you her number!"

I'm already halfway down the sidewalk when I call back, "Maybe!" I shouldn't have left that door cracked.

∞

Back at the bakery, I slump in my office chair with my head in my hands. Carol pokes her head in the office, and I smear my palm down my face.

Her face scrunches. "Ugh, you look terrible."

"I feel terrible."

"Was it the date?"

I groan, flopping my head into my folded arms on the desk. "It was a mistake," I grumble.

"Of course it was. It wasn't Michelle."

The tension in my arms pulls taut again.

I turn with my cheek now on the table and mumble, "You're more annoying than me—you know that? And that's saying something."

Carol cocks her head. "Why'd you go?"

It's a good question that I've asked myself over and over. I went because Michelle asked me to, is the simple answer. But that's unfair to Michelle. Ultimately, it was my decision. She didn't force me to walk over and ask Sara out. She didn't shove the sports coat over my shoulders. I chose to try dating. I stupidly hoped my feelings for Michelle were exactly what we'd said they were—those of two horny divorcés.

I was wrong.

When I don't answer, Carol slides into the steel folding chair in the corner.

"I wish you knew how good a guy you are."

I lift an eyebrow. "That was a nice thing to say."

She shrugs. "You're my brother. I'm allowed to be nice every two to five months." We exchange smiles. "So, why wouldn't it work with her? Michelle—not her sister."

I snort. "Because . . . she's got Seattle. A life she loves so much. And I've got my whole life here. A very busy life. I work long hours. I have two kids. She didn't ask for that."

Carol blinks, opening her mouth to maybe say something, but a *ding* echoes from the front lobby.

I grit my teeth. "If it's someone else with a picture of some woman, so help me God."

She snickers. "Don't worry about it. You mope."

"I'm not moping."

"It's okay; you can feel sad."

"I'm not sad!" I insist, but she's already left my office, which is good because I don't have the energy to argue my obvious lie.

I wait a few minutes, until the bell over the door chimes again. I leave my office and poke my head out. Lars is in the lobby, giving a goofy wave. I groan through it.

"How'd the hot date go?"

"Don't ask."

"But I—hey, wait, what—"

I walk past the display cases and toward the door painted in turkeys and pilgrims.

"Where are you going?" Carol asks.

"For a walk."

"To mope?" Lars asks.

"Yeah, yeah. Funny."

I walk outside, and to my dismay, Lars follows. We pace down the sidewalks and through the center of the square. Little pilgrim hats rest on leftover Halloween skeletons. Standing cardboard cutouts of cartoon turkeys hide behind haystacks. Their beady eyes mock me—I can feel it.

"It's okay that it didn't work out," he says. "I mean . . . what did you expect to happen though?"

"Lars?"

"Yeah?"

"I'll give you a dozen doughnuts if you don't talk right now."

"Deal, man." He claps me on the back. "But I'm not leaving you like this."

"Fair enough."

We emerge on the other side of the park and cross the street. I feel aimless. And I'm cold.

A single raindrop hits my forehead. I sigh and tuck myself under the nearest awning for cover. I peer through the floor-to-ceiling glass windows and exhale again. It's the video store, and Emily is inside once again, leaning on the counter across from Josh.

At the sound of the front doorbell, Emily turns around. Her eyes bug out in fear. Her mouth drops open to argue.

I hold up my hand. "Nope. I'm too tired to be upset. Help me find some movies."

She and Josh exchange wide-eyed glances. From the corner of my eye, I spot Lars giving them a reassuring thumbs-up.

I know how I look. My hair is damp from the sprinkling rain outside. My hands are shoved in my jacket pockets. I didn't sleep much last night either, so I probably look like a dead man crawling from the grave.

Emily scrambles away from the counter and down my aisle, sidestepping past Lars.

"Dad, you good?" For the first time since Halloween, my daughter doesn't look like she wants to lock me out of her room.

"I'm good," I say with a half smile.

It's not convincing because her eyebrows furrow together.

"What's wrong?"

"He's moping," Lars cuts in.

"That's eleven doughnuts now."

"Ah, come on."

I turn back to Emily. "I'm looking for some movies for while you kids are gone."

"Ugh," she groans.

I huff out an exhausted laugh and rub her back.

"Hurts me too, kiddo."

I turn the corner to a different aisle, bumping my fingertips over cases. I freeze in front of *Pretty in Pink*. My heart skips. It's the movie Allen didn't like Michelle to watch.

Such a stupid man.

I grab it.

Emily clicks her tongue behind me. "It's funny you're here actually. Me and Brittany were talking . . . and before we leave, we'd like a girls' night with Aunt Carol."

"Sounds fun," Lars says. He's trying his best to cover for my pessimism.

"That's fine," I say. "When have you ever asked for permission to do that?"

"Well, we wanna invite over Michelle and Sara too."

I freeze. Even her name is a blow to the chest. It shouldn't be. She's *Michelle*. My friend, my neighbor. *Michelle*.

Lars's face is pulled into a comical grimace. "Uh . . ."

I blow out air. "What are some good movies out right now?"

"Wait, what about the sleepover—"

"Go with *Braveheart*!" Josh calls from the counter through cupped hands.

"Huh." I poke out my bottom lip and murmur, "First good thing he's said."

Fig roll might have upgraded to something better. A Swiss roll maybe. More spongy.

My daughter stares at me, tucking her blond strands behind her ears.

"Are you actually dating again?" she asks. "Like, *really*, really?"

The day keeps getting worse. I didn't want to cross the dating bridge like this. I wanted to present the right woman at the right time—not be the dad who dates around.

"I'm gonna go over . . . yep." Lars shuffles into the next aisle over, leaving me with Emily's worried expression.

"They got to you too, huh?" I joke.

"Well, there was Sara last night, and now everyone is asking me if my dad is single. Which is *so* mortifying." Then she gives a sheepish shrug. "It probably sucks for you, too, though, huh?"

The corner of my mouth pulls up.

"It hasn't been fun," I admit. I hold up a tape and yell, "What do you think about *Twister*, Josh?"

"Fantastic, Cliff—"

Emily groans. "Since when are you two pals?"

I chuckle. "Josh and I are two peas in a pod. Didn't you get the memo?"

"So, is it true? Are you dating?"

"No."

"Okay, but don't you want to get back out there, Dad?"

"Why does everyone think I should do that?" I murmur under my breath. "Josh! *Independence Day*?"

"Dude, yes! The best movie last year for sure."

"That's the one, then," I muse, tapping it on top of the other movie.

I attempt to walk back to the counter, but Emily blocks my path.

"Em—"

"You've got a problem, Dad."

I raise my eyebrows. "I have a problem?"

"Yeah. You're the divorced dad who owns a bakery. That's your thing."

A laugh bubbles out of me. "How's that a problem?"

"Because I think you *like* the reputation of being the divorced guy. You hide behind it, so then you don't have to think about the possibility of dating again and being in love."

I blink at her. "What the hell are they teaching you in school nowadays?"

She slouches. "I don't like it when you mope."

"I'm not moping. Wait, did Carol tell you to say that? Or Lars?"

"I wouldn't mind if you dated Michelle."

My stomach drops. I know time has passed, but I always assumed Emily would feel betrayed, having another woman in the house who isn't Tracy. Brittany is too young to remember me and her mom as a unit. But Emily is sixteen; hell, at this point, she probably knows more about dating than I do.

I tilt up my chin. "Aren't you supposed to be mad at me?"

"Yeah," Emily agrees. "Gotta keep that up for another few days at a minimum."

"Makes total sense," I say through a half smile. I sigh. "And, yes, Michelle and Sara can come over for a girls' night. As long as we never talk about me dating ever again."

With a grin, Emily jerks out her hand. "Deal."

I shake it. "Pleasure doing business with you."

With a satisfied *hmph*, Emily strides away from me, leaving me in the drama section by myself to cope with this news of a sleepover with a woman I can't be with.

There's some irony in there somewhere.

Chapter 30

MICHELLE

Popcorn topples down from the couch cushion again, missing Sara's mouth by almost a foot.

"Okay, try one more time," she says, leaning on her knees.

Brittany rears back and tosses the kernel. Sara twists, it lands, and she raises her arms in victory. Carol, Emily, Brittany, and I clap and cheer.

I've never had a girls' night with anyone except my sister. Then again, I've never had many friends aside from Sara either. At least not close enough to be invited to pajama parties. I don't know what that says about me.

We're in the Burkes' living room under a makeshift fort of pillows and blankets. Bedsheets hang from the top of the couch, knotted to corners of kitchen chairs with hair ties and scrunchies and pinned behind the television, so the entire world is blocked out aside from us and *Rock-a-Doodle*. Snacks fill bowls, plates, and the ground.

"Miss Shell, can you braid my hair?" Brittany asks, squirming on a pillow.

"I'd love to." I sit on the couch as she straightens up on the floor below me.

A door outside our fort creaks open, and my spine stiffens the moment I hear it.

"How's it going in there?" Cliff's voice asks.

I haven't spoken to Cliff in nearly two days. Forty-eight hours of only seeing his daughters and waving from afar. But now his voice strikes a bolt through my nerves, and I'm stock-still.

"It's fun!" Brittany calls.

"So-so!" Emily answers sarcastically with a wide grin toward me. She's continuing to get her kicks messing with her dad.

"Terrible!" Carol adds.

"Good," Cliff says with a low chuckle. *His laugh* . . . "Don't have too much fun without me."

"Dad, are you going to the kitchen?" Emily calls.

"Yeah. What do you need?"

"Gummy worms."

"How many have you eaten?" he asks suspiciously.

All of us stare at the large bag with four remaining worms.

"None," she lies.

"Who cares?" Carol amends. "It's a girls' night!"

"Girls' night!" Emily adds through cupped hands.

"All right, all right," he says with a husky laugh. "Be back."

The moment his footfalls disappear, I feel like I can breathe again.

My fingers thread through Brittany's hair strand by strand, and when I finally look up, Sara is staring back at me with one gummy worm hanging between her lips.

She sucks it in and mouths, *Are you all right?*

I nod stiffly and return to braiding.

I'm not all right. I've been thinking about Cliff's words for two days now.

"Because I'm really confused about us and I'm trying to sort through it."

"Because you mean more to me than just a simple, confusing kiss."

We haven't talked about it like we said we would. The inn has been too busy, he's been trying to soak up as much time with his girls as possible before they leave for their mom's, and honestly, we've been avoiding each other.

I want to talk to him, but I don't know what I'd even say. I miss talking with him so much that it hurts. I miss our nights on the front porch. I miss racing down the inn steps together. I miss his sarcasm. I miss the way he challenges me.

My neck tingles again when I hear Cliff approaching. The curtain to our fort slides to the side, held by Cliff's big hands with trailing veins and defined knuckles and wrists. I miss those hands—touching my knee, my back, my hair. I hate that I miss those hands.

And then his head pokes in.

It's a weird thing, seeing someone you know so well but feeling like they're a stranger. He's only a few feet away, but it's so distant at the same time. My hands, tangled in Brittany's hair, suddenly feel clammy, like he's a popular boy in high school I have a crush on instead of Cliff Burke. My Cliff Burke.

"Having fun?" he asks.

Cliff pokes at Brittany's feet—so close to mine—and she giggles, nodding over and over.

"Em?"

Emily purses her lips. "We're having a good time."

"Good." He looks at Carol with a lopsided smile and waves to Sara.

I keep anticipating that he'll look at me. I'm buzzing with nerves. My knee bounces on the floor.

See me, see me, see me.

Finally, he does.

And our gazes *snag*.

They always do.

There isn't Brittany, Emily, Sara, or Carol. It's me, Cliff, and his blue eyes. Cliff and the little line in the corner of his mouth that deepens when he starts to smile. Cliff and the barely there bend in the bridge of his nose. Cliff and the small scar above his upper lip that I traced with my fingertips. Cliff and his tense jaw.

"Because I'm really confused about us . . ."

What do we say? Nothing. I'm leaving, and I don't know when I'll come back, and ultimately, it doesn't matter. He's got a life here. I've got a life elsewhere. We can't get close.

It makes me sad. It makes me upset. Angry with myself.

I like control over my own life, but somehow, I can't get my wits about me around Cliff. He's been the tornado barreling toward me since the day my taxi drove into town.

I want my life back. I want normalcy. And he's messing it all up.

"Dad!"

Cliff blinks, and so do I, my tunnel vision widening back to the pillow fort and my hands tightened in Brittany's hair, mid-braid.

Emily groans. "Can't you see we're *busy*?"

"Right, right, right," he says, shaking his head. "You girls have fun."

I expect him to steal one last glance at me. I'm desperate for it, but the curtain drops, and I'm left without him again.

I swallow and finish Brittany's braid.

"Hair tie?" I ask.

When none lands in my hand, I look up.

Emily, Carol, and Sara are staring at me.

"What?" I ask.

All three look away, saying, "Nothing," "Nope," and, "Not a thing."

"I wish Rocket were here," Brittany says in a low whine.

Emily's head jerks up. "You do?"

Brittany nods. "I miss him."

I stroke my fingers through the ends of her braid, undoing it to try again. "He misses you too."

Brittany gasps. "Did he tell you that?"

I tilt my head side to side. "In a way, yes." I keep braiding halfway down her neck. "Hey, how about when you get back, we have a whole playdate in the front yard?"

"It'll be cold."

"Then we'll wear jackets."

"Will Rocket be there?"

"Yes, and we'll find him a jacket too."

A steady smile rises onto Brittany's cheeks as she murmurs, "Okay."

"Hair tie?" I insist again.

This time, Sara tosses me one. I tie off Brittany's braid and pat her back. She, Carol, and Sara roll over to the nail polish station, leaving me to slide down the edge of the sofa to the pillowed floor. Emily sidles up next to me, leaning her head on my shoulder.

"I'm sorry he went on a date with your sister," Emily whispers.

My stomach curls. It was my fault. I told him to. I pushed it. I have nobody to blame but myself.

I force a smile. "Why?"

"Because."

I remember how hurt he looked the other morning, and it kills me to think I did that to him. I'm causing all of our problems, and it's so par for the course that I'm almost sickened. He doesn't deserve that.

"Hey, do me a favor?" I ask.

"Yeah?"

"Cut him some slack about Halloween."

Emily giggles. "I like to make him sweat. He thinks he's *all that*, so I've gotta set him straight."

I huff out a laugh. "Well, try not to make him *too* nervous, okay?"

"I promise." Then she nudges me. "And you too."

My heart hammers, but all I manage is a small "I'll try."

Chapter 31

CLIFF

Three days pass without Michelle. I'm exhausted. I miss her.

It doesn't help that tomorrow is Thanksgiving. I'll be at Bird & Breakfast, like I was last year, but this time, Michelle will be across from me, laughing and smiling and being beautiful. And tonight, she'll be staying under my roof.

Christ.

I'm not in the mood for celebrations this year. Thanksgiving can go gobble elsewhere for all I care, especially as I pull up to the bus station parking lot to send my two girls off to New York without me.

I attempt a smile as I pull the parking brake, looking over at Brittany's slumped shoulders and Emily's thin, straight lips. She pulls her headphones down around her neck as the Discman in her palm continues to spin.

"You girls ready?" I ask.

"Woo," Emily deadpans, pushing the stop button.

Brittany's big eyes peer up at me. "Do you think Rocket will forget me?"

I chuckle and run a palm over her head. "Of course he won't."

She nods to herself, hugging her stuffed unicorn closer to her chest.

I open the door and climb out, handing Emily her black duffel bag with key chains and patches and grabbing Brittany's sparkly pink rolling suitcase, almost blinding in the sun's reflection.

I roll their bags over the craggy concrete to the covered bus station with my free hand holding a small box of pastries for their trip. The bus is already here, humming and whining. The three of us ran behind this morning because we always do, and now I only get minutes with them. It feels unfair.

"Hugs," I command, and both girls barrel into my arms.

I sigh against them, gripping each of their sides closer to me. I reluctantly pull back once they do, twisting my lips to the side.

"You be good for Mom, okay?"

For the first time since Halloween, Emily hugs me again, leaning her head on my shoulder. Brittany looks like she's on the verge of tears, so I cup behind her head and pull her close.

"What if I don't want to go?" Brittany asks.

"You'll see the parade though." I grin down at her. "That's gonna be really cool."

"Sorry I've been mad at you," Emily murmurs. "I don't even remember why I was in the first place."

"Halloween," I clarify.

"Oh yeah. You suck."

I chuckle. "I know."

"Were you mad at me too?" she asks.

"No," I say sarcastically with half my mouth tilting in a grin. "I could never be mad at you."

Brittany giggles at the same time Emily does.

Emily punches me in the side. "I'll miss you, idiot."

"I know that too."

I look at my watch. Their bus is set to leave soon. They need to board. It doesn't feel like enough time.

"All right, here we go!"

They hold me tighter. I wrap my arms around them and hold them as close as I can until they're both laughing and pushing me off.

We say final goodbyes. I load both of their bags onto the bus, hand off the box with too many apple fritters and chocolate chip cookies, then walk down the stairs. They wave from the window.

"Say hey to big Garfield for me!" I call out.

Emily cups her palms around her mouth and yells back, "I'm gonna pop his balloon!"

"That's my girl!"

With Brittany's face mashed against the window, the bus rumbles away. I watch and wave until it's out of sight. I stand there for a minute in silence—the wind as my only companion—before strolling back to my truck. I casually lower my forehead against the steering wheel and let the monotone honk echo through the parking lot.

It's a weird sensation, sitting at a bus stop one day before Thanksgiving. There's a heavy knot tied in my gut, pulling tighter and tighter until it's painful.

They're gone.

I exit the car, slamming the door closed as I stride back to the bus depot. I dig in my pocket for coins and push a quarter into the pay phone. My fingers shakily mash over the small numbers, and then I hear the ring of the number I'm calling. Over and over as my heart pounds more and more.

Then the line clicks.

"Thanks for calling Bird & Breakfast. This is Michelle. How can I help you today?"

My heart rate slows. Her voice is soft. Warm. Comforting. It doesn't matter that we haven't spoken in days. I'm addicted to the sound, and I'm letting myself indulge.

"Michelle," I breathe.

"Cliff?"

"Hey."

"Are you okay?"

"Yeah." I push my head against the pay-phone box. "No. I . . . I dropped the girls off. I don't feel good."

And I needed to hear your voice, I don't say.

"Is everything okay? Are *they* okay?"

"Yes, sorry. Yes." I huff out a laugh. "They're on the bus. Didn't mean to worry you. I . . . I needed to talk. Sorry. This is—can you . . . distract me for a second?"

"Oh," is all she says.

It's quiet.

I sigh. "That was—"

"Dad's been greeting the guests this morning. He's really staying active. I think he's playing chess now with some guest. You can tell the man's family wants to leave the inn, but my dad's got him in a match he can't escape now."

The knot inside my stomach slowly unravels, like her words are gentle hands untying it herself.

I choke out a laugh. "Sounds like Paulie."

"And this morning, Lisa and George stopped by to help set up place mats and stuff for tomorrow. Lisa, of course, told me I needed more silverware. And then I told her that if she wanted more—because I have enough already—then she could bring some herself. But then *she* said they wouldn't match."

I chuckle again. "What a morning. Wish I could be there."

There's a long pause before she asks, "Why are you really calling, Cliff? What's going on?"

"The girls left, and . . . I'm not doing okay. And we haven't talked in days and . . ." *And I feel dumb for even bringing it up.* "I'm fine. Having trouble breathing a bit. I ran to the pay phone, so that's probably why."

"Why'd you run?"

To talk to you.

"I forgot something," I lie. I wonder if she can tell.

On her end of the line, I hear a door open and close. There's a distant clicking on linoleum—maybe Rocket— then a hiss of wind. She must have stepped outside.

"It's breezy here today," she says. "Smells kinda like fall, kinda like Christmas."

I breathe in, the smell of dank bus stop air like a swift, unwelcome kick to my senses.

"Smells like garbage here," I say through a laugh. "I think there's sewage nearby. Nothing to phone home about."

"Well . . . except you did."

I can picture the teasing at the edge of her lips. God, I can imagine how beautiful it is.

Home. I smile to myself even though she can't see me— *especially* because she can't see me.

I grin. "I guess I did, huh?"

Michelle sighs. "I'm sorry the girls left, Cliff."

I shuffle my feet against the concrete. "Yeah . . . thanks."

A silence passes between us, at first a little nice and comforting like before, but then it lasts too long, and Michelle makes a small, breathy noise, like she wants to speak but can't.

"So, I set up the bed for you," I finally say.

"Oh. Well, I won't be over until probably late," she says almost aimlessly. "Working, you know."

"Right. Well, I'll be in Emily's room if you need me."

I hike my shoulders up to my ears as a gust of wind blows by. I know my unease isn't from that though.

"Good," she says.

"Yeah. So, I'll . . . see you tonight, I guess."

"Good," she repeats. "Sounds like a plan. And thanks again, Cliff."

"Absolutely," I answer. "Uh, hey, I should let you go," I say. "Off the phone." I don't know why I felt the need to clarify, but the fact that I did stabs me hard.

"Sure," she agrees on a breath. "I'll see you at Thanksgiving tomorrow."

The implication of not seeing each other before then hangs in the air.

"Yeah. I'll see you then."

I hang up and groan in the empty parking lot.

She's stubborn. I guess so am I. But when you like someone—as a friend or more—you take the good with the bad, and I like Michelle *because* of her stubbornness and not in spite of it.

I have a feeling I'm the biggest sucker in the world.

∽

I stare up at the starry ceiling in Emily's bed. Leonardo DiCaprio stares back. I avert my eyes to the clock on the side table. It's one in the morning. I've been awake since Michelle came in at eleven, but I haven't moved an inch. Just me and Leo.

Inhaling, I throw back the covers and open the door. I need water. Air. Something.

I quietly take the stairs down to the kitchen, but when I reach the tiles, Michelle is already sitting at the nook, papers drawn out in front of her. Rocket lies at her feet.

I halt in the doorway. My entire body heats. She has her legs crossed at the knees, poised in a matching dark gray silk pajama set. Unwrinkled and pristine. Over her chest is the pendant necklace she now winds between her fingers. Her face is bare. Lashes aren't as long as usual. Her complexion is uneven. Lips are light pink. It's the first time I've seen her without makeup, but even without her armor, she's stunning.

Her eyes travel down to my chest and back up. I'm in my boxers, and I'm not wearing a shirt. My chest, covered in wisps of brown hair, is on full display.

"I didn't think you'd be up," I say stupidly.

"Working."

An empty coffee cup rests by her hand.

"I see."

"Sorry if I was making noise."

"You weren't. I like your pajamas."

She looks down at herself. Her chest flushes red. It always does when I compliment her. It's the best part.

"Do you want some crepes?" I ask.

The corner of her mouth rises. "You don't have to bake for me whenever you see me."

I chuckle. "My burden in life is to bake for everyone."

She eyes the stove, then me. "If you must."

"I must indeed."

I click on the stovetop as she goes back to her papers. The silence is weirdly uncomfortable—something that doesn't make sense for us—but it doesn't last long. I'm not capable of quiet.

"I'm sorry," I say. "For the other morning. Not talking about things."

"It's all right. I didn't talk either."

Then the kitchen is silent once more. I pull down a plate.

It gently clatters to the counter. Every cabinet is an echo as I find ingredients. The fridge is a loud whir.

I don't know what I expect from a midnight encounter with Michelle, but it's more than this. More than a silent one a.m. session of quietly making crepes while her pen scribbles over paper.

Rocket walks over, nudging his nose against my calf.

I tear off a piece of finished crepe and say, "Sit."

He drops down.

Well, look at that.

"Good boy."

I raise my eyebrows at Michelle. She manages a small smile before turning back to her work. That's all I get.

It takes me a total of twenty minutes to finish up. I slide the dish across the table to her and save none for myself.

"Weird baker thing?" she teases.

"Sure," I answer.

These won't be her favorite—I know her tastes well enough by now—but I remain shameless when she takes a bite. Yes, I'm absolutely tactless as I watch the fork disappear between her gorgeous, plush pink lips. A dab of honey is nestled in the corner of her mouth, and she easily licks it away.

God.

"These are great," she says.

"Good," I reply.

She stands to take her plate, but I rise with her, grabbing the opposite side.

"I've got it," I say.

Her eyes meet mine, and we freeze. Still as statues. Breathing in tandem. She's close. So close. I could be closer if I dared.

I swallow, pulling in a deep breath. The plate pushes

against her pajamas and my bare chest. I look down at her lips again, to the necklace resting in the divot of her collarbone, down to the gap in her pajamas with no bra and a peek of cleavage. My tongue flicks out to lick the corner of my lips, and I exhale.

When I look back up, her brown eyes—warm like the autumn leaves—flick between my eyes and my lips. They dip past my chin to my chest, to my checkered boxers, and back up to me. She chews on her bottom lip.

I want to say something. I always want to say something to her. But what is there to talk about now? We've gotten in this precarious situation with no real exit. She's going to leave Copper Run. I'll stay here. What is there to discuss?

I crane my neck closer. Her eyelashes start to flutter. I can feel her exhale on my chin. I want to reach out and place my thumb on her lips. I want to tilt her head back. I want to kiss her again.

It would be so easy . . .

But it's never going to be easy with us. To wish for that would be naive.

I take a step back. Her breath leaves so shakily that it sounds like it hurts.

I walk over to the sink, rinse off the plate, then deposit it in the dishwasher. When I turn back around, she's staring at me like a deer stuck in headlights.

"Good night, Michelle."

Her throat bobs in a swallow. "G'night, Cliff."

With all the strength I have, I cross the threshold out of the kitchen and go back through the dining room and upstairs again.

MICHELLE

I normally like Thanksgiving. Normally.

"You're a grinch," Sara says, waving a floppy piece of ham my way.

I bat it away.

"The Grinch doesn't like *Christmas*, Sara. Wrong holiday."

Dad chuckles from the corner of the kitchen, mixing gravy. "I bet he loves Thanksgiving actually. Because it's not Christmas."

"Or," Sara offers, dangling the ham piece down to Rocket, who jumps to snap it up, "he hates Thanksgiving because it's the last holiday before Christmas. He knows it's coming. It's like the day before school. Nobody likes the day before school."

My dad and I exchange a look, then both shrug.

"Good point, honey," he says with a twitching smile.

I didn't realize I'd missed these conversations with my family. It's been years since we've spent this much time together. I always spent holidays with Allen's family.

Thanksgiving was Mom's favorite holiday. There were turkey-themed plates and thick cotton napkins with little autumn leaves. A cornucopia sat in the middle of the dining room table, overflowing with fruit. And the turkey was *always* burned. I tried many times to make my own. Hours and hours. Years and years. But at a certain point, it was a beloved tradition to have terrible turkey.

Once I was married, my traditions with Allen became quiet Thanksgivings. Dishes with neat garnishes instead of hefty butter. Polite politics and no dessert. It's like I've taken steps back into childhood, like the last five years didn't exist.

Sara didn't make it out the last year either. She couldn't afford the plane ticket across the country. I wish we had now. Dad is smiling again. I wonder if having his daughters close is the thing he's most thankful for. Everything is different now, yet the same.

"This looks so good," Sara says, dipping her finger in the gravy.

At that moment, Lisa storms into the kitchen and shoos her away. Sara, Dad, and I aren't cooks. Lisa, however, is spearheading Thanksgiving almost as well as some project managers at my company. They should consider hiring her.

"Touch nothing, dear," Lisa snaps.

George pokes his head in, flashing my dad a raised eyebrow.

Dad stiffly nods in understanding. "How can we help?" he offers.

Smart man, my dad.

"Lars is bringing deviled eggs." Lisa crosses to the oven, pulling out a green bean casserole. "Carol is bringing potato salad. The girls . . . well, normally, Emily makes a boxed brownie recipe that Cliff hates," she says with a chuckle.

Cliff.

My palms shake every time I pass the back door. I know he'll be walking in at any moment, and after last night, I'm even more on edge than I should be. I can't endure another night at his house.

Even in the short time I've known Emily and Brittany, it feels wrong that the girls aren't here for a holiday. It's only been twenty-four hours since one of them ran through my kitchen and stole a banana or a cup of coffee, but I'm already missing the patter of little shoes and snapping of sneaker shoelaces.

"Who's bringing the burnt turkey?" Sara asks with a teasing grin.

"Burnt? Lord, no. Cliff is in charge of the turkey," Lisa says. "And last year, it was the best damn turkey I'd ever eaten. Even your mother didn't mind sacrificing tradition."

Leave it to Cliff to conquer the hardest item on the menu. And for my mom to accept it.

I take the last few dishes into the dining room. We installed the table's center leaf to gain extra room. With the inn guests joining and too many people in Copper Run, we needed as much space as we could get. It's already crowded and stuffy in the house, but everyone seems too distracted by the TV and Macy's Thanksgiving Day Parade to care.

"Oh my God, is that the Backstreet Boys?" Sara says, scrambling to the coffee table and clicking the remote.

The volume grows louder with sounds of the boy band singing. I smile to myself. It's windy in New York—more than usual—and everyone is bundled in coats and hats. But I know Brittany is jumping with joy to see them anyway.

"Hey now, look at that turkey!"

I turn at the sound of George's impressed voice. His arms are outstretched as he approaches the dining room threshold. Standing in the doorway with a tinfoil-covered pan is Cliff.

He looks so undeniably *Cliff*. His jaw is freshly shaven. His hair is a little more windswept, forcing small strands onto his forehead and the little hidden specks of gray along his temple to peep out. His heavy jacket is pulled over a yellow-and-orange sweater, and that ever-familiar grin pulls up one side of his mouth.

Lisa takes the turkey from him, and I stare as Cliff shucks off his coat. His broad baker's shoulders fill out the sweater so well. He pushes up the sleeves. His strong, veiny forearm leads down to his watch-covered wrist and long fingers with that faded burn on the back of his hand.

I finally look back up, and his blue eyes are already locked on mine. My feet won't budge, and my heart is only racing faster.

"Hey, Michelle," he says. It's stiff. Unfamiliar. His forced smile is even worse.

"How are the girls?"

"They called me this morning. Brittany was very excited about the parade." Cliff breaks our stare, looking beyond me at the TV. His smile fades.

More people filter in until, eventually, Cliff stands in the corner with Lars, hands tucked in his pockets as they discuss news or maybe the parade or something. I feel so small, so insignificant, being so far away from him.

Lisa claps her hands. "Everyone ready?"

There's a humming assent and additional claps.

"Shells, mind turning off the TV?" Dad asks.

I do, but I don't miss Cliff's face falling when it clicks off. I wonder if he was hoping to see his daughters. I almost turn it on again, but Sara steals the remote and pushes me toward the table. She pulls out a chair and sits me right next to Cliff.

He side-eyes me with a wry smile, shifting in his seat uncomfortably.

"Hey," I whisper.

"Hey." He smiles, but it doesn't reach his eyes. The fan of

wrinkles doesn't crease even a little. His words are cordial. Nice.

We dig into the food, passing around small dishes between conversation—though none between Cliff and me.

I'm quiet. I've always been quieter in crowds, but I watch Cliff carry on seamless discussions about sports or books because that's the man he is. I wish I were half as approachable.

I stare as his lips press against his water glass. I admire the bob in his throat when he swallows. He laughs at something someone said, and his casual smile shows slivers of his white teeth.

I inhale and exhale.

"Have you ever been to the parade? Shelly?"

I look up at the sound of Lars's voice. Half the table is staring at me. Heat travels from my chest up to my throat. There's no way my face isn't beet red. My dad has his fork half raised to his mouth.

"Oh," I answer. "No. I live in Seattle, not New York."

"And are you excited to go back to the city?" George interjects.

I hesitate, and I can't help but steal another look at Cliff. His jaw is set as he stares down at his forkful of mashed potatoes, as if waiting for my answer. But he won't look at me.

Irritation spreads through my chest and down to my fingers.

Why the hell won't he *look* at me?

I smile with pretend pride. "Yes," I answer. "Of course."

"Wow. It must be a great life there," Lars marvels.

"It is. I love it."

"You would never know it though," Sara chimes in. "She's a natural at running this place."

George raises his wineglass. "Hear, hear!"

I manage a weak, affirming laugh. But it drifts to nothing when Cliff also politely raises his glass.

My heart stops as he finally looks at me—finally gives me a smile, one that isn't entirely forced, but maybe sad—before drinking his water, then setting it back down.

And that's all the acknowledgment I get from him. Of course it is. Because I did what I always do. I tried to hold everyone in my life with a tight, ruling fist. I can do that at work—it's why I'm great at what I do. It's why I love it. But I can't control someone like Cliff. He's the least influenceable person in the world.

How could he, at any point, think I don't have feelings for him?

I have feelings.

Happiness.

Longing.

Frustration.

The tightness in my chest is so all-consuming that it feels like I'm getting shoved deeper and deeper into a six-foot grave I dug for myself.

Oh, I have feelings for him all right.

I have—

The next thought makes me freeze.

I think I might be in l—

The whole room shifts, and I'm a little dizzy. My fork clatters to my plate, and the lump in my throat is so heavy that I feel like I might choke.

Sara's hand touches my forearm. "Shells, you okay?" she whispers.

Beside me, Cliff's eyebrows tilt inward. His lips part. I jerk my eyes back to my plate with untouched cranberry sauce and potato salad.

"I'm fine," I murmur.

I grip my skirt in my fists as conversation passes in the blink of an eye. I don't know when lunch transforms to the late afternoon, but eventually, I rise from the table to put out dessert.

Apple crumble cake, chocolate-filled croissants, and pecan pie. Cinnamon rolls oozing with icing. Pumpkin cheesecake. Only one person could have baked all this.

I find Cliff staring as he crosses the living room with a cup of coffee in his hand. He laughs with my dad, then Lisa and George, and the guests. His blue eyes sparkle when he finds something extra funny, and the smile reaches the little crinkles beside his eyes. Other people laugh with him, like he's a battery of energy for everyone here.

I grit my teeth and curl my lips in. My chest tightens. My fists clench.

And all at once, I know it as clear as day.

I love him.

I love *him*.

Sarcastic, floppy-haired Clifford Burke.

I love the man I—*damn it*—set up with my *sister*. The man who told me he's sorting through his feelings for me, and I was too stubborn to address them. The man who called me in a panic when he lost his girls. The man who depended on me, who gave me a bed under his roof, even when we hadn't talked for days.

I love this man.

I pinch my eyes closed. And instead of feeling elated—I'm in *love*—I'm angry. I don't know if it's with myself or him. For making me fall in love with him so suddenly that I realize it on *Thanksgiving*, of all times. I figure out I love this stupid man when he packs away the remainder of the turkey into Tupperware containers and slides them into the inn's fridge, taking none for himself because, damn it, he's a good guy.

I'm in love with a *good guy*.

I'm seething in the corner as he hugs my dad and my sister goodbye. I grit my teeth when he walks over, tensing his jaw and reluctantly pulling me into a hug.

He's warm. He smells like baked bread and vanilla and cinnamon, but underneath all that is the citrus. The real Cliff I know. Me. Not anyone else.

I'm so angry that I could be split from the inside out, and when he lets go quicker than he did for anyone else, it only infuriates me more.

I stare as Cliff leaves through the back door. I watch with narrowed eyes as the chill from outside winds through the kitchen, sending goose bumps over my skin. I focus on the blinds as they snap shut on the glass when he closes the door.

I stand there for too long, focusing on the bare trees outside. The dead grass.

I should probably give Cliff space. Let him heal from my mistakes.

But I've never been that kind of woman.

So, I pass by Sara, rip open the back door without a jacket or a care, and storm my way through the setting sun, right over to Cliff's house.

Michelle

I don't knock on the door. I haven't knocked on Cliff's back door in more than a month, and I'm not starting now.

Cliff isn't in the kitchen, so I stride past the dining room and into the dark living room, where only a dim lamp illuminates Cliff reading on the couch. He twists around, eyes wide as he takes me in.

I stand there like a statue. Air whirs through vents. The house settles with a low creak. The couch cushions whine as he leans forward and sets his book down on the coffee table.

He checks his watch. That beautiful leather watch on his irritatingly gorgeous wrist.

"Why are you here already, Michelle?"

"I'm talking to you. Like we normally do. Like *friends* do."

He blinks. "Okay, and what are we talking about?"

"I'm irritated." I close my eyes. "I'm *so* irritated."

His head jerks back. "Irritated?"

"Yes."

"And why's that?"

"Because you're frustrating."

His eyebrows furrow, and guilt rolls through me.

"Don't look at me like that."

He scoffs out a disbelieving laugh. "Last I checked, you're the one here, picking a fight."

I pinch my eyes closed. "I wouldn't if you weren't so infuriating."

"You keep saying that, but you're not clarifying," he answers through a tense jaw.

"And now you're angry with me."

Cliff slowly stands from the couch, running his tongue over his teeth and shaking his head.

"Yeah," he confirms, blinking through thoughts again, as if trying to center himself in this new argument. "I guess I am now."

"Why?"

"What do you mean, *why*?"

"I'm mad at you. Why are you mad at me?"

He slaps his palms on his thighs and looks off to the side, toward nothing on the wall, before swiveling his eyes back to me. They're like two sharp points, locked on me.

"Because you come over with no introductions. No agenda, except to tell me my flaws." He huffs another laugh.

"Well"—I lick my lips—"you're irritating."

"I know I'm an irritating guy. You think I don't know that?" Now, he *is* getting frustrated. "I was told that for fourteen years. And, listen, I'm not changing anytime soon."

I don't want you to.

I fold my arms over my chest, and he squints at me.

"You're not saying something. What are you thinking?"

"Why did you go on a date with Sara?"

His mouth drops open, and he tongues his cheek. "I don't know."

"You didn't have to."

He pauses, then breathlessly says, "Excuse me?"

"I didn't like it."

"You . . . you . . . God, well, you know what? I didn't like it either. It was actually kinda shitty."

"Shitty?"

"Yeah, Michelle. It was really shitty. I felt like shit."

"You said you needed to get back out there."

"No," he counters, pointing a finger at me. "*You* said I needed to."

I grit my teeth. "And you agreed."

He blinks at me repeatedly. His mouth opens, then slams closed. His frustration is picking up now. He's adding fuel to my fire, and I'm thrumming with energy. I want to raise my voice. I want to argue with him. I have so many emotions; I'm boiling over with them.

"Seriously?" An arrogant grin pulls onto half his face. "What? Am I gonna *argue* with you? Do you know how impossible that is? It's impossible *now*, and I don't even know what we're arguing about." He exhales and holds up his palms, as if trying to calm himself down. "I shouldn't have said yes. That's my fault. Not yours."

No, I think. *It's me. I'm the one with problems.*

I keep circling it over and over. I did this to us. We were doing just fine until this. *He* was doing fine until I came along.

Cliff pinches the bridge of his nose and closes his eyes. "God, stop thinking for half a second, Michelle. I can never tell—"

"You don't need to. I don't owe you or anyone anything."

His eyes snap to mine, and he's speechless for a moment. "Fine."

"Fine," I answer.

But I don't move. I don't want to be done. I'm far from it.

"Well, then where do we go from here?" I ask.

"What do you want to happen now?" he asks me.

"No," I drawl. "No, stop being so accommodating. Stop asking me what I want. You're so—"

"What am I—"

"You're always—"

"Do you even—"

"This is so complicated!" I raise my voice above the jumble of a nothing argument I've created. "I want you to be happy and—"

His next words almost come out in a whisper. "Have you ever thought I might be happy with you?"

I tense, taking in a shaky breath. "You can't mean that."

"I almost wish I didn't."

"But you said—"

"I say so many things that I don't know what comes out of my mouth half the time," he says. "But you do . . . you make me happy. So, there. I'm stuck in my own damn head with thoughts of you that I can't get rid of. So, what do I do? Huh? What do I do?"

Suddenly, our fight is too real. I pushed him too far.

He lets out a slow exhale. His hands fall by his sides, defeated. "Come on, Michelle. Talk to me. Please." He sounds so desperate.

His head tilts to the side. His eyebrows turn in.

It's too much. It's all so much. I've *done* too much damage.

I *deserve* to be alone.

I turn on my heel to leave.

But in a stern crack of words, Cliff says, "Don't you dare walk away."

I freeze in place and turn around.

"I'm not letting you leave this discussion like that. Let's

talk through this. Stop overthinking what it is you have to say and say it." He's trying to stay collected, but the flush on his cheeks is betraying him.

"I'm done."

His blue eyes dart between mine. If I didn't know better, I'd think he'd forgotten where he was.

"You're done," he echoes.

"Yes."

He shakes his head. I start to turn again, but then he says in the most matter-of-fact way that it punches through my soul, "No, you're scared."

"Scared?" I ask with a sardonic laugh. "Of what?"

"You're lashing out at me because you're scared. That's why you came over. You're scared of being happy for one single second." He inhales, swallowing and staring at me with a pointed look. "And maybe you're even scared of . . . of falling in love again."

"Love?" I ask with wide eyes, but my heart is hammering. Because maybe he knows. He *knows*. And what do I do with that? What will happen if he knows? "You're one to talk."

"What?"

"You, Mr. Copper Run, with your relentless charm and selflessly helping with town events and making stupid, perfect turkeys. You want to be the dad who has it all together. But *you're* scared."

"Michelle—"

It's a warning. I don't heed it.

I stalk toward him. "Look at you. Some innocent baker who offers to help out the new innkeeper next door—"

His teeth grit together. "What are you doing?"

"The guy who invites her to dinner on her first day here and makes her spend time with him and . . . and . . . you think you're hilarious and"—my words start to choke out now—"you don't understand..."

"Michelle!"

"Sometimes, you're so irritating, and you make me crazy, and I can't believe I even came over here to tell you that maybe you don't even make me all that crazy at all."

It's silent. Eerily silent. The ticking clock on the wall. The whirring of the fridge from the kitchen. The house settling all around us.

"What the hell?" he finally breathes out, blinking at my finished outburst.

He looks at me like I'm damn near crazy. My fists are clenched, and the place behind my eyes burns, and I can feel my chin starting to shake.

"Tell me like it is, Cliff," I whisper out. "I'm a mess. I deserve to be alone."

"I'm not going to tell you—"

"Tell me I deserve to be alone," I snap, the words louder than I intended, bouncing off the walls of his serene house with photos of his daughters and this town and everything that shouldn't be tainted by me and my curses. "I know you think it. I know that's what's been going through your mind for weeks now. I know—"

His fists clench. "Stop saying that."

"But it's true."

"No," he says through gritted teeth. "It's not."

"Don't lie to me."

"I'm not."

"Tell me I deserve to—"

"Fine! You want me to?" He storms forward.

I take a step backward, my heart pounding.

"You really want me to, Michelle?"

A chill runs over the room. My yells, which once permeated the air, are lost to his closeness. To the intensity of his gaze. The way he flexes his hand beside him.

"Yes," I say, breathing heavy.

He's so close. His chest is almost touching mine.

"Please."

He grits his teeth. "Really?"

"Yes," I whisper, but it's more like a desperate whine. My whole body shakes.

I love him.

I love him so much.

Cliff takes another step. I suck in a breath. He exhales sharply through his nose.

And slowly, he clutches my jaw, traces a thumb over my lips, and murmurs, "God, you're so stubborn."

And then he presses his lips against mine.

It hurts, like I deserve. It's painful, like I need. And I'm melting into it faster than either of us can breathe.

Our mouths move in heady, rushed kisses. I clutch the fabric of his sweater, curling it into a fist and jerking him closer. He walks me back against the wall. His hand stops my head from bouncing against the picture frame before threading through my hair, bunching it up to my ears and tangling it around his palm.

I try to catch a breath, but it barely slips between our lips as I push against him and he pulls, as if we're fighting for something.

Then, finally, he murmurs against my lips, "I would never say you deserve to be alone. Because you don't. And I never want to hear you say that again."

I groan into his mouth, rising taller on my toes, gripping strands of his hair in my fists as I press my lips closer, harder.

"Do you hear me?" Another muffled kiss. "Never." He crowds me closer to the wall, pushing his hips against mine, gripping my waist. He kisses against my lips so hard that they might bruise.

Then he suddenly pulls away.

We both gasp, inhaling and exhaling, our chests heaving, desperate for air or each other—I can't tell. Our eyes search each other's. I can smell the cologne beneath him—the Cliff behind the mask he puts out for the world. My Cliff. All mine.

He leans his forehead on mine and stares directly into my eyes as he says, "God, I like you so much. I like you when you lash out. I like you when you come up with a thousand reasons to hate me." He cocks his head to the side. "And when you run to my house to tell me all those reasons. And even when you put up so many walls that even God can't break them down." He grabs my chin between his thumb and forefinger, his eyes razing me on the spot, blown out and wide and seeing me—always seeing me—right through to my core.

I open my mouth to speak. To say, *I love you. You can break my walls down.*

But then Cliff traces his thumb over my bottom lip and says, "I like you because you're Michelle. And that's enough."

Chapter 34

CLIFF

Her lips part as she stares at me like I'm a stranger.

"Why would you say that?" she whispers.

I might be offended if I were a lesser man.

"Why wouldn't I?"

I cup her cheek in my palm, and she leans into it.

The corner of her lips tilts up, and I return the lazy smile, bending down to press my lips against hers. I can feel her smile widening against my lips as she winds her arms up my shoulders to tie around my neck.

"I like you," I murmur against her mouth.

She moans into it.

My hands roam over the waist of her velvet dress, up her spine, over her shoulders, holding her closer—as close as she can get. I've touched Michelle in quiet ways for weeks, little bumps or strokes along her knee and forearm, but the freedom to touch wherever I like is like carrying heaven in my palms.

And to be touched by her—to have her slender hands trail up my neck and dip into my hair—is all-consuming. The gentle thumb strokes over my temples, the way her lips open for me to sink my tongue into, the little breathy moans when I glide my palms back to her ribs . . .

I walk us backward. The backs of my knees bump against the couch arm. I perch against it and tug her hips between my knees, my hand dipping down to palm the plump curve under her tight dress with my other resting behind her head.

I could kiss her forever. I could spend hours tasting her until our lips were sore. But I'd be lying if I said that's all I want. I want *her*.

I try to push off the couch—to carry her to my bedroom—but we only walk a couple of steps before she pushes me backward. I topple, off-balance, landing on the couch cushions with her standing over me.

I'm stunned, pressing into the cushions as I look up at the woman before me. She's so proper with her black tights and Mary Janes and that emerald dress, hugging her hips and hanging off her shoulders. She's a gorgeous city girl, dressed more for a New Year's party than being here in my living room with a quilt draped over the couch and photos of my family hanging on the walls. We're from entirely different worlds, but she's here. With me.

Michelle slowly climbs on top of me, straddling her knees on either side of my thighs. The skirt of her dress rises, exposing the outline of her thong beneath sheer tights.

I run my palms over her legs, gripping tighter, rippling the fabric against my fingers as my thumb finds the crease of her hip. I trace along the deep line between her legs and the hem of her underwear.

She cups the back of my head and presses her hips down, grinding against my strained zipper. My head falls back against the couch headrest, but I keep my eyes locked on her. I'm breathing so heavily. I slip my thumb under her skirt, touching the warm, pulsing area in the center of her, only separated from it by her sheer black tights.

Her lips part, a small breath leaving her as I rub my thumb in a circle. My other palm holds her hip, coaxing her to roll over the hard length of me again, and she gifts me with a near-imperceptible whine.

The corner of my lips quirks into a smile, and very subtly, so does hers.

She dips her finger into the loop of my belt, slipping it through its hold and tugging to unhook it. The rattle of the buckle echoes through the quiet room, clanging as she guides the leather through.

I've wanted this for so long. Maybe as long as I've known her—as far back as noticing the absence of that ring on her fourth finger. Or maybe the first time our eyes crashed together back in Seattle.

I manage a half laugh at the thought and shake my head.

"God, I'd like to rip your beautiful clothes off."

She gives me the most wicked grin. All for me.

"Would you?" she asks, half inquiry, half challenge.

"Would I?" I mock, bending up to kiss between her breasts, biting the velvet between my teeth and pulling the neckline of her dress lower.

I raise my eyebrows at her, peering up through my lashes. A breathy exhale leaves her. I place my thumb into the crease of her thighs, finding a taut section of the tights and tugging it toward me. It only takes a moment for the fabric to stretch, rip, and allow my finger through to the other side. She gasps.

"I would have double-checked whether you wanted to lose these, but . . ." My words trail off as I dip a few fingers into the new rip and tug, threads snapping and unstitching as the center of her tights is torn apart under my palm. "I'll buy you more."

Through the open rip is dark red satin. I murmur her name under my breath.

"Michelle, Michelle, Michelle . . ." I repeat low, as if I'm admonishing her for being so indiscreet.

My knuckles greedily trace along the lacy hem as she fiddles her fingers into the button of my jeans, sliding it through the slit, then tugging down my zipper. I'm practically busting through my boxers when she runs her beautifully painted nails over the outside of the fabric. They're a mossy green today, and I want to see them everywhere.

My body tenses when she slides her hand into the slit of my boxers. My breath catches. I've never slept with anyone except Tracy, and the fact that I'm nervous at all is so ridiculous. I let out an exasperated laugh.

As if reading my mind, Michelle whispers, "Cliff."

My head jerks up to meet her gaze.

Her stare feels like being dunked into warm water after so long in the cold. My nerves are almost shocked before melting, dissipating down my chest and to my hands. My palm winds up her neck and behind her head, burying my fingers in her hair.

I tuck my opposite thumb around the fabric of her underwear, tugging it to the side and tracing my middle finger along the outside of her. She's warm. So wet already, practically dripping down my knuckles.

It's been so long since I've made a woman come. I want it so bad that I can taste it. I want *Michelle* so bad that it hurts. I slowly curl two fingers inside her as her head falls back. The column of her neck is gorgeous against the dim light. A silhouette of beauty in the palm of my hand.

I pump my fingers inside, searching for every exhale, every

tense movement, every piece of her she'll allow me. And she grants me so many.

Her throat bobs in a swallow. Her knees on either side of me shake. She lifts up and lowers down, grinding on my fingers, pushing down as I pulse in. I twist my thumb to trace over the outside of her, and she bucks against it, pulling her lower lip in.

She's so close. I can feel her tightening, and, God, I want to watch. She's quiet, whining through it all. Too quiet, but that's a problem for later. With a hitched breath, her thighs tense around me, her palm grips my shoulder, and I can see her eyebrows pinch in the middle as her mouth opens as she releases.

Her chest is rising and falling. Her mouth, open wide and exhaling. When her eyes meet mine, I try to exist with her, stuck in space with her. Floating in her orgasm as long as she needs.

Steadily, shakily, she reaches out to pull down my boxers, releasing my already weeping cock to bob against my thigh. I scoot up the couch. She rises onto her knees again, tremors running through each movement. I grip myself and position the tip directly against her, rubbing a line over her smooth center.

It's sensuous. It's hesitant.

"I haven't been with anyone since Allen," she says quietly.

My eyes shift up as a heavy breath leaves me. Our gazes catch.

"I've only been with Trace."

"Then don't do something you think you'll regret," she whispers.

I shake my head with a crooked grin. "Oh, I wouldn't regret this, Michelle."

Her beautiful lips tip into a smile. "Me neither."

On a single synchronous inhale, I sink into her.

It's hard to explain the way my body tightens under her, how the rush of sensitivity tickles over my cock as she slides over me. It's hard to explain how perfect we are together. She can't take all of me at first, but it is so sweet as I watch myself slowly disappear inch by inch with each gradual thrust.

Her hands hold my biceps as our hips finally touch. I reach up to trace my thumb over her jaw. I can't help but admire her. And for some reason I don't deserve, she's looking down at me in the same way, trailing her palms over my neck and down to my chest.

Then we move. It's slow at first. She's pushing up on her knees, and I'm gripping her waist, slowly pumping up into her. But it's also automatic, like we're practiced. Like we've been doing this together for so long already. Maybe in a way, we have. I know she likes it when I touch her neck. She knows I like it when she strokes my arm. We haven't been this sexually intimate, but, God, don't we know each other just as personally?

We work into a rhythm. I hold her hips. She uses my chest as leverage. And I'm watching her fall onto me over and over.

I run my palms up her spine, around her ribs, over her stomach. In the area between her breasts, the arch of her shoulders, stroking my fingertips in the dip of her collarbone. I can't get enough of her. I want to touch every curve of her body, hear every glorious sigh, and taste the amber perfume on her neck.

She bounces up and down. I grip her jaw between my hands and pull her down to kiss me again. She bites my bottom lip, and I groan against her, sliding down her sleeve and bra strap and tugging at the neckline until her breast is exposed, at mouth level so that I can break our kiss and take her nipple into my mouth. She sighs above me. Her breath catches if I run my tongue over it. It's a whine if I nip it.

I roll my thumb at the area above where our hips meet, finding the one spot that has her breath instantly hitching. She's so quiet. I don't want that.

"Moan for me," I command.

She blinks down at me. "Wh-what?"

"I want to hear you."

"Why?"

I chuckle. "Because you're stunning when you sigh. And I want to know those sweet noises are for me." I hold her shoulder and pull her hips down to meet mine again. "So, moan for me."

She's quiet for a moment before whispering, "Nobody's ever talked to me like this."

Allen really was a sad excuse for a man, wasn't he?

I grin. "Well, I am. Now, let me hear you."

Slowly, hesitantly, she lets out a low, heady sigh.

"That's right," I say, the need rumbling in me.

The next one is more daring. Less of a sigh. More of a gasp.

"Just like that. There we go."

My name leaves her lips on an exhale, and, God, my body tightens beneath her.

I thrust harder, groaning out a throaty, "Love it when you say my name."

"Keep talking," she sighs.

"You like it when I talk?"

"Yes."

"God, you're so wet for me."

"Cliff, please—"

"And you beg so good."

Her head lolls back with a loud huff of air. I praise it with a bite on her shoulder.

With every noise, every additional thrust and slap of my body against hers, the tension in my stomach gets tighter. She takes control, pushing against my chest, grinding faster. My legs start to shake. I can feel my own pleasure building. And even though my mind is practically buzzing and I can almost see spots in my vision, I move to pull out. But Michelle tightens her knees around my thighs.

"I'm on birth control," she breathes sharply.

And, God, the smile that explodes over my face must be wild because her matching grin is so fucking *seductive*.

"Lucky me."

We both laugh, and I'm not sure I've ever had fun during sex like this, but I'm tied up in knots over her.

I roll my tongue over her nipple, pushing my thumb against the apex of her thighs. She exhales, and the sound is so sweet, so precious, that I'm moving faster. Rubbing small circles, burying my other palm in her hair . . .

Her head falls back. I tip it forward again.

"Look at me," I demand.

Our gazes snap together. I watch her lips part, her eyebrows scrunch together, and I breathe in to savor every gorgeous piece of her crumbling apart in front of me.

I think she might moan out, "I'm close again," but I'm not sure because the tail of it comes out in a whimper as she suddenly tightens around me and releases.

I've never orgasmed at the same time as someone else before, but now, as her hair cascades like a curtain around us, my orgasm floods over me like a tidal wave, sending my head rolling back on the couch headrest as I jerk into her, releasing every ounce of me with a low groan.

I might say her name. I might mumble something about how gorgeous she is. I don't know what nonsense leaves my mouth, but I know that, one moment, I'm seeing stars, and the next, her bubbled-up laughter is tickling against my neck as she places kiss after kiss along my collarbone.

She rests her chin on my chest, smiling up at me like I've never seen Michelle smile before.

I tuck a strand of hair behind her ear.

"Hey," I whisper.

I cup her cheek, and she leans into my palm.

"Hey," she echoes.

"You are . . ." I start, but the words fade off. I press my lips to her forehead and murmur, "Spectacular."

Her face, already flushed with pink, deepens to a red. I run a thumb over the color with a smile.

And it hits me.

I love this woman.

I don't know when it happened. It slipped over me so softly, like the changing of seasons. The seeping scent of baked bread first thing in the morning. A wistful sigh on a perfect fall day.

I love Michelle. I've loved her for far too long.

She's complicated. Difficult sometimes. She tastes like caramelized sugar and cinnamon and all the layers of flavors in between.

And suddenly, I know exactly what that is. She could never be something as simple as croissants or muffins or even cinnamon rolls. She's something else entirely.

Michelle places her cheek against mine and nibbles my earlobe.

I chuckle, running my palms over her spine and up to her shoulders. "Careful there."

But Michelle leans back and raises her eyebrows in challenge.

"Will you talk to me again?" she asks.

I laugh. "You really liked that, huh?"

She nods.

I bite the inside of my cheek and shake my head, grinning from ear to ear. "You're playing with fire, woman."

Her hand slips over my chest, trailing back down between us. A wicked smile tips at the edge of her lips.

"Fine," I say with a grin. "Have it your way."

December 1997

MICHELLE

"What's with the Santa suit and no Santa?" I ask.

We stand on the sidewalk, looking out at Winston's winter wonderland yard, where every patch of snow-covered grass is crowded with either a candy cane, snowman, or light-up reindeer. A loose red suit hangs from the roof.

"The myth is that he magically popped away when a kid saw him," Cliff explains.

"And he left his clothes?"

"Yeah," Cliff says, tilting his head to the side curiously. "Winston's Santa is a weird guy."

I cock my head to the side as well, then peer over at Cliff. He smiles, reaching out, dusting snow from my hair. But the fuzz from his mitten only separates strands of hair more. I give a pursed smile. He huffs out a defeated laugh.

"Oh, hush," he says.

"I didn't say anything."

"You didn't have to," he teases, lowering his arm to brush his fingers against my sleeve.

I press into the touch, letting it linger for longer than a normal touch should.

It's been one week of this. Hand-holding. Stolen touches. Exchanged laughs and constant smiling. If I think about it too long, my nerves kick into my throat. It feels so real. Too real.

With Allen, it was all serious conversations and work. I think I craved the adult feeling of being wanted and respected. But with Cliff, it's . . . easy. It's respect, accented with adoration. It's flannels instead of suits. It's not going to fancy parties; it's playing in the snow.

"Are you two coming?" Emily asks.

She stands across the street, squinting and hunched with her gloves tucked in her denim jacket, as if she can scare off the flakes by appearing disgruntled enough.

Josh, on the other hand, rolls up a snowball on the ground, beaming up at her. "Hey, Em! Look! A snowman!"

Brittany and Rocket—reunited after Thanksgiving with a giggle and a bark, respectively—dart through Luke's yard, leaving prints in the fresh snowfall. He runs after them.

"Let's snowball fight!" Luke yells, already balling up snow in his mittens, aimed toward Brittany.

Cliff and I exchange glances.

"Nah, let's go inside," he says. "I've got peppermint brownies to make."

"Yes!" Emily yells, pumping the air with her fist and tugging on Josh's coat to coax him to his feet. "I haven't had those in forever!"

"All right, all right," Cliff says, crunching across the street. He pulls her in for a side hug that she squirms against. "Stop yelling. Somebody'll think I don't feed you or something."

"You do?" Emily asks.

Cliff rolls his eyes and smiles. "Hardy har."

I walk through the snow behind him. The snowplow hasn't come through yet, so the streets are piled high with fluff. I'm not used to seeing this type of snowfall. In Seattle, the plows are practically on the roads before the meteorologist even says there *will* be snow. But here, there's some time for it to settle—for it to really *feel* like winter.

Rocket runs past, leaping snout-first into a snow pile, sending Brittany into a fit of giggles. His head pops up in an explosion of flakes.

Shelly, this is the best.

"Dinner?" Emily asks impatiently, already halfway down the street, hand in hand with Josh.

"Coming!" I call.

"Not yet," Cliff says, murmuring the innuendo under his breath.

I whirl to find one side of his mouth crooked up and his wicked eyebrows raised.

Friendship with Cliff Burke was fun. Friendship with benefits is even better.

Allen liked the lights off and silence. Cliff likes talking. He likes praising. He likes roaming his eyes all over me in the dim lamplight, sliding his palms over every inch of my body. He likes flirting.

We trail down the street, parting ways with the girls in Bird & Breakfast's driveway. Emily, Brittany, and Rocket dart between the bushes to their house as Cliff walks me to the inn's back door. Once the girls finish knocking snow off their boots and disappear inside, he immediately walks me backward until I'm caged against the inn walls by his palms. He leans down for a slow kiss.

I'm so accustomed to his lips now, to the gentle way they trail over mine, to the way his hand threads through my hair. I thought Cliff liked touch before, but now it's like he can't get enough of me. Like he was a man starved and he can finally feast.

We haven't told the girls about us yet. We agreed that it would be too difficult to explain, simply because we don't understand the situation ourselves.

I'm here until after Christmas, and then . . . well . . .

My natural inclination is to have a plan, but Cliff says we'll make one when we cross that bridge. Normally, I'd fight him on it, but the alternative is to face the inevitable. The lonely plane ride out of Vermont. So, for now, I enjoy the brush of his winter gloves running over my hips and try to ignore my thoughts.

"Save me some brownies," I say against his lips. "Or some pie if you have some."

He hums against me, kissing me again and murmuring, "I'll bake anything you want."

I laugh, placing a final kiss and pulling apart. "What happened to the weird baker thing? Watching me while I eat."

"Oh, I figured that out."

"Did you? So, you don't want to watch me eat anymore?"

He chuckles, leaning down to bite my earlobe, pressing a gloved hand against my pelvis. "I'd rather you watch me eat."

I can't help but stammer out through bubbling laughter, "Cliff . . ."

"Is that a yes?"

I lightly push him away, pointing an accusatory finger. "Down, boy. I'll be over in ten. I wanna finish some paperwork real fast."

His glove winds up my waist to finally stroke over my cheek.

"All right," he concedes. "Go do your job before I do unspeakable things to you in the snow."

My heart zips at the thought, but I force myself to turn

and leave. When I do, he grabs the crook of my arm and pulls me back into his chest for another kiss. I sink into it for a moment, then push him back.

"What happened to me doing my job?" I tease.

He shrugs. "You look too good in those jeans. I'm a simple man."

I shake my head through laughter—laughter that feels so natural now—and finally open the back door. His boots crunch away in the snow, and before the door shuts, I look behind me. He looks over his shoulder at the same time, and my body thrums with excitement.

I bite back a smile and close the back door.

Strolling to the front desk, I sift through recent reservations. We've been busy lately. In fact, we have a wait list for bookings, which, according to Dad, has never happened. He told me over the phone that, while Mom had the hospitality part down, they could never quite figure out advertising. They depended on word of mouth. I changed that for Bird & Breakfast.

Newspaper ads work, sure. And there's the internet—a new frontier for search advertising I'm steadily grasping as each day passes. But the biggest advantage was my tiny connection at a small northeast travel magazine. We somehow made the December issue. It was a short paragraph about cozy Vermont small towns, but sometimes, the smallest things have the biggest impact. The phone has been ringing steadily since.

It's a good time for Bird & Breakfast. And I did it.

I expected maybe someone would call from my office to congratulate me. But they're out west. I suppose the article wouldn't have reached them. Or maybe they wouldn't have called regardless. Weirdly, I find I don't care.

People sift in and out of the bed-and-breakfast over the

next few minutes. It's a revolving door of Copper Run residents and inn guests. With the snow outside, people are walking instead of driving. Playing instead of working.

Lisa pops in while passing by, to say hello. I give her a to-go cup of coffee and a newspaper before she goes back out.

Sandra drops off a new bouquet of flowers for the foyer table. She said she noticed them wilting on the way to work. I reach in my pocket to pull out cash for her troubles, but she waves me off.

"On the house, Michelle."

The guest in the bay window flicks through the local Copper Run newspaper. Listed on the front page are the winners of the Thanksgiving potluck, an announcement for the Snow and Sips Festival mid-month, and weather reports that read we should expect more snow for the following week—more for this idyllic snow globe.

I sort through the small stack of mail in the corner of the desk, but the addresses bleed together. They're no longer addressed to Birdie; most are written to me. They're Christmas cards from guests that I slide in the space beside Mom's black binder and the reservation log.

I haven't looked at the binder in weeks. I haven't had to because this place runs like a well-oiled machine. And there's one thing in particular I haven't looked at.

Dear Sara.

At this point, do I want to know what Mom wrote? Does it matter? This place is alive—thriving—and I'll politely pass it on to my sister, as planned. Mom's wishes will be fulfilled. What else do I need to know from a letter that isn't addressed to me?

The desk phone blares with a ring, ripping me out of my thoughts. I pick it up.

"Thanks for calling Bird & Breakfast. This is Michelle. How can I help you today?"

There's a quiet pause, followed by a gasp. "Michelle?"

"Hi. Hello. This is she."

"Hi." The voice is breathless. "Wow, this is Cheryl. I'm from Topsy's Travel Agency."

My eyes widen, and my heart leaps into my throat. "Oh, hi, Cheryl. It's so lovely to hear from you."

Topsy. My best client. The client that—hopefully—Mark hasn't completely upended. Their paperwork has been scattered over my counters and desk for months, but here they are, calling me.

"Hi," Cheryl repeats on an almost-exhausted sigh. "Oh gosh, I'm so happy we found this number."

"How are you?" I ask. "I hope Mark is treating you well."

"Heh," she says on an uncomfortable laugh. "Well . . ."

"That's not something I love to hear," I answer with an equally nervous laugh.

"That's actually why I'm calling," she says. "We are . . . not very satisfied with your company."

"Oh?" My stomach drops—absolutely plummets to the inn's carpet.

Shit. Shit. Damn it, Mark.

I knew this would happen. I left my best client to Mr. Thirteen Handicap, and he's better at driving business into the ground than driving a ball across the course. Now I'm here to clean up his mess.

I quickly stumble out, "I'm happy to help clarify anything or—"

"Well, we were actually wondering if you'd like to work with us. We're creating a position for an in-house advertising manager. If you're interested."

If my heart wasn't already on the ground, it'd be burrowing beneath, swallowed up in molten lava. I can't catch my breath.

They want me?

"Michelle?" she asks on a laugh.

"I'm sorry." I blink, and a near giggle bubbles out of me. "But, Cheryl, are you attempting to *steal* me?"

She lets out the most delightful laugh.

"It's fun when you put it like that," she says.

"It sure is," I agree. My fingers fidget with my earring. "I mean, wow. This is . . . well, of course I'd love to discuss this further. Please send any information you have over. I can give you the inn's fax number."

I tap my pen on the blank pad of paper, glancing out at the snow falling in thick, fluffy flakes. A guest walks down the stairs next to his wife. He opens the door for her, and they both wave their mittens in my direction. An easy smile slides onto my face as I wave back.

"That's fantastic to hear, Michelle. Well, listen, we'll send over what we have, and if it's not too last minute, we'd actually like to fly you out right after Christmas for an interview. Formalities, you know."

My stomach curls in on itself, tightening in a coil, like metal squeaking over metal.

"Oh."

"That won't be a problem, will it?" she asks.

That's four fewer days in Copper Run. Four days without Cliff.

But this is *my dream*.

Isn't it?

Starting a new advertising department. My *own* department.

"No," I say quickly, shaking my head to get through the fog. "No. Gosh, no, it's not a problem at all."

"Fantastic. Well then, I'll fax you—wait, what's the fax number?—anyway, once I have that, I'll send a packet with some information. Nothing official, some things to look over. There's a number on there, too, for our internal booking. They'll get you set up with a plane ticket."

"Thank you," I say.

"Mm-hmm. And, hey, welcome aboard. Hopefully?"

We share laughs, but the moment I put down the phone, I'm overwhelmed.

This is unreal.

But something—*something, something*—shimmers down my spine in a sudden pool of unease.

This is perfect. So . . . why doesn't it feel as good as it should?

I hold my hand to my uneasy stomach.

This is good. This is fantastic. This is . . .

I tuck the rest of my paperwork into the desk, grab my mom's purse from the hook, and head back out and over to Cliff's. The chill outside bites, and the wind hissing over my cheeks is too loud, but I push through the back door of Cliff's house at a run.

Boots and jackets are piled near the kitchen table on soaked towels. The air is warm from the oven. The kitchen is coated in smells of melted butter and jam. On the stovetop, some type of berry compote bubbles. The girls laugh in the living room. The *Rugrats* theme plays from the TV. Rocket taps into the kitchen with a wagging tail, his tongue lolling out from the corner of his teeth.

Cliff comes around the corner behind Rocket, laughing that beautiful laugh of his as he straddles over Rocket to pass by. He's already changed from the swishing windbreaker coat to his white cable-knit sweater. But the moment he sees me, his brow furrows.

"Everything okay?"

I don't know how to answer. There's no easy way to.

"Yeah," I say breathlessly. "I . . . I got a call from the travel agency. That top client, you know?"

"Oh," he says. And then, as if it dawns on him, he echoes, "*Oh.*"

"They . . . they want me. They offered me a job. There. Building their advertising from scratch."

"Oh!"

His eyebrows rise to his hairline, and he grins from ear to ear. He strides forward, pulling me into his chest, stroking a palm through my hair. He kisses my forehead, and I close my eyes as it lingers before he pulls back, ducking to look into my eyes.

"That's great. Congratulations."

He's so supportive. So overjoyed for me.

I swallow, leaning forward to bury my nose in his neck. He holds me tighter.

"It's great," he says. "You deserve every bit of success you get."

I let Cliff be optimistic. I let him be happy—feeling emotions for the both of us . . . because I'm not sure how to feel at all.

Chapter 36

CLIFF

After two weeks, the girls are out of school for holiday break. By the time I get home from the bakery every afternoon, stuffed animals are strewn all over the living room, the TV is blaring, and bits of snack crumbs litter the coffee table. But the house is always empty.

I drop off my wallet and keys and cross over to Bird & Breakfast, where the real party is. Brittany sits at the breakfast nook with a Christmas coloring book. Lisa is across from her with markers of her own. Rocket lies on the floor at their feet. I grab his leash and click my tongue. The inn is full these days, and Michelle is always busy, so I imagine he hasn't been walked in a few hours.

Rocket trots to me in good spirits. I scratch behind his ear. A month ago, he might have turned the other cheek, but he leans into my palm now.

I can even say, "Stay," and he'll halt as I clip him into his leash.

After a chilly walk around the block, I give him a treat and start the coffeepot before beginning the search for my busy woman.

I pass under the collection of Thomas Kinkade holiday

cards hanging along the kitchen doorjamb, walking down the hall and back toward Michelle's bedroom. Emily flips through a *Seventeen* magazine on her bed, where Michelle notably isn't. She lies on her stomach, her feet kicked up in the air. A music video for Chumbawamba's "Tubthumping" plays on the TV.

"Where's Michelle?" I ask.

Emily shrugs, mumbling, "She's fixing a room, I think."

"Thanks." I turn to leave but grab the doorway and pull myself back in. "Wait, where's Josh?"

Emily's back stiffens, her feet kicking a bit harder. "Working."

"And you're not sitting on his counter?"

"We don't have to be tied at the hip," she shoots back to me.

I raise my hands. "Singing a different tune than two months ago, but, hey, not my business." I rap my knuckles on the doorway, taking one last look at the TV. "Have fun burning your eyes out."

"Whatever."

I lift my eyebrows and chuckle. "What's with the attitude?"

Emily's been crankier lately, especially with mentions of Josh. I was starting to like the guy too. He gave me a Billy Joel CD as an early Christmas gift, and I can't fault a Billy fan.

"Nothing," she murmurs, nonchalantly adding, "I'm just PMSing, I guess."

"Need anything? I can go on a tampon run."

For some reason, that has her slumping more. "No. Thanks," she mumbles.

Emily doesn't normally get embarrassed about that stuff around me, but it's been the season for changes with her, so I'm not gonna question it.

"All right, kiddo. Well, cheer up."

"Thanks, Dad."

I cross through the foyer and ascend the stairwell to the second floor.

"Marco!" I call.

I hear Michelle's airy laugh from a room down the hall. I grin, following the sound to the last room on the right. Michelle is halfway in the closet, hanging up a new robe and wiping out the wrinkles with her palms. I knock on the threshold.

"Marco?" I ask again.

"Polo," she answers.

I walk through, kicking the door closed behind me. I cross the room, wrap my arms around her waist from behind, and bury myself in the crook of her neck. This is the highlight of every afternoon. The new ability to touch Michelle whenever I want—as long as it's in private, away from prying eyes—is my new obsession.

I place kiss after kiss up the column of her throat. I can feel her pulse against my lips. She smells like amber and sugar. My favorite smells.

"Hey."

"Hi." I can't see her face, but it sounds like she's smiling.

I purse my lips behind her ear and murmur, "How was your day?"

"Busy," she says on a breath.

"Busy how?"

"Lots of check-ins. The days feel like they're blurring together." She exhales and adjusts the hanger that doesn't need adjusting before dropping her hands to her sides.

She looks a little exhausted. I don't blame her. It's too soon before she moves back to Seattle. Every day feels like the sands of time slipping through my fingers, and I can't catch it fast enough. After Thanksgiving, our situation has felt both better and worse. Better because we're together. Worse because we've made our situation impossible to win. We were friends, parting ways one month ago, and now she's a woman I love, leaving Copper Run. Again.

"They'll blur together, and the next thing you know, you'll be working your *new*, fancy executive job."

She rolls her head to the opposite shoulder.

"I'll be happy to no longer be working two jobs."

I scoff. "No, you won't. You love it."

She laughs and nods to herself.

I kiss her neck. "You workaholic, you."

Honestly, I'm terrified of what will happen after the holidays when this woman moves across the country, back to her old life. But I'm not here to make it worse than it already is. Michelle worked hard to be where she's at in Seattle. And I'm just some baker from a small town in Vermont.

She twists in my arms, turning around to wrap her hands behind my neck. She opens her mouth to say something, then closes it.

She's the loudest thinker I've ever met.

Michelle smiles, but it's a little weaker than I want. She feels bad for leaving, and I simply cannot have that.

I tilt her chin up, and her head lolls to the side. She has that defiant look about her. I kiss it away.

"We're gonna make it work, okay?"

"How?"

"Hmm," I muse, pulling her closer. "Well, because you're a wonderful, stubborn woman, and I'm the kind of man who will pay *astronomical* phone bills to reach you." I grin down at her. "So, how can I help?"

"With what?"

"Anything. To make you a little less stressed."

She snorts. "Coffee?"

"It's already brewing."

"Well . . . Rocket hasn't been out."

"Just finished doing that too."

Her head jerks back, and a slow grin spreads across her face. "You did all that?"

I shrug. "Yeah."

"Why are you so irritating?"

"Gonna be honest—not the reaction I expected."

She chews her bottom lip and shakes her head. "You are. You're . . ." She lightly beats a fist against my chest and sighs.

I stroke her back. "Well, since I'm irritating already, I can irritate you in some more fun ways."

The little crease in the center of her brow slowly relaxes, and a small twitch at the edge of her lips appears instead.

She holds back laughter. "You're ridiculous."

I lean down, my words shifting the small strands of hair hanging in her face as I whisper, "Would you like me to irritate you, Michelle?"

"Cliff . . ." she says, the word fading off.

It's as if she's debating this, but I know she's already made up her mind. I can tell in the way her heart rate picks up. How her fingers stroke along the back of my neck.

I tuck a piece of hair behind her ear. My hand slides from her back, over her ribs, and over the outside of her shirt. The satin fabric is thin. When I ghost the back of my fingers over her, her nipples harden underneath. I pinch one between my index and middle finger knuckles. Her hand snakes down my stomach to the bulge straining against my zipper.

I kiss behind her ear, using my other hand to dip into her hair, exhaling out, "You're so beautiful."

Her hand cups the outside of my jeans, and I hiss in a breath.

She strokes slow movements with her palm. "Keep talking."

It's funny; I've always been a talker in the bedroom. I can't help myself. But this is new for Michelle, and now it's all she wants. I'm not complaining.

I run a thumb over her jawline, burying my nose in her hair, and murmur into her ear, "What do you want me to do? Want me to touch you here?" I slide my hand down to her jeans, tucking the top button through its hole. I pull the zipper, the hiss of it a harsh sound in the room's silence. "Want me to taste here?" I trail my fingers below the hem of her underwear.

She's slick between my fingers, and suddenly, I'm hard as a rock.

She nods against my shoulder, lowering her chin into the dip of my collarbone. "Please," she whines.

"I love it when you beg," I groan. "I love—"

There's a knock at the door, and both our heads swing back.

"Michelle?" It's Emily.

Shit.

My erection is dead immediately. Michelle zips up her pants, buttoning them back up. My eyebrows rise in question. Emily can't know I'm in here. We've been trying to keep our relationship a secret from my girls, especially while we try to figure it out for ourselves. There's no point in breaking their hearts too.

I look around, but Michelle pushes me against the wall beside the door and out of sight. She slaps her palm over my mouth before cracking the door open enough to see Emily.

"Hi. Sorry. Cleaning up," Michelle says. "The guest left, and . . . well, I don't want to get into it."

"Ew," Emily says with a sneer, and I can picture the little scrunch in her nose. "Something gross?"

"Yeah," Michelle answers, letting the word drag.

I twist against Michelle's palm to look at her. I kinda like her hand over my lips. I open my mouth against her palm, tracing a small line with my tongue between the crease of two fingers. She grips my mouth harder.

"It might be ten more minutes or so," Michelle tells her.

I gently nip her finger between my teeth.

"Twenty," she corrects.

"Oh. Okay." Emily's words fade out.

Instantly, my dad alarms blare at Emily's sullen, disappointed tone. I tense. So does Michelle.

"Why?" Michelle asks. "What's wrong?"

"I wanted to talk to you about something. It's important."

My stomach drops. She sounds nervous. Maybe even scared. I turn my head to look at Michelle, but, smart woman that she is, she doesn't look back.

"Okay. Well, hey, let me wrap up this room in five, and we'll talk."

"I thought you said it would take twenty."

"I overestimated."

Even with my eyebrows furrowed in concern, I weakly smile against Michelle's palm. Why does this feel so easy? My daughter confiding in her. Make-out sessions in guest rooms.

Just the thought of her leaving makes my nerves tighten everywhere. My heart feels erratic. I wish we had more time. I wish she could stay. I wish we didn't live on opposite sides of the country, living opposite lives.

I notice that Emily hasn't left. She stands quietly outside the door.

"Actually, can I . . . can I talk to you now?" she asks Michelle.

"Oh," Michelle says, her eyebrows rising in surprise. "The room is—"

"I don't care how messy it is," Emily interrupts. "I'm really nervous right now. I can't keep it to myself anymore."

"Em—"

She interrupts again, this time shakier, "Please?"

Michelle is at a loss for words.

Emily fills the blank space for her. "I think I might be pregnant."

Chapter 37

CLIFF

I think I black out for half a second. Blurry dots crowd my vision. My knees nearly collapse. The only thing keeping me upright is Michelle's palm, but even her fingers are now shaking against my lips.

"What did you say?" Michelle breathes.

My daughter might be *pregnant*.

My mind is swimming. Drowning.

Emily might be pregnant.

I have a half-second thought of, *I'm going to murder Josh and string him up in the square, Middle Ages–style.*

But once that fantasy is out of the way, I hear Emily shakily asking, "I . . . I think . . . You aren't mad, are you?"

My daughter is scared. She's as scared as Tracy was when we were her age. Terrified of a different future than the open path available to her now. She doesn't even know what she wants to go to college for—or if she even wants to go. She's barely considered the future before losing it for another one.

I push off from the wall, and Michelle drops her palm from my mouth. I turn the corner. Michelle steps back to give me room. My body crowds the doorway, my shoulders nearly touching either side of the threshold.

Emily's eyes widen until they are so big that I can see every edge of the white surrounding them.

"Dad," she breathes.

My heart is pounding. I can't tell if I'm angry or sad or scared.

Scared. I'm definitely scared.

But when Emily's bottom lip shakes, I know she's more scared than I am. Being scared isn't my job right now.

"Em," I say, keeping my tone as even-keeled as possible. I don't know how to have this conversation. So, I default to business. It's my only option if I'm going to stay sane right now. "How do you know?"

"I don't. I'm late on my period." The words rush out. She hasn't averted her gaze from mine, as if she's frozen on the spot.

I nod to myself. "You were using protection?"

"Dad, I'm so sorry—"

"Were you using protection?" I repeat, closing my eyes as tight as I can.

"Y-yes," she replies.

I open my eyes, and she's clenching and unclenching her fists. I reach out to grab her hand, gingerly unfurling the fist with my fingers. Immediately, she entwines hers between the grooves of my own.

"Good. And, hey," I whisper, "it's fine. I'm not angry."

"You aren't?"

"No."

How could I be? It would be hypocritical to be angry over something I did myself. I'm far from angry. I'm concerned, yes. But angry? No.

Emily swallows and amends, "Well, one time, we couldn't find a condom and . . ."

I groan. "Em."

"You *said* you weren't mad!"

I could laugh at how quickly her attitude turns on. I can't tell if she gets it from me or her mother, but then the thought of her having a tiny version of herself baking brings me back to reality.

"I'm not," I say through an exhale. "I'm not, kiddo."

"I . . . what do I do?" she asks.

What do *we do?*

Footsteps creak slowly up the stairwell. Emily jerks her head to the hall. Maybe it's a guest, or maybe it's Lisa. She's discreet. But I know Emily wants nothing more than to keep this to herself.

Herself and Michelle.

She came to Michelle for this.

She trusted Michelle enough to have this conversation. A small piece of my punctured heart mends even a little.

A guest rounds the corner, gives us a smiling wave, which the three of us somehow manage to return, then disappears into the room at the opposite end of the hall.

"Have you taken a test?" Michelle whispers over my shoulder.

I raise my arm higher up the doorway, allowing Michelle to duck beneath and join our circle.

Emily quietly shakes her head. "No."

"Okay," I announce quietly, looking between Emily and Michelle.

Both their jaws are set, like they're ready for battle.

"Here's what we're gonna do. I'm gonna drive out of town and pick up a pregnancy test. And then we're gonna try it out, okay? No reason to be scared."

"I'm not scared," Emily counters.

But her words don't match her heavy breathing. It feels

like yesterday that I held her in my arms with the same labored breaths between ear-splitting cries. Her arrival into this world was with kicks and screams. I know my girl. She doesn't do anything without a little ferocity.

Michelle claps her hands together, as if to end this conversation. "All right! Em, want to help me set up the guest room next door?"

She silently nods, peering at the room behind Michelle and me. "I can help with this one too. I didn't mean to stop you."

Michelle shakes her head. "It's finished. Don't worry."

Emily squints. "But you just said—" She swallows, and maybe she doesn't connect the dots, or maybe she doesn't want to right now, so she stiffly nods once more.

Michelle slides past me, gliding a small, reassuring hand along my waist as she does, and walks to the hall closet. Emily, in a distant haze, follows, but not before glancing back at me once more. I give a wan smile.

"I'll be back," I say.

Her lips pull up at the corners, but the smile doesn't reach her eyes. "Thanks, Dad."

Michelle, Emily, and I lie, arm to arm, on Michelle's mattress. I stare at the popcorn ceiling as the fan above whirs in slow whooshes. If I stare at it too long, it looks stuck, like a broken record.

"Has it been ten minutes?" Emily murmurs.

I look at my watch. "We've got seven more."

"It's only been three minutes?"

"No, it's two. I didn't want you to worry."

All three of us pull in a deep inhalation and let it out

slowly. The silence in the room is sending shocks of nerves through my heart, pounding all the way down to my fingers.

Emily licks her lips. "What happens if I am . . . you know?"

She can't even say the word *pregnant*. I remember Tracy couldn't either when she showed me the stick with two pink lines. We were both at a loss for words.

I reach my arm up and over Emily's head, twirling her long blond strands between my fingers.

"Then you are." I assure her, "And you'll be fine."

"You won't be mad?"

It's the fiftieth time she's asked me that, and at this point, I huff out a laugh.

"Of course not."

"Or mad at Josh?"

I exhale heavily. Josh—his Swiss roll self—wouldn't be the worst option for her. I almost smile. Not many people could handle Emily. But he can.

"No," I answer. "I won't be mad at Josh."

"What happened when you found out? You and Mom?"

"We were scared," I confess. "Then, very quickly, we were happy. Because it led to you."

She groans. "Dad, I'm serious."

"So am I."

Michelle shifts on the opposite side of Emily, letting out a shaky exhale. I wonder if she's nervous too.

"Michelle, did you ever . . . go through this?" Emily asks slowly.

"No," Michelle answers honestly, then laughs lightly. "I was too uptight in high school to have a boyfriend."

A short, giggly laugh bubbles out of Emily. "As if. I bet you were bangin'."

"Far from it. You should have seen my prom dress. Very poofy."

The two of them laugh together, and a delayed chuckle escapes me too.

"You went to prom?" Emily asks. "I thought you said you didn't date."

"I didn't. I went alone."

My heart sinks.

I wonder what Michelle was like in high school. I would have asked her to prom.

I've always considered the possibility of Emily getting pregnant. It was less about the act and more about her having to grow up too fast. I don't want that for her. She's my girl.

The moment she told me about her first boyfriend, my stomach plummeted down and has never really found its way back up. I always assumed it would be Tracy on the other side of her, talking through this with her with compassion. But it's Michelle instead, and the way Emily lets out a funny laugh when Michelle talks soothes the ache in my soul.

When the laughter settles down, Emily audibly gulps. "What if Mom finds out?"

"Well," I say through an exhale, "whenever you start to show, I imagine she'll figure it out."

Emily groans, as if that wasn't in her list of possibilities. "I forgot about the whole belly thing."

"You'll be fine."

Then, in a silence that lasts too long, Emily whispers, "What if I'm like Mom?"

It's a gut-wrenching sentence. I stiffen and sigh. It's long. It's steady. It's there to fill the loss of words.

"Your mom is a wonderful woman," I say.

"She doesn't like me."

"She loves you," I correct.

"She left us."

"She was here at this moment sixteen years ago," I say, poking the mattress. "And she knew she'd love you, no matter how it changed her life. She loves you like you wouldn't believe. Life is complicated, Em. She had dreams, and she needed to go find them. But that doesn't mean she loves you any less."

Tracy is complicated. Flawed. But she spent fourteen years cherishing Emily. The first time she bounced Emily in her arms—the way her face lit up with happiness—is a memory I wish I could revisit countless times. It would be easy to fault her for leaving if I didn't know how much she adored her children.

Her leaving and our divorce were inevitable. We had gotten married so young, with factors beyond our control. It was a time when shotgun weddings were the norm, not the exception.

The mattress shifts as Michelle reaches her arm up, finds my hand, and hooks her pinkie in mine. I have a theory she can read my mind, and she has yet to prove me wrong.

"I wonder if I'll be a bad mom," Emily murmurs.

"Impossible," I say.

"Michelle, you were lucky," Emily says. "You had Birdie."

Michelle grows quiet. I squeeze her finger with mine.

"My mom was kind and generous, but sometimes it was complicated. All child-parent relationships are. She was . . . sad when I was younger. Very sad. And when she came out of it, she tried very hard to fix what she could." Michelle exhales. "She *did* try." The words sound as if she's realizing them at the same time she says them. "She tried her best."

The three of us listen to the ambient sounds of Bird & Breakfast. The clattering of flatware from the dining room.

The creaking and thumping footsteps above our heads. The TV in the parlor, playing a *3rd Rock from the Sun* rerun.

I look at my watch again. We're past the ten-minute mark.

"All right," I exhale. "You ready?"

Emily's chest expands quickly, and she shakes her head. "No. You look. I can't."

"Are you sure?"

"I can't," she repeats, turning her head to face me with worried eyebrows.

I release my hand from Michelle's and cup the top of Emily's head. I kiss her forehead, then swing my legs over the side of the bed and stand. I stare at the two of them for a few moments, watching Michelle thread her fingers through my daughter's stringy hair cascading over the bedspread. Emily scoots closer to Michelle.

My heart pounds as I walk into the bathroom. The small stick is resting half on the counter and half over the sink. I feel like I'm the bridge between Emily's old life and potential new one. Earlier this month, we were playing in the snow. Now, I'm next to a toilet covered in pink shag, and reaching for a pregnancy test.

If she is pregnant, it will be another wonderful person added to our family. It will be fine.

All will be fine.

I pick it up, inhale, and flip it, and looking back is one single pink line.

A single line.

I close my eyes and finally break out into an exhausted laugh.

A single fucking line.

"What?" Emily asks, scrambling to the side of the bed. "What, what, what?"

"It's negative," I announce.

The air in the room rushes back.

In one smooth motion, Emily's eyes roll to the back of her head, and she falls backward onto the bed with a giant, loud, exhaled groan. "Oh, thank *God*."

I can see the weight fall from her shoulders. Michelle shakes them with a grin.

"I never want to do that again," Emily groans. "That's it. No children for me. Ever."

"Music to my ears," I tease.

She grins at me, but it falls quickly. "We can't tell Mom."

My stomach twists.

Impossible.

"No," I say.

Emily's eyes widen.

"Sorry, kiddo. She deserves to know."

"Why?" she whines.

"She's your mom. It wouldn't be right. But how about this? I won't tell her while she's here, okay? That way, you only have to deal with her over the phone."

Emily exhales. "Okay. Deal."

She jerks out her palm, and I roll my eyes, shaking her hand.

"Good." I clear my throat. "Now, back to business . . . where is Josh?"

She tilts her chin down. "Dad."

I playfully hold up my palms. "I want to talk to him—"

"Dad," she warns again, a sliver of a smile on her face.

"Me, Josh, and a machete."

"Dad!"

Suddenly, she breaks into laughter, and I do too. Then I'm hugging her again and kissing her forehead even though I get more whines of protest.

"Love you, kiddo."

"You love Josh too?"

I snort. "I'm heavily indifferent."

"Who wants a cinnamon roll?" Michelle asks, breaking the tension.

"*Please*," Emily groans.

Emily hops off the bed, rushing to the doorway. I gesture her through, peering over at Michelle, who is grinning from ear to ear. I can't stop smiling either. It's the nerves of the whole situation pounding through me. The thought that *we* went through this together. Michelle was here for my daughter when she needed her. And Emily *did* need her.

The unspoken truth rings through my head, as it has for weeks now.

I love Michelle.

I love her, and I'll have to let her go.

Michelle's face falls. Mine must have too.

It's all going to end.

Emily stops short of the threshold, spinning to face us. She points a finger between me and Michelle, breaking our eye contact.

"You were in the guest room together," Emily states.

My stomach knots.

"Are you two . . ." Her words fade, as if she's expecting an answer, but I don't know what response to give.

Are we dating? Are we in love?

There's no clear-cut answer to our complicated problem.

I exhale out a nervous laugh, clapping Emily on the shoulder. "Our business is between us, Em."

A smirk slides over Emily's face so slowly and sinisterly that it could rival the Grinch's. "But there *is* business?"

I lightly shove her back into the hall. "Get out of here, kid."

Emily bites her bottom lip and snickers.

But when I glance at Michelle, her eyebrows tilt in too. I reach back and drift my fingertips over hers at the same time she reaches for me. We exchange a weak smile, then walk into the kitchen behind Emily.

Chapter 38

CLIFF

The morning Tracy rolls into town is, of course, the one day we get multiple orders placed for holiday parties around town. I called George and told him his usual order wouldn't be ready until tomorrow. Considering he and Lisa are attending two out of the three other parties I'm catering, he didn't hem and haw much.

Once everything is either finished or in the oven for Carol, I frantically rush back to the house with flour on my arms and probably smeared somewhere on my face. My tires screech over the driveway with the key fob jangling against the ignition. Emily walks out the back door with lifeless, bored eyes.

I barely have the car door open before she's whispering, "Mom keeps asking Josh about his plans for the future. Make her stop asking Josh things."

"She's your mother; be nice."

"She's also asking where you've been."

"Perfect," I breathe out sarcastically.

"That's your ex-wife; be nice," Emily mocks.

I ruffle her hair, and she pushes my palm away.

Creaking open the screened back door is a Herculean effort because I know in two seconds, I'll see—

Tracy.

Standing in our kitchen, with one hand pressing buttons on our phone and the other clutching her beeper, is my ex-wife. Her lips are pursed tightly, but her hair is pulled back in an even tighter ponytail. Her sharp, tailored blazer and slacks look like they popped out of the pages of Michelle's *Cosmopolitan*. The city life suits her.

Years ago, she wore T-shirts and denim. She went through a funny leg-warmer phase in our early twenties and a padded blazer phase years later. As time passed, I realized she always hinted at wanting more than the small-town life. She always wanted to be more put together, and now she has the money to do so.

Tracy's eyes dart back and forth between the two pieces of technology until the door snaps shut behind me. She jerks her gaze to mine. I hold up a hand in a wave. She returns it while tucking the beeper back on her belt loop and leaning the kitchen phone between her ear and shoulder.

She holds up a single finger in my direction. *Please wait.*

Brittany, sitting at the breakfast nook, flashes me a piece of paper with crayon-doodled stick people.

"Look, Dad! I drew you and Michelle!"

"That's great, Britt Britt."

"Did you see Rocket too?" She shakes the flopping, crinkled paper closer.

It's a drawing of me, Michelle, and the two girls. My mouth crooks into a smile. Michelle is wearing a short red skirt. Emily has big black circles for eyes, probably to show how doe-eyed she is. In the corner, there's a black-and-white dog with stick legs.

"I love it," I say. "We'll put it on the fridge."

"Yay!" she squeals.

I press my finger to my lips, and Brittany mirrors the motion.

"We gotta be quiet while Mom's on the phone though, all right?"

"Why?" Emily asks loudly from the corner.

I run a palm over my face.

Emily passes her mom like she's not even there, reaching in the fridge to grab some pop and take it into the next room. Josh follows dutifully.

Tracy crosses her arms, peering into the dining room to look at Emily, silent on the phone. Suddenly, she straightens up, switching the phone to her other ear. "Hi. Yes, this is Tracy Marie."

She's going by her middle name now?

"Mm-hmm."

As Tracy continues her conversation, the back door opens, almost slamming into my back. Michelle's head pokes through.

"Trying to kill me?" I whisper with a grin.

"Sorry," Michelle says, snickering. Her voice isn't low, so it cuts through the kitchen like a knife.

Tracy flicks her eyes at Michelle, like laser beams ready to fire.

Tracy was always stiff around women. She had a few friends in Copper Run, but I don't think she's talked to them since moving. Most of all though, she never liked when I made other women laugh.

I move to the side, guiding Michelle in with a hand on her lower back.

Emily traipses back into the kitchen with a grin on her face, leaning against the doorway, loudly slurping on her can. She's here for the drama.

"Hey, Michelle," she says at normal volume, obliterating the quiet again.

I roll my eyes, and Emily grins wider.

Tracy covers the receiver. "Let me call you back, Doug. Mm-hmm. Yep. Mm-kay. Buh-bye." She jabs her finger against the phone's button, staring at our motley crew.

Emily slurps again. It echoes.

Michelle takes the first step forward, extending her hand. "Hi. You must be Tracy."

Tracy turns her head to the side, as if analyzing Michelle's entire being—her body, her face, her hair, which has that freshly washed bounce to it.

It's weird, seeing them side by side, because, aside from the hair color (Tracy's high blond ponytail and Michelle's brown) and the complexion (Tracy's ivory and Michelle's almost olive), they're similar. They look like they could be friends. At minimum, colleagues. Like two sides of the same coin.

Tracy takes Michelle's hand and shakes in a definitive way. Almost jerky.

"This is Michelle," I say. "She owns the inn next door."

"She's Dad's *best* friend," Brittany throws in, mindlessly coloring, not realizing she threw a grenade into the room.

"Really?" Tracy asks, blinking at Michelle.

Michelle rolls her eyes with a smile. "He helps with the inn a lot."

"Sounds like Cliff. Did he force you to be his friend?"

"I forced him actually," Michelle says matter-of-factly.

I bark out a laugh without thinking. It's not true, and we both know it, but I can see what she's doing.

He's not a burden, she's saying.

And, God, I love her for it.

Tracy and Michelle might be equally intense women, but they're undeniably *different*.

Michelle's posture is tall. Her look is effortless. She's not wearing a blazer, like Tracy. Michelle's only in a button-up and jeans, but it's somehow nicer. Tucked in. And Tracy keeps looking at all of her with hawk eyes.

"So"—Tracy claps her hands together—"what's new out here, family? What are we doing?"

I don't miss the *family* dropped in there, and I also catch the side-eye Tracy gives Michelle.

I don't like that. Not one bit.

Brittany shrugs. "We play in the snow."

"That's fun," Tracy says with raised eyebrows, but the words are stilted, then quiet.

I'm not sure she knows how to interact with her girls anymore. Emily moaned about how uncomfortable Thanksgiving was for the entire week afterward. I didn't consider it might be this bad though.

Tracy takes in Michelle again, eyes flicking from her face down to her black loafers. We're probably standing closer than best friends should, and Tracy clocks it from a mile away. But neither I nor Michelle budges.

Tracy's eyes narrow.

What the hell?

I work out my stiff jaw with a forced smile. "Hey, how about we put up the Christmas tree, huh? We've been waiting for Mommy to arrive to do that, haven't we?"

"Yes! Yes, yes, yes!" Brittany gasps, leaping up and running into the living room with a happy squeal.

Yesterday, I brought down rattling boxes of decorations from the attic. I almost dropped them halfway down the ladder, but Emily and Michelle fumbled to catch my fall. All four of us laughed about it for a while after. It felt comfortable. It felt like home.

Now, with Tracy flashing a big smile to us and following her daughter into the living room, the house feels still, like the static air before a storm. Emily raises both eyebrows at Michelle and me and exhales.

"Fun," she whispers sarcastically.

I give a weak smile as she leaves to go in the living room too.

The kitchen is quiet again.

"So, that's your ex," Michelle announces.

I nod solemnly, trying to gauge her reaction, but she seems unaffected. So sure of herself. I smile. Of course she is; she's Michelle. But I also know she hides behind a lot of walls.

"She's not so bad," Michelle says.

"She's not," I agree. Except I keep thinking about that look she gave Michelle and how much I didn't like it.

"This won't be an issue."

I smirk at Michelle. "Oh, really?"

"I've handled harsher women. *I'm* a harsher woman."

I wrap my arm around Michelle's waist and tug her into my hip. I run my thumb up to her ribs and lean over to nip her earlobe between my teeth. She hisses in a breath, followed by bubbling laughter. Having her in my arms instantly makes me feel better.

Her eyes cling to the threshold Tracy passed over. She might not want me to think she's self-conscious, but I can read her like a book.

Pressing my forehead against her temple, I whisper, "Have I told you lately how badly I want to rip off these pants?"

I tuck my palm into her back pocket and squeeze a handful of her cheek.

A small smile slides over her lips.

There we go.

"Many times," she whispers back.

"Ah, I was afraid of that."

"You can tell me again, if you want though."

"How about I show you later?" I murmur. "Maybe unzip them with my teeth, if you're lucky."

Shivers break out over her neck. I trace my finger over them.

"You want that?"

"Of course I do," she answers defiantly. If she'd tacked on the word *idiot*, it would have fit seamlessly.

I run my nose over her neck. She leans back, exposing herself to me more as I place kiss after kiss down her jaw and onto her collarbone. I feel her swallow.

God, she's intoxicating, and she's *mine*. For some reason, this quiet, closed-off woman chose *me*. She lets my hands roam where they like. I didn't know something this healthy could exist, yet here I am, with a woman who longs for my touch.

Michelle leans back and traces her fingertips over my jaw.

"Are you doing all right?" she asks. "Seriously."

I smile, kissing her once more, tucking my thumb under the hem of her jeans and murmuring, "Come on. We've got a Christmas tree to put up."

She inhales an offended breath, then grabs a fistful of my shirt and pushes me away.

"You tease," she snarls with a grin.

I chuckle. "I don't think I've ever been called a tease."

I walk behind her through the dining room, and she halts in front of me. Instinctually, I grab her hips to steady us both, but she takes the opportunity to push her ass against me.

I choke out a laugh. "Michelle—"

"Good luck with your boner," she whispers, reaching behind her to pat the growing bulge in my jeans for good measure.

I let out a frustrated growl as we cross into the living room.

Brittany digs through the box of ornaments. Emily sifts through her CD collection next to the stereo. But from the armchair, Tracy stares at Michelle and me with tense, pursed lips.

Chapter 39

MICHELLE

Our group grows exponentially in a short amount of time. Sara and Dad arrive back in town shortly after Tracy. Cliff helps carry Sara's suitcases inside, and the moment they fall onto my bedroom floor, the weight in my stomach plummets like an anvil to my gut.

Sara's officially moving in to run Bird & Breakfast.

I must have been staring at the suitcases for too long because Sara leans her head on my shoulder.

"Sweet suitcases, right? I bought them with your graduation money."

I couldn't make it out to California for her graduation due to all the business around the inn. But I heard all about it over the phone, and I sent her probably more money than she needed.

"It's a pretty suitcase set," I agree.

It's a nothing conversation, interrupted by Cliff, who yells from the kitchen, "Michelle, you want mustard on your sandwich, right? The entire bottle's worth?"

I smirk, and Sara laughs with me because he knows I hate mustard. Both of them do.

Is this the life I was missing while married to Allen? Are

these the fun conversations I could have had instead of quiet, polite ones with his friends?

Once Dad and Sara settle in—Dad in the only open guest room and Sara sharing the bed with me—I walk her through basic inn tasks through the afternoon and evening. Check-ins, checkouts, daily issues, like the faulty handle on the hall closet or the creaking stair near the attic. Things that feel like second nature that will no longer be part of mine.

It's hers.

The inn is hers, like it was always meant to be.

Once the sun sets, we gather up our two-house troop and walk to the square.

The Snow and Sips Festival is in full swing when our party arrives. Bing Crosby and the Andrews Sisters croon "Jingle Bells" through speakers. Multicolored lights dip between lampposts with wreaths. Booths pop up every few feet, and their sloping red covers are coated in snow. Forest-green garland is wrapped around the gazebo roof with strings of candy canes and mistletoe dangling over every set of stairs. It smells like peppermint and chocolate and a hint of the smoke coming from the popping bonfire in the middle, where a crowd roasts marshmallows.

Emily runs ahead to find Josh near the nativity scene. Tracy trails behind Brittany as she snaps pictures of plastic reindeer. My dad walks off to find hot chocolate with Sara. Carol spots George and Lisa, stalling them from walking over. I have a feeling that was intentional.

It's me, Cliff, and Rocket remaining under a sprig of mistletoe. The corner of Cliff's mouth tips into a playful grin. I roll my eyes, sighing as puffs of warm air float in front of our faces. He runs the outside of his gloved pinkie against mine. It's our little secret.

"How are you feeling?" he asks.

"I was gonna ask you the same thing."

"I'm jolly. According to ol' Bing anyway."

I huff a laugh out my nose, and his grin grows wider.

"How are you really, Michelle?" I open my mouth and close it, managing a smile when he leans in to murmur, "You think so loud."

"It's a pretty festival," I admit. "Copper Run's best so far."

His smile falls almost imperceptibly before he pulls the corner of his mouth back up.

"I bet Seattle has some great ones. A big tree or something. An ice-skating rink."

"It does," I say.

Rocket looks between us, his tail slowly wagging.

Shelly, you've never *been ice skating.*

I tongue my cheek as Cliff suddenly says, "Can't wait to see it."

My head jerks to him. It's the first time we've acknowledged visits instead of calls—something *real*.

"Yeah?" I say on a breath.

The little crease beside his mouth deepens. "Yeah."

Brittany jogs over and holds up her yellow disposable camera to Cliff. We jerk our hands away. Tracy, trailing behind Brittany, looks down at where our joined hands were only moments before.

"What's up, Britt?" Cliff asks.

"I need another camera," she says, clicking the button uselessly.

He chuckles. "Isn't this your third one since Halloween?"

"I want another."

Cliff peers up at the line winding through the park, leading to a golden armchair, where Santa—very obviously Lars in a costume—bounces Luke on his lap. Luke's arms are stubbornly folded across his chest as he frowns with red cheeks. His mother snaps a photo of his scowl.

"Why don't you tell Santa?" Cliff suggests to Brittany.

She pouts. "But he's supposed to get me my other pictures."

"You haven't developed the photos yet?" I murmur to Cliff with a laugh.

He side-eyes me with a smirk.

"Well," he says down to Brittany, "I'll check with Santa and see if he can handle both things."

"Promise?" Brittany asks.

"Absolutely."

"*Promise*, promise?"

"Yes, yes," he says. "Or you can tell him first." He playfully pats her back. "You want to go get in line?"

"I'll take her," Tracy interjects, sidestepping past me with a small bump of her shoulder against mine.

I jerk my head back in response. In any other situation, I'd acknowledge it. But as ours stands, I bite back my response through grinding molars.

It's taking every ounce of control for me to force a smile for Tracy. I almost said something yesterday when she passed the broccoli dish to Emily, deliberately bypassing me in the process. I don't like it when someone starts a cold war without my consent. I only start arguments if I plan to end them and win, and she's gotten an unfair head start.

Brittany tugs Cliff's hand into her mitten. "Can you come too, Daddy?"

"Oh." Cliff looks awkwardly from me to Tracy, then back down at Brittany.

She beams up at him, and he returns it.

"Of course."

He'll always be weak for his daughters, even if it requires more time with his ex. That's the kind of dad he is.

I pinch his side. "Go be a good dad."

Cliff tosses me a playful wave as he stumbles forward, forcefully pulled by a six-year-old, and the tether between us pulls taut with the distance. Tracy follows, exhaling sharply in irritation before peering back at me.

That's the weirdest thing of all. Tracy doesn't *like* Cliff, but she doesn't like me with him either.

The three of them walk to the line for Santa. Tracy holds out her hand for Brittany, who eagerly takes it, now gripping one hand from each parent. My stomach twists at the sight. It's so domestic. Brittany doesn't have three hands, so where would my puzzle piece slip in?

Emily's pregnancy scare took me by surprise. When Sara was a teen, she was too distracted by acrylic paint and charcoal drawings to care about boys. But even without experience, helping Emily felt natural. As we lay on that bed with her between me and Cliff, solving problems . . . it felt like we'd been doing it for years.

Dad nudges my shoulder, startling me. He chuckles and holds out a paper cup, steaming with hot chocolate. I smile and take it.

"Thanks. Where's Sara?"

"She's on the hunt for pie."

"Oh."

It's the first time Dad and I have been alone since Thanksgiving. He seems happy again. He's smiling.

"Happy to be back?" I ask.

He shrugs. "Sort of."

I give him a curious look, and he laughs.

"I love Copper Run," he corrects. "But the inn? It was your mom's passion. Not mine."

I clutch my hot chocolate tighter. The steam rises to my cheeks—or maybe it's my own heat.

"Let it be Sara's, then," I say, looking out at the crowd, where Lisa and George each try a bite of funnel cake from the same plate. "Let yourself retire out here. Enjoy the town."

"Yeah," Dad says, drawing out the word and squinting at me. "I was thinking about that. What about you?"

I lift an eyebrow. "What do you mean?"

"Have you been thinking about Copper Run?"

I clear my throat. "Not sure I follow."

"You know, you're very similar to your mother," he says. "You have her motivation. Tenacity. Confidence."

I shake my head. "Sara has all that too."

"Your sister got her spirit—that's true. Birdie gave that to her in spades." He gives me a weak smile. "But you like a good challenge. So did she."

My heart sinks as I slide my—no, Mom's—pendant across its chain. As I grip her purse on my shoulder. I finally take a sip from my paper cup, and the hot chocolate stings my tongue.

"I'd be lying if I said you girls were raised by the same mom. She was a different woman with Sara. And it wasn't your fault. And it wasn't fair either. But nothing in life is. I'm sorry you got the short end of the stick, Shells. But I'm proud of you. And I know she would be too."

I tighten my fingers around the paper cup. It dents and pops back out again, sending small drops of hot chocolate over the side, singeing me through my glove.

"I was perfectly fine back then," I murmur into my sip. "And I'm fine now too."

"You've always said that." Dad looks around the park. "But this might be the first time I believe you." He smiles gently. "You fit in here."

"In Copper Run?" I ask. "No, I . . . I like the city. I miss Seattle."

But the words feel so defensive now, like a knee-jerk reaction.

I hesitate for a moment, open my mouth, close it, then take a sip of my hot chocolate. I find myself subconsciously searching the Santa line again, spotting Brittany dangling her feet over Santa's lap, grinning from ear to ear. Cliff stands off to the side with his arms crossed, beaming and talking to Tracy, who gives a wry smile in return.

I'll miss these events. Maybe I could come here specifically for the holidays. September through December. But what fun events do they host in the spring or summer?

I glance down at Rocket. His tail is no longer wagging, but he takes a step closer, nudging his head against my leg. For once, I can't decipher what he's saying.

I find Cliff, like a magnet searching for its opposite pole. And, like Cliff always does, he somehow finds me as well, staring from the Santa line and tossing a wink my way.

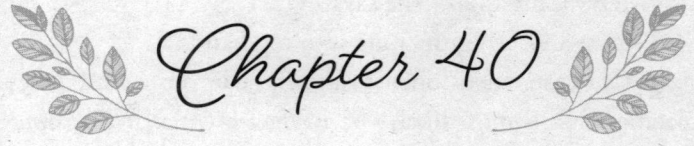

Chapter 40

CLIFF

I wake up to a tickle on my foot. I kick the sensation and roll over on the couch, throwing the sleeping bag comforter over my head.

"Wake up, Dad," Brittany whispers at the opposite end of the couch.

She tickles my foot again, and I tug my legs up into a fetal position.

"The birds aren't chirping yet," I murmur into my pillow. "If they're asleep, we should be too."

"But Santa came!"

"And I bet he's tired after delivering presents," I argue.

I hold up my palm to shield my eyes from the bright tree lights, which kept me up all night. At one point, I unplugged them, but Brittany's pitter-pattering feet woke me up somewhere between three o'clock and five o'clock as she plugged them back in. It was too much energy to get up and turn them off.

A finger wiggles into my ear. A shiver skitters down my spine. I bat the hand away.

"Up and at 'em, old man," Emily says above me.

I peer up through my folded arms to find her perching on the couch's arm with a steaming coffee mug.

I point a finger. "Is that for me?"

"Merry Christmas," she says.

I sit up and bring the mug into my hands.

A CD case cracks open to the right of me. I find Tracy placing what is most likely the *Billboard Greatest Christmas Hits* on the open stereo slot and sliding it back in. For sixteen solid years, we've listened to it every Christmas morning without fail.

"Dad, do you think Michelle and Rocket can come over?" Brittany asks.

I almost choke on my own air. Tracy's head jerks to me. Even the beginning of "White Christmas" by Bing Crosby can't make her expression pleasant.

It's hard to make out her expression without my glasses, but I think I see a single eyebrow rise in question. When you raise children together for as long as we have, you form a type of unspoken parent language. A few years ago, I might have been able to decipher exactly what she's thinking. Now it's a shot in the dark.

The front door slams inward, sending a snow chill into the living room as Carol thumps her boots on the welcome mat. A thick scarf is pulled up to her ears, and her woolly coat is covered in fluffy snow.

"Is that coffee for me?" she asks through chattering teeth, kicking the door closed behind her and snatching the mug from my hands.

I blink to myself, but I'm too sleepy to question it.

"Em, is there any coffee left?" I ask, swinging my legs over the side of the couch.

"Duh," Emily answers, putting her finger into my ear again.

I swat at her.

"Dad, can Michelle and Rocket come over?" Brittany repeats.

I rub my palm over my face. "Heard you the first time, Britt Britt. Let me get some coffee, and we'll see."

I grab my glasses from the side table and blink through the remaining grogginess on my way to the kitchen. I hear Tracy following, the *fwick-slap* of her house shoes hitting the linoleum behind me.

I look out the kitchen window toward Michelle's bedroom. There's a curtain of snow falling between our houses, so it's difficult to see if her lamp is on. I wonder if she's already awake, making cinnamon rolls.

I sniff and cross to the cabinet. I pull down a mug, gesturing it toward Tracy, as if to say, *Want one too?*

She nods. I take down another—the one with the Burke's Bakery logo—and shuffle over to the full pot gurgling on the counter.

Tracy clicks her tongue and sighs.

"If they want to invite Michelle, that's fine," she says stiffly.

I peer over, pouring coffee. "You're kidding. This feels like a trap."

Her lips straighten into a thin line, and she crosses her arms. "She's nice enough."

I snort. "It's your holiday," I say, grabbing the second mug and pouring more. "I'm not here to ruin Christmas with the girls."

Tracy's jaw tightens. "And I'm not here to ruin theirs. If they want your neighbor over, I'm fine with it."

It's uncomfortable, talking about Michelle with Tracy. The words are all wrong. *Neighbor* feels too casual. Then again, so do words like *best friend* or *girlfriend*.

Tracy clears her throat. "Cliff."

"Hmm?"

"Call her."

"You're sure?"

"Yes."

I don't believe her, but Tracy's gaze doesn't break from mine for a solid few seconds. She's either convincing me or persuading herself. With a straightened back, she snatches her coffee from my palm—a small splash springing to the counter—and leaves the kitchen.

I cautiously walk to the phone, dial Bird & Breakfast, and lean the receiver between my ear and shoulder.

"Merry Christmas!" Michelle's customer service voice is enough to wake me from my blurry slumber. I could listen to her talk all morning. "Thank you for calling Bird &—"

"Merry Christmas, Michelle," I interrupt with a low laugh.

"Cliff." Her voice goes soft.

I love when her voice goes soft.

"What are you doing this morning?" I ask.

"Dad and Sara are sleeping."

"And what are *you* doing?" I repeat.

I hear her smile as she says, "What *am* I doing, social planner?"

I set my coffee down, lean against the counter, and place one ankle over the other. "You're invited to our Burke Family Present-Opening Ceremony."

"Wow, is that a big deal?"

"Huge."

There's a beat before she asks, "Is Tracy fine with it?"

I smile to myself. "It was her suggestion."

Silently, she murmurs, "This feels like a trap."

"That's what I said."

"Well, I'm in pajamas."

"So are we."

"Let me—"

"We have coffee," I say. "So, put on those cute fuzzy slippers of yours and get over here," I demand with a grin. "Don't make me come get you. And bring Rocket."

"He'd get mad if I didn't."

We both hang up, and it suddenly hits me that I'm spending Christmas with Michelle. I feel like . . . well, like a kid on Christmas, I guess. I tuck my feet into house slippers, rip open the kitchen door, and trundle along through the snow.

By the time I make it past our rosebushes, Michelle is out the door with two bags in her hand and Rocket trotting by her side. She laughs when she sees me and laughs even harder when I tuck my arms under her knees, lift her over my shoulder, and carry her back to my house with Rocket barking the whole way.

When we're back inside, I plop her down on the linoleum. She reaches out for my glasses with her free hand and adjusts them.

I wiggle them up and down with a smile. "You still like them?"

"Maybe."

I want to bury my lips into her neck, but I have to pull away when I hear tiny footsteps pounding over the carpet toward the kitchen.

"Michelle!"

Brittany barrels into Michelle's legs, nearly knocking her backward. She holds tight, hugging on to her as Michelle attempts to walk. Rocket bounces alongside them, his tail whooshing through the air, hitting against the breakfast nook's legs.

"Did Santa come to your house?" Michelle asks.

"Yes! We haven't opened presents but—"

"You *haven't opened presents yet*?" Michelle gawks, looking at me with a broad grin. "Cliff, how dare you!"

"I'm revoking your coffee privileges," I say.

"No, you're not," she counters.

I smirk and dutifully grab her a mug from the cabinet.

Brittany gasps. "Are those for us?"

I finally look closer at the two bags in Michelle's hands. They're illustrated with snowy cottages and horse-drawn carriages. Red tissue paper sprouts from the top.

"They are," Michelle says.

The smile that bursts over my face is almost embarrassing. *She got my girls a gift.*

"You didn't have to—" I start, but Emily runs in, yelling, "She did!"

Michelle tells them which bag is theirs, and the girls snatch the presents, running back into the living room together. Following them with a coffee mug each, Michelle and I walk into the living room. It's oddly domestic, but I love every second of it.

I sit on the opposite side of the couch from Michelle and Rocket—not too close in case the girls notice, even though Emily's eyes swing from Michelle back to me with a broad grin. Tracy's gaze follows, staring pointedly at Michelle.

Brittany and Emily rip into their gifts like animals.

New CDs quickly stack up for Emily. "Whoa, you got me the Smashing Pumpkins, Michelle?"

For Brittany, there's a new Barbie, a Tickle Me Elmo, and finally, a rectangular box she shakes in her hand. She looks at me curiously, and I nod.

"Open it up, Britt."

She slides open one side. Slick, glossy photos slide onto the carpet.

Her eyes shine as bright as stars. "Santa got my photos, Dad!"

"See? Told you he'd listen," Emily says with a smile, performing her older-sister duty of keeping up the Santa myth.

I think she enjoys it more than I do.

Brittany holds up the top photo. "Look! It's Rocket!"

Rocket perks up at the sound of his name.

I laugh. Sure, the photo has Rocket, but it also has half of Brittany's thumb in the shot.

"You're a natural," I say.

Brittany continues pushing through the photos. I skimmed the stack before wrapping it. There are crooked shots of the inn and Rocket's snout. There's one of me at the bakery, arm deep in the oven. Some are from Halloween, but most of those ended up blurry from the flash.

Carol scoots behind her and looks through them over Brittany's shoulder. Laughing, she grabs one and holds it up. It's Michelle and Carol sitting on the front porch.

"Paparazzo," she teases.

"Oh, look, there's Josh," Tracy says, joining in.

I can tell she feels left out. She points to a photo tossed closer to the fireplace. In the picture, Emily and Josh are curled on Bird & Breakfast's couch under a big blanket.

Tracy tilts her nose up. "I can see how you two get into trouble."

Emily goes stiff as a board. "What?"

Tracy shrugs. "Just remember to be safe."

Her wide eyes instantly dart to me and Michelle.

"You *told* her?" Emily snaps.

Michelle's eyebrows rise. So do mine.

"You promised you wouldn't tell her."

"Tell me what?" Tracy cuts in. Her face is turning red at the same rate Emily's cheeks are suddenly draining of color.

"Tell her what?" I ask too.

Then it hits me. I can feel my own heart sinking as I uncomfortably adjust on the cushions. I glance at Michelle, whose eyebrows stitch inward. She probably realized it seconds before me. The pregnancy test.

"Em . . ." Michelle says, but the word fades off.

"We didn't," I finish for her.

Emily's posture falters as the realization suddenly settles in.

"You didn't tell her?" Emily whispers.

Michelle quickly shakes her head, pulling in her lips.

Emily's shoulders drop, and she breathes out a small, "Shit."

"Emily Theresa Burke," Tracy snaps. "Language. You tell me what's going on right now."

I immediately pinch my eyes closed. That type of demand will get her nowhere with Emily, and predictably, Emily scrambles to stand with a glare pointed at her.

"I'm not telling *you* anything," she snaps.

Tracy's ears are bright crimson. "But you told *her*?"

For a moment, I'm confused. But then I follow her line of sight to Michelle, and heat from my chest rises up my throat to my cheeks.

Michelle is stunned to the spot, but hidden beside her is a very tight fist.

"Her name is Michelle," Carol points out.

Tracy's mouth gapes in a scoffing laugh. "I don't care *who* she is."

"Trace . . ." I warn.

This is escalating quicker than I'd like, and even Carol's eyebrows get more furrowed by the second. Poor Brittany sits on the floor, confused, holding photos and smearing her fingerprints all over them.

"I should know what's going on with my daughter before someone else does," Tracy says.

"You'd know if you ever *talked to me*," Emily spits back.

Tracy pinches her eyes shut, ignoring Emily to say, "I should at least know before that . . . that—"

I rise to my feet without thinking. My heart is pounding. My knuckles are white from clenched fists, painfully forcing my nails into my palms. My chest is on fire.

"I'd watch what words come out next, Trace. Before we all say something we regret. Something the girls shouldn't hear."

The room turns cold. Jimmy Boyd's "I Saw Mommy Kissing Santa Claus" slices through the living room. The fireplace lightly pops. Wrapping paper awkwardly crinkles as Carol sets down a present on the ground.

Tracy's eyes blink up at me, her lips wide and parted. This fight feels too much like old times. Useless, instigated arguments. But that I can handle.

Words against Michelle?

Not in my house. Not anywhere.

Emily audibly swallows. "I'm going for a walk."

Tracy's head jerks to Emily. "In the snow? No, you aren't."

"You can't tell me what to do," Emily says with a sneer.

"I'm your *mother*."

Emily blows out a breath. "Psht. Whatever," she says as she strides past me.

I sigh. "Em, it's cold."

"I don't care."

"It's snowing."

"I don't care!" she repeats louder.

"Fine. I'm gonna have to follow you."

"No!" Emily yells, walking quickly from the living room.

Stumbling to stand, Tracy also yells, "I'm coming too!"

"Fuck off, Mom!"

Tracy's whole body jerks backward. She looks like she got slapped across the face, blinking over and over. Stunned to silence.

Damn it, Emily.

"I'll be back," I grumble, striding from the living room.

Emily slams the back door shut. The blinds crack against the glass. I rip it open again and step out into the cold after her.

Chapter 41

MICHELLE

I'm doomed to cursed holidays in Copper Run.

I sit on the couch, my feet curled up under my butt, with my fuzzy slippers on the carpet in front of me. Rocket is half curled in my lap after the loud noises. I look completely at home in a house that isn't mine—with a family that belongs to the woman staring in my direction with her thin eyebrows perched high on her forehead.

"I should get going," I say, unfurling my position and dusting my pajama pants off, as if specks of the awkward moment remain.

"Oh, Michelle—" Carol moans.

Brittany crawls, then stands, running to me and hugging my legs again.

"Don't go," she whines.

I pat her head and twirl my earring with my other hand, cutting my eyes to Tracy. She hasn't stopped staring at me. I'm not the kind of woman to be intimidated, if that's what she's going for. But I understand when I'm unwanted.

"I'll be back tomorrow, okay? Merry Christmas," I say with a wave to Carol.

Brittany buries her head in my thigh, and I stifle a laugh by chewing on my bottom lip.

"Promise you'll be here tomorrow?" she whispers.

"Promise."

"Okay." Then, reluctantly, she pulls away.

I give her the best smile I can muster. Carol exhales in frustration, narrowing her eyes at Tracy. I throw Tracy a gentle wave, but she doesn't return it.

Fair enough.

I walk down the hall and back to the kitchen with Rocket beside me, but harsh footsteps follow us the whole way.

"Michelle." Tracy's voice comes out like a demand.

I sigh through my irritation and squeak around on my heel. "Thank you for inviting me, Tracy."

She shakes her head. "The girls wanted you here." Her eyes roll to the side, catching on something in the corner. "Cliff did too."

I open my mouth and close it but say nothing. I don't know what I'd say anyway.

Tracy stalks over to the kitchen window, peering out to the road. Through the thick, falling snow, Cliff and Emily sit on the curb in their loose pajamas and no jackets.

Tracy's shoulders pin back, and she tilts her chin higher, watching her daughter outside without her. She grips the edge of the wooden chair with white knuckles.

We're too similar. I know because I do the same thing when I'm hurt—I attempt to cover any uncomfortable truth with pride, like a shield.

She darts her eyes to mine with the speed of a hawk.

"Tell me something," she says like a cracking whip.

"All right," I agree tentatively.

"Does Emily seem happy?"

I don't hesitate. "Yes."

"And Brittany?"

"She's a kid," I answer with a twitch of my mouth. "She could build a house out of sand and live inside without a care in the world."

"You seem to know kids very well."

"I don't. But I know my sister, and she was like Brittany." I tilt my head side to side. "Still is."

"How old is she?"

"Old enough to probably not act that way."

Tracy's eyes dart between mine. "Are they happy with Cliff?"

I swallow. I don't feel comfortable discussing Cliff with his ex, but the way her chin trembles, I find myself nodding.

"Yes," I answer.

Tracy inhales and glances out the window again. She lets out the breath. "She chose him over me," she says matter-of-factly, as if she were reading about their relationship in an encyclopedia.

I don't answer.

I peer down at Rocket. He silently stares back at me. We're at a loss for words today, I suppose.

"They . . ." Tracy pauses. "They really depend on him, don't they?" The words start confident, and then with each syllable, she frowns further. All pretenses of confidence drain from her body.

"Yes."

It's sad to watch as her jaw tightens, but I don't pity her. I see myself through her. It's the same part of me that longed for my mom to want me the most.

"That's good," she says quietly. She finally turns to me. Her cheeks are blotchy. Her nose is red. Her jaw tenses.

"Well, thank you for coming over." It's sharp, like disappointment is burning through as the reality she so carefully constructed in her mind immediately falls apart.

I turn to leave, but my heart suddenly beats so fast at the thought of not standing in this kitchen anymore, of not walking between our houses every afternoon. And not seeing Cliff. I have a couple of more days, but this feels weirdly definitive.

I won't see his cocky smile burst at the sight of me. I won't hear his low, husky laugh. I won't hear his sarcasm and non sequiturs. I won't hear his terrible jokes that make me laugh despite myself. I won't feel his palm roam over my knee, onto my waist, and against my cheek. I won't feel his hair tickle between my fingers.

But most of all, I'll be across the country, where I won't be *seen*. Not really. Not like Cliff does.

"Michelle?" Tracy asks.

I blink out of my reverie and back to her. She's staring at me again.

My nose feels hot. The area behind my eyes stings.

"I'm heading out," I say stiffly.

My bottom lip trembles despite myself, and I hate it so much for doing so.

Chapter 42

CLIFF

"It's cold out here."

"Really?" I ask. "Huh. I'm feeling great."

"Shut up, Dad."

We sit on the curb outside the house. The street has a thick layer of snow that almost covers the line between the sidewalk and the road. I forgot a coat. I'm in my Bulls T-shirt and thin pajama pants, soaked through from sitting on the ground. I genuinely wonder if my balls will be ice in the next few minutes.

I exhale out a misty fog of warm air.

"So . . . do you want to talk about it?" I ask.

"No."

I nod to myself. "All right, then."

Emily pulls her arms closer to her chest. She isn't wearing a jacket either. Thankfully, she's at least in a long-sleeved striped shirt and thicker sleep pants than mine. Her long blond hair is braided down her back, exposing pink ears. When she visibly shivers, I sling my arm around her shoulders. She leans closer.

"Are you gonna sit here until I talk?" she asks through chattering teeth.

"No. I'm gonna sit here until you want to go back inside.

Doesn't matter if you wanna talk or not. You're not freezing to death alone out here."

"I won't freeze to death," she insists.

"And what if those are your last words?"

"I'm gonna be fine."

"I won't even be able to say *I told you so*."

"That's because I'll be the one saying *I told you so*," she counters.

"How? You'll be dead."

Emily smirks. I squeeze her shoulder. She buries her head in my chest. I smile to myself.

Muffled against my shirt, I think I hear her murmur, "Sorry for yelling at Mom."

I hum in acknowledgment.

"Are you angry?" she whispers.

"Yes," I admit. I rest my chin on her head. "That was inappropriate. You should never say that to someone. Especially not your mother."

"She thinks she can tell me what to do even if she's not here anymore. It's crap."

"She's trying her best," I say. "Your mom is only human. But I will say that things are complicated."

Emily grumbles, "Is this when you tell me I'll understand when I'm older?"

I shrug. "Maybe you will. And honestly, maybe you won't."

There's a lot about Tracy I don't understand and a lot of things I don't agree with. But I won't poison the waters for Emily or Brittany. I wouldn't like it if Tracy did that to me, and I definitely don't do it to her.

I wish there were a way to explain both sides of the story. That Tracy had dreams. That, sometimes, life doesn't always go the way you want, and it's never ideal to abandon your previous life to pursue a new one. But sometimes, if you don't, life isn't a life anymore. Tracy resented Copper Run. She resented me. Even the girls. And she would have continued that for the rest of her life. Sacrifices had to be made. Tracy leaving was the best outcome for our girls. It was like mixing oil and vinegar—Tracy and Copper Run—and we needed to let them separate. It didn't seem like it at the time, and maybe it will never make sense to Emily.

"But either way," I continue, "you are not to talk to your mother like that again, okay?"

Emily silently nods. "Okay."

"Good."

"I hate it when you get all dad-like on me."

"We can't be best pals all the time."

A gust of wind passes by, making us huddle closer. I keep waiting for Emily to get up, but when she doesn't, stubbornly shivering instead, I hunker down and endure with her.

"I'm not your best friend," she suddenly mumbles.

I bark out a laugh. "That's mean."

"Michelle is your best friend."

My gut clenches. My hand probably squeezes her shoulder more than it should as I try to ground myself again.

"She's a very good friend," I answer, more fact than opinion.

If I were to be honest, in my opinion, Michelle is the closest friend I've ever had—man or woman. We're closer than Tracy and I ever were. Trace and I were parents out of necessity. We didn't date long enough to get to know each other on a friendship level. We were running on hormones alone. I wanted the hot cheerleader. She wanted the funny class clown. But there was only so much of that she could take.

Michelle doesn't *put up* with me. She *chooses* to be around me. I like making her laugh, and she likes my jokes and sarcasm. She's realistic when I don't want to be.

"Are you and Michelle dating?" Emily asks.

"That's kind of between us, kiddo."

"Are you?"

I exhale and finally admit, "Yes. No. I don't know actually."

"She's leaving in two days," Emily says.

"She is."

"Are you gonna miss her?"

"Of course," I say, the answer choking out of me.

"I'm sorry."

I huff a half-hearted laugh. "It is what it is."

Emily kicks her bare foot out, breaking up a small bit of snow on her pink toes.

"Em, you're gonna get frostbite."

"Make her stay," she blurts out.

I growl under my breath in frustration. I would if I could. If it was the right thing to do.

I shake my head. "I can't do that."

"Why not? You said you're gonna miss her."

"Because making people stay in Copper Run when they don't want to isn't a nice thing to do," I say.

"Maybe she wants to stay," Emily argues.

"She doesn't."

"You don't know that."

"I have a pretty good idea. Her dream is in Seattle, and dreams don't go away. She deserves to have hers."

I know this better than anyone. Dreams never go away. That whole saying about loving someone enough to let them go is true. I wish it hadn't taken me thirty-three years to realize it.

Emily scoots away. "What if her dream is here? With you? And she needs you to tell her how you feel?"

How I feel.

I run a cold hand through my hair and shake it back out. I can't tell her I love her. It would only make things worse.

"Tell her," Emily whispers.

I snort and side-eye her. "Are you stealing Cupid's job?"

Emily shrugs. "Michelle's great is all."

"She *is* pretty great, huh?"

"Yeah."

We fall silent. The neighborhood of Copper Run has never been so quiet. The wind, me, and Emily. And maybe the low hum of excessive yard lights from Winston's house.

A shiver rolls down Emily's spine again. "It's cold out here."

"Hey, you're the one who chose to sulk on a curb. Not me."

She doesn't respond with a snarky comment. Instead, she leans her head on my shoulder and exhales another puff of warm air. "I'm gonna miss Michelle."

I lean my head on top of hers. "Me too, kiddo. Me too."

Michelle didn't stay after the Christmas morning disaster. I didn't expect her to, which is good because Emily turns her nose up at her mom with a ferocity I wouldn't wish upon anyone.

The three of us stand in the kitchen, with Carol in the other room, watching over Brittany.

"You're happier in New York," Emily says matter-of-factly.

Tracy looks from me to Emily with wide, offended eyes, as if I'll help her. I don't intend to step in.

"Not because of you," is all Tracy can think to say.

"I know you blame me for . . . why you had to stay here,"

Emily says. "I didn't ask to be born though, and you don't get to treat me how you do."

Tracy gawks and shakes her head. "Em—"

"I'm serious. I want to be treated like I matter, Mom."

Tracy blinks and sighs out a small, "You do. I . . . I've considered having you move—"

"*Having* me move? You don't get it at all. We're happy here. Me and Brittany? Super happy. I don't *want* to move. I get a say sometimes, you know. What we have here is enough for us, and we're happy. You're happy there, and there's nothing wrong with that. But we wanna be happy here."

Tracy is stunned for a few minutes before nodding to herself. Emily storms back into the living room after her outburst. I shrug and follow. My girl needed to get it off her chest.

Tracy didn't have much of an argument for that, and her snappy comments lessen after that conversation. When she warms by the fire, she makes sure to ask more tentative questions about Emily's life. She asks about Josh. Emily still doesn't tell her about the pregnancy scare. That will be my responsibility, but that's fine. It's what I'm here for—to have the rougher conversations.

Emily makes chicken potpie that night, proud now that her home ec class is done. Tracy says it's the best potpie she's ever had—which is a little generous—but I agree to press home the point. We have dinner on the early side because Tracy's bus leaves that evening. By the time I'm carrying her suitcase to the front door, things have settled enough that half smiles are all around in the living room.

Brittany runs and hugs her mom goodbye. Tracy swings her back and forth, placing a gentle kiss on the top of her head before smoothing down her hair.

"Be good. And tell that boy Luke that he can ask you on a date when you're sixteen."

Brittany nods in agreement. I'm pretty sure her mind is stuck on her new Lisa Frank coloring book instead. Good. I'm exhausted with boys around the house.

Emily stands from the couch and reluctantly pulls her mom into a weak hug. It's awkward and almost uncomfortable to watch. But when Emily's eyes close, I can tell it's maybe the start of something good. She needed that hug more than her mom did.

"Be good?" Tracy asks.

Emily nods. "I'll try."

I grab Tracy's luggage and gesture toward the door. Outside the window, a taxi rumbles in front of our house, blowing puffs of exhaust on the plowed street beneath. Tracy nods, and I walk her out to the sidewalk with her suitcase carried over my head. It couldn't roll on the icy sidewalk even if I wanted it to.

Setting it down, I pull her in for a hug. "Nice to see you, Trace."

"You too." She looks back at the house and sighs. "I feel . . . like I should be here more. I don't even know them anymore."

"Don't feel guilty."

"I should."

I shake my head, holding her by the shoulders. "Feel how you feel. But don't do it because it seems like something you *should* feel."

She sucks in a shaky inhale. "I do feel bad, Cliff. Every day, I do."

"They're safe here. They're happy. So, go do what makes you happy. Come visit when you can. Don't change what's been working. No need to be annoyed by me more than you need to."

She blinks and shakes her head. "You don't annoy me." She looks down at her shoes and shrugs. "It . . . didn't work out. But you're a wonderful dad. You're doing good here. Really good."

"Thanks."

"And by the way," she says, "I can tell she really loves you."

"She?"

"Your neighbor."

The smile slides off my face. Tracy straightens her posture and nods assuredly.

Love?

I swallow and laugh.

Tracy scowls and interjects a cutting, "Don't be an idiot, Cliff."

I tuck my hands in my pockets and hike my shoulders up to my ears. "I try not to be."

She pokes a finger at me. "I'd better see her again."

I grin. "Bye, Trace."

"Bye, Cliff."

We hug again, holding each other a bit tighter this time.

She gets in the taxi. I load the suitcase in the trunk, and then I pat the side of the car. It putters away. Tracy doesn't turn back around. She never really has though.

Chapter 43

MICHELLE

The doorbell rings. I crack open the front door of Bird & Breakfast, only to see Cliff on the other side.

"Can Michelle come out to play?"

Then he's smacked on the side of his head by a snowball a second later.

"Get back out here!" Lars yells from the sidewalk, rounding a ball of snow in his palms.

"We've got a war," Cliff says with a grin, running down the stairs toward Brittany, who takes off across the yard, heavy breaths puffing into the air.

I run out without grabbing a jacket to roll my own snowball. Cliff barrels toward me. His arms grab around my waist and pull me against his chest, kicking my feet up into the air.

"Let me go!" I call through laughs. "I need to hit you!"

Another snowball hits his head with a *poomf*, barely missing my own.

"I think Emily's already got me covered," he says, releasing me to the ground, where inches of snow have accumulated. I was so busy packing to leave and walking through the inn with Sara that I didn't take time to notice.

I finish rolling up a snowball, rearing back to aim toward Lars, Emily, Carol, then Cliff. I have no clue which person is on what side of the war. Maybe we're all lone agents. Or maybe it's all of them against me.

"You'd target your own team?" Cliff asks on a laugh when I point my snowball toward him.

"I assumed I was on my own team," I answer with a grin.

Cliff slowly shakes his head. "I'm always on your team."

The smile that erupts over my lips feels like an electric shock zipping straight from my heart. I kiss him, then smack the snowball over his head anyway.

It's our last full day together before I board a flight back to Washington. I try to savor every moment I can. I listen to the album I gifted to Emily as she breaks down every song, explaining why it's brilliant. Cliff makes us thumbprint cookies with raspberry preserves, and I watch shamelessly as he pushes into the dollops of dough, all pulsing forearms and bony wrists under his flour-coated watch.

Brittany steals a cookie only minutes after they leave the oven, then asks if she can have another. Cliff ushers her back to the living room.

"You're already gonna barf up the last two you ate," he says through a laugh.

"So?" she whines. "Rocket got one!"

"Rocket *stole* one," I correct, flashing my eyes to him.

He jumped his paws onto the kitchen nook table and chowed down before we caught him. The baking sheet was too hot for him to grab more, but he would have eventually if Cliff hadn't moved them to the counter.

I admonished Rocket with a "Bad dog," but he shot me a look that said, *Since when, Shelly?*

But even now, as he peers up at me from the dog bed Cliff added to their kitchen, Rocket seems content with any title, as long as he's here.

My stomach smarts. I wonder if he'd be happier in Copper Run. Maybe Sara will take him in. He's a very good dog. But then what will I do?

At midday, Sara walks in the back door with packets of hot chocolate, which Cliff offendedly puts to the side before making us his homemade recipe. Sara gives me a secretive, pursed smile, as if that was her plan all along.

Lisa and George drop off leftover fruitcake in the evening.

"I didn't know George could bake," I whisper to Cliff.

He chuckles and shakes his head. "He doesn't."

As it turns out, the fruitcake is terrible, but George's pride keeps anyone from saying a word.

Lisa and George decide to stay for dinner without an invitation, and they call Dad, who lugs over his chessboard and laughs in the corner, challenging anyone who will dare walk by. Lars, in particular, is adamant about winning, so much so that he plays three times. He loses all three times.

Cliff watches the busy living room scene and pulls me closer into his arms.

I wish I could pause this moment. Maybe keep it on my shelf like a beautiful snow globe I can shake whenever I like. But that isn't how life works.

It's a little after eight o'clock. Dad went upstairs to read before bed. Cliff is at his house, putting Brittany to sleep. Emily is with Josh and a group of other teenagers in the square, enjoying the continued snow. Sara and I remain at Bird & Breakfast's front desk as I walk her through final instructions.

Eyeing the binder tucked beside the handprint-littered pencil holder, I finally draw it out and lay it on the desk.

"If you are ever unsure, this binder has been my holy grail."

"Mom wrote this?" she asks, opening it with a near-silent crack echoing in the empty foyer.

"Yeah."

"It's so organized." Sara peers up at me through her lashes. "Like mother, like daughter."

I smile to myself. The page protectors, filled with local takeout restaurants and numbers I've memorized, crinkle as Sara turns each one. But closer to the end, she stops on a handwritten letter.

Dear Sara.

Heat rises from my chest up to my head, sending my brain swimming. And then the feeling settles, and the tide of nerves draws back into my chest. I'm floating on the surface, bobbing with each passing of my slow heartbeat.

I haven't thought about that letter in weeks. At some point, it no longer mattered. This place *is* Sara's. My mom gave it to her because it made sense—not because she loved me less. It was always complicated, like Tracy and her daughters. Sometimes, we forget our parents are humans too.

Sara removes the letter from its sleeve, tracing a finger over the raised pen scratches.

"Did you know about this?" Sara asks.

"I forgot," I confess. "I haven't read it."

"You haven't?"

"It's written to you."

Sara chokes out a laugh. "You're far less nosy than I am."

The rolling chair whines as Sara leans back, tucking her knees up to her chin. Her eyes skim over the letter. A smile grows, lingers, then suddenly falls. Her hands grip the paper tighter.

She looks at me again. "You didn't read it?"

I furrow my brow. "No."

She holds it out to me. "You should. For your peace of mind."

I swallow, taking a half step back. "It's written to you," I repeat.

"Read it, Shells. It's nothing. Really."

My heart is suddenly racing as my quivering hand takes the paper. I pinch my eyes closed, inhale, then open them and read.

May 20, 1997

Dear Sara,
I'm writing this to you in hopes that you'll one day take care of my heart and joy—Bird & Breakfast.

First, I left instructions in this binder with everything you might need. There are lovely people in town who will help if you ask. Lisa lives one block over at 225. Hopefully, they're alive when you read this—Lord willing. They're the most generous people I know. You can bribe George with pastries—biscuits are his favorite. Betty will give you free sandwiches if you agree to try her new recipes. Lars is a sweetheart but a gossip; visit him to meet more people. And if Cliff Burke still lives next door, he will bake for you. I made him promise he would, and he is a man of his word.

You are a bright light in this world. You have been since the day you were born. I always tell your father that you were born giggling. You are hope and wonder and heart. I trust your glow will shine through every day. Keep glowing, my little sunshine.

And as a little note: please take care of your sister. Shells has always watched over you, but it's your turn to protect her. She will need you—even if she never shows it. She's like me in that way. She's too strong for her own good. Tell her you love her always. Encourage her to be happy. She might need a little help, but I trust you to be her guiding light.

I love you both so much. You've filled me with so much life.

Love,
Mom

I reach up to my pendant and run it up and down the necklace chain. Sara watches.

My breath leaves in shaky exhales. My shoulders are tight. My jaw won't move from its clenching hold.

"Are you okay?" she asks.

"Are you?"

She smiles. "Are *you*?"

I laugh through a derisive snort. "I'm . . . fine."

It's funny; the letter was nothing like I thought it would be. It was a simple letter. Instructions more than anything. But I'm realizing now that I wanted there to be more to it. Maybe I wanted something revolutionary. But it's nothing. This is all she left. It is what it is.

"Where did you get that, by the way?" Sara asks.

"Get what?"

"Mom's necklace."

I glance down at it and let go. I was tracing the pendant up and down the chain.

"She gave it to me," I say.

"When?"

"It was in Mom's surgery bag. They took it off her before she went in. I tried to give it back after, but she said I should keep it."

I've never seen Sara freeze so quickly.

"Do you think she knew?" she whispers.

Now it's my time to freeze.

"How could she?" I ask. "She had just gotten out of surgery. She probably thought she was fine. We all knew she was."

Sara shrugs, staring at the necklace lying on my collarbone. She curls her shoulders in and bites her lower lip. She reminds me of Emily in that moment. When Sara was her age, we occasionally had conversations like this—existential things. I was always more of a realist, but Sara always thought along the lines of stars and dreams.

"Maybe she felt it," she says, flicking her eyes to mine. "Knew it was her time. Maybe it's why she wrote the letter so soon before."

I want to tell her that's ridiculous, but I don't. Sometimes, Sara needs a dose of reality, but now is not that time. I instead set the letter on the desk and cross my arms.

After a moment, Sara murmurs, "What if I said I didn't want the inn?"

My eyes flick to her. "Why would you say that?"

She audibly swallows, then firmly nods. "I . . . I want to make art. How can I do that here?"

"Sara . . ."

"And . . . well, this place should be yours. It *is* yours."

Those words hit me harder than they should.

I shake my head. "No, Mom left it to you."

"But she also said to make sure you're happy. And you're happy here." I open my mouth to counter, but she cuts in. "You never smile like you do in this inn. Like when you're talking with guests." She breathes in slowly and lets it out. "Like how you smile with Cliff."

"I like it here, but this isn't my life."

"But it can be," she says, almost on a plea.

I jerk my head back.

"Why not, Shells?"

I turn my head, looking at the stairwell—anything to not see her.

"I can't," I answer. "I have a life in Seattle. A life I love. A dream I'm living."

"But you're in love!" Her hands flail in the air before slapping down on her thighs. "Isn't that good enough, Shelly? You're in love with this town. This place. And Cliff. You are *so* stupidly in love with Cliff, and it's so frustrating, watching you throw all this away. Him and the inn. And for what? To live in the same stupid town house you had with Allen?"

I clench my jaw. "It's more than that, and you know it. I can't pick up my life and move here. I have a *dream* offer. An offer I've worked so, *so* hard for, Sara. You don't even understand. You have no idea what I've sacrificed to make this career. I've done *so much*. My own damn marriage couldn't stand up to it. So why shouldn't I get what I've worked for? This is what I have. What I deserve. This career. I have nothing but this, and I love it. I can't leave it." The words leave so wildly that they surprise even me.

Sara stares at me for too long, then shakes her head stiffly. She huffs out a sardonic laugh, slams the binder closed, and walks toward the kitchen. She stops short of the doorway.

"You ever stop to think that maybe you deserve more?"

I open my mouth and close it, running my tongue over my teeth and sighing.

Sara shakes her head. "Just a thought. See you tomorrow."

I mumble a small, "See you tomorrow," but I don't think she hears me.

○○

That night, I don't sleep in my own bed. I sneak between the rosebushes and push into the Burke house with a quiet creak of the back door. A gurgling coffeepot brews in the corner, and Cliff sits with a book at the kitchen table.

His lips pull at the corner, the crease beside his mouth deepening so beautifully, and I hope I can remember it exactly as it is when I'm across the country.

I walk to him and lower into his lap. He turns the book spine up on the table and wraps his arms around my waist.

"Excuse me, ma'am. Do I know you?"

I smile. "No, I don't think we've met. I'm Michelle."

I hold out my hand. He gently slides his palm into mine—large and rough compared to my smooth fingers.

"Cliff. And might I say, you are an absolutely stunning woman."

Shake.

"Someone told me that once."

He laughs through a bitten lip. "Well, you should be told every minute of your life."

Shake.

"You're funny," I say.

"Not a single person has told me that."

Shake.

"You should be told that every minute of your life," I whisper back.

He stops shaking my hand and leans his head into the crook of my neck.

"Hey," he murmurs.

"Hi."

"Figured you'd be here eventually," he says. "Made you some coffee." He nods toward the coffeepot. He aimlessly runs his palm up my spine. Touching me. Always touching me. "And . . . I have your Christmas gift."

I straighten up. "Oh, really?"

"Really."

He pats my butt so that I rise off his lap, then walks to the counter. He swivels around with a small white box.

"I've missed your weird baker thing," I say with a sigh.

"I think I've mastered the baker thing this time." Cliff sets the box on the table. "Try it."

I look at him, then back to the box, sliding open the lid and looking inside.

I've never seen a pastry like this before. It's not a muffin, but it's not a sweet roll either. The dough has that croissant texture, but it's also compact. Small. Round. And it smells exactly like burnt sugar.

I pick it up, take a bite, and . . . *melt*.

It's buttery. Flaky. There's a soft crunch with a bit of the sugar flaking off onto my lips. It's messy, but every crumb is a delicate balance of flavors.

It's so unique, so wonderful, that I take a second bite, trailing my tongue over my lips after.

"What is this?" I ask.

I glance over at Cliff. He sinks into an exhale, and the little line beside his mouth deepens.

"It's kouign-amann."

I laugh. "Kwe what?"

He leans from one hip to the other, sauntering over to my side and placing a palm around my lower back.

"It's a French pastry. A pastry that is"—he leans in on an

exhausted exhale—"*incredibly* difficult to make. With many layers. A lot like you."

"I'm difficult to make?"

"You're difficult. In the best of ways."

I smile. "Well, it's my favorite," I announce, dropping the last bite into my mouth.

His eyes pinch closed as he grins. "God, that's so hot. Say it again."

I lean closer. "It's my favorite, Cliff."

Peering down at me through hooded eyes, he grabs my hand and tugs me down the hall.

The moment his bedroom door shuts, we're reaching for each other. Cliff cups my head and kisses me. It's wild. Eager.

He lifts my shirt over my head as I grip his jaw. I bite his lip as he pushes the hem of my tight skirt up around my waist. Together, we fall backward on the mattress.

Cliff kisses over my chest with low, barely there hums, like he's singing a hymn in his church and I'm the icon he's praying to. He gingerly tugs down my bra cup, kissing the peak of my breast and then the other. Licking. Biting. His tongue traces a line down the middle of my chest, between my ribs, and over my stomach. He places kiss after kiss between my thighs and over my underwear before hooking his thumbs in the fabric and pulling them down.

I watch as his eyes flick up to meet mine. That very reliable *snag* locks us in place, and slowly, with his eyes steady, his tongue rolls over me. I gasp out a breath.

He dips his fingers inside, curling with ease, sending zips of nerves through my stomach and to my chest. I'm on fire with every stroke of his tongue and every subsequent pump of his fingers. It's magic. Thrilling. My chest heaves up and down as I try to gasp for breath. My fingers thread through his hair.

I try to stay quiet as sensation rolls through me, but it's fruitless with how his tongue is moving. Eventually, Cliff reaches up and cups his palm over my mouth. That alone—the grip of his rough palm over my lips—sends my orgasm barreling over me in a rush.

I'm breathless when I pull his arm to coax him back up to me. I reach for his belt, and it clangs apart, the zipper pulling down in a quick hiss. He's inside me within moments. I close my eyes, letting every thrust push me closer and closer. Every beat of his heart against mine thrums over my chest and down my stomach before pulsing between my thighs.

His thumb strokes over my cheek. "Open your eyes, Michelle."

I find him looking down at me, searing me to my soul, like he always has from the first day he laid eyes on me. His hand lands beside my head. I entwine my fingers through his.

And suddenly, our quickness slows to a crawl.

"I love watching you," he says.

I love you.

"Please," is all I can say.

His husky laugh follows as he thrusts deeper. "God, you're beautiful," he huffs out, cupping my cheek in his palm, stroking a thumb over my bottom lip and tugging.

"Keep talking," I breathe.

"You like feeling me inside you?"

"Yes."

"I love this."

I love you.

"You feel so good," he exhales. "Like you were made for me."

I wonder if it's true. If I'm the only woman who sees him for the man he is. Funny and sarcastic, but selfless and good.

And I wonder if he was made for me, if he's the only man who will ever *see* me. I don't believe in destiny or stars, but I have to believe Cliff's constellation would align right beside mine.

"You think so loud," he says, pumping into me harder. "Let it out."

I moan, and his palm roughly covers my mouth again. I remember the first time he held me like this. The first night we kissed. The night he caged me against that house and told me, "Screw it," and we fell into the abyss together. The night I realized that I *wanted* him.

I loved him in that moment.

I didn't know it yet.

But, oh, how I did.

The sensation hits me suddenly, zipping through my chest, over my shoulders, and down to my fingers. My mouth widens in a breathy whine as I orgasm. He thrusts inside me, giving an equally low, muffled groan as we come together.

I wouldn't call what we did *sex*. It's too crude. But I wouldn't say it was *making love* either. It was something different altogether—something that didn't feel like it should have been mine—but I sure hoped whatever it was didn't mean *goodbye*.

I look at the clock. It's ten minutes after midnight. I officially leave Vermont today. I pull in a heavy, shaking breath. Cliff glances at the red digital numbers, too, then kisses the dip in my collarbone.

His silence speaks louder than anything either of us could say.

MICHELLE

I don't expect a big send-off, but when I walk out of Bird & Breakfast with my suitcases and Mom's purse hiked on my shoulder, I'm grateful that so many people are there.

Dad slings his arm over my shoulders and exhales a big sigh. "You're gonna do great things, Shellfish."

I manage a half smile. "You gonna be okay here?"

"Stop worrying about other people," he says sternly. "And know that if you ever want to come back, we'll have a room for you."

"There are only three guest rooms."

"We'll always have a room for you," he repeats.

I swallow, nodding as he pulls me into a hug. It's warm and close and something he hasn't done since before Mom died. He's piecing his heart back together. I hope he finds the remaining bits here.

I take one step forward but am immediately tackled again.

Carol wraps her arms around me so tight that I have to tilt my chin up to get air. Her hair smells like stale smoke and roses. Maybe four months ago, this might have felt awkward and suffocating, but I smile and lean into it. It smells like Carol.

She swings me side to side until finally letting me go.

I grimace. "You've gotta stop smoking."

"You sound like Cliff."

"Good."

Lars is behind her, holding out one arm for a side hug. "Don't be a stranger."

All I can do is nod in response.

Brittany stands behind him, winding her fingers through the overalls straps under her coat. Her unicorn stuffed toy is gripped in her fist. I crouch to meet her eye level.

She shoves the toy toward me. "I want you to have him."

"Oh, I can't," I say, tucking a strand of her curly blond hair behind her ear. "He's yours."

She jerks her head side to side and shoves it at me again. "Keep him."

I smile, gingerly taking it and nodding. "How about I babysit him for a while? He can see the other side of the US, and then I'll give him back the next time I'm here."

"Okay," she murmurs.

"And, hey, Rocket's gonna stay here for a while," I say. "So I'm trusting you with him too, all right?"

She nods, staring down at her light-up sneakers. "Because you'll be back?"

"Right," I say through a swallow. "Because I'll be back."

"Promise?"

I manage a smile. "Promise."

She barrels into me with a hug, burying her face in my chest.

I pull back and smile. "And don't forget to put Luke in his place when he talks about Steve."

Her head bobs up and down. She runs the back of her hand over her nose. I pull her into another hug and don't let go until she does.

I rise back up and turn to see Emily standing with her arms crossed, leaning against the front porch column.

"This sucks," she drawls.

"Totally," I say, mocking her teen tone.

"Whatever," she says on an eye roll, peering out the corner with a half smile.

I know she's not a big hugger, so I give a smile and start to walk away. But then her hand grabs me, pulling me back into a hug.

"I'll miss you," she murmurs.

I hold her and squeeze. "I'll miss you too."

"I can call, right?"

"Anytime you want. I'll call you too."

She leans back. "You will?"

"Of course. How else am I gonna know about what stupid things you and Josh get up to?"

Emily grins. "Okay. Cool."

"Cool," I echo, stroking through her long hair and smiling.

Sara stands at the bottom of the stairs, and if all those hugs weren't enough, she gathers me in her arms for yet another. She holds me in silence, and eventually, I try to tug apart, but she won't let me.

Instead, with her lips close to my ear, she whispers, "This place is yours if you want it."

"Sara," I say, but the word catches in my throat.

Yours.

She leans back, peering into my eyes. Her blue eyes are so much like Mom's, and for a second, I can see her through them as well.

"It's yours," she repeats. "Just say the word."

I blink to the ground. "I . . . I can't think about this right now."

She hugs me again, and it successfully hides my shaky exhale. Maybe she could sense it was coming. Sara's always had a knack for knowing my feelings better than I do.

I pull apart and stare back up at Bird & Breakfast with its porch awning over the same swinging bench where I sat on most chilly nights. Lace curtains hang in front of the bay window. Inside the open door is the stairwell I descended countless times; the front desk, where I figured out how to run this place; and the kitchen door down the hall with that STAFF ONLY sign I pushed through every single day.

The kitchen is where I colored with Brittany. The backyard is where Rocket played. The living room is where Emily watched too much TV, and the dining room is where I sat with guests every single morning with my shitty cinnamon rolls and my pretty-okay coffee.

Sara opens her mouth. "Remember—"

"Thanks," I interrupt. "But I should go."

Her face falls. "Okay. Have a safe flight."

I nod, but I can't look at her anymore. I can't look at anyone. It's best if I leave with my head held high and no regrets.

Lisa runs at me with a hug, mashing her thick glasses against my face. George stands stoically behind her with his palms resting together.

"So, you're going back," he announces.

"Yes."

"Must mean a lot to you." And somehow, the words feel hollow.

I tongue my cheek as he pulls my shoulders in for a quick hug.

"Watch Sara, okay?" I whisper to Lisa.

She gives a wink and a thumbs-up.

Rocket taps down the front porch stairs, trots casually

across the cobblestone walkway, and drops in a sit right in front of me. *You're not leaving.*

I snort and murmur, "I am."

He turns his head to Cliff's waiting truck, rumbling in place, with the engine sending exhales of smoke into the snowy air.

Rocket's head swivels back up to me. *No, you're not.*

I bend down and pat his head. "Be a good boy."

No.

Cliff walks around the side of his truck, swinging his keys over his fingers. He's such a beacon of light in this winter weather that I swear even the snowflakes part for him. He walks toward me with long, confident strides, looking exactly like he did the first day I arrived. Flashing that handsome grin with a heavy hand threading through his thick brown hair. He tucks that hand in his denim pocket and leans against the truck.

"Ready to go?"

He's so calm when I'm simply *not*. But that's who Cliff is; he's the glue keeping me together. He has been since day one.

"I'm ready," I announce.

He loads my luggage into the truck bed and opens the passenger door for me. The passenger seat is filled with various items from the girls, which makes me laugh. I move a Barbie and a pack of playing cards to the floorboard. Glossy photos scatter in the middle of the bench seat. I tuck them into the glove box over napkins with the Burke's Bakery logo.

Before I can close the door, Rocket speeds down the sidewalk. I startle when he leaps into my lap.

His brown eyes stare back at me. *I'm riding with you, Shelly*, they say.

Cliff climbs into the driver's side and chuckles. "The more, the merrier, I guess."

I shut the passenger door, and Cliff shifts the truck into gear.

We drive down the road as my family waves to us. Bird & Breakfast disappears around the corner. We roll past the sidewalks, cross in front of Burke's Bakery, and go around the square until it fades away too. We drive under the covered red bridge, and I see the back side of Copper Run's latticed sign.

Thank you for visiting! Come back soon!

Rocket curls closer in my lap. I run my fingers over his feathered black-and-white fur and lean my cheek against his neck.

Chapter 45

CLIFF

Copper Run's sign gets smaller and smaller until I can't make it out through the sticks and bare trees. I know I'll be coming back, but I'll be coming back without her.

We talk the whole ride to the airport—everything from recent news to Copper Run gossip. I make sarcastic comments, and she laughs, as always, her head beautifully falling back on the headrest. I hold her hand the entire time, stroking my thumb over the back of hers, holding as tight as I can.

The tall buildings appear faster than I would like. Planes take off from runways in the distance, booming overhead. The drop-off car line is long and agonizing. My nerves pick up in my chest, and I can tell hers do, too, because she starts running Birdie's pendant over the chain. I kiss the back of her knuckles.

"It's fine," I whisper.

She nods quickly, over and over.

Rocket is restless in the seat, walking over her thighs to mine, pressing his nose to the window, leaving wet nose marks against the glass.

"Rocket," I say through a laugh, lifting up to peer over his body.

Michelle claps her hands. "Rocket, let him drive."

Suddenly whining, he paces back to her, pressing his muzzle against her window instead.

We finally pull to the curb, and I put on my emergency lights. I look over at her. She's already staring at me, absent-mindedly stroking Rocket's fur as his paws shake on her thigh.

I reach out to bury my palm in her hair.

"Come here," I murmur.

She leans across the bench seat, pressing her lips to mine. The kiss is slow and lingering and doesn't last nearly long enough.

I lean my forehead against hers. "This is good," I whisper.

She nods. "Yeah." But it doesn't sound sure.

I force a laugh. "You're Michelle. You're going to thrive out there, like you always have."

She silently nods against me.

I want to keep holding her, but a car behind me honks, and I groan.

"Time to go, huh?" I say with a laugh.

She doesn't return it, instead repeating a small "Yeah."

I open the door and shut it before Rocket can jump out. He's a wild card today, and I'm not risking it. I lean over the side of the truck bed and pull out her suitcases, lowering them to the ground with a definitive *thunk*. She stares at me, and I let out an exhale with a smile.

I throw my thumb back to the truck. "Rocket kinda ruined my chances of walking you to your gate."

She looks at the ground, playing with the long strap of her purse with a breathy laugh. "I know."

I'm mentally cursing that dang dog, but I know he wanted to see her off. I couldn't deny him that.

I walk forward, pulling her into my chest and placing my chin on her head. "I'm so excited for you."

My heart is pounding. I can feel it thrumming in my ears. But I can't show her this is killing me. She doesn't need that right now.

"Watch the inn, will you?" she murmurs, tilting her head to the side. "I know Sara is gonna . . . I don't know . . . burn the biscuits or . . ." She sniffs and looks at the sky, shaking her head. "God, she won't pay the bills—I know it. Make sure she checks the mail daily."

I chuckle. "I'll check it for her."

"And the honeymoon quilts. Don't let her forget those."

"The ugly pink things. Got it."

She smacks my arm, and I chuckle as she buries her face in my chest again. My nose stings, but I can't be sad. I have to be certain for her. I have to be.

"Take care of my favorite place, okay?"

I laugh. "I will."

"Okay," she says, swallowing. "Okay. I'm gonna go."

"Call me when you land?"

I kiss her again, and she clutches my arms so tight that I wonder if it'll bruise.

"I'll talk to you soon," she says, and the words sound almost strained. Desperate.

I've never heard that sound from her before.

I cup her cheek and kiss her again.

I love you.

"I'll miss you," I say instead. It's easier. Kinder.

She grabs the handles of both suitcases with whitened knuckles and shaking hands. I place my palms over them.

"I'll see you sooner than either of us can blink," I reassure her.

"You're right," she says with a smile that doesn't reach her eyes. "I know."

Michelle shakes her head and laughs. Then, finally, she turns, dragging both suitcases behind her, and walks away.

My breath catches. My nose stings. My chin is wobbling.

Michelle turns around to see me again, and I let out a choked exhale. I hope she can't hear it.

I force a smile and hold up my pinkie and thumb, wagging my hand beside my ear and mouthing, *Call me.*

She laughs, turns back around, and walks through the sliding doors into the airport. I stand there for a moment or two, staring at the empty space she left behind, then climb back in my truck.

The drive back to Copper Run is so quiet compared to the drive with Michelle. Rocket sits stoically in the passenger seat, staring at the bare winter trees flying past. He doesn't make a sound and doesn't move an inch. I'll need a drink with Lars the moment I get back.

I flick through the radio stations, one right after the other, then pause when Eddie Vedder's voice croons from the speakers. Pearl Jam's "Black."

And that's when it all hits me.

She's not here.

She's not here.

And suddenly, I'm choking through tears as they fall shamelessly down my cheeks. My eyes burn. My vision blurs. I'm sniffling and coughing and gripping the wheel tighter.

Rocket gingerly walks across the bench seat, stepping onto my lap to sit. I inhale and exhale shaky breaths, resting my chin on his shoulder, sniffling over and over. Rocket twists and tries to lick the tears from my cheeks. I can barely see the road.

The driver behind me lays down on his horn. I realize I'm

going ten under the speed limit. I pull off to the side of the highway.

As the car angrily revs past, I feverishly roll down the window and stick out my middle finger, croaking out, "Yeah, keep moving, buddy!"

I lay my forehead on the wheel, tightening my grip and loosening it. Rocket tries to shove his head under my arms. I lift my head up, draw in a deep breath, and slide my palm down my face, dragging my cheeks with it.

"All right." I sniff. "Let's pull it together, right, boy?"

I reach for the glove box to find napkins to blot my messy tears, but when I jerk it open, glossy photos flutter out and fall to the floorboard. I bend down, but staring up at me is Michelle.

My breath hitches as I snatch the photo. It's us on Halloween. I'm in my black costume cloak, holding that scary mask in one hand. My red flannel pokes out under the sleeves. I look silly, but Michelle—standing across from me with her palm over her mouth—is absolutely radiant. She's laughing with me, her smile so broad that her eyes squint. She only gets that type of laugh when she's so happy that it's hard to keep it in.

She looks so happy.

God, I love her.

I blink through my thoughts, zooming past in a whirl.

I love her so much. This can't be it. This isn't the end of us.

"I have to tell her," I breathe out. I scuff my feet across the floor mat to sit up straighter. I slam my palms on the steering wheel. "Damn it!"

Rocket starts pacing back and forth again, whining. I peer at him from the corner of my eye. He barks in my face.

"Yeah," I agree. "Let's go, mutt."

I push Rocket back, pull down the seat belt to buckle him in, and slam the car into gear. I rip the wheel to one side. His ears fly back. The truck skids us back onto the two-lane highway, fishtailing into the opposite lane. I slam my foot on the pedal, and we take off.

Chapter 46

MICHELLE

I stare out the airport's floor-to-ceiling window. The runway is full of planes either parked, rolling, or soaring into the air. I clutch Brittany's stuffed unicorn closer to my chest. My other hand fists around Mom's purse strap. My flight takes off in five minutes. My section was called ten minutes ago. I'm the only one left standing at my gate, but I can't seem to move.

If I get on that plane, I'll have to watch Vermont disappear beneath me.

I'll be back, sure. But when?

I wonder if Sara remembered to make afternoon coffee. I wonder if Emily feels comfortable, watching TV in the parlor with Dad there. I wonder if Rocket's made it back to Brittany already.

I wonder if Cliff misses me.

He kept encouraging me to go, and the words at the tip of my tongue couldn't find their way out.

I love you.

The moment he drove off, it felt like a piece of me went with him. Just like how the last white dot of Copper Run's sign felt like a puncture in my heart that won't go away.

I cough out a laugh and roll my stinging eyes, but not before wiping the corner because God forbid I cry in an airport.

God, why am I crying? I feel nauseous. Sick to my stomach. It's so ridiculous.

I reach into my purse, fiddling through makeup and keys. I could have sworn I dumped travel-size Kleenex in here. I zip open the back pocket, and my hands fumble over something else. I pull it out. It's a folded piece of notebook paper, faded to a light tan with a small wine stain in the corner.

I slowly unfold it, my hands somehow shaking as a letter stares back at me.

Dear Shelly.

I pull in a deep, shaking inhale, stumbling toward the window and catching myself, my palm slipping on the glass.

January 1, 1997

Dear Shelly,
Happy New Year! Your father told me I shouldn't write this, but damn it, I'm going to. Life is too short to have regrets.

It's a new year with new moments. I know you make many new year's goals, and you probably keep them, too, because you're the kind of woman I strive to be. But I want all your moments to be special, so consider this resolution too.

A quick story first.

You should know that your father and I spent this new year drinking with our new friends. I've never had a best friend before, aside from your father, but Lisa and her husband, George, are spectacular. I told them I'd never stayed up all night. A full twenty-four hours without sleep—can you imagine? So, Lisa suggested we walk around town all night until we saw the sunrise. We ended up in a graveyard, and, Shelly, I was so scared that I almost ran for the hills. But your father said I'd regret it if I didn't walk through, so I did.

I'm sure you think that's nothing wild. It's only a graveyard. But I felt alive. I felt freedom in a silly graveyard. And I don't even believe in ghosts! Sometimes, you have to do the silly, irrationally scary things.

So, here's the long and short of it. Allen sucks. He's terrible. You think we don't know, but we do. Your father and I see every time you fight because it's every moment you're not smiling. And you haven't smiled in years. We haven't always seen eye to eye, but you're more like me than you know. You're strong. And we strong women deserve better.

It will feel scary, starting new, but it's that irrational type of fear—the graveyard-at-night-with-no-ghosts fear. You'll be fine. I promise.

I wish I could see you more. I wish we talked more. We have a lovely neighbor next door who is a total hunk. And newly single! He's more talkative than you, but something tells me you two would get along swimmingly.

Don't be too serious, Shells Bells.
And call if you need anything.

Love you forever,
Mom

My teeth start to chatter. My jaw clenches.

Why didn't she send this? Why am I reading it now, when it's too late?

I look at the white tiled ceiling, pulling in a heavy breath.

Why did she move to start a new business after she retired? What secret to happiness did she know that I don't?

"Last call for flight 347 to Seattle, Washington!"

I let out my shaking breath. My nose stings with tears. I stuff the note back in my purse, gripping Brittany's stuffed unicorn tighter and tighter against my chest.

Why am I about to cry?

Why can't I get on this plane?

I've worked hard for my life in Seattle, but it feels . . . empty now. Not like Copper Run. Not like the inn.

Mom's right; *this* is the silly, irrationally scary thing. *This* is freedom.

A small town with people who *see* me.

BARK!

I freeze. I heard a dog bark.

Or what I thought was a bark.

I swivel my head to the gate attendant at the same time she looks at me, as if we're both checking to make sure we heard the same noise.

And then it happens again.

BARK!

The gate attendant looks behind me, and her eyes widen. I follow her gaze, twisting on my heel to look. The moment I do, my stomach drops.

Two security guards fumble down the hall, past the airport bookstore and convenience store.

They're barreling straight toward us, yelling words like, "Stop!" and, "The dog can't be here!"

And in front of them, sprinting with his arms pumping at his sides, is Cliff Burke.

My feet are glued to the floor as I watch him grow bigger. Closer.

It's him.

He's here.

And ten feet ahead of him is the dog.

My eyes flick to the rush of black-and-white fur. Rocket is zooming forward so quickly that I can't see his feet touch the ground. His border collie legs push him faster than anyone can keep up.

He barks again, running faster when our eyes meet. I drop the unicorn toy on the ground and crouch in time for him to leap into my arms.

Rocket whines in my hair, licking my face and wagging his tail so hard that it moves his whole behind. My mind is spinning.

Footsteps thump closer, and when I look up, Cliff is jumping over a bench with one hand and landing so hard on the opposite side that he stumbles. I gasp, covering my mouth with my palm and laughing, watching him break into a sprint toward me again.

God, he's *here*.

Cliff is here.

His heavy chest tightens against his flannel with each inhalation. And then, suddenly, he's standing over me, bending down with his palms on his knees and a grin pulling halfway up his cheeks.

"Miss me?" he asks breathlessly.

"I thought you said—"

"Yeah, I say too much," he says with a laugh.

He grabs my hand and pulls me to stand. My eyes dash between his. My chest is rising and falling almost as quickly as his. I don't know how I'm breathing.

All I know is, he's *here*.

Through another choked exhale, he says, "Don't get on the plane."

"What?"

"Don't get on the plane, Michelle."

"I don't—"

"I love you."

All the warmth in my chest rises up to my neck, my ears and cheeks. And it's so overwhelming, so all-consuming, I'm halted in place with my lips parted in disbelief.

His eyebrows pull in, and the corner of his mouth tips into a smile. "God, I love you," he says, shaking his head. "I love that you roll your eyes when I make stupid jokes. I love that you argue with your dog when you think nobody's watching. I love that you have coffee at night and that you don't dress up for Halloween. And I love how great you are with my girls. I told myself I would never ask someone to stay with me again. But I love you. And that's gotta mean something, right?" His eyes dart between mine, and he echoes on another breath, "That's gotta mean something."

I can't find words. I can't think at all.

Rocket nudges his nose against my leg, but it's stock-still.

"I . . ." I lick my lips. "Cliff . . ."

His face slowly, agonizingly falls. "I'm sorry," he cuts in. "I . . . That was . . . I—"

"I don't want to go," I interrupt.

His chest heaves up and down. "You don't want to go."

"I don't want to go," I repeat, a slow smile spreading over my face. "I love you."

"You love me?" And there's relief, sadness, then disbelief.

I smile even wider. "I love you, Cliff."

He exhales, his face going slack as he cups my jaw. "Oh, thank God."

And then he kisses me.

Just like that, the little piece of my heart that he took clicks back into place. I sink into him, wrapping my arms around his neck and pulling him as close as I can. And maybe we should stop—maybe I'm making a scene in a public place, being reckless and embarrassing—but Cliff continues kissing me.

Even as the guards around us start to say words I can't decipher; even as Rocket barks over and over, jumping on my leg; even as the attendant tells me this is my last chance to board—I'm so lost in Cliff that I don't care.

Then he pulls away, gathering his breath, running a palm through his hair.

"Oh my God, I'm sorry, ma'am. I forgot to introduce myself." He sticks out his palm. "My name is Cliff. I can't believe I showed up and kissed you. So rude of me."

My heart leaps so high that it cuts into my throat and stings my eyes.

I slide my hand into his.

"I'm Michelle," I say. "It's nice to meet you."

Shake.

"God, you're beautiful," he says. "I actually think I might love you."

"I think I might love you too."

Shake.

He looks at the security guards, standing with their arms crossed.

Shake.

"I need to go," he says. He leans forward to murmur, "I'm about to be arrested."

I laugh. "You or Rocket?"

"I shouldn't have let a dog run through an airport."

"Probably not."

Cliff looks down at Rocket and smiles.

Rocket wags his tail, beating it against the airport carpet. He barks again. For once, I know exactly what that dog is thinking without a single doubt in my mind.

I smile. "I think Rocket wants to go home."

"Yeah. Me too."

Chapter 47

MICHELLE

My new favorite Copper Run holiday is New Year's Eve.

Papier-mâché stars hang over dim tea lights in the square. Streamers in white, gold, and black twist and drape over archways and lampposts. A small ice rink has been created in a corner of the park, only big enough to fit three skaters at a time. It snowed earlier today, so ice clings to the ground, making each step a little slippery.

Cliff and I run the small booth with the Burke's Bakery sign hanging over the top. The line hasn't been long enough for Cliff to need help, but I wouldn't want to be anywhere else.

I open the cash box, digging out a couple of quarters for George, whose hands are cupped around a coveted chocolate scone. I hold out my hand to empty the change into his palm, but he shakes his head.

"Keep the change."

I toss it back into the box and click it shut, peering at Cliff, who is already staring at me.

"What?" I ask with a laugh.

"You look good in my flannel," he says, the side of his mouth tilting up into that halfway grin.

I push up the baggy sleeve of his coat, which engulfs me. My luggage is currently in Seattle, where I notably am not.

I called Topsy's and said that I would have to, happily, decline the offer of employment. I then faxed my resignation to my former manager as well, all while proudly adjusting the plaque at Bird & Breakfast's front desk reading, MICHELLE CADELL, OWNER AND OPERATOR.

We're working out how to get my luggage back, considering it holds every piece of fashionable clothing I own. For the past four days, I've been wearing Sara's cropped shirts layered under Cliff's baggy sweaters. It's not much, but it'll do for now.

I traipse over to him, resting my chin on his chest and looking up into his blue eyes.

"I could look better without it," I tease.

He sucks in a breath and lets it out with a laugh. He chews his bottom lip and shakes his head. "I love you—you know that?"

"You can tell me every minute of my life."

His eyes shadow over, and he leans down to whisper, "God, I love—"

But Brittany runs behind the booth, tugging Rocket on a leash behind her. They both crouch down.

Cliff looks at me, then back at her. "Uh, what's going on, Britt Britt?"

She scrunches her nose. "Luke keeps following me."

Cliff sighs out a low groan. A grin slides over my mouth, but I curl my lips in to hide it. He's not ready for another boy chasing his daughter—literally or figuratively. I can't blame him.

"Hide here all you like," I say, patting the top of her bouncing scrunchie, poking out over her earmuffs. But she's only there for a moment or two before running out again. Kids have short memories, I suppose.

Sara slides up to the booth next, breathing heavily in exhaustion. "Sorry I'm late. Trying to get things cleaned up."

"You've got"—I peer over the crowd at the giant clock ticking down on a makeshift stage—"thirty seconds."

Sara pumps her eyebrows. "Just in time, then."

I reach out and run my thumb over the small dot of yellow paint on her forehead. "Missed some."

She laughs. "Thanks."

When I came back to Copper Run, Sara moved out of the innkeeper suite and is staying in a vacant apartment above Betty's store on the square. I don't know how quickly she found it, but Sara's always had that kind of charm and resourcefulness about her. Half the town already loves her, and the other half simply hasn't met her yet.

Her studio apartment has Bird & Breakfast's air mattress on the floor and clothes strewn in the corner. The walls are already coated in half a mural. When Sara paints, she disappears. I had to convince Betty to key me in when twenty-four hours had passed after Sara moved and we still hadn't heard from her. She'd stayed up all night, painting half of one wall, coated with a sunny mountain.

She's decided to assist with the inn, but it's not long term. Her dreams lie elsewhere. She's already talking about opening a studio for local artists in Copper Run. Winston had his name in the hat the moment he heard about it.

I look out in the crowd as she runs off.

Emily and Josh skate three circuits in the tiny ice rink until Josh slips, causing a collective "Ooh" from onlookers.

She helps him up with a cringe, and they slip and slide on the ice until they're on level ground again. Carol pulls Emily up to steady her, twisting her lips until her cigarette hangs out the corner of her mouth.

Lars comes up behind Carol, plucking the cigarette from her mouth and tossing it on the ground.

"You're littering!" she whines, but he shrugs nonchalantly, traipsing over to us and leaning on the counter.

"Doughnut, please?"

"Yes, sir," I say, holding out a palm for Cliff to drop it in my hand on a neat napkin.

"All yours."

Carol saunters over with another cigarette between her lips.

Cliff sighs. "Carol, you promised you'd try to quit."

"I always do, and it never sticks."

"Try again," Lars says, elbowing her.

She tilts her head to the side in defiance.

"It's a new year," Cliff says. "Don't you want to have a fresh start?"

She looks to the darkened midnight sky as if thinking, then shrugs. "No. Not this year."

I peer from the corner of my eye at Cliff. That makes only two of us, then.

Cliff and I talked a lot about fresh starts, about what staying in Copper Run would mean for me and for us. But we're trying to not plan too far ahead. We both want to live in the moment more—for the now instead of the anxious future.

So, all I know is, for now, I'm here with him. With this town. And my mom's inn. My inn.

And that's more than enough for me.

"Oh, oh, it's happening!" Lars says.

Suddenly, all of Copper Run starts counting down from ten. Nine . . .

Lisa and George linger alone outside the white fence surrounding the park, clutching champagne and a scone, knocking them together in a toast and smiling.

Eight . . .

Emily and Josh hold hands beside a lamppost. He kisses the top of her forehead.

Seven . . .

Sara runs to join Dad by the clock, hooking a hand into the crook of his elbow and leaning her head on his shoulder. I can see his shaky inhale and the smile that looks relieved on the breath out.

Six . . .

Carol pushes her cigarette butt into the top of the city trash can's ashtray. She pulls the pack from her pocket, flips it over once, then twice, and then tosses it into the trash can.

Five . . .

Cliff's arms wrap around my waist. I close my eyes, breathing in his cinnamon and vanilla scent, the leftover smells of his afternoon baking for the booth. And beneath it, that citrus smell. The uniquely Cliff scent.

Four . . .

He slides his hands up my hips, around to my spine, and over my shoulders. Touching, always touching. But I love when he touches me.

Three . . .

He cups the side of my cheek, turning my head to face his.

Two . . .

I search his eyes—the blue eyes that I saw from across the chapel. A man I knew before I even met him. A man who loves me in the same way I love him. For exactly who we are. Flaws and all.

One . . .

Fireworks launch into the air, popping and crackling as Cliff's mouth meets mine.

It's officially 1998—a new year—and I plan to spend every day of it as happy as possible in the arms of a person who loves me. I think we both deserve that.

Epilogue

ROCKET

EIGHT YEARS LATER

This walk is longer. We've been going to the same building for years, but now we're walking farther to a bigger building I don't recognize. We never go out this far.

People run all around me. Some kick off from skateboards. They all laugh and step around us. Somebody pats my head, which feels good, and I recognize him as the guy who watches TV with Little Girl sometimes, grinning and laughing together. But Little Girl isn't laughing much right now. She stands beside me, her fist clenched around my leash as she bites her lip. Something about this building isn't sitting right with her. The thumping inside her is pretty fast and loud.

Funny Guy walks up beside her. He says something that has her punching his shoulder. I nudge her leg because when she pets me, the thumping inside her always slows down a bit and she seems to smile more. But Funny Guy says something snippier—he always does that—and she erupts into giggles.

If I can't help her, he normally does. We're a team like that.

Little Girl transfers my leash into Funny Guy's fist, then

bends down to pet my head again. I don't make out much, but the words *good boy* make sense, and that makes me happy because that means I did what she needed *and* I get more pets.

I *am* a good boy.

Funny Guy looks down at me and raises his eyebrows. He's got that funny look about him—*typical*—where his eyes are rimmed in red. He mumbles something to me, and I think I make out *home*, which is good because I'm really tired and I'd like to lie down. The walk was long today. I guess this is where Little Girl will be during the day now instead of that other building. I wonder if it's because she's getting taller. A lot of changes are happening because of that.

Little Girl and I stay in her den more often. She likes talking into some box a lot, which means she pets me for a long time, and I don't mind that. Though, sometimes, she picks up sticks with fur on the bottom and spreads sticky stuff over a paper. The first time I tried to lick it, she told me not to do it again, so I haven't. She spreads the sticky stuff a lot now, and the papers are all over the walls. Funny Guy says it's *art*.

Sometimes, I go to the other den and lie down when she's doing *art* since she doesn't like me walking on it. That den smells like Sassy Girl, even though she doesn't live with us anymore. One time, she came back for a while, and we all went to the park, where Sassy Girl stood in a big white dress and said some words to someone else. Then they mashed their faces together and ran away. I don't know who they thought they were hiding from because we all watched it happen, then saw them a few minutes later with food and music. I don't question their weird rituals.

We're getting closer to *home*. I sniff my usual spots, making sure nothing new is happening or someone new isn't here.

Some people come and go, but usually, *home* smells like food and *her*.

Funny Guy walks me through the grass and up the stairs. When he unhooks me from my leash, I take a right through the door with the food smell.

Then I see her.

My Girl.

It always feels like I'm gone from her too long.

Right now, she's flipping through papers at the kitchen table. She does that a lot, and sometimes, if I see her do it too much, I'll nudge her so she can go outside with me instead. But she's already standing, which is good because I don't have enough energy to nip at her heels today.

Funny Guy walks in after me. He always wraps his arms around My Girl. It's the first thing he does, holding and holding until, finally, they mash faces. Sometimes, they mash faces for so long that I get bored and go to another room, where someone else will pet me. But today, they stop pretty quickly, so that's nice.

They walk outside again to the swaying seat and sit down. I wait for it to steady before jumping up between them and burying my nose in My Girl's lap. She always smells better than anyone else.

Years ago, there was some extra thumping in her that made me really uncomfortable. I was scared she was sick or something. But then, one day, it stopped, and that same thumping rhythm came from some raised bed in My Girl's den. The wriggling thing in there smelled like My Girl and looked a little like Funny Guy, so I figured this New Guy wasn't a safety risk. Plus, he giggles like Little Girl used to, and I love that sound. Now that New Guy is bigger, sometimes he chases me. It's fun for a bit, and I wish I could play longer, but running gets me a little out of breath nowadays. I much prefer sitting on the porch, especially with these two.

Funny Guy says stuff that makes My Girl laugh, and I love it when she laughs. When I first met her, she didn't laugh at all. She was really quiet. There was some other person with her, but he left, and I barely remember him now. All I know is that I took care of her, and she took care of me, and now we sit outside every day and are happy, and that's really great.

As long as I have My Girl and as long as Funny Guy makes her laugh, I can't complain.

Not one bit.

> Enjoy this exclusive
> New Year's Eve bonus scene!

December 31, 1999

BRITTANY

The world is ending.

At least that's what Emily tells me every night before I go to bed. She says it's something about how computers won't work. She says we'll be in complete darkness. She says there's some song by a band called R.E.M. that totally predicted this.

Dad groans about how she's just scaring me, but when Shell and I went to the corner store for milk a few days ago, the entire aisle was empty. When we told Aunt Carol, she immediately called Dad to ask if we should go one town over to see if they have any left.

Dad laughed and so did Shell. Their laughing made me laugh too. Dad said milk would go bad if the fridge didn't work. Shell ensured Aunt Carol that computers probably don't work like that anyway. Carol still got in her car, and Dad's best friend, Lars, said he'd go with her to get some milk, even though he was snickering as they drove off.

But now we're one minute away from midnight, and I'm lying on my stomach on the bed in Shell's room with my feet kicking in the air behind me, and I can't help but feel some tension in my chest at the countdown on the TV.

"*My* mom got tons of bread and water," Luke brags, swinging his feet off the bed.

All the adults in the living room are loud and Rocket didn't like the noise, so I came to Shell's room to watch the ball drop on the TV with him. Luke followed. For some reason, Dad said we had to leave the bedroom door open. I'm not sure why it matters but he said something like "We're getting too old," which sounds weird, but whatever.

"Did you guys get any water?" Luke asks.

I snort. "My dad says it's dumb to be scared."

Even Rocket huffs out a breath. I bet he agrees.

Luke doesn't. "Well, maybe *he's* dumb."

"My dad isn't dumb."

"He is."

"Shut up."

"Make me."

I push his arm but it only makes him laugh. Luke always laughs when he can push my buttons. Emily keeps teasing that maybe he likes me but that doesn't make sense. He wouldn't irritate me if he liked me.

The hardwood creaks as someone walks down the hall. Luke and I exchange a look, then peek around the corner. It's Aunt Carol, wringing her hands together with a sigh. She looks too worried to notice us, or maybe the house is too loud.

"See?" Luke whispers to me. "*She* knows the world is ending."

"Shh," I hiss at him.

Maybe Aunt Carol knows something none of us do.

The floors creak again and my dad's best friend walks down the hall. Lars has that funny mustache of his that always wiggles when he smiles, and he's grinning so big right now.

He stops in front of Aunt Carol and crosses his arms.

"Are you seriously scared?" he asks through a laugh.

Aunt Carol's lips purse as she pushes him the same way I just pushed Luke. Maybe Lars is annoying like that too.

"We have no clue how computers work," she says.

Lars places a comforting palm on her forearm. "You're being ridiculous. You know that, right?"

"No, I'm not."

From the living room, everyone starts counting down from ten. We're close to midnight.

Lars smiles. He always has the kindest smiles.

"We'll count together," Lars says, stroking a line up her forearm.

Aunt Carol's eyes dart down to the hand. I wonder if she's worried he's rubbing something on her. Lars always has sticky doughnut glaze on his fingers. But I think Dad made pie instead of doughnuts tonight.

"You're trying to scare me more," she says.

"Or I'm trying to distract you."

She snorts, like she doesn't believe him. But it does kinda seem like he's being nice to me.

I glance back at the bright shiny ball on the TV, getting closer and closer to the crowd in New York.

"Eight seconds until the end of the world," Luke says.

I groan. "Stop it."

"Four . . . three . . ."

"Luke, stop it!" I whine.

The countdown feels slower than usual. I try to remember Dad telling me I'm not supposed to be worried, but maybe things *will* end.

"One . . ."

There's an outburst of "Happy New Year!" from the living room and everyone cheers. I freeze, waiting for an explosion outside or maybe even total darkness. But everything feels the same.

I watch Lars take Aunt Carol's cheeks in his large palms. He grins.

"See?" Lars says. "Happy New Year, Carol."

She blinks at him as if in shock, but something tells me it isn't because the computers didn't explode. I've never seen Lars get this close to her. She looks like she hasn't experienced this either.

"What are you—" Then Lars leans in and kisses her.

Luke immediately lets out a "YUCK!"

And that's when the lights and TV shut off.

The world goes dark.

Luke screams, making me scream, and then Aunt Carol screams. A firework sparks off outside. Rocket scampers into the bathroom, his claws skidding on the hardwood. There's a *plunk*. I think he jumps into the tub.

"I told you!" Aunt Carol screeches at Lars.

But then the lights turn back on. The heater lurches, then hums back to life. From the living room, laughter roars through the house, followed by Shell's yells of "Cliff!"

From the hall, Lars bursts out laughing.

The world didn't end? The world didn't end!

Carol's face falls. "It's . . . not the end of the world?"

"Your asshole brother just turned off the lights," Lars says. "Trying to scare everyone."

Then Carol lets out a hesitant laugh. Her words are shaky as she says, "He's . . . he's ridiculous."

"A family trait," Lars says, and they look at each other for a lingering moment before Aunt Carol takes his face this time and kisses him. I expect to feel grossed out like Luke was, but instead I smile. It's kind of cute. It feels like something from all my princess movies. I wonder if Aunt Carol feels like a princess.

Maybe that's silly. Maybe I look silly to Luke. I look back at him, but his eyes are wide, staring at the blank TV.

"It's not the end of the world?" he asks breathlessly.

And suddenly it all seems so funny.

"You screamed," I say.

Luke shakes his head, like he's coming back to reality again. He furrows his brow. "I did not!"

I giggle. "You're a total scaredy-cat."

"Well . . . you screamed too!"

But then I'm laughing and eventually so is he, and we're falling back on the bed in fits of laughter neither of us can stop. Each laugh feels lighter and lighter until all the tension coiled in my chest is in the room instead of inside my chest.

"Want to go see the fireworks?" I ask.

He laughs. "Definitely."

Rocket tiptoes out of the bathroom.

"Want to come, Rocket?"

He disappears again, but that's fine. He'll realize Emily was wrong.

It's *not* the end of the world.

And we feel fine.

Acknowledgments

I always hope readers will love my stories. It's why I love writing them. But halfway through writing this book, I found myself thinking, *If I'm the only person who loves Cliff and Michelle, I'll be all right with that.* That's when I knew both: (a) This story officially had a piece of my soul that it would keep forever, and (b) I was in danger of being blissfully unaware of its flaws. Thankfully, I have some amazing friends, family, and editors who make sure that isn't the case, and they deserve all the love I have (and more!).

Thank you to my fantastic agent, Kimberly, for being an absolute badass at what you do, making dreams come true, and having endless patience and support as I stumble through traditional publishing like the newborn baby deer that I am.

Thank you to the amazing team at Berkley who worked on bringing Copper Run to life again, and to my fantastic editor, Sarah, and Liz, for loving Cliff and Michelle as much as I do. Thank you for believing in all my silly ideas.

Shout-out to my wonderful indie editor, Jovana. I promise I removed the fifty thousand *just*s in this one. You are an angel.

To my dev editor, Becca. I trust you with my life and my books, which are basically the same thing. I love you.

Jenny B. You're the glue holding my sanity together. Thanks for always listening to my panicked audio messages, for sharing in our mutual love of mac and cheese when we both need it, and for refocusing the wild hamster running on a wheel in my brain who is always attempting to juggle fifty off-the-wall ideas.

Dad. For inspiring every wonderful father I write.

Rusty. For loving nostalgia as much as I do.

Allie. For being the platonic love of my life.

Jillian. My sunshine.

Caroline. My vacation soulmate.

Jere. My inspiring, starry-eyed Capricorn.

Thank you to my OG beta team: Jenny, Allie, Angie, Carrie, Emily, Elizabeth, Erin, Rebeca, Caroline, and Kolin. Special shout-out to Danielle and Jenny Z., who double-checked the nineties accuracy!

To my reader group and all the lovely romance readers . . . thank you for your endless support and passion for reading.

And finally, as always, thank you to my husband—my nineties punk rocker at heart. Thank you for supporting all my "Yoda was a gnome" ideas. For listening when I randomly spout story ideas in the middle of watching *Survivor*. For watching endless nineties movies and documentaries while I was writing this. For keeping our lives afloat when I'm on a deadline. You're the reason why I love writing friends-to-lovers. Thank you for being my forever best friend. I love you, I like you, and I love you.